WEDDIN...

At the entrance to the wegiwa, Tag cleared his throat to announce his arrival, drew aside the flap, and entered. Caro knelt on the other side of the dim room, her weight set back on her heels and her hands demurely folded in her lap. Tag stopped and caught his breath at the deceptive picture of utter innocence.

She floated to her feet. "Welcome, my husband." Before he could speak, she padded across the dirt floor to stand in front of him. Close enough to make him forget she was English, or Indian, or anything but a woman. Her hands burned on his shoulders and she looked up at him, her lips so close to his. He bent and brushed his lips against hers with a lingering touch.

"Oh." She gasped and looked up. "What . . . ?"

He smiled at the reaction. "A kiss. Have you never been kissed?"

"Never."

He gripped her shoulders and thrust her from him. *She was a virgin.* "Dammit!" His fingers dug into her shoulders with each word. "Why did you let me think . . . ? Damn!"

She watched his face, her eyes wide. "I don't understand. You are angry because I don't know how . . . ?" She bit her lip and looked toward the entrance, then back at him. She stepped back away from his hands, which he had left on her shoulders. With a deep breath, Caro straightened to her full height, and took two determined steps toward the door.

"Where are you going?" he roared. He grabbed her wrist and she came to a jerking halt.

"To learn what you need me to know."

Other *Leisure* books by Judy Veisel:
FLIGHT OF FANCY

UNTAMED Love

JUDY VEISEL

LEISURE BOOKS   NEW YORK CITY

To Cathy, Susan, Theresa and Steve, who gave endless joy and new meaning to the word "mother."

A LEISURE BOOK®

February 1999

Published by

Dorchester Publishing Co., Inc.
276 Fifth Avenue
New York, NY 10001

ISBN 0-8439-4481-1

Printed in the United States of America.

Untamed Love

Chapter One

Ohio Valley, April 1816

"Jake . . ." Taggart Asherton's whisper rasped through the still afternoon air. "Jake, I have the feeling somebody is watching." His horse sidestepped to protest Tag's tightening thighs.

As a veteran of two campaigns against Napoleon, the Earl of Elmgrove had learned to trust his instincts. The trail he and his guide had followed for three days hadn't changed visibly, but something was hardening Tag's stomach muscles into a tight knot. The same something was causing the back of his neck to feel uncommonly exposed.

Jake Fletcher turned toward him with a wide flash of yellowed teeth. " 'Bout time you noticed somethin'." His American drawl held no hint of stress.

"You feel it, too?" Tag asked. Jake's lack of concern eased the tension in Tag's shoulders. "Then somebody *is* watching?"

"Been watchin' for the last ten miles. I'd be surprised if they didn't." Jake chuckled. "By now every ten-year-old in the village's had his look at you."

Tag again searched the surrounding woods for any sign of human life. He saw sprouting, green underbrush and solid brown tree trunks. The muted padding of the unshod horses sounded unnaturally loud in the stillness, offset only by an occasional territorial chirp. Nothing rustled or snapped to betray a human presence.

Before Jake spoke again, he pointed to a spot in the distance where the trail broke from the woods into a small clearing at the crest of a hill. ''We'll stop up there and let you do your lookin'.''

Tag slowed his horse. One hundred yards, he thought. One hundred yards to curse the capricious nature that had brought him three thousand miles to keep a promise to a dying man.

With a mental shrug he thought of all the places a man with any sense would have turned back. New York, Albany, Niagara, and that last wretched outpost of civilization, Detroit. Instead, he had dredged out his stubborn streak, discounted every vicious tale he had heard of the savages who inhabited the wilderness, and followed the trail of a man who had left England thirty years earlier. Now he was about to ride into a village of Shawnee Indians to ask if they happened to be borrowing Wendell Fenton. And if so, did they mind giving him back?

Now that he had confessed to his insanity, a surge of anticipation rushed over Tag. He was about to see a sight most Englishmen only read about—a genuine Indian village. A good third of the people he talked to, including his untroubled guide, had assured him the savages wouldn't cut him open and eat his heart while he watched—as long as he didn't show any fear.

Hell, that should be easy. If he had the good sense to be afraid, he wouldn't be here.

At the crest of the hill, Tag pulled his horse to a halt beside Jake and scanned the panorama a hundred feet below. For a long moment he just stared. ''A bit of a disappointment.''

''What'd you expect?'' Jake's words were fraught with suppressed laughter.

''I'm not sure. The stories . . .'' The village below could

8

have been almost any roughly constructed town. The largest structure, toward the far end, sprawled a full eighty feet long and thirty feet wide. Smaller square or rectangular houses—*wegiwas*, Tag recalled—lay scattered in an irregular pattern. The graying walls and roofs appeared to be made of bark with a frame of branches on the outside. "I guess I never expected such a peaceful-looking place." Men and women sat or moved about at an unhurried pace.

"Don't let it fool you. Things have been quiet for a spell now, but it ain't a good place to go making enemies."

"You never seemed uneasy before."

"Ain't uneasy now. Just that I've been tradin' with them for years." Jake inhaled for a dramatic pause. "And I ain't English."

Tag grinned. "You've never confessed to being anything but some kind of mongrel. Now you want to make being English some kind of a crime."

"Out here, may well be. Two times runnin' your generals didn't bother to show up when the Shawnee were fightin' the Americans. Last time out cost the Shawnee their greatest chief."

Tag grinned to conceal his surprise. "You conveniently didn't mention that when you agreed to bring me." Tag managed to keep his tone light, in spite of the words of caution, he trusted Jake.

"Reckoned you knew. Maybe it didn't matter none. You don't get 'em riled, and these are just plain folks. You'll do all right so long as you mind your manners." Jake grinned again and his saddle creaked as he shifted.

Their arrival had attracted attention. Many of the the people below had ceased their activities to stand in silence and look up the hill. Occasionally someone pointed.

"Do your gawkin' now," Jake said, " 'cause once we start down, you're gonna look straight ahead, real unconcerned, till we get clear to the chief's lodge."

Tag did his "gawkin' " because he had quickly discovered something that made this village different from any he'd ever seen. If clothes made a man, these people barely qualified. A few of the men wore leggings. Most wore a lot less. A belt and a flap of something to cover the essentials, and they were dressed for the day.

Being male, and not much interested in what a sudden wind might reveal, Tag let his gaze seek out the women. While not quite as sparingly dressed as the men, they offered some interesting possibilities. Most wore dresses but shorter than any he'd ever seen. Short enough to make him grateful Indian women had nice legs. Obviously, they didn't subscribe to the notion that bared legs belonged only in the bedchamber.

This would be an interesting day.

"Seen enough?" Without waiting for a reply, Jake nudged his horse into a slow descent of the easy hill.

Tag moved down with him, and the three packhorses lumbered along behind. A cluster of rowdy dogs raced from the village to greet them. Tag imitated Jake's indifference and didn't even glance down. He fixed his eyes on a spot at the end of a wide avenue through the center of the village and refused to acknowledge the stares that followed their progress. Behind him he could hear children's voices and the whap-whap of unfamiliar syllables.

The ride took the longest five minutes of Tag's twenty-eight years. He had spotted their destination well before Jake reined in his horse. In front of a twenty-foot-square hut stood a tall, gaunt man, about fifty years old. His affected nonchalance defined his position—and he wore more clothes than most.

His deerskin leggings had fringe along the outer seam. A matching shirt decorated with quills and bound tightly with a red sash at the waist came almost to his knees. The shirt had no sleeves. Twin bracelets of pounded silver banded his biceps.

Without speaking, he stood motionless until Jake dismounted and took the two steps that brought them face to face. Paying no heed to either Tag or the horses behind him, the Indian raised his right hand. "You come at a good time, Fletcher."

Jake raised his own hand and smiled as comfortably as he ever had at Tag. "Howdy do, Chief Seven Feathers."

The chief's gaze shifted to Tag. "You bring a friend. Do I know of him?"

Tag found himself staring into a pair of dark, assessing eyes. The penetrating appraisal searched for any weakness and judged him as surely as any commanding officer ever had, and the clipped English put Jake's to shame. Mentally, Tag squared his shoulders, refusing to be intimidated into any visible movement. "No reason you would hear of me. I just came from England."

"British." Seven Feathers spat the word like bitter fruit. If anything, Jake had understated this chief's distrust of the English. There wasn't anything Tag could do about that.

"Well, now, you gotta take into account he just got here." Jake's comment exonerated Tag of responsibility for whatever atrocities the British had committed in the past.

"He is a friend of yours?" The chief asked the question without shifting his gaze from Tag.

"So far," Jake answered.

If Tag had dared to move he would have nodded his compliments to the clever American. In an incredibly few words Jake had done his best to absolve Tag of responsibility for past crimes committed by the British, and himself of any future blunders on Tag's part.

The chief nodded. "How do I call your friend?"

"His name is Taggart Asherton, but the Englishmen call him Elmgrove because that's the name of the place he's chief of."

Tag suppressed a smile. That was about as clear an explanation of his name and title as any he'd heard. At this point he didn't much care what the Indian chief called him

11

so long as they got this introduction business over with and let him get off his horse.

"Elm Grove." The chief tested the name, breaking it into two words. "Elm Grove. It could be an Indian name. Not a good one, but better than most English names that have no meaning at all. Welcome, Elm Grove."

Tag swung a leg over and jumped down from his horse, relieved to finally stretch his legs. "Thank you, Chief Seven Feathers."

The chief turned, raised the animal hide covering the entrance of the *wegiwa*, and motioned. Tag and Jake entered. Tag blinked his eyes to adjust to the dim light. Though not exceptionally tall, he had to walk three feet into the room before he could stand erect and study his surroundings. Wooden frames, inside as well as out, pressed bark walls between them. Nearest the walls, animal hides and household goods covered the dirt floor for three or four feet except for the far end, which contained a blackened fire pit. Most of the light in the room came from an opening in the roof over this pit, and a rough wooden bench provided a seat on one side.

Without hesitation, Jake walked over and plopped down on one of the benches. He signaled with his eyes for Tag to sit beside him.

A moment later the chief entered, followed by four other men. One of the men dealt out animal skins from a pile, and the others sank down to sit cross-legged opposite Jake and Tag. Tag noted that the breechcloth was a single long strip that passed between the legs and seemed in no danger of wandering off.

As soon as everyone was settled, Jake shot off a question in the rapid-fire language Tag had heard as they moved through the village.

The chief frowned and shook his head. "In English, please, to honor our guest."

"Thank you," Tag said. "I noticed you speak English well."

Rather than glowing at the compliment, the chief looked sad. "We have been fighting the English and the American long knives for fifty years. A warrior must speak English to know his enemy."

So much for making a new friend. Tag clamped his lips shut and belatedly vowed to follow Jake's advice and speak only when addressed.

Jake rephrased his question in English. It proved to be a polite inquiry about the chief's wives. Plural. It seemed the chief wasn't quite as stiff-laced as he appeared.

Chief Seven Feathers frowned and discussed one wife, then smiled and reported on the other.

Tag shifted, making himself as comfortable as he could on the wooden bench, which felt even harder than his saddle. According to Jake, it would be hours before they could even mention the object of their visit. The men in the room dove into an animated exchange about weather, hunting, friends, old battles, and all the other topics men discuss when they meet after a long separation. In spite of the chief's order, they often slipped into Shawnee, and only changed back after a gentle reminder.

A woman came in and distributed cups of strong, bitter tea. Tag had tasted worse, but he couldn't remember when. He smiled and emptied his cup as quickly as the others. Two hours later the woman returned and served bowls of thick white gruel made of mashed corn with chunks of meat, then left as silently as before.

After the meal the chief smiled. "You have chosen a fortunate day for your visit. Breath of a Panther will marry tonight. His bride will be pleased you have come." The chief straightened his legs, signaling his intention to rise. "We must prepare for the ceremony."

Jake stiffened and nodded to Tag. The moment had come.

13

"We thank you for the invitation," Tag said, "but before we separate, perhaps I should tell you why I have come."

The chief halted his movement.

Tag accepted his silence as permission to continue. "I am looking for an Englishman, Wendell Fenton. I understand he has been living with you for many years."

Two of the warriors paused, their legs half-unfolded, and dropped back into place. No physical movement drew Tag's attention to the weapons the Indians wore at their belt, but he was suddenly uncomfortably aware of them. The men stared at him, silent and impassive. Tag couldn't tell if the crime that caused the sudden tension was Wendell Fenton's or his own.

Seven Feathers broke the heavy silence. "Why do you seek this man?" His eyes had narrowed with suspicion.

"I have a message from his family."

"You have come a long way to deliver a message."

The moment didn't seem right for a lengthy explanation. "Yes."

The chief spoke in unintelligible staccato syllables to the stony-faced man on his right. The man rose and left without a word.

"We will wait." Seven Feathers again crossed his legs in front of him.

Since no one spoke, Tag assumed they would wait in silence.

Caro Fenton sat on the ground in front of the *wegiwa* she shared with White Fish, the medicine man. The ceremonial shirt she had been finishing the beading on lay forgotten in her lap. Around her the women chatted with their usual animation, but she scarcely heard their words.

She had seen the two men as soon as they crested the hill and, after a moment's disappointment, recognized Jake Fletcher, who had come to trade for the winter furs. The village had been expecting him for weeks. She paid him scant attention, but the sight of the man beside him both excited and terrified her. From the cut of his formal clothes and the stiff way he sat his horse, she knew he must be English.

Over the years such visitors had occasionally arrived bearing letters for her father. He would read the letters, and for a few days he would talk of the life he had left behind, even promising to take her to England someday to meet the family she had never known.

When she had first come to the village, she'd spent days dreaming of returning with him to the world she had been born to. He would proudly introduce her as his daughter. His father would forgive him for being gone so long because he'd brought her with him. She would have aunts and uncles and cousins who would love her stories and beg her never to go away again.

But these were the fantasies of a lonely child. Without White Fish, her last vague longings for England would have died months ago—with her father. But White Fish had opposed Seven Feathers's plan to marry her to Breath of a Panther, and counseled patience. "Even a chief cannot change your destiny," he'd warned.

White Fish would know if the stranger was the sign he had predicted.

Her fingers fluttered on the beads. What if the visitor truly had come for her? What if her grandfather had heard of her father's death and finally sent for her? What would she do?

The thought of leaving made everything around her a thousand times more precious.

A shadow fell across her hands. She looked up into Breath of a Panther's warm, dark eyes. He glanced toward the hill where the visitors had first appeared. "Did you think it was Billy Boy? Do you still hope he might get back in time for the wedding?"

"No." She had, but only for an instant. "He is doing what he must. I am proud of him."

A month ago Breath of a Panther would have recognized the lie and teased her about it. But their relationship had changed. He treated her more carefully now. "Seven Feathers has sent for us," he said. "He thinks we should both hear what the visitor has to say."

Her mind returning to the visitors, Caro rose and fell into step beside Breath of a Panther. Seven Feathers often summoned her to listen to English visitors. Later he would question her about her impressions, using her intuition to evaluate the negotiator's words. Perhaps he now felt he needed to include her future husband in such invitations.

Together they walked to the chief's lodge. Breath of a Panther drew aside the flap and entered. She followed. Though curious about the visitor, she looked first at Seven Feathers and silently knelt in the place he indicated at his side. "This man has come from England," Seven Feathers said. Caro settled her weight back on her heels, accepting the chief's words as permission to study the stranger.

The man sat bent forward on the uncomfortable bench, his knees apart and his hands folded between them. A triangle of sunlight from the opening in the roof illuminated him clearly. She inhaled as if she could physically drink in the sight of his golden hair—as blond as her own, as blond as her father's. That would explain the surge of kinship she felt toward him. He came from a world where fair hair didn't set a person apart.

Perhaps he felt the same, because he offered her the ghost of a smile. His eyes softened with a twitch of his lips, and again she had to make an effort not to let a sharply drawn breath betray her curious excitement. Unlike the solid brown eyes of everyone she knew, his were gray, but a soft gray that might have been torn from newly formed rain clouds. Those eyes watched her as if no one else in the room existed.

Jake Fletcher coughed, but he would know better than to speak before Seven Feathers gave permission. Seven Feathers liked silence, which often made white visitors uneasy. Despite his formal English clothes, this other visitor gave no sign of discomfort. His hands remained quietly between his knees and his face became expressionless after the brief smile.

Seven Feathers broke the silence. "Elm Grove, you may continue with what you have come to tell us."

Elmgrove. Caro mentally tested the name as one word, the way the English would say it. Solid like a tree, but cool and sheltering.

Elmgrove glanced at her and then back at Seven Feathers. "I have not met the young lady."

Caro's heart quickened at the cadence of the words, so like her father's. Even after all these months she missed the sound of his voice. The stranger spoke with the same quiet assurance.

Seven Feathers didn't react quite so warmly. "As you can see, she is of English descent. She will listen to what you have to say." His tone served as both a rebuke and a command to continue.

"Very well. I have come from England seeking Wendell Fenton. I hope to persuade him to return to England with me."

No. Why would this man come now? Months too late.

"Fenton has no wish to return to England," the chief said.

Caro almost betrayed Seven Feathers with a startled look. He had not told Elmgrove of her father's death. Seven Feathers briefly covered her hand with his, signaling patience. Perhaps he was right. Perhaps they should learn more before the stranger learned he couldn't get what he wanted.

"I believe he will come now," Elmgrove said.

He couldn't know how his suggestion opened the wound

17

of her father's broken promises. So often in the first years after she had come to the village he had promised, "One more spring, then we'll go, child. We'll go and you'll have aunts and cousins and enough family to fill an entire village." But those were just words to placate a lonely child. Her father had once had a family of his own, and he could never really understand why she still felt like an outsider in spite of all the love she'd found in the village.

"It has been many years since he has even spoken of England," Seven Feathers said.

Elmgrove nodded. "But men returning from here have carried stories of him. He is a brave fighter, and only he can prevent a very evil man from profiting by what he has done. I must at least see him."

"Why?" Years of training couldn't keep the question from Caro's lips. Without looking, she felt the reproof that stiffened Seven Feathers's grip.

But Seven Feathers loved her, and he repeated the question for her. "Tell us what has happened and we will decide what should be done."

Elmgrove's brows drew together. "It might be better if I talk to him. It concerns his family."

Caro's patience snapped. "My family," she said in Shawnee, turning sharply to face Seven Feathers. "Please, let me talk to him."

"Control yourself, child." Seven Feathers said, also in Shawnee. His eyes turned hard with disapproval and a hint of fear. "We do not know this man. We may not want him to know who you are." He looked thunderously at Fletcher and spoke still in Shawnee. "You will forget what you should not have heard."

Jake gave a lazy smile and spoke in the same language. "Sorry, Chief, I wasn't listening."

"And you will not." Seven Feathers turned back to Caro. "Be patient. I promise you, this man will tell us all he knows." His face softened, and Caro knew he understood her feelings even if he didn't approve.

"Please, let me question him," she said.

Without replying, Seven Feathers turned his attention back to Elmgrove. "The Englishwoman knows Fenton well. She will ask you what he would want to know."

Elmgrove hesitated long enough for Caro to wonder what he was debating. Then his face relaxed. "Very well. None of it is any great secret. What do you know about why he left England?"

"A little." In truth, Caro knew almost nothing. Her father would never talk about it. "I know he was very angry." When that summary of her knowledge didn't prompt him to continue, she added, "But tell us about it if it has anything to do with why you are here."

"As a young man, Fenton fell in love with a very beautiful woman. His father disapproved, cursed the woman, and wished her dead. When she did die, Wendell Fenton wished the same fate on his father and left England, swearing he would never return."

Caroline, Caro thought, and remembered the flicker of pain in her father's face the only time he had mentioned the woman she had been named for. "I am glad he never returned," she said.

"If it makes any difference in whether he will see me, I was to tell Fenton that his father regretted his words."

Caro's lips tightened. "Regret is easy for a man who wants something. I assume his father wants something now."

"Needs something. But I have heard him speak of the incident and I believe he has suffered enough for words he spoke in anger. At the time he was very stubborn and thought he could live without his last son. He had three other male children. All had married women who pleased him. But the second of these sons died with his wife and three children in an epidemic in Italy many years ago."

An epidemic would be the same in any world. Caro

19

couldn't harden herself against the pain of that sweeping loss. "We too have lost many people to sickness. I would not wish that grief on anyone."

"In any case, Fenton's father still had two sons and a grandson, so whatever his grief, he still had an heir, which is the most important thing to a man of his stature. Then two years ago, his oldest son never returned from a hunting trip to Scotland."

Caro reached out involuntarily as if the gesture could halt the story. The dread welling up inside her warned of what he would reveal. Aunts, uncles, cousins, the family that had lived in her imagination for so many years—they were all dead. That was why this man had come. So a selfish old man would have a son left. "Stop. I don't think we need to talk anymore."

She had her family here. She had the life she had built with the people who had raised her.

"Wait," Tag said in a tone that stiffened Caro's already rigid spine. "Hear me out," he said more softly. "Even if he still harbors his anger against his father, I know Wendell Fenton cared about Oliver, his youngest brother. Oliver told me they still corresponded."

"Oliver," Caro whispered the name softly. She remembered the laughing young man her father had described. Though it meant losing the last of her real family, she had to hear what had happened.

"Yes, Oliver. He was a soldier and a good man. He and his only son fought with me last year in the great battle they now call Waterloo. On the first day of the battle, the son was killed. Shot in the back."

Seven Feathers growled. "A warrior should not be shot in the back."

For the first time, Elmgrove shifted his attention from Caro. He nodded to the chief. "I know. Oliver mentioned this shame to no one. He just mourned and went on with his soldiering. The next day, he was also shot in the back."

Elmgrove turned his attention back to Caro. His eyes had hardened into gray pebbles. "But Oliver Grover Fenton didn't die on the battlefield. I found him in a field hospital where I went to visit one of my men. He swore to me he had never turned his back on the enemy. The shot had come from behind him."

The warriors surrounding Caro murmured comments, their faces angry. Seven Feathers waved his hand sharply to silence them. "British!" His disgusted shudder matched his tone. "One of your own warriors shot Fenton's brother?"

"That's what Oliver believed."

Caro's blood pounded with the rage that filled the room. The last of her family. Shot by a man who should have been protecting his back. "Who did such a thing?" she asked.

"Oliver's cousin was behind him that day. He had also been in the regiment with Oliver's son the day before. And he now stands to inherit the estate that belongs to Fenton's father."

"That man deliberately shot my—" Just in time, Caro remembered Seven Feathers's command to conceal her identity. "—Shot Fenton's brother and nephew for money?" She clenched her fists to control her rising anger.

"That is what Oliver believed."

"Did he kill this cousin?"

"No." Elmgrove's voice tightened and his eyes narrowed. "Oliver died before I left him that day."

"You were his friend. Did you kill the man for him?" Caro's cheeks blazed as if she were sitting too close to a fire.

"No." Elmgrove glanced at the floor, refusing to meet her angry gaze. "I wanted to but . . . no."

"Why?" She challenged him. He didn't look like a coward. "Were you afraid?"

His jaw tightened and he met her gaze without flinching.

"It does not take great courage to kill a man. English law demands some proof before taking a man's life."

"I would have cut his heart out."

"I doubt that, though I felt the same at the time. An Englishman does not dispense justice without proof. Even Oliver understood that."

Finally understanding why he had come, Caro released an impatient whoosh of air. "So you came to find Fenton to do your killing?"

Elmgrove stiffened and glared at her. "Can we please stop this talk about killing? It is not the English way."

Caro refused to be brushed aside so easily. She could think of no other reason for his presence. "If not to find someone to do your killing, why have you come?"

Elmgrove spoke with exaggerated patience. "Oliver knew he was dying. That didn't bother him as much as the fact that his cousin would succeed. He would inherit everything unless I could stop him. Oliver begged me to come here, find his brother, and persuade him to come back and claim his inheritance. If Fenton will do that, then Oliver will win, even in death. The villain will get nothing."

Caro could barely keep the disgust out of her voice. "And that would punish him for killing two brave men?"

"Not necessarily just that. Oliver and I thought a man who has killed twice might not give up so easily. Wendell Fenton wouldn't be an unsuspecting victim. We thought—"

"A trap." Seven Feathers nodded his approval. "The evil man would not willingly let go of what he thought would be his. He would have to try again and then your English law would permit you to kill him."

"Precisely. Fenton will avenge his brother and inherit a fortune. He can even return here if he chooses to."

"I—" Caro got out only the single word before Seven Feathers's tight grip silenced her.

"This would be a dangerous plan," Seven Feathers said,

his words as much a warning to Caro as a response to the visitor.

"Not for a man of Fenton's stature," Elmgrove said. "Oliver spoke often of his strength and courage."

"And if Fenton cannot return with you, Elm Grove, what then?" the chief asked.

Elmgrove shrugged. He shifted his gaze to the doorway. "There will be little I can do." He looked again at the chief, pursed his lips, and spoke slowly as if first considering the alternatives. "When Fenton's father dies, I suppose I might announce there is a missing heir. Tie up the estate. It will take the murderer a longer time to claim the money."

"This will defeat him?" Seven Feathers spat out the words with the scorn Caro felt at such a meaningless action. "You live in a very spineless world if a man kills your friend and you talk of money. You must take this man prisoner and send him here. We will see to his punishment." Everyone except Elmgrove nodded in agreement. "In this village it will take him many days to die."

"That has no more honor than killing him myself. The law—"

Seven Feathers's warning hand prevented Caro from rising to shake the Englishman who would cloak everything in words, but he could not quell her anger. "The law!" she cried. "This man deserves to die, and you talk of the law."

"Hush, little one," Breath of a Panther said in Shawnee. He rose and stood, a proud warrior accepting his quest. He looked down at Caro. "I will kill this evil man for you and bring his scalp back to decorate our *wegiwa*."

The other warriors murmured their agreement, accepting Breath of a Panther's right to avenge her family.

Seven Feathers exhaled a long breath and studied the far wall for several long seconds. Slowly he shook his head and looked at Breath of a Panther. "I am sorry, I cannot let you go. We have too few hunters as it is. Even with your skill, many of our old ones went hungry this year.''

''I will return.''

''But not before the cold comes again. Though it shames me to say it, this man has already done his worst. We must let it go.''

Breath of a Panther began to nod in agreement; then his eyes widened and he looked at Caro with compassion. ''Perhaps he has not done his worst.'' He turned to Elmgrove. ''You said this murderer could not have the money until Fenton's father dies. Do you not fear he will kill the old man as well?''

Caro's heart skipped a beat. A grandfather. She had a grandfather. In the turmoil of learning that all the uncles and cousins her father had spoken of were dead, she had not thought of the living. Her grandfather.

''Perhaps not,'' Elmgrove said in a too reasonable tone.

''Perhaps—'' Caro couldn't find words. At this very moment a murderer might be smothering her grandfather in his sleep and this ineffectual Englishman said, *Perhaps not.*

''I believe the villain has no immediate need to harm the old man, and good reason not to,'' Elmgrove explained.

Elmgrove didn't sound as certain as Caro would have liked, but she bit her lip to curb her impatience. She wanted to believe what he would say. ''Tell us.''

''Others heard Oliver's tale and have talked about it. There were rumors. If anything untimely happens to his father, it will arouse suspicion.''

''You said suspicion means nothing.''

''Legally, no. But it is enough to pause a man if he does not need to hurry. In England a man can live a considerable time on the expectation of a fortune, if he is modest in his needs.''

''And if he is not?''

''Then . . .'' Elmgrove turned his palms up. ''That is one of the reasons I am certain Fenton will accompany me to England. His father's life may depend on it.''

His words washed over Caro. She had found a family and already lost them. Found a grandfather and even now might be losing him. And nobody was going to do anything.

Her father would have gone. Caro knew that. But would he want *her* to?

Despite the touch of Seven Feathers's hand on hers, she felt as if she were standing alone in a vast empty space.

Elmgrove had come with a message for her, but not as the lonely child in her had dreamed. Not with an invitation from people who wanted her. He had come because there was no one left to protect what was hers.

Even Seven Feathers wouldn't help her now. He might be angry at the white man's wickedness and sorry for what she had lost, but he had to protect his own people first. His touch warned her against speaking.

Later they would talk. He would have reasons why she shouldn't go in her father's place. She would listen to him as she always had, because he was the chief and because he loved her. If she hoped to do anything, she had to speak now.

The men around her talked, but she couldn't hear their words. Her inability to hear the voices sharpened her other senses. She felt the individual hairs of the mat on her shins, the warmth of Seven Feathers's fingers on her wrist, the blanket-like heaviness of the air. Could she leave everything important to her to protect an old man who might not even want her? If she didn't, would she always wonder what would have happened if she'd had the courage to speak?

In a movement that seemed to take as long as a sunrise, she drew herself to her feet to address the group. She had failed her parents, but she would not fail the last of her family. "I must go," she said. "I must go to England and protect my grandfather."

Chapter Two

"What . . ." The question died unspoken on Tag's lips. *Fenton's daughter.* Of course he should have realized she wasn't some random American woman who happened to be living with the tribe. But nothing in her uncle's appearance had prepared Tag for this tiny slip of a thing.

It appeared that she had Oliver's courage, though. The chief looked like he wanted to strangle her. Tag wanted to applaud.

Not much more than five feet tall and slim as a willow tree, she stood before the doorway, framed by the golden glow of the afternoon sun, daring Seven Feathers to challenge her right to protect her grandfather. In a rare moment of insight, Tag realized he would carry the image of her dramatic pose to his grave. A portrait in hues of gold and tawny beige.

Wisps of blond hair escaped from her thick braid, and framed fairy-like features and skin the color of toasted almonds. The soft tones emphasized the only vibrant color in the picture, eyes as deep and blue as a Scottish lake.

The silence gave Tag time to indulge his fantasies. She would smell of leaves and sunbaked air. His gaze drifted downward to her soft doeskin dress. The material curved gently over her breasts and hung loosely to her knees. Rounded calves tapered to trim ankles. Tag's ears warmed as he realized he was staring at the bared legs of an English gentlewoman. Worse, he'd just thought she'd make for some interesting nights if she decided to accompany him to England.

No more. Thoughts like that showed on a man's face. Tag forced himself to wrench his gaze back to the chief and the fierce-looking warrior beside him.

Chief Seven Feathers gave a dark scowl. Fenton's daughter had obviously spoken out of turn. "You will do as we decide."

"I . . ." The girl's jaw moved with a few syllables of unspoken protest, then she nodded.

"Come here," Seven Feathers's command cracked like a rifle shot.

Tag leaned forward, his muscles tensed. Foolhardy or not, he would protect this delicate creature if the chief decided to punish her physically.

She resumed her seat next to Seven Feathers, who ignored her and returned his attention to Tag. "As you have guessed, Elm Grove, this is Wendell Fenton's daughter, Caro."

"Fenton is—?"

"My father is dead." Her direct gaze rejected both his sympathy and his quixotic impulse to protect her. "You must forgive my interruption." She looked at Seven Feathers to extend the apology to him as well. "I know I should not have spoken yet."

"You are too much like your father." Seven Feathers smiled and shook his head. "I should only be surprised you waited so long to speak."

"If I had waited, you would have thought of too many reasons why I should not go."

"I already have such reasons, but I am sure that will not stop you from telling me what you would do if I let you go in your father's place."

"Exactly what my father would have done. I will go to England and avenge the murder of his brother. I will kill this man before he can harm my grandfather."

27

Tag blinked to be sure the words came from the same fragile woman who had aroused his protective instincts only a moment before. "You will hang," he said quietly.

She threw him a scornful look. "Would you have brought my father to England to kill and then let him hang?"

Tag took a deep breath to control his impatience. "I had no intention of asking him to kill anyone. Not unless his life was in danger."

"Tell me, Elmgrove, would I not serve as well as my father?"

"I . . ." Tag cursed himself for being so distracted by her appearance he hadn't prepared an answer. "You would certainly rob your cousin of the inheritance he expects, but—" He thought of Oliver's certainty that his cousin would stop at nothing after he had killed twice. He shuddered. "But no. You must not think of it."

"Is there a reason other than the danger you mentioned?"

"It would have been dangerous even for your father, a soldier. It is unthinkable for a woman alone."

"I have been raised here. I am not some helpless Englishwoman."

"She would not be alone," the hulking warrior on Caro's other side said. He looked at her. "As your husband, I would go with you."

"Your husband," Tag said, speaking quickly to cover the stab of envy he felt. "That would change everything."

"No." Seven Feathers glared at the brave. "I have said I cannot spare you."

The warrior's shoulders stiffened. "Caro must not only avenge her relatives, she must protect her grandfather. Surely to protect him—"

"That man is a stranger. Your skills feed many of our people in the winter. We cannot let them die to save the life of a stranger."

28

Caro put a calming hand on the arm of the frowning warrior. "You could never be happy away from here, and you are not my husband yet." She turned her attention to Tag. "You said a husband would change everything. How is that?"

"In England, once a woman is married, everything she owns belongs to her husband and his family. You only need a husband with a large enough family that even your cousin Edwin couldn't dispose of them without attracting too much attention."

"Could I find such a husband in England?"

He laughed. "You could find a dozen in an afternoon. Your only problem would be selecting one to suit you." Tag recognized the truth of the compliment even as he automatically spoke the words. Men would write sonnets to her eyes and hair without even considering the fortune she would inherit.

The compliment deserved a smile, but Caro bestowed that reward on the warrior next to her. "You are saved, Breath of a Panther. You may stay here. If I need a husband, I will find one in England."

"Enough." Seven Feathers muttered a few unintelligible words and made a circular motion with his hand. The warriors jumped to their feet. "We all have much to think about."

Jake rose. Obviously the meeting was over. Tag stood, curbing the impulse to offer his hand to the young lady, who remained seated beside Seven Feathers.

Even though he remained seated, the chief's presence dominated the room. "Tonight you will stay in my *wegiwa,* Elm Grove. We will talk again tomorrow." His gentle hand on Caro's arm kept her at his side. Her protector hovered over her.

"The wedding," Caro reminded the chief.

"There will be no wedding until we settle this matter." Tag hesitated at the doorway. No point in turning his back on a man he had just deprived of a bride. To his astonishment the huge warrior brushed past him without a glance, his expression that of a man whose hanging had been postponed.

Caro sat in the shadows, her stomach churning from the meal that should have been her wedding feast. The moon gleamed high overhead and the familiar sounds of night comforted her. Wood smoke and the lingering smell of roasted elk and squirrel filled the air. Bathed in the dying firelight, a warrior had just completed a tale of a battle many summers past. How could she have said she would leave all this?

For those few seconds the idea of going to England had felt so right, but the certainty had disappeared as quickly as it had come.

Seven Feathers was right. She owed nothing to the old man in England. After the others had gone, she had waited for Seven Feathers to forbid her to leave. But he had said none of the things she had expected, just shaken his head sadly and said, "You will decide, child." Then he had caressed her cheek and smiled. "But you will not decide right now."

All afternoon she had covertly watched the visitor, looking for something that would make her despise him and reject the mission his presence imposed.

Late in the day he and his guide had strolled around the village, exploring as casually as if they had been born there. The trailing herd of children quickly discovered the guests had not arrived empty-handed. Within minutes Elmgrove had draped six of the youngest boys in fine cotton shirts several sizes too large for them. An equal number of girls pranced around him in jangling necklaces. The children, obviously thinking they had to give him something in trade, had presented him with three-year-old Calling Bird. He had laughed and carried the child in the crook of his arm for the rest of the afternoon, only setting him down when they returned to Seven Feathers's lodge to prepare for dinner.

Unlike many visitors who adopted informal dress as soon as they arrived in the village, Elmgrove had stepped from the chief's *wegiwa* dressed in a spotless white shirt with ruffles at the neck and a tight-fitting gray coat. With crisp elegant movements he tugged the cuffs into place and straightened the coat on his shoulders. Then, with a shrug and a smile, he totally ruined the effect by bending to scoop up the waiting Calling Bird before joining Seven Feathers and the other men at the cook fire. So English, but so gentle. A good man.

He ate every bite set before him, and conversed with Seven Feathers and the other warriors as if he had been in the village for months. If she had to go with him, at least he would be an entertaining companion. The thought of leaving upset her stomach once more.

Gray Wolf rose and moved to the center of the circle. Caro sighed. She had heard his only tale too many times to have any patience with it tonight. Others in the village felt the same. Low-voiced talk broke out even as Gray Wolf began his story. He spoke louder, demanding attention for his sorry feat of bringing back two mangy horses and the scalps of an old man and a young boy.

Chief Seven Feathers spoke quietly. Elmgrove responded. Seven Feathers laughed. If Gray Wolf's look had been a tomahawk, both would have died. Gray Wolf's narrative came near to shouting, but he finished his tale more quickly than usual and waited for praise. Only a few of the older warriors in the circle even bothered to grunt approval.

Gray Wolf turned to stomp back to his place. Then he stopped and towered over Elmgrove. "Is this man even a warrior?" he asked in Shawnee. "If he is, we should hear his story."

Fletcher spoke softly to Elmgrove, obviously to translate

the request. Elmgrove looked up at Gray Wolf, smiled, and shook his head.

Gray Wolf turned and addressed the group. "If Elmgrove is a warrior, not a woman, he has a story."

Several of the other braves echoed the demand. Everyone loved a new story. Elmgrove again signaled his unwillingness. The chief spoke to Elmgrove, words Caro couldn't hear. Fletcher whispered something. The muscles of Elmgrove's jaw tightened.

A moment later he pushed himself to his feet and stepped to the place in the circle reserved for the storyteller. He waited. The snap of the log in the fire and the rain of cinders broke the silence. Finally he began to speak. "A year ago the English had a great battle with the French at a small village called Waterloo."

Fletcher must have translated the earlier stories for him, or else Elmgrove was a natural storyteller. He drew the English words out in the rolling Shawnee way and waited patiently for Fletcher to translate what he said before continuing. He pointed to the surrounding woods. "You couldn't hold such a battle here. The armies stretched from horizon"—he threw his arms widely apart—"to horizon and the battle went on for two days." His face hardened with the memory and he spoke with the voice of a war-hardened veteran.

In ringing tones, he told of being a messenger for the great chief Wellington, of having two horses shot from under him, and killing three of the French with his sword. Finally he clasped his left hand over his right arm to show where he had been wounded. He stopped speaking, and the listening braves shouted their approval. Chief Seven Feathers nodded the respect of one warrior for another.

Elmgrove took a long stride toward his seat.

"And the second day?" Gray Wolf planted his feet apart and hurled his words at Elmgrove. "Did you watch from the woods like a woman because you had a small wound in your arm?''

Elmgrove may not have understood Gray Wolf's Shawnee words, but he stopped in mid-step, knowing he'd been challenged. He looked to Fletcher and waited for the words in English. He hesitated only a moment, then returned to the center of the circle. He spoke so softly Caro and the warriors had to strain forward to hear, but the emotion shimmered in the air.

"On the second day my arm was bound to my body so I couldn't hold a gun or a sword in my right hand." He paused and looked at the sky, the painful memory gouged into his face. "And yes at the start I watched from a hill. I watched my friends being slaughtered by three times their number. They fought until every officer lay dead. Then the men broke into a run. It would have been a massacre.

"I don't know how I managed to stay on my horse or hold my sword in my left hand, but I tore out of the woods. We fought like madmen, close up with hands and swords, and we turned those troops. We fought until the French stopped coming, until only four of us were standing." He shot a fierce glare at Gray Wolf. "No. I didn't watch like a woman, but too many men died there for me to talk about it any longer for your pleasure." He stalked over and sat down heavily beside Seven Feathers.

The seated braves waited for Fletcher to repeat the words in Shawnee, then clamored for more, calling out the all-important question, "How many did you kill?"

When Elmgrove understood, he just shook his head and said, "Too many." He refused to say any more even when Seven Feathers asked.

Gray Wolf, however, wasn't finished. "How many scalps did you take?"

"The English don't take scalps."

Gray Wolf strutted to the center of the circle. "Perhaps

the English do not always want to prove their brave words.''

Elmgrove ignored the taunt and said something quietly to Seven Feathers. The scene might have ended there if Seven Feathers hadn't looked at Gray Wolf and laughed.

Enraged, Gray Wolf continued taunting. ''How do we know any of his words are true? Englishmen are cowards and liars. I say he lies.''

Caro gasped at the insult.

Silence froze the warriors. Seven Feathers glared at Gray Wolf.

Elmgrove stood as slowly as a cat uncurling from sleep, his face a mask, white and hard. Each slow deliberate step across the hard ground slapped in the silence. Only inches from Gray Wolf he stopped. The firelight cast their flickering shadows to the edge of the circle. The Englishman spoke slowly, and every word echoed. ''In England, a man who called me a liar would live until dawn and not one minute longer.''

Caro tensed. This was lunacy, not bravery. Gray Wolf towered over Elmgrove. Even a coward could tear apart a man half his size. She held her breath, afraid for Elmgrove but relieved she was not the one staring into the chiseled rock of his face.

Gray Wolf retreated, one step, then another.

Caro's clenched hands relaxed. Gray Wolf wouldn't fight.

Everything would have ended there if three of the braves hadn't snickered. Gray Wolf pulled out a knife and slashed, but Elmgrove jumped faster than a coiled snake. In a blink, Elmgrove also had a knife. Gray Wolf fell back another step, and the two men circled each other. Nothing moved but the two men and their shadows.

Seconds crawled by. Fletcher pushed himself to his feet and strolled casually into the circle as if totally unaware of the drama. His path took him between the two combatants and he very deliberately turned his back on Gray Wolf and shook his head at Elmgrove like a mother scolding a child. "Now I told you to mind your manners, and here you are showin' off with a knife." He looked toward the chief. "You have to excuse him, Seven Feathers, he just got that knife and can't hardly resist showin' it to everybody he meets."

The chief whipped the air with his hand and two braves jumped up to stand on either side of Gray Wolf.

Caro exhaled. The Englishman would live. Was the stab of fear that had clutched her heart the sign she was seeking? Not a sign that she should stay here, but the instinctive message that she wanted him to live so she could leave with him?

On a bed of animal skins, Tag lay in Seven Feathers's *wegiwa*. Despite the warm summer night and the glow of the dying fire, he pulled a woven blanket over him. That way, if anyone glanced his way, the embarrassing direction of his thoughts wouldn't be so apparent. Visions of women in dresses that barely reached their knees flickered in his mind.

Nothing like talk of war to bring on the need for a willing woman. And right now he couldn't think of much else.

At first the scanty garb of the women had only mildly amused him. That was before his body had become fully aware of the possibilities. From the satisfied looks of the couples who returned after slipping away from the fire circle, he wasn't the only one aware of how easily those dresses could be raised.

It had been much too long since he'd had a woman.

The murmur of voices drew his attention to the other side of the room, where the chief lay with the wife he had chosen for the night. Deep regular breathing told Tag the other wife and children slept. He coughed to warn the chief he was awake and now wouldn't be a good time to be fumbling between his wife's legs.

The soft growl of the man's voice came again, followed by what sounded like a moan from the woman.

They wouldn't.

Not with him in the same room.

The covering over the two heaved in an unmistakable movement. Dammit, they were going to do it. Why the hell hadn't Jake warned him this might happen?

A determined flip onto his side shut out the sight, but the sounds continued to assail him. He clenched his eyes closed. It didn't help. His mind provided its own pictures. The English girl. Caro. The way the hem of her dress crept above her knees when she sat back on her heels. The space between her knees just wide enough for a man's hand. Her eyes would widen with his feather-soft stroke. A soft moan would invite more. He'd find—

Dammit. He counted to one hundred. He counted backwards to zero.

The slapping sounds ceased abruptly. At least someone was satisfied.

Caro dressed hurriedly and slipped from the village just minutes before the sun crested the hill to the east of the valley. Without conscious thought she followed the familiar paths. She had come out early—to decide, she told herself. The heaviness in her heart forced her to acknowledge the lie.

She had come out to say good-bye.

How could she bear to never smell the earth again at dawn? Or to feel the kiss of the dew-heavy air against her arms?

She found the rock with the body-sized niche carved by generations of wind and rain. Today she didn't sit, but just ran her hand over the smooth stone. Where did the English go in their big houses when they were troubled? To another room? Could a person really think with walls pressing in on them? Could they even breathe?

She followed a path from her secluded glade. Even in her happiest moments she had known that someday she would leave. She had known it yesterday, though throughout the night she had tried to hide from the knowledge.

She could expose her skin to the sun to become as dark as the bark of a maple tree. She could boil dye and wash her hair black, but she could never send out the invisible roots that bound her adopted people to the land of their ancestors.

Such things had never troubled her father. He had stepped between the two worlds as easily as she would cross a narrow stream: More Shawnee than the fiercest warrior when it pleased him, but casually donning the English ways as easily as slipping into the British regimental coat.

Even the wiliest chiefs, who trusted no one, would organize a feast to welcome Fenton to their village. They trusted him because he didn't speak with broken promises. He donned the war paint and fought beside them, took scalps with the boldest of them, and returned to the campfire to boast in Shawnee of his triumphs.

And he trusted them to raise his daughter.

Her heart twisted with the need to ask him whether he wanted her to go or not. A meager smile forced itself to her lips. His idea of wondering where he belonged was to ask who had a sleeping robe in their *wegiwa* for him.

If she left, it wouldn't be because he expected it of her.

She bent to pick a wild herb and twisted the stem in her fingers, releasing its tangy, wild aroma. She let the leaves flutter against the palm of her other hand. *If she left*, she thought, and knew she wouldn't stay long enough to see the leaves dry to a crackling brittleness. Last night White Fish, the medicine man who had taken her in as a sickly child and taught her the things her father could not, had told her she would leave—in a way so vivid it hurt to recall.

She had waited up for him until the fire in the lodge had become nothing more than a bed of glowing coals. "Should I go?" she had asked, her tight muscles willing him to say no.

He had brushed her hair from her face and let his hand rest on her shoulder, but his answer had been the same as Chief Seven Feathers's. "You will tell me that in the morning." He had waited until she lay down and pretended to sleep before giving his real answer.

His shoulders hunched like a woman carrying a heavy weight, his fragile frame casting a long shadow on the bark overhead, he had moved about quietly.

He'd opened his well-worn medicine satchel and began packing it with roots and herbs as he'd done a hundred times when getting ready for a trip. From his wooden chest he selected carefully, occasionally shaking his head and returning an item to the chest. He looked like a very old man. Only when he turned toward her and she saw his face, collapsed into loose wrinkles like a hide pulled loose from its frame, did she realize he was packing the satchel for her.

He wasn't going on a journey. She was.

Now the rye grass of a rich meadow grazed Caro's knees. The new day's sun caressed her back. She murmured a greeting to a startled doe, which should never have been this close to the village, but had appeared to share this moment with her. "I am going away, little mother. You would protect your family. I must go and protect mine."

She would go and kill the evil man because the village couldn't spare a warrior, and a Shawnee couldn't let an enemy kill his family without striking back. She would go because game was scarce and one less woman would be one less hungry belly in the empty months of winter. And she would go because she and White Fish had always known she would go someday.

She turned to face the east and the path she must follow,

straightened her shoulders, and tilted her chin towards the sun's rays. If she had to go, she would go as a Shawnee woman, tall and proud.

A half-smile played at her lips. Maybe not so tall, but at least proud. No one would see her whimper for what she left behind. No one would feel sorry for her.

Firm strides carried her along the more direct route back to the village. The decision made, she looked for a sign to confirm her choice. A small woodland creature happily scampering along a path to the east would do nicely, she thought.

She cut through the underbrush at the edge of the village and found her sign.

Breath of a Panther stood in front of the council house talking with Little Dove. They stood apart, not even within arm's reach of each other, but her imagination framed them in sunlight like a single person. If nothing else, Caro would go with the visitor to give the gift of happiness to these two people she loved.

Breath of a Panther looked up and called a greeting. Caro walked toward them. Little Dove smiled and echoed the welcome, but she slipped away before Caro came close enough to speak. Little Dove's heart might be alive with hope, but she would never intrude.

"Not only did I wake this morning without a new wife," Breath of a Panther said, "but I couldn't find you anywhere. Already I shall have to think about beating you, Caro." His voice held the falsely hearty note she had grown used to since he'd announced he would marry her, the tone he had adopted so she would never know the command to marry her was tearing the heart from his body.

Caro glowed with the happiness of anticipation. Today she would offer Breath of a Panther the joy he deserved, and perhaps she would have the comfort of their old easy friendship for the time that remained. "I am afraid you will have to look somewhere else for a wife to beat. I am going to England.''

So quickly that even she who knew him so well couldn't swear she saw it, a flicker of hope flashed through his eyes. ''You have decided?''

''Yes.''

''Then I will ask Seven Feathers again to let us go together. You are to be my wife and even a chief cannot forbid me to avenge the murder of your family.''

''I *was* to be your wife. Now I am a grand lady of England.'' She tilted her nose to the air as she had seen the women in Detroit do. ''What would I want with an ordinary Shawnee brave like you?''

Breath of a Panther bristled like a porcupine. ''A man to kill your enemies.''

Caro produced her fiercest scowl, finally finding something to enjoy in the wrenching day. ''One miserable enemy. Do you doubt that I can kill a single Englishman, a coward who shoots people in the back?''

Some of the old affection lit Breath of a Panther's eyes. ''I think if we had sent you to England a hundred years ago, we wouldn't have to worry about so many white men here today.'' He put his arm on her shoulders and guided her back in the direction she had come. About twenty feet into the brush they found a huge log worn smooth by the many who had rested there in the coolness of the woods.

There, in gentle tones he tried to talk her out of her decision. She let him have his say, knowing no man could be completely happy until he had said everything he thought in eleven different ways. Her chin set, she let his words wash over her, remembering all the times they had argued. His voice soothed her, and she relaxed against a jutting banch. They had not talked so comfortably in weeks.

''Even if you must go, I cannot like your going off alone with this stranger. We know nothing about him. I think—''

40

"I think you have to stop treating me like the frightened child you had to teach to walk tall. I am a Shawnee woman now. If Elmgrove annoys me, I will tie him to a tree and light a fire between his toes."

The warrior grinned and shook his head. "Do not be deceived by his soft eyes. He has the heart of a warrior. He proved that to us all last night. He can be a dangerous man. Do not provoke him, little sister."

Little sister. His words sang through Caro. Breath of a Panther had accepted she was leaving and understood that he was free. She had back the brother she adored rather than the reluctant bridegroom. The joy of it sent a laugh bubbling from her lips. "I never provoke."

He cuffed her softly on the side of the head. "Then you better behave much better with Elmgrove than you do with me."

"With you! My only problem is what to do with you."

"Do with me?"

She shivered with the pleasure of her gift. "Now that I cannot marry you, I will have to find you a wife." She shook her head and pretended concern. "Shadow Tree might accept you," she said, naming the toothless woman they had laughed about as children because she fawned over every brave who came to the village, "if I do not tell her you eat more than twelve men."

"I don't—I will find my own wife." His eyes softened with the look that belonged only to Little Dove.

Caro couldn't even tease any more. "Then you had better do it quickly before Seven Feathers finds somebody else who needs a husband and orders you to marry her."

"I—" His mouth dropped open and his eyes widened. For a moment he stared at her without speaking. "You knew . . . ?"

"That Seven Feathers ordered you to marry me? Of course."

Judy Veisel

His face took on an expression of pain and bewilderment. "How? I was so careful. I—"

Caro reached out and put her hand on the warm skin of his shoulder, the first time she had touched him comfortably since the disturbing day he had informed her she would be his wife. "Yes, you were. And I loved you all the more for it."

"But how . . . ?"

She hadn't known at first, but had felt a terrible emptiness in his words. "Even though you called me Caro, not little sister, your eyes still said sister. But I didn't know for sure until I saw Little Dove."

A furrow appeared between his brows and his voice crisped. "She swore she wouldn't—"

"She didn't. You forget, I am trained to heal. I felt the pain she hid. Then I saw her look at you, and I knew."

"Why didn't you say something?"

"I did. As soon as I understood, I went to Seven Feathers." She grimaced at the memory of the chief's towering rage when she had fought against his decision. "He doesn't like a woman disagreeing with him."

"You wouldn't argue with—yes, you would." He shook his head. "What did he say?"

Caro studied the cloud formation over his shoulder to avoid meeting his eyes. "At first he tried to explain. He said many braves have asked for Little Dove. She could have many husbands. While I . . ." Again the familiar pain of being different burned through her.

She could see that Breath of a Panther sensed the hurt as he always had, from the day she had arrived. "Everyone in the village loves you. You are kind and caring."

"I am blond and fair."

"You are sunlight with eyes of water."

"But warriors do not marry sunlight and thin white blood. Nor do they want a wife who may bear a child with the white man's blue eyes."

42

"Your child will be beautiful."

"My child will be your child if you don't stop being kind." She laughed to take the pain from his eyes. "I told Seven Feathers you were ugly as a toad and I would rather marry a tree stump."

His rich laugh rang through the forest. "And such a wise chief would never believe that. You should have told him you are an annoying little dog flea who does not deserve me." His banter was so wonderfully familiar it warmed the air around them. So many times had he tried to chase her away with the same manner, only to turn and motion her to follow him. A cloud came over his face again. "Why did you never tell me this?"

"Nothing could change Seven Feathers's mind. He said if I spoke of it, I would only make all of us more unhappy."

"I think it would have." He winced. "I am sorry, little sister. I would have cut my heart out before I hurt you."

Caro smiled at him. "I think you already have. A little piece each day. Now, I have the happiness of giving it back to you." The smile turned into a small laugh. "Though now I suppose you are just going to throw it away on Little Dove."

"Do you think . . . ?" His gaze darted toward the village where he would find his happiness.

"I think in a minute her eyes will be shining as yours are now. Go to her."

He rose and looked down at her, still tentative in his newfound joy. "Are you sure?"

"I have never been more sure of anything."

Her words gave him permission to release a wild whoop of joy. He reached down, lifted her from the log, and swung her around until they were both dizzy.

She laughed. "Put me down and go to her before she finds somebody with sense enough not to be dancing around in the forest."

He obeyed with a suddenness that left Caro scrambling

with tiny steps to keep her feet. "She will have me," he declared. He started toward the village, calling over his shoulder, "You will dance the marriage dance with us? You wouldn't go without . . ."

Caro didn't need to hear the rest of his words. She wouldn't go without wishing them joy. But she would have to go without saying farewell to Billy Boy, the boy who belonged to her as no one else ever had. Perhaps that would be best as well. Her one final way to release him to take his place among the men. She glanced toward the glade where she had taken him so often. "Good-bye, Billy Boy," she whispered.

Content for the first time in almost twenty-four hours, she entered the village. A cluster of children immediately surrounded her, all calling for her attention.

"Where have you been?"

". . . Seven Feathers has been looking every place . . ."

". . . wants to see you right away . . ."

". . . wants to discuss his plans for your wedding."

Chapter Three

A litany of curses trailing behind him, Tag lurched through the opening to the lodge where he had left Jake.

Jake set aside the half-mended moccasin. "Either you're practicin' good for a cussin' contest or somebody has provoked you real bad."

Leaving deep boot prints on the dirt floor, Tag reached the far side and whirled. "Well, aren't you going to ask me what happened?"

"Figure you'll tell me flat out when you're ready. Least you ain't got a dozen fellas comin' after you with knives. Reckon it can't be that bad."

"Worse than that. I'm getting married." He choked. "Tonight."

"Well, I'll be damned." Jake's grin lit the inside of the lodge as he held out his hand. "Congratulations."

Tag brushed his hand aside. "Not congratulations. Tell me what to do."

Jake gave an imitation leer. "Iff'n you don't know what to do on yer weddin' night, I reckon I can explain it. But it sure does seem to me . . ." His voice trailed off into a throaty chuckle at his own joke.

"Dammit. It's not funny."

Jake stifled his laugh, though his eyes continued to twinkle. "Okay. Tell me about it."

"I was fool enough to tell Chief Seven Feathers that the girl would be safer in England if she had a husband. He doesn't believe in wasting any time. Since I'm the only Englishman here, he scheduled my wedding for tonight.''

"Gather you told him what you thought of the idea."

"He went so far as to make it very clear I wouldn't be leaving without marrying her. Did he mean it, do you think? Or was it just a threat?"

"Doubt it was a threat." Jake stood, walked to the opening and glanced out. "Them two braves out there are bound to make certain you don't take a notion to leave before the ceremony." He scratched the stubble on his chin. "I don't see what you're carrying on about. That Caro's a damn fine-looking female."

"I don't care what she looks like. I can't marry her, dammit. I don't want to marry her. I—"

Jake held up both hands to ward off whatever Tag might have said next. "Sure don't see why not. These here Indian women make damn fine wives. They don't grow up with fool notions 'bout how they're not supposed to enjoy being in bed with a man."

Tag ground his teeth until his jaw ached. "Why not is because I plan to choose my own wife and already have the perfect woman in mind. As soon as I get back to England—"

Jake shrugged. "But you ain't back in England now. Half of the white men who come into these woods sleep with a squaw for the winter."

Tag reared back "Caro—Miss Fenton is not an Indian squaw. She is the granddaughter of a very wealthy man. And if you tell me once more marrying her is no problem, I'll—"

"All right, you wanna jaw on this serious-like." Jake settled back onto the floor. "I say you marry up with her. You ain't leavin' unless you do. And it ain't like your Church of England is going to pay any nevermind to a backwoods weddin'."

Tag rose. "Are you saying I should—"

"Sure. Marry up with the gal. Hell, it's just a ritual, and it sounds like it might make Seven Feathers happy enough to let you ride out of here still wearin' your hair."

"I can't do that."

"Would you take her to England with you if you didn't have to marry her?"

"I'd have to. She's been trapped here since her father's death. I may be her only chance to escape. I owe it to Oliver to escort her safely to England."

"Then I don't see how a little marryin' makes much difference. Besides, you don't have much choice." He glanced toward the opening at the gathering twilight. "Or much time."

Tag exhaled, his shoulders releasing the weight of his resistance. A ceremony here in the middle of the American wilderness wouldn't make much difference to anybody. He relaxed onto a heavy deerskin mat. "Seven Feathers said you would explain about the ceremony."

Jake chuckled. "You're bound to like that part of it. Leastwise you will iff'n you've got red blood in your veins. No clergyman. No fancy words. Just two people doin' a dance. After that, if they want to be hitched, they're hitched."

"And if they don't?"

Jake laughed, obviously enjoying himself. "Not many people don't. That's the purpose of the dance."

His words confirmed Tag's suspicion this wouldn't be a traditional ceremony. "I am not going to have to get naked for this thing, am I?"

Jake didn't answer quite quickly enough. He angled his head and studied Tag. "Probably be enough if you just slide outta that fussy shirt. Now, once you're standin', we kin start practicin'."

Tag rose, but still held back. Seven Feathers certainly hadn't been overly concerned about an audience for his performance last night. "I'm not going to have to . . .

to . . ." He cleared his throat and pointed to the opening in the *wegiwa*. ". . . right out there in front of everybody?"

Jake frowned, then his face lit with comprehension. "You're just gonna dance. A lot of other people will be dancin' too. After that, you and this gal'll sashay over to your own *wegiwa*. What you do there is your own business."

Tag relaxed. "Show me this dance."

Jake gripped the awl he'd been using to punch holes in the moccasins, bent, and drew a line on the ground. "You'll be dancin' with fifteen or twenty men. Just watch them fellas on either side of you. Do what they do. Once the dance ends, if either you or her says, *Ouisah meni-e-de-luh*, that means 'good dance,' then you both walk away and forget about the whole thing."

"And if we don't say the oushey thing?"

"Then you say, *Ni haw-ku-nah-ga*, you are my wife. And you are married up with her."

Convinced he would never leave the village if he didn't learn to say *Ni haw . . .* , Tag practiced the phrase until Jake was satisfied.

Awkward at first, Tag imitated the steps and fell into the rhythm. He produced a grim smile. "I believe I can manage that. You said that is all. I doubt that is likely to unleash much unbridled lust."

Jake pointed again to the lines he had drawn. "These women ain't gonna stay put over here, and you ain't stayin' there. You'll be dancin' right close time the thing ends. And you'll be talkin' at her."

Tag sighed in exasperation. "I'm grateful you remembered to mention that. What the hell am I supposed to say?"

Jake laughed. "Now don't get all riled up again. You're just gonna be spoutin' the usual things you say to a woman you wanna be climbing all over."

48

"I don't know any Shawnee except *Ni haw,* and she'll probably get tired of that pretty quick."

"You'll pop up a thought or two. And she'll be jawin' back at you."

The idea rather pleased Tag. "What will she be saying?"

Jake continued grinning. "For your sake I hope she'll be sayin' it in Shawnee 'cause a bone-proper Englishman like you'll surely faint dead away at some of them things that cross a woman's mind."

"You may as well tell me. And you can stop that infernal chuckling before I throttle you."

"Well, now, I can't say precisely what Caro will pop out with." He eyed Tag slowly as one might a stallion he meant to buy. "But I can purely tell you what my little gal said to me." He nodded significantly to Tag's groin. "She said I had a tallywhacker as big as a buffalo."

Caro moved about the *wegiwa* she had shared with White Fish for ten years. She had asked for a few minutes alone, and the women helping her dress had filed out. To prepare herself, she had said. To say good-bye, she meant.

Everything she did brought the same feeling. Not a sadness, just a soul-deep awareness of what would never be again. Her fingertips caressed the inside of a wooden bowl, worn smooth and oiled by a thousand meals. She had eaten for the last time from this bowl. She would never again turn automatically and reach for the familiar curved spoon.

A female voice came from outside. "Hurry now."

She would never again tense at Drifting Stick's impatient tone. She would come when she was ready. For now she had these moments.

Only a day ago she'd thought the idea of leaving would tear her apart with a terrible grief. But the grief had never come. The moment she'd made the decision, a heavy weight had floated from her shoulders. She had grown, feeling tall, as if a single stride might cover an entire meadow.

In the hours since then, she had turned repeatedly toward the east, as if her eyes might see across the distance to the land of her people. A land where she would truly belong as she had never belonged here.

How often had she sat on a hill overlooking one of the white-man's towns and envied the people who claimed a piece of land and defended it to the death. Perhaps that was what made her different. The desire she shared with the other world to set down roots like the mighty oak tree. To build a home as the English did, and know her family would live there for the next hundred years. A home where every bush would be familiar. No one else ever seemed to feel the wrench she did every time that Seven Feathers announced the game had thinned and they would move on.

Every fiber in her body stirred with the rightness of what she would do. She would say this final good-bye and move on to a place where she could stay forever. In spite of the many people who wanted to share her final hours, she had spent much of the day alone, visiting her favorite places.

She had stood in the middle of the cornfield, felt the sun on her face and listened to the rustle of the leaves. She had bathed in the pool by the waterfall, savoring the caress of the warm water and remembering how the icy water prickled her skin in the early spring. But mostly she'd walked the paths she'd walked with others, saying good-bye to the spirits of close friends who had fallen in battle or been wrenched away by sickness.

Though he had already left to join the others outside, Caro said a silent farewell to White Fish. She filled his home with her spirit and her gratitude. He had taken her in as a sickly child and given her strength and wisdom. She would take much of him with her and leave much of herself here.

The flap covering the entrance shifted. Little Dove came in, hanging back, afraid to look, as if fearing what she would find. "Are you . . . ?" Her eyes widened with hope. "You are not terribly sad, are you?"

Caro laughed and hurried over to take her hand. "Sad I don't have to marry a man who has always loved me like a sister? Of course I'm not. Though I will be terribly angry if you don't stop asking me that." She stepped back to look at her gentle friend who had spent the last hour preparing for her own wedding. "You are lovely. Your hair is gleaming like the hard black rocks when the water rushes over them."

Like herself, Little Dove wore a white doeskin dress. Though elaborately decorated with beads and porcupine quills, Little Dove's was not new because she had not expected to marry tonight. But Breath of a Panther wouldn't even notice the dress. He would see only her soft smile, her glossy black hair tumbling to her waist, and her huge black eyes glistening in the firelight. "Breath of a Panther will probably disgrace you by carrying you off to his lodge before the marriage dance even begins."

"I came to be sure. Are you . . . ? Oh, Caro, do you have to marry this white man? You can—"

Caro smiled at her friend, born with so much kindness and so little selfishness. "If you tell me one more time I may marry Breath of a Panther, I will go to him right now and tell him you have the brain of a spider and he should marry Shadow Tree."

Little Dove refused to be teased out of her concern. "Please, don't joke any more. I didn't know when Breath of a Panther talked to me this morning that you would have to marry this stranger. Why do you have to marry tonight?"

"Seven Feathers has ordered it. The same way he ordered me to marry Breath of a Panther."

"But why? He loves you. He must know—"

"He only wants me to be safe. Because of English laws about money, he believes I will be safer in England if I have a husband."

51

"But this man is a stranger."

The noise from outside increased. Caro recognized the boisterous comments. The men had arrived for the marriage dance. They had only a few minutes. She couldn't let Little Dove's tender heart spoil her wedding night. "He is no more a stranger than many of the men who come from distant villages to ask Seven Feathers to choose a bride for them."

"But even if we don't know them, we know of them. We know their families."

"Seven Feathers always chooses wisely. I trust he has done so in this case."

"Even our wise chief knows nothing about this Elm Grove. None of us do."

Here Caro felt on surer ground. "That is not true. We know he traveled many thousands of miles to keep a promise to his friend. And I have watched him from the moment he came into the village. He came bravely into a place where he knew he might find enemies of his people."

"He might not be brave, merely foolish."

"I thought so at first. But he moved cautiously and took care not to offend anyone."

"He offended Gray Wolf."

Caro laughed. "Squirrels offend Gray Wolf." She sobered, remembering her terror when the stranger had faced the huge warrior in the firelight. "And Elmgrove met his challenge with courage."

Gentle Little Dove had less regard for bravery than one who had had to stand alone among strangers. "We have known many brave men. They are not always good husbands."

The first hollow sounds of the drums resonated through the walls. Suddenly Caro needed to reassure herself as much as Little Dove. "You have seen how he carried Calling Bird about the village and how he smiled when he gave his gifts to the children of the village. If I could choose a husband, I would choose one who is gentle with children.''

Even Caro's strongest argument failed to convince her friend. ''But will he be kind to you? Why would he even accept this marriage? You are as much a stranger to him as he is to you.''

''In his country such marriages are common. My father left England because he didn't want to marry the woman my grandfather had chosen. Besides, I think . . . I hope . . .'' Caro let her voice trail off, unable to express her secret hope even to her closest friend.

''Tell me, please.'' Little Dove clasped Caro's hands. ''Tell me why you think you will be happy.''

''I . . . It is very hard to find words, because it is more a feeling. Even when I have no reason to, I find myself watching him, hoping he will notice me.'' Her words dropped to a near whisper. ''Hoping he will like me.'' Her heartbeat quickened. She had not meant to confess so much even to herself.

''I feel like that with Breath of a Panther.'' Little Dove's eyes sparkled. ''How could Elmgrove not love you? You are very beautiful.''

''Only to you because you love me. But possibly to a white man . . . Perhaps after tonight . . .'' She felt the rush of color to her face at the thought of how intimately the stranger would touch her. ''After tonight, perhaps he will look at me as Breath of a Panther looks at you.''

As flushed as Caro, Little Dove embraced her. ''He will. I know he will.''

They had no more time to spend on idle wishes. With her more usual teasing laugh, Caro twisted from her friend's arms. ''Best of all, Elmgrove is not a large, clumsy oaf like Breath of a Panther. When your husband crushes you, you will envy me with a gentle white man.''

''Never.'' The outside sounds became louder. Little Dove looked to the entrance, back at Caro, and back to the entrance. She surrendered to her happiness, glowing with excitement. "They are starting. Come, let us go." She grabbed Caro's hand and together they ran from the *weg-iwa*.

Outside they joined a group of fifteen waiting women who would honor them by joining the dance. All wore their finest dresses, with their hair tumbling loose about their shoulders. The excited group surrounded them to exchange whispered greetings and suggestive comments. Seven Feathers's first wife hushed them sharply and led them toward the campfire.

In the center of the large circle of watchers, seventeen men were lined up two feet apart, facing the direction from which the women came. Most tried to appear casual, but their shifting gazes searched the group until each found the woman he sought. Each women likewise had no doubt which warrior belonged to her. They swiftly traded places and Caro found herself opposite Elmgrove.

She had done the dance many times before, but always to celebrate with a friend. Always with a man who made the proper motions, and tempered his advances with respect. Tonight the wedding dance would be for her, and before the night ended she would lie with the stranger.

A sudden shyness gripped her. She stole the quickest glance across the open space and saw the sea of bodies before she dropped her gaze to the bare feet of the man who would be hers. She had vowed to meet her fate bravely. Curling her fingers, she squared her shoulders and tossed back her head. Unaccustomed to her loose hair, she tensed as it fluttered across her neck.

She wondered if she was pretty. Would her man ever look at her with his heart the way Breath of a Panther looked at Little Dove?

Not if she never did anything but stare at the hard-packed earth. The drums began to beat in earnest. She raised her head and met his gaze for the first time. He stood as straight and proud as the others, looking directly at her. He allowed her a moment to accustom herself to his regard; then impossibly, he winked at her. No one had ever winked at her before. She imitated the gesture, only to realize she had merely blinked both eyes and wrinkled her nose. He grinned. She had expected heat or passion, not this slow relaxing of guard and tension. This would surely be all right.

He had removed his shirt, and the stark white of his chest evenly divided the row of bronze warriors. If he felt uncomfortable with the difference, or even noticed it, she couldn't tell, because he didn't appear aware of anyone but her. Even across twenty paces his look warmed her.

An elder stood and added the sandy shiver of his rattles to the drum beat. *"Ya ne no hoo wa no,"* he chanted. *"Ya ne no hoo wa no . . . ya ne no hoo wa no."* The line of women began to move in unison, stepping and swaying from side to side. Hands behind their backs, they joined the chanting, then as one took a single step forward. One step closer to the line of men.

The men mirrored the motion; stepping, swaying, and chanting, they took a pace forward. The distance between the lines decreased. The tempo increased. The watchers took up the chant. The lines stepped and the distance decreased again. *"Ya ne no hoo wa no."*

Caro's blood throbbed with the beat. She no longer had trouble meeting Elmgrove's gaze, no longer worried about the decreasing distance. Without a shirt, he was larger than she remembered. Broad powerful shoulders, muscles shifting and moving in his chest, making it a living thing. Her awareness of him caused the crowd and the other dancers to fade into the background. They might have been alone in the clearing. Only the two of them moving closer in the flickering firelight. Why had she never thought white men attractive? His skin looked to have the smoothness of a wild mushroom.

Her gaze traveled lower to his slim waist, where the pale

skin disappeared into the harsh black of his tight English breeches. His narrow hips swayed comfortably with the music. She stepped forward with the line. Only a few more feet.

Always aware of her body, she felt it come alive under his gaze. Her breasts tightened, nipples brushing against the warm doeskin. Her thigh muscles grew taut. Her chest rose with each short quick breath.

Now only a foot of space separated them. Through the mental haze that had isolated her from the other dancers she heard Little Dove abandon the ritual words to chant her greeting to Breath of a Panther.

Caro tried to speak as she had done at this moment many times before, but this dance was different. Never before had her mouth been too dry to say the opening words.

What did she want to say? It was too early to speak of the things she found beautiful about him. Too early for her blood to feel so hot. But she must greet him and she couldn't remember what to say.

A warrior. All men wanted to be greeted as a warrior. *"Psai wi ne noth tu,"* she chanted. "You are a great warrior," she translated.

"You are a beautiful woman," he responded keeping the intonations of the chant.

Caro's heart sang. He thought her beautiful. His eyes feasted on her body with a heat that echoed his words.

Before she could respond again, his eyes softened. *"U le thi ski she quih."* He carefully chanted each word, then grinned. "I hope I said that right. I meant to say you have eyes that a man could lose himself in forever."

She couldn't help returning his smile. "You said, 'Pretty eyes.'" Never before had she abandoned the ritual and simply responded to the man. This dance would be different. From both sides she heard the formal words of the other dancers, but couldn't regret her own amused response.

He had taken the trouble to learn some Shawnee. In return she spoke rather than chanted. ''Your eyes are the color of fire smoke, but they burn like the sun,'' she said in English. She stepped forward again, only a half-step this time, but that left only inches between them. He exhaled his warm breath on her face. She inhaled the freshness of pine, the lingering wood smoke, and the pungent aroma of male body. ''I drink in your scent.''

She could hear the murmur but not the words of other couples. The tempo of the drums increased. She shuffled her feet forward until their bare toes touched. Then she began to sway forward. His brow furrowed, and instinctively he leaned back. ''That's right,'' she said, ''bend backward.'' He bent until she hovered over him at a slight angle. Her hair fluttered across his naked chest, and he gave a soft moan of pleasure at its touch. Obviously, whoever had prepared him for the ritual had not prepared him for this part.

''Now, come with me.'' She began to straighten and willed him to follow her.

He drew himself up, darting a quick glance at the other men to confirm that they were doing the same. She arched back, and he followed until he hovered over her, their bodies almost touching, his breath warm on her neck. He smiled. ''I think I like this.''

She rose toward him, forcing him back, deeper this time. Her breasts brushed his chest. ''Your chest is hard with your strength.''

His eyes widened with the contact. He hesitated when she leaned back, remaining straight up while the rest of the men leaned forward. She felt a stab of disappointment.

He understood he had made a mistake, glanced to the side again, and watched Breath of a Panther bend over Little Dove. Understanding, he hurriedly bent. Though his eyes turned soft and liquid, he didn't lean close enough to touch her with his body.

It was her turn. Slowly she forced him back until the strain showed on his face. His chin rubbed against the side of her forehead and she brushed her breasts gently against his hard chest, letting them linger for a moment before beginning to move back. "I like your hard muscles against my body," she said in Shawnee.

She more than liked the feeling of his hard muscles. Heat surged through her as it never had during this dance. She knew many of her friends went with the men without waiting for the ceremony of a marriage dance. But that was one of the few restrictions White Fish had imposed on her. He had ordered her to wait, and now she was glad she had. This man would be her first, and she would open her legs willingly to him when he came to her.

He leaned forward and she arched back, feeling him shudder at the momentary contact, but he didn't speak.

The dance continued as they alternately swayed forward over each other. Next, when she leaned over him, she let her tongue dart out and taste the warmth of his chest. "Speak to me," she whispered. "Tell me what you like."

His eyes clouded. "I am not sure I can speak. Right now I am having a very hard time thinking. I can't remember what I am supposed to say."

She arched back and her hips touched his for a fleeting second. "Just say what you are thinking."

He shook his head, but continued with the prescribed movements. "You don't want to hear what I am thinking."

She smiled. "It is a marriage dance. I am not afraid of your thoughts." This time when she hesitated over him, her hips again brushed his.

He bit his lip until she began to move back. "Do that again and I won't have to tell you what I'm thinking."

Caro surrendered to the sensations that washed over her, glad that she had waited for this Elmgrove. It would be good between them.

*   *   *

Beads of sweat broke out on Tag's forehead. He curled his fingers and tried to distract himself by digging his nails into his palms. The pressure of Caro's hips and thighs against him obliterated any lesser feeling. *Dammit.* Jake should have warned him. He'd thought he'd been prepared for anything. Naked savages dancing around. Women with bare breasts jiggling. Even a particularly uninhibited couple demonstrating. Anything but this slow, fully clothed invitation to the most erotic night he could imagine.

Every time he leaned over the beautiful woman before him, he knew exactly how she would look as he lowered himself onto her, her hair tangled about her face and shoulders, her eyes inviting and glowing with a heat that went straight to his groin.

She came toward him again, talking in Shawnee. He had to fight the urge to grab her hips and bury himself in her. Her breasts brushed lightly against his chest. Her hips hovered so close to his she had to sense his hardness. She smiled and said something unintelligible but wonderful.

The drum pulsed with the rhythm of sex. *Thump. Thump Thump.*

His turn. She leaned back. Her bare feet bracketed his. Her short dress pulled up, exposing white thighs and her parted knees. Damn, someone should have told *her* they were not going to consummate this thing. Someone had better remind him of that too, because he was losing control fast.

The dance continued with Caro murmuring in Shawnee. If she didn't say he had a tallywhacker as big as a buffalo's, it wasn't because she hadn't noticed. The only place her eyes didn't explore was the back of his heel.

He surrendered to the night and the music. He could no more have kept his eyes from exploring than he could keep his ears from hearing the insistent beat of the drum and the sensuous cadence of the rattle. He clamped his lips shut and didn't say anything because there were some things a

gentleman didn't say to a woman. And just about everything in his mind fell into that category.

With a few final, resonating beats, the music stopped,
leaving the silence of the night and the uneven rhythm of
the dancers' heavy breathing. For several heartbeats nobody
moved. Then around him the couples began shouting the I-
don't-want-to-marry phrase Tag had learned. And forgotten. They melted away into the shadows, leaving only Tag
and Breath of a Panther standing with their women close
in front of them.

Tag's chest tightened with fear. The words. He couldn't
remember the words. Hell, he couldn't remember his own
name. His groin ached with the need to bury himself in the
woman beside him.

Before Tag could mentally form the phrase, Breath of a
Panther's voice rang out. *"Ni haw ku nah ga."* You are
my wife.

Tag looked quickly at Caro to judge her reaction. Her
face glowed in the flickering light. If she minded that her
bridegroom had just claimed another, she concealed it well.

"Ni wy she an a." Breath of a Panther's woman had
shouted the words. He beamed down at her. The watchers
roared their approval.

Now what? Tag looked at Caro for a clue.

She looked up at him expectantly and waited. And
waited. "You must decide," she whispered urgently.

Evidently the wedding was still on. *"Ni haw ku nah ga,"*
he shouted. "You are my wife," he repeated in English.

She smiled and touched his hand. *"Ni wy she an a.* You
are my husband," she yelled back.

Again a raucous noise broke out amongst the watchers.
Everyone looked pleased. He had survived the ceremony.
Now he just had to survive his wedding night—without
dishonoring his non-bride.

She looked up at him, her heated gaze an invitation. Her
tongue moistened her lips, increasing Tag's discomfort. "I

will wait for you.'' She glided into the darkness before he could speak.

The softer beat of the drum continued in the background. Jake appeared at Tag's side. "You made me proud." Jake looked around grinned. "Looks like half the village will be celebratin' your wedding night with you."

"I'll be damned." A quick scan of the clearing showed that everyone between puberty and ninety seemed to be disappearing—not saying a polite good night and leaving, but slipping off in pairs towards the woods or the huts. It didn't take much imagination to guess what they would be doing for the next hour or so. "I'll be damned," he repeated more softly.

Caro couldn't have done this wedding dance with such skill if she hadn't done it many times before. He remembered the luminous softness in her eyes. How many times had she whispered the same invitation to her partner?

Tag shuddered, picturing a darkened woods and her lithe body straining towards a hungry warrior. The desire that had begun to abate came back with triple force. Perhaps the restraint he planned wouldn't be necessary. If she was not a virgin, he could bed her as casually as he would an English widow.

He would be taking nothing she had not already given to others.

With a curt good night to Jake, he started toward the *wegiwa* the chief had pointed out earlier. Blood had already begun to throb at his temple.

At the entrance he cleared his throat to announce his arrival, drew aside the flap, and entered. Caro knelt on the other side of the dim room, her weight set back on her heels and her hands demurely folded in her lap. She wore the same dress and her hair cascaded over her shoulders, gleaming in the fading firelight.

Tag stopped and caught his breath at the deceptive picture of utter innocence. She had known from the first beat of the drum this moment would come, and she had set him up well for it.

She floated to her feet. "Welcome, my husband." Before he could speak, she padded across the dirt floor to stand in front of him. Not as close as she had stood for the dance, but close enough to make him forget she was English, or Indian, or anything but a woman. Her hands burned on his shoulders and she looked up at him, her lips so close to his.

So close that he realized he had never kissed her. He had touched her intimately but never kissed her. He bent and brushed his lips against hers with a lingering touch.

"Oh." She gasped and looked up. "What . . . ?"

He smiled at the reaction. "A kiss. Have you never been kissed?"

"Never."

"Did you like it?"

"I . . . I don't know."

"I can show you again." He rested his hands on her waist and put his lips to hers again, but she had drawn hers into a tight, hard line. Against her fluttering lashes, he said, "Soften your mouth." He moved his against hers so she could feel what he was asking. Gradually she responded, and he forgot about teaching and concentrated on the kiss, angling his head just right.

Her hands slid from his shoulders to his neck. One crept into his hair. Her nails tingled against his scalp. She learned quickly. "Yes," she whispered against his mouth.

"Yes, what?" He didn't care what, but he wanted her to speak again. He had missed the fleeting chance to slip his tongue between her lips when she spoke.

"Yes, I like—oh." Her mouth rounded with surprise and gave him the full entry he sought.

He lowered his hands from her waist to cup her rounded buttocks and draw her against him. She came willingly, with a small sigh of pleasure.

He searched again with his tongue. She understood and opened her mouth to welcome him. He retreated immediately, then thrust again. His blood pounded with the remembered beat of the drum. He simulated the rhythm, first with his tongue, then with his hands, drawing her to him. He ran his hand up her spine, feeling the warm softness of the finely tanned doeskin and her response in every muscle. He lowered his hand to knead her buttocks again and feel the satisfying pressure of her softness straining towards his ache.

No. Not like this. Not standing, coupling like a pair of paupers in the street. Slowly he uncurled his fingers, releasing her.

She continued to move against him for a moment, then sensed the change and quieted. Her ragged breaths rasped in the silence.

He forced his own breathing to slow. A delay would only make it that much more satisfying.

She looked up, he blue eyes troubled and bewildered. "Did I . . . ? Am I not . . . ?"

He soothed her, drawing a hand along her spine. "No. It is all right, but we need to lie down."

"Oh. I'm sorry. . . . I . . ." She produced a troubled frown, followed by the most endearing smile he had ever seen. "You will have to tell me what to do. I don't . . ." Her hand fluttered nervously.

Nervously. Sweet bloody hell. It couldn't be. Not the way she moved her body against him, so sure of where he needed her. "You have done this before, haven't you?" The paralyzing coldness that swept through him echoed in his tone.

"No. . . ." Her eyes shifting apprehensively from his face to the place where he planned to take her.

He gripped her shoulders and thrust her from him. "Dammit!" His fingers dug into her shoulders with each word. "Why did you let me think...? Damn! Damn! Damn!"

"Don't be angry. I am sure I can learn quickly."

"You won't learn anything because we won't... can't..." His jaw trembled. Despite every rational thought, he still wanted to tumble her to the floor. Damn the consequences. Damn everything.

She watched his face, her eyes wide. "I don't understand. You are angry because I don't know how...?" She bit her lip and looked toward the entrance then back at him. "I... Somebody could teach me." She looked again at the opening. "Not all of the braves are asleep...." She stepped back away from his hands, which he had left on her shoulders. With a deep breath, she straightened to her full height, and took two determined steps toward the door.

"Where are you going?" he roared. He grabbed her wrist and she came to a jerking halt.

"To learn what you need me to know."

Chapter Four

A lifetime of living hadn't given Tag the language that statement deserved, but he tried. He used every Old English word he knew and borrowed a few from French and Spanish. "Dammit," he finished, "you're not going anyplace."

She tried to wrench her wrist from his tight grip. "I don't understand. You are angry because I don't know how to please you. Why should you be more angry when I say I will learn? Someone will teach me."

"You will stay right here." Tag released her hand so he could circle the confined space. He had to do something to keep from *teaching* her right there where she stood. He clenched his fist, but stopped himself from pounding it into the wall. Nothing looked solid enough to withstand a vicious kick. He couldn't even stand up straight without tangling his hair in the crude roofing. Finally, with a deep breath, he turned to face her. "Your husband will teach you, but that husband won't be me. Is that clear enough?"

Her brow furrowed in confusion. "But you are my husband."

"I am not your husband. I am no more your husband than any other man you have done that dance with."

"But the marriage . . . Seven Feathers said you understood."

"That wasn't a marriage. That was a heathen ritual with no purpose except to make a man forget everything but his . . . everything from the waist up."

She shook her head, determined not to accept his words. "I am your wife."

"You are an Englishwoman. You will be a wife when you marry in an English church, with a clergyman and a license. Until then you are a goddamn English virgin."

The blood in Caro's veins turned to ice. *Englishman. Lying, lying Englishman.*

Whatever made her think she could trust an Englishman just because she had been born with the same fair skin?

He had said she needed a husband. He had said he would be that husband. Less than an hour ago he had been smiling and making promises with his eyes and body. Now he was cursing her because she didn't know how to please him.

Damn him. If she were a true Shawnee, she would cut out his black heart and serve it to the village for breakfast.

"I am sorry. . . ." He spoke, but she would hear no more of his words. She had to plan how she would expose his deception. Her mind feasted on visions of his punishment.

"Go to sleep, Caro." He turned his back on her and spoke to the wood that framed the walls. "We will leave early in the morning." He still did not know he was a talking dead man. She would expose his treachery and listen to him die. And after he died . . .

Her shoulders sank. After he died she would still have to face the village with her humiliation. She would be a woman whose man didn't want her because she did not have the skill he wanted.

Caro closed her eyes, as if by not looking she could keep from thinking about tomorrow. Seven Feathers wouldn't let her leave the village alone. He would still have to face the problem of what to do with her. A second wife to Breath of a Panther? Or would he try to find some other man to marry her?

No. She drew in a long breath and knew she could not pay that price for her wounded pride. The Englishman would have to live long enough to leave the village with her.

"We cannot stand here all night," he said in an impatient tone. "You need to sleep and I need to get out of here." He stepped toward the opening.

"Stop."

He froze at the command.

"You cannot go out there."

"I sure as hell can't stay in here. If I do I will—" His hands clenched and he turned to look at her with a searing look that made her believe he did want her. A lying look, but she still couldn't let him die for his treachery.

Not yet.

"If you go out there, you will die."

"Say that again."

"If you go out there, you will die. Everyone will know you lied."

"I didn't lie."

"A man doesn't walk in the village on his marriage night. The Shawnee will not deal kindly with a white man who came to mock their customs."

"I am not mocking their customs. I just—"

"The chief arranged the marriage. The warriors will kill you for defying him. And they will enjoy doing it. If we are to leave here tomorrow, you will not step outside tonight."

"I see." He looked around, his hands clenching and unclenching. "I will just—I don't know what the hell I will do, but I wish you would lie down—someplace far away from me."

She should say no more, but he didn't deserve an easy night. "I will sleep, and you can spend the night worrying whether I will denounce you in the morning. I can think of few things that would give me greater pleasure than exposing a man who has come to scoff at the customs of my people."

She lowered herself to the bed she had planned to share with her husband. Before dawn she would have to decide how far they must go from the village before she could use her knife to cut out his still-beating heart.

Caro woke the next morning. Immediately a new wave of humiliation washed over her.

Her new husband didn't want her.

For the first time in her life she didn't rise as the faint whispers of light from the smoke hole turned the room an ever softer gray. Morning sounds filtered in from the village: snorting horses, the shuffling thump of hoofs, and the creaking of a pack strap being tightened.

Seven Feathers shouted a sharp rebuke above the murmur of voices. She swallowed hard, aware that he was supervising the final preparations for her journey.

She would have to face him. Would he look for the happiness of a new bride in her face and find only shame? She drew her sleeping robe tighter around her shoulders. How innocent she had been to think she might finally belong to someone simply because Seven Feathers had ordered a man of her own kind to marry her.

Fool, she told herself, *wretched simpleton*. Why should Elmgrove want her? She no more belonged in his world than she belonged here. But at least she could hate him. She did hate him.

She hated him and hated needing him, but somehow she would have to get through the next hour without exposing him.

Sounds from outside intruded again.

She flung aside the blanket covering her. She would go with Elmgrove, telling no one of her shame. Her first test would come before she even left the village. Could she keep Seven Feathers from seeing the icy ring of anger around her heart?

She searched the dim room for evidence of the Englishman. The robes he should have slept on were smooth. She couldn't feel his presence.

Rising, she moved through her morning preparations, dressing in breeches because of the long ride and a white cotton shirt of her father's, which she belted at the waist with a red sash. The hushed voices of Elmgrove and Seven Feathers came through the thin wall, warning her she would have to face them together. She tested a smile, but the stiff muscles of her cheeks made it feel like the grimace of a dead person.

Better not even to feign happiness. If they could leave the village quickly enough, Seven Feathers would think he understood. She was leaving him. He would not expect the usual glow of a new bride during their final minutes. As long as she didn't look at her deceitful husband, she would escape with her pride intact.

With a final tug on her braid, she pushed aside the flap and bent through the opening of the *wegiwa*. The finality of the moment overwhelmed her. Her step faltered. She had said her good-byes last night, but most of the village had assembled to see her leave. A silent circle in the rose-gray light, they would not speak. All the words had been spoken, but their love and final wishes hovered in the morning air.

Caro's searching gaze found Little Dove, her arms folded over her chest, her back pressed against Breath of a Panther as if she might melt into him. Caro knew she could have practiced a smile until every lake in the valley dried up and never produced the soft look of happiness Little Dove radiated.

"Thank you." Little Dove mouthed the words without sound and offered a wavering smile.

Caro nodded a silent response. Little Dove especially should not guess how alone she felt.

Seven Feathers had reserved for himself the privilege of the last words. "We thought you would sleep until spring," he called, his tone too gentle for the words.

Caro turned to where he stood with Elmgrove. Prepared, she quickly averted her gaze before either man could see the anger flare in her eyes. Why couldn't he have stood anywhere else? Deliberately relaxing the tension in her shoulders, she vowed to concentrate only on Seven Feathers. They would have only these few minutes together.

Even as she began to walk toward the two men, Elmgrove drifted back to wait with Jake, apparently to say his good-byes. She stopped in front of Seven Feathers and looked directly into his eyes. The softness in them squeezed her heart. For all her earlier determination to avoid his searching gaze, part of her wanted to bask in his love forever.

Seven Feathers cupped one hand around her shoulder. "White Fish has already left to pray for your safe journey." He held his clenched fist toward her and waited until she put her palm under it before easing his fingers open. "This will keep you safe."

Caro knew immediately what she held. Only the knowledge that the sacred token would have fallen to the ground kept her from drawing back in horror. She had grown up hearing of Seven Feathers's certainty he would die if he lost the ever-present cougar tooth from around his neck— the cougar tooth she held in her hand.

"No." She spoke softly, gripped his hand, and returned the gift. "I am leaving. It is my right to choose what I will take." She reached up and plucked one of the eagle feathers from his bound hair. "My *unsoma* will be an eagle feather. That way I will always have a part of you with me." She held her breath and waited for his reply, uncertain if she saw a flicker of relief in his eyes.

He gave a single abrupt nod. "The eagle's wing will carry you safely."

She exhaled and risked a smile. "Now they will have to call you Six Feathers." Her fleeting lightness evaporated with his second, softer nod. If the entire village had not

70

been watching, she might have thrown herself into his arms and begged to stay. Instead, she inhaled slowly and waited for his final farewell.

And waited.

The chief, who sent his warrior sons to almost certain death without a flicker of an eyebrow, became a fluttering old woman with his warnings of dangers. "Test the waters before crossing a stream. Listen to the music of the forest. Trust your heart and not the words of a stranger." A dozen more and then the first few again.

"But your feet grow restless," he said finally.

She bit her lip to keep from agreeing.

He raised his hand in an abrupt signal.

She couldn't tear her gaze from his. She would never again see him hide his heart behind an angry frown.

Seven Feathers glanced toward where she knew the horses waited. The moment had come. She could no longer avoid looking at Elmgrove. Was the disdain with which he had looked at her last night even now in his eyes for all to see?

A warm flush tingled in her cheeks. She bit the inside of her lower lip and turned. Whatever she saw in his face, she would mount her horse and ride from the village with her back straight.

Raising her eyes, she saw Jake standing next to the horses, Elmgrove at his side. For a heart-stopping minute his placid gaze met hers.

The few steps that separated them seemed too short for the traitorous thoughts that tumbled through her mind. Thoughts of what it would be like if he were truly her husband. The memory of the way his laugh rang out when he lifted Calling Bird to settle the child in the crook of his arm.

No. She wouldn't let herself think like that.

She came to a stop in front of him, conscious of the

unearthly silence. Even the village dogs must have sensed the finality of the moment.

"We had best be on our way," he said. He stepped back, allowing her to move past him to the smallest of the three waiting horses.

As if the leaden weight in her heart were a physical thing, Caro wondered where she would find the strength to leap onto the animal's back, something she had done a thousand times without thought.

Elmgrove held out his hands to help her mount in the English way. Panic surged through her. She wanted this to look so right and she had no idea what he wanted her to do.

"Allow me." Without waiting for a response he gripped her waist with both hands and lifted her onto the horse.

Another minute and they would be away. Seven Feathers, for all his love and power, would no longer control her destiny.

As if spurred by the same thought, Seven Feathers stepped forward again, not for a last word with her, but to speak to Elmgrove. "You may still need my help," he said. He reached up and removed the silver band that encircled his arm. "My allies will recognize this as belonging to me. Produce it and they will follow your orders as they would mine."

No. Caro's hand leapt to snatch at the symbol that gave Seven Feathers's authority to the man who didn't want her. A word from her would change everything. For a moment her hand trembled in the air; then she lowered it, tangling her fingers in the coarse hair of her horse's mane. She would leave in silence as she had promised herself she would, and Seven Feathers would never know how he had betrayed her with his last act of kindness.

Back straight, she nudged her horse into a walk, leaving Elmgrove to gather up the reins of the packhorse and follow.

*   *   *

Tag urged his scrambling horse over the crest of the hill and exhaled. He would probably go to his grave wondering what would have happened if his new bride had decided to expose the wedding as a sham. For now he wanted just to bask in the warmth of the rising sun and breathe without fifty pairs of eyes watching.

His relationship with his new traveling companion required some thought.

He could think about that later, he decided as he followed her onto the trail he and Jake had traveled two days before.

As if to celebrate the start of his journey back to a world he understood, nature had produced a perfect spring morning. Tiny diamonds of dew sparkled on the lime-green of the newly opened leaves. The moist air caressed his face like a soothing balm, rich with the heady odor of moist tree bark and the promise of blossoms to come. The spongy earth muted the horses' steps. It was a perfect day to be alive.

Within a few miles Tag realized that his general appreciation of springtime had narrowed to an infinitely more specific appreciation of the woman in front of him. She rode astride, her tight breeches taut over the fluid muscles of her thighs. It was enough to make a man envy the horse those thighs encircled so firmly. Even more interesting, she seemed to be indulging in a healthy sulk because he hadn't made love to her last night.

His blood began to hum with the memory of her soft curves molded against him.

This could be a problem, and a big one if they were going to travel three thousand unchaperoned miles together. Particularly if she persisted in wearing just a thin layer of clothing that outlined every curve. He had as much restraint as any man, but if she ever again looked at him the way she had last night, he'd have to be made of stone not to respond.

By Jove, he never thought he'd be in the position of explaining to an English virgin she couldn't let a man take liberties with her. He didn't even know if it was possible to talk about such things with a woman.

He shrugged. He certainly couldn't do any worse than whoever had had charge of her education so far.

He cleared his throat and mentally practiced an opening line. *Miss Fenton, we must both forget about last night.* Excellent, except that they would both immediately begin thinking about last night—which would certainly defeat his purpose. He tested a few similar opening comments, all of which left him thinking of her blond hair tumbling over his bare chest and his hands cupping her rounded buttocks.

The hell with it. They would discuss it this once and then never think of it again. He urged his horse into an ungainly canter that brought him up beside her. "Miss Fenton, awkward as it may be, I believe we must talk about last night." The trail was barely wide enough for them to ride abreast.

She turned her head slowly to favor him with a withering glance. "I can't think of any reason I would want to talk to *you* about anything. Except possibly to say good-bye."

He was right. She was angry. "I realize now we should have discussed the wedding beforehand. But there was no chance, and I assumed . . ."

"Yes?" She waited for him to continue. Tag had no idea what he had been going to say. "What did you assume?" she asked.

"I assumed that since you were English . . . since you would be living in England, you would not regard that ceremony as any more than—" He winced, remembered the fire in her eyes when she spoke of *the customs of my people*, and knew he shouldn't finish that sentence. *A heathen ceremony* didn't seem an ideal word choice either.

Fortunately, she had some choice words of her own. "And I foolishly assumed that since you told Seven Feathers I needed a husband, and since you agreed to be that husband, you would behave like one.''

"It is not as simple as that. Surely you know enough about England to understand that a man in my position cannot simply go about marrying every woman who needs a husband. I mean no offense, Miss Fenton, but I have a very specific idea of what I need in a wife.''

She glared at him, her jaw tight. "Then you shouldn't go about offering the position to women who don't meet your standards.''

He should have known she wouldn't make this easy. "It is not a mistake I usually make. And I am trying to apologize.''

She gave an angry toss of her head and rode for several paces before turning her upper body so she could face him again. "For a man who doesn't usually make that mistake, you seemed remarkably agreeable until you discovered I didn't have skill enough to please you.''

"Your *lack of skill* was not the problem. Quite the contrary.'' Tag hadn't intended the remark to sound quite so cutting. They needed to discuss this, but calmly.

He tried again. "Your lack of skill had nothing to do with my decision.'' A gentleman certainly wouldn't mention that her skill had everything to do with the fact that he had entered that hut with his functioning mind located somewhere below his waist. Or perhaps in this case, he would. "If anything, your expertise during the dance led me to make a very unfortunate assumption.''

"Oh? And what was that?'' Her voice chilled the balmy air for a mile in all directions.

Damn her. She knew perfectly well what he had assumed. Or perhaps she didn't. Except for the fact that she was English and spoke the language impeccably, he knew nothing about her. He had never wondered who told English virgins not to lie down with the first man who suggested it. He'd thought they were born knowing that.

But if she was a virgin, she certainly wasn't obsessed with staying that way. That would have to change if he was going to be responsible for her virtue for the next three thousand miles.

"Your assumption, Elmgrove. What did you assume?"

Damn. He was going to have to be very specific. He'd never even said the word virgin to a female.

A hearty flush warmed the back of his neck. He cleared his throat again and resisted the temptation to look straight ahead, or anywhere but into her wide blue eyes. "Miss Fenton, how much do you know about what goes on between a man and a woman?"

"I am trained as a healer. I know about such things."

"Are you familiar with the term virgin?"

"Of course."

"Then you must know I would never have behaved as I did if I had known you were a virgin."

She gave an impatient shake to her head. "Every woman is a virgin until her first time."

"That is precisely what we need to discuss. For an Englishwoman that is something she must reserve to please her husband." Tag couldn't believe how priggish he sounded, but he also couldn't believe he had to state something so obvious.

"Last night you were my husband, and it did not please you."

"But it would have if I had been your husband."

"But you have said you are not, and this conversation is annoying me."

"It is annoying me too, but I am afraid we must continue." It was more than annoying him. It was making him think how very much he would like to be looking down into her eyes as they widened with wonder and surprise when she discovered how very much she didn't know yet. "Last night I almost made a very serious mistake. That must never happen again."

Her tongue darted out and moistened her lips. "Are you suggesting you intend it to happen again?"

"No, dammit, I don't, but—"

She looked at him, her eyes frankly curious. "But?"

"We will be traveling alone. At least until we can procure a chaperone. And you are a very attractive woman."

"You didn't think so last night."

"I thought a lot of things last night that I managed not to say." Tag heard the sharp bite to his words and bridled his impatience. It wasn't her fault that even now her upturned face and moist lips were making him fantasize about stopping the horses and lift her down onto him so she could discover exactly how attractive he found her.

He bit his tongue to control his rampant thoughts. He had come this far and he would finish the conversation so neither of them would have any doubt about how they should behave. "In England we have very strict rules regarding men and women traveling together simply because a natural attraction sometimes leads to unfortunate consequences. We must be very careful."

"Situations can flare up." She gave an irritated huff of air. "What are you trying to say?"

"You are a very provocative woman, Miss Fenton. Physically provocative. I am a normal man, not always immune to temptation. I hope that is clear enough because I have no intention of saying any more."

She frowned as if she found him particularly dull-witted and irritating. "I doubt there is any danger of repeating our wedding dance."

"I am talking about how we will behave from here on. We must be very careful that nothing we say can be construed as an invitation to something more intimate. Most of all, we must be aware of proximity." He tried to ease his horse from her to the far side of the path to provide a few more inches between them. At least his awareness illustrated his point. "Even now, I am finding it distracting to be riding with your leg so close to mine.''

''The trail is narrow. You could ride behind me.''

''We must finish this conversation because I am certain I will never have the courage to speak of such things again. Last night I almost made a dreadful mistake.'' Tag shuddered. ''If I had not recognized my error in time, we would have been married today. The English ceremony would have been merely a formality.''

Her brow furrowed. ''I don't understand. You insist we are not married.''

''In England when a gentleman takes a woman's virginity, he has no choice but to marry her.''

She continued to study him, her eyes still narrowed. ''You mean, if you had . . ,''

''Yes, Miss Fenton, if I had proceeded with what we began, I would have been honor-bound to marry you.''

''And you are concerned that you might still proceed?'' She didn't wait for an answer. To Tag's amazement she began to laugh. Not a soft ladylike titter, but a full-bodied laugh that had her shoulders shaking and her hands reaching to cover her mouth. ''But that is perfect,'' she said, the laughter still bubbling in her voice. ''I plan to hate you forever for casting me aside last night, and you have given me the perfect revenge.''

With a motion Tag couldn't even detect, she cued her horse to move sidewards so her leg brushed his. ''If I merely use the methods you suggest and coax you into lying with me, you will have to be my husband.'' She chuckled again, enjoying the joke immensely. ''And you will hate that, won't you?''

Tag cursed. He drew on the reins of his horse so he was no longer beside her. Then he cursed again because the tingling nerves in his thigh remembered not the laughter but the startling softness of her leg.

*   *   *

Caro's spirits soared. The plan had come to her in the instant she understood what he was trying to say in his awkward fashion. While it might not be as innately satisfying as pummeling him about the head with her fists, for the Englishman with his strict regard for dignity, it might be worse. She regretted she would not be able to repeat the wedding dance. She would have to find small ways to make the fire return to his eyes. Small reasons for standing too close to him.

He might prove remarkably easy to torture. She might not be able to make him bleed, but she could make him sweat.

She could make him worry in a thousand ways.

He liked to have things all neatly arranged and clearly understood. Something had kept him awake half the night. Perhaps her threat to expose him. He'd certainly made no attempt to conceal his relief when the village dropped from sight behind them. Then he had immediately begun agonizing over what would happen if he couldn't obey his strict laws of propriety on the journey.

She smiled again at his bumbling attempts to make certain she didn't tempt him beyond his limits, and his look of horror when she promised that was exactly what she would do. Her smile became a small laugh. Even now he was probably planning how to defend his besieged honor and save himself from the unspeakable fate of having to marry her in a righteous English ceremony.

If she could make him worry enough, he would reach England such a shriveled shell of his former self that none of his worthy English maidens would even look at him. She settled back to enjoy the journey and ponder what else she could give him to fret over.

Reluctantly, she discounted the obvious, attacking war parties and ferocious wild creatures. She didn't doubt his physical courage. But he had the oh-so-English regard for rules and law. He had been appalled at the idea of Breath of a Panther going to England to kill her cousin, and equally aghast at the idea of delivering the villain to the village for the Shawnee to dispatch. English law, he had kept repeating. English law.

He would certainly lose a month of sleep if he truly believed she might kill the murderer. And he probably wouldn't sleep all the way to England if he thought she planned to dispatch the villain as soon as she stepped off the boat. The prospect of watching him gnash his teeth again pleased her, so she turned with the half-formed idea of sharing that plan immediately.

He looked properly thunderous and preoccupied. Her newest arrow could wait to be loosed.

Just before the sun set they came upon a sheltered grove beside a small stream. "We will camp here," Caro said.

Elmgrove trotted his horse across the clearing, nodded, and jumped to the ground.

Caro reined her horse to a stop, but didn't jump to the ground. He took two steps toward her, checked his movement, and turned to tend to his horse.

"Aren't you going to help me dismount?" She fought to keep the smile lines from twitching in her face.

"I am sure you can reach the ground safely yourself." The coolness in his eyes yielded to his own amused smile. "Much too obvious a ploy, Miss Fenton. You will have to do better than that."

With brusque movements he began unfastening the straps that bound their belongings to the packhorse. He slapped the bundles to the ground in a series of solid thunks. His manner certainly kept his promise to avoid giving any false impressions of intimacy.

Caro concealed a half-smile as she dismounted. Then she knelt with her back to him, and began to scoop out a fire ring. She heard a few more thumps and then silence. A long silence, unbroken even by a whispering movement of his feet.

"Dammit, it didn't take you long to figure out how to do better, did it?" he asked, his tone both annoyed and amused. "Do you have any idea how you look right now?"

Startled, Caro raised her head. She knew she looked tired, wind-blown, and too hungry even to think of her plan. But she looked over her shoulder to find what she had done to succeed.

He stood staring directly at her raised buttocks, his lips tight. "At least stand up, for God's sake." His eyes had the warm look she'd hoped to provoke if he'd come near enough a moment ago. "We will deal with the question of your attire right now."

Caro rose and turned to face him. "My attire—?" She had dressed with no thought but of comfort on the long journey. Certainly she hadn't planned her clothes to tempt him.

"You are an Englishwoman. And from now on you will begin dressing like one." He pointed to the bundles on the ground. "Surely you must have something in there that is suitable."

"A gown perhaps?" Some of Caro's exhaustion faded with her amusement at his request.

"Anything but those . . . those . . ." He pointed in the general direction of her legs. "No Englishwoman . . . not even a tart, would dream of going about in breeches. They leave nothing to the imagination."

"I have a dress, but—"

"Splendid. Put it on." He turned to begin rubbing down his horse, then whirled to face her again. His eyes narrowed. "Do I need to ask you to describe this dress?"

Caro smiled, now thoroughly enjoying his discomfort. "Not at all. You found it attractive enough last night."

"You are deliberately provoking me. You said you had been to Detroit. You must have something else."

81

"I went to Detroit two years ago. I have grown. I saw no point in bringing a gown I couldn't button."

"Well, what the hell did you intend to do when we got there now?"

"People in Detroit are quite used to the way my people dress. I can purchase what I need before we go on."

"And what did you think I would do in the meantime with you running around in breeches or a dress that barely comes to your . . . your . . ."

"Can't an Englishman even say knees?"

"Of course I can say knees." He sputtered, then actually smiled. "I simply can't say knees about a lady's knees." He exhaled, but the smile remained in his eyes. "I'm sorry. I suppose none of this is your fault, but we can't have you running about in those things." He pointed to her breeches." "Put your dress on over them, and I should be able to succeed in thinking only the purest thoughts." He waited. The horse at his side snorted for attention. He ignored it. "The dress, please." He softened the words to a request rather than a command.

Still amused by his soft smile, Caro crossed to the rolled bundle containing her few clothes and located the dress she had made for her wedding. She shook it out and looked at him to see if he would sense a victory in her obedience to his ridiculous request.

He nodded. "Please."

She complied, but stored the knowledge that he found her breeches unsettling. There would be ample time for using that insight. The rolled cuff of her father's shirt caught in the sleeve. Her head poked twice at the shoulder before finding the opening, and the dress tangled at her hips so she had to shuffle and tug the soft leather to her knees. Worse, when she had completed the process, she found herself shyly reluctant to look at him. She shouldn't want his approval, but she did.

He gave a short, disbelieving laugh and shook his head.

"That should help, but it doesn't. A moment ago you were an enchantress. Now you are an absurdly dressed enchantress." He shrugged. "I have dealt with sorceresses before and survived unscathed." He softened the words with another rueful smile.

Not this time, Caro vowed. But the attempt to regain her hostility lost the war with the warm glow his smile produced. To cover her confusion, Caro knelt with what she hoped was a cool expression and began unpacking the wrapped meats Seven Feathers's wife had prepared.

He moved to the far side of his horse so he could watch her while he continued rubbing the sweat from the marks the straps had produced on the packhorse. He sang a few bars of an unfamiliar ballad and broke off abruptly. "The devil of it is, Miss Fenton, I have no idea whether you even understand my concern. Tell me about yourself."

"I don't like wearing many layers of clothes for your comfort."

He laughed. "And I don't like long periods of abstinence. But it seems we must both rub along as best we can."

"So you will not have to accept me as a wife."

"Precisely. When we get to England I will find you a splendid husband." He began to sing again, matching his currying strokes to the rhythm of his voice.

For a moment Caro sat back on her heels, captivated by the sound of his deep rich voice. A bird scolded angrily.

Fool, Caro chided herself. How had she fallen victim to his charm so easily? A few smiles, a haunting song, and she found herself wanting to please a man who would keep humiliating her. A man she had wanted to kill only twenty-four hours ago. He wouldn't sing with such vigor if he knew why she was going to England.

She rose and glared at him until his song trailed off. "If you are a sample of the kind of husband I might expect, you may save yourself the trouble. I will not be staying in England.''

His circling hand stopped abruptly on the horse's back. ''What are you saying?''

''There will be no need for a husband. I will accomplish my mission and return here.''

Trailing his hand along the horse's back, he circled the animal, his step deliberately slow. ''And what, precisely, is your mission?'' She had his complete attention.

''What you and your paltry English friends do not have the courage to do. I will kill the murderer of my uncle.''

Thwack. He slapped his hand too hard against the pack-horse's rump. ''That is absurd.'' The tired animal turned its head to regard him with a reproachful stare that Caro wished she could imitate.

''I told you that was my intention the afternoon we met with Seven Feathers.''

His jaw tightened. ''I didn't believe you.''

Caro smiled. ''You believe only what suits you.''

''I believe in English law.'' He took a step towards her, then paused as if he might lecture on the subject.

Caro spoke before he could continue. ''I am aware of that. That's why you had to come for my father. And why I have to go in his place.''

''I came for your father with some hope he might help trap the murderer. Even that is out of the question for a woman. It is too dangerous.''

''Dangerous and unnecessary. I will do what needs to be done and I will return here.''

Elmgrove studied her for a long moment, angling his head first to one side and then to the other. ''It seems I have been wrong about you again.''

Satisfied her announcement had had the effect she anticipated, Caro waited for him to explain.

''I thought you were an Englishwoman.''

She drew herself up proudly. "I am a Shawnee woman as well."

His fists clenched at his sides. "Fortunately you saw fit to explain that before we wasted more than a single day."

Caro laughed. "Do you plan to spend the rest of our traveling days trying to change that?"

"No." He threw aside the rag he had been holding in his clenched fist. "I plan to return you to Seven Feathers in the morning. I have no intention of taking a murderer with me to England." He lowered his voice so Caro could scarcely hear his mutter. "Not even one as seductive as you."

Chapter Five

Tag watched as Caro recoiled as if she'd been slapped and stared at him with her mouth agape. "You want to go back?"

Her disbelieving tone would have tempted Tag to smile if he hadn't felt a stab of regret at the prospect. "Yes."

"No."

Just once he would have liked to see her smile meekly and say *yes, my lord* instead of dragging him into a lengthy discussion. But he couldn't very well turn the horses and head back the way they had come without her cooperation. "Your announcement that you plan to kill a man leaves me very little choice. Even if I were certain I could resist you flaunting your legs and your tempting little backside all the way to England, I no longer have any idea what I would do with you once we arrived."

"Then it is just as well you refuse to acknowledge our marriage, because once we arrive in England you will not have to concern yourself with me at all."

"Unfortunately, I promised Seven Feathers I would protect you."

"You also promised Seven Feathers you would marry me." She tossed her head and stormed across the clearing to the fire ring, where she knelt and began unwrapping a bundle of foodstuffs. "Your promises have little meaning." She might be angry, but she wasn't going to starve.

"I did not give my word lightly." Tag surveyed the area

86

and spotted a moss-covered rock that looked only moderately uncomfortable. The position would allow him to face her head on, and offer the least enticing view of her desirable curves. "Seven Feathers wanted only a husband for you. I even had the ideal candidate in mind." The rock proved more uneven than it looked. He endured. Standing again so quickly would let her know how much her accusation nettled him.

She favored him with a withering glance. "Not quite as ideal as you, I am sure."

"Alan McSoley is a good man." He spoke slowly, though he had no idea why it was so important she understand his intentions had been good. "Poor as a chicken egg, but he is courageous, fiercely proud, and as warm-hearted as any man I know. He lacks only a fortune to be the perfect husband. And you, of course would provide that. I even spent a few hours last night envying the bastard."

"Then I will marry him. And when I leave England, he may have my fortune."

Tag found himself on his feet and pacing across the clearing before he remembered his resolution to appear unconcerned. He decided to ignore the fact she planned to marry, then leave the poor blighter when the mood struck her. "You will not marry him because you are not going to England." His new position gave him the disconcerting view of her backside he had maneuvered to avoid. He paced back to stand by his rock.

She slapped some grain into rounded cakes with considerably more force than necessary. "Nothing has changed since this morning."

"Everything has changed. Imagine me telling Alan about the bride I have selected for him. 'She is beautiful. She is passionate and incredibly wealthy, but she does have one small fault. She plans to murder a man, and will probably be hung for murder.' Even Alan would have some reservations about that."

Judy Veisel

Her pounding stopped. She regarded him with enormous blue eyes. "You think me beautiful?"

In spite of himself, Tag smiled. "I think I have made that obvious enough."

"And passionate?"

"I should not have said that." He made another circuit of the clearing.

"And this Alan person will think so as well?"

Her expression was so intent Tag laughed. "I wouldn't have married you to a blind man."

"Good." She nodded and went back to her preparations. "You will tell me how to locate him when we get to England."

"You forget. *We* are not going to England. You are going back to your village."

"If you want to eat, you will pick up some of those sticks you keep kicking about and bring them over here for a fire." She sat back on her heels and waited in silence while he complied. Except for her determined expression, Tag might have thought he had won an easy victory. He clattered a small armload of dried branches into the ring in front of her and waited for her to protest his declaration.

She said nothing.

He gathered a second load of sticks and placed them on the edge of the ring while she arranged the first load to her satisfaction. He waited for a few seconds for her attention, then returned to his rock. Her silence unnerved him, as did the feeling they had settled nothing.

She struck a spark and blew life into a small flame. She hovered over it for a moment, then settled back to watch the setting sun.

Tag didn't believe she would give up so easily. "I'm glad you've decided to be reasonable."

Slowly she drew her gaze back to his face. "Reasonable? In what way?"

"I thought you might protest."

88

She gave a small laugh. "I forget, you need everything in words. Very well. Tomorrow you may go where you please. I am going to England."

She hadn't protested. She had simply stated a fact. A fact that wasn't going to happen. "You need me," he said "And—"

She dismissed his words with a flick of her hand. "I *needed* you. I needed you only so Seven Feathers would permit me to leave. Now you annoy me."

A wise man would have said good-bye and wished her a splendid trip, but he had made a promise to the chief. "You have no idea how to get to England." Someday he would learn to think before making promises.

"Exactly the same way you plan to. I will ride east until I come to the ocean. Then I will get on a ship." She arranged several rocks and set their meal to cooking as if she could deal with a three-month journey just as efficiently.

He mentally listed a hundred reasons why her elementary plan was absurd, the most obvious being she would be raped and murdered in the first town she came to. He settled for one she might consider less debatable. "You will need money to pay for your passage."

"I have my father's gold."

Which again brought images of robbery, rape, and murder the first time she produced the gold. Or worse, robbery and a short lifetime of bondage to some foul-smelling innkeeper. Again he ignored the obvious and kept his objection immensely practical. "How much gold?"

"Enough." The tantalizing aroma of roasting meat filled the twilight air with distracting odors.

"Do you even know how much?"

"If it isn't enough, I will find a way to get more."

She would probably deal with his other ninety-eight rational reasons just as cavalierly, which left him a limited number of choices. "Let us eat and rest," he said. "Fortunately, I am still stronger than you. Tomorrow we will return to your village if I have to physically put you on your horse and tie you there."

She angled her head and challenged him with a steady gaze that prickled the hairs on the back of his neck. "Does your life mean less to you today than it did last night?"

Tag weighed her words, and decided he would rather face Seven Feathers than travel to England with a single-minded woman planning a murder. "Seven Feathers is a reasonable man. He has dealt with the English all his life. He will understand."

"He will understand you took a wife last night and discarded her this morning."

"Nothing happened between us last night."

"You may not want to take me to England, but you cannot claim nothing happened. You admitted you wanted me as a woman."

"Dammit, that happens. It means nothing. You are as innocent as you were twenty-four hours ago."

She folded her arms over her chest and smiled. "Only you know that. Seven Feathers will order you killed when I describe our wedding night."

"You would lie?"

"No more than you."

"You wouldn't." She might. He knew nothing about her except that she was angry and determined to go to England.

"But are you willing to gamble your life on that?"

"Then you will go back alone," Tag said.

She smiled as she would at a child. "Why would I do that?"

"Because you are not coming to England with me. And because I cannot leave you here. You have to go back."

"Come to the fire and eat, Elmgrove, before you realize how absurd that idea is. It would be a shame to waste good food on a man who plans to do nothing but sit and gnash his teeth.''

Tag crossed the clearing and sat on the ground opposite her. Still sifting his thoughts for an adequate response, he accepted the bowl she held out to him. The smell of the roasted meat made his mouth water, and soft clouds of steam from the heated cakes warmed his nose. Only a fool would argue rather than eat.

She ate looking off into the distance. Her silence gave him time to study her face for any sign of weakness. Escaping wisps of hair framed hollow cheeks and a straight nose with only a hint of a curve at the bridge. Even in repose she held her well-defined chin at a defiant angle. The hint of wistfulness he imagined might have been a trick of the firelight.

In the distance a bird swooped from the sky and snatched a fish from the pond. She watched without a flicker of change in her expression. Would she order his execution and watch with the same composure? Instinct said no. Reason said yes.

However fair her skin, she belonged with the people they had just left. That left only the problem of how to get her there. He could drag her back to the village. A grand gesture, but probably not the action of a rational man if he could find another way.

For the past hour he had been thinking as if they would always be the only two people in this whole deserted valley. But he and Jake had met several parties of Indians both in Detroit and on the trail. Tag put down his bowl and let his hand drift to the pocket where he had put Seven Feathers's armband. With relief he found the token still nestled there, the token and the power to order Caro's return to her village.

Touché, Miss Fenton. He needed only to find someone who recognized Seven Feathers's authority and she would be returned whether she liked it or not. The solution should

91

have brought triumph, not the war that erupted in his mind. *She's English. She's heartless. She's your responsibility. She's a murderer. You don't know that.*

He must have groaned because she turned and regarded him questioningly. When he said nothing, she put aside her bowl and reached up to unbraid her hair. Darkness had fallen and shadows from the firelight flickered over her face. Every action demanded his full attention. She worked intently with just the tip of her tongue protruding from the corner of her mouth. When she had freed her hair, she reached up and combed the fingers of both hands through it, an intimate, uninhibited gesture. She looked deliciously fragile and vulnerable. Perhaps he should be executed for depriving London of the sensation she'd cause there.

He tensed. Sleep would never come with that image of her hovering in his mind. "Are you really so heartless, Miss Fenton, that you would travel three thousand miles to kill an unsuspecting man?" he said viciously. "Does human life really have so little value to you?"

His harsh words at least interrupted her languorous movements and brought rigidity back to her posture. "At the moment yours does."

"Would you truly order my execution without regret?" He leaned forward, some part of him willing her to deny the accusation.

She smiled. "With pleasure."

"I thought so." At least she had helped him control his lust. Like most men, he had only a modest desire to make love to someone determined to act as his executioner.

She stood up and walked three paces toward the pond. Pausing at the edge of the firelight, she turned back to face him. "You don't know me, Elmgrove. You have no right to judge me."

"No. I suppose not." He looked toward the darkness, but she had already disappeared. She was right, dammit.

He had no right to judge a person who had been raised in her harsh world, and he couldn't help a lingering pang of regret. She was unlike any woman he had ever known. He couldn't bring her to England. Hell, he probably wouldn't draw a comfortable breath until he found someone to escort her back to her village. The night already seemed emptier.

They rose at dawn the next day. Caro showed no surprise at Tag's willingness to continue the journey. He didn't feel he would improve their shaky relationship by communicating his plan to part company as soon as he could find the proper escort for her. For several hours, they rode in a silence broken only by the wilderness sounds. Twice Caro signaled him to draw his mount off the trail. The first time a lumbering bear passed within several feet of them. Tag never did detect the danger she thought she sensed the second time.

Late in the afternoon they stopped at a bubbling spring to water the horses and quench their own thirst. Just as they were about to mount, Caro froze and warned him with her eyes to do the same. She listened for several seconds, then pointed for him to follow her deeper into the underbrush. As quietly as possible with three horses, they sought deeper cover. Two hundred feet into the brush she stopped and tethered her mount. Tag did the same. When she reappeared from behind her horse, she had a dangerous-looking pistol in one hand and a knife in the other.

"What is it?" Tag mouthed silently as he collected his own weapons.

She ignored the question and signaled him to follow her back toward the spring. Halfway there she selected a position behind a waist-high boulder, where an overhanging branch shielded them from sight. The concealed spot offered a perfect view of the spring.

Tag still had heard nothing when the first Indian stepped

into view. A second followed, and a third. Seconds later there were five, all laughing and jostling for position at the small spring. They drank, then carried water to the horses that they had left just out of sight. Moments later they drifted back to settle themselves on the ground and eat. The staccato sound of their conversation reverberated through the afternoon air.

Tag waited for Caro to call out a greeting. She remained rigidly posed with the barrel of her pistol resting on the boulder and her eyes wary and shifting. If she hoped to convince him these five were not an ideal escort, she succeeded. After ten minutes when nothing more exciting happened, her tense posture slackened. "We will wait until they go," she whispered.

"These are not friends?"

"Iroquois. They have stolen some horses and furs and are returning home. They will not go near my village."

It was an hour before the group got to their feet and left, another half-hour before Caro relaxed and turned to Tag. "I believe we can go on now."

"I am surprised you didn't kill them all just to keep in practice."

His attempt at a joke did not amuse her. She gave him a cool stare. "I only kill men who annoy me. You would do well to remember that."

"It's difficult to forget." He pointed to the dangling pistol in her slack hand. "I assume you can really use that."

She nodded. "All Shawnee women can use a gun." Her face relaxed into a smile. "I can just use one better than most."

"And the knife?" Tag pointed to her other hand.

For an answer, she drew back her left arm in a movement too swift to follow and threw. The knife sliced through the air and buried itself in a tree thirty feet away. Tag's last doubt she would be capable of killing Edwin Boyle if she got to England evaporated.

94

They rode for another hour before Caro again signaled Tag to stop and dismount. "There may be someone ahead." She handed him the reins to her horse. "You stay here with the horses. I will go on and be certain it is safe."

He accepted the reins, but stopped her with a hand on her arm. "We will tether the horses and go together."

She smiled. "I am not questioning your bravery, Elmgrove, merely your ability to move quietly. I'm sure they can hear your boots in Detroit when you walk."

"But—"

"I have grown up in these woods. I will be as safe as you would be in London." Before Tag could protest, she slipped silently away, leaving only a single shuddering branch to mark her passage.

Tag tethered the horses deep in the woods and followed. Each step took an eternity because he had to debate where to put his lead foot, but he moved without noise. He stayed a few feet off the trail, confident he would eventually come upon Caro crouched behind a boulder, knife and gun in hand.

A sharp clatter of voices checked his step. A rapid-fire exchange of syllables. A masculine voice. Caro's voice. The masculine voice again. Tag lengthened his stride, heedless of the noise. Caro had found herself an escort to take her home.

Tag stopped at the edge of the woods to give her time to prepare the others for his arrival. Caro stood with her back to him exchanging bursts of words with two men slumped against a fallen tree. A third man shifted on the ground about ten feet from the group.

"These men have been injured, Elmgrove," Caro said in English. She didn't even turn to confirm his presence. "Please, bring my things at once."

When Tag returned, Caro was standing next to the reclining man. She moved directly to the packhorse. Brushing aside Tag's attempts to help, she untied the straps with efficient movements. She ignored the large bundles that fell to the ground and scooped up a worn satchel and a water pouch.

Her face an impenetrable wooden mask, she held the pouch out to him. "Would you—"

"Of course." Grateful for a way to help, Tag marched to the river and filled the container with icy water. He brought it to where she knelt beside the younger of the two men by the tree. She had already cut the side of his breeches to expose a jagged wound on the outside of his thigh. Still without a trace of feminine emotion, she reached up and accepted the dripping pouch. With the same crisp movements with which she would wash a haunch of meat for dinner, she poured the water over the gaping wound. The young warrior stared straight ahead without flinching.

"Can I help?" Tag couldn't help adding, "Show them a little compassion perhaps?"

She didn't dignify his question with a reply. He waited another moment, then retreated to see what he could do for the reclining man. His first look caused him to wince and turn his face away. The victim's hands seemed the only thing keeping his insides in place. Blood and entrails oozed from between his fingers. Worse, the boy couldn't be more than fourteen.

He was conscious and his hungry, liquid gaze followed Caro's every movement. He had to be in terrible pain, but no sound betrayed that.

"Caro." Tag's first attempt at her name was little more than a croak. "Caro, you can tend those men later. This boy is dying."

"And these two can benefit from my attention." She had begun stitching and didn't even turn to look at him.

"Damn you," Tag cursed too softly for her to hear. No boy should die waiting for just a sign that someone cared. He dropped to his knees beside the boy. "It's all right,"

he said quietly. "It will be over soon. I'll stay with you."
The boy might be Indian, but dying was always the same.
Always ugly.

The boy's eyes rolled briefly to take in Tag's presence,
but returned immediately to watch Caro. She finished
bandaging the younger brave's leg and turned her attention to the older man. With practiced efficiency she
quickly washed and sprinkled some gray powder on a mi-
nor wound in his shoulder. They talked in clipped syllables while she worked. She secured a bandage on his
shoulder and wrapped another long strip around the
wound on his forehead. She tied a final knot and he
stood.

The brave caressed her cheek and said something in a
tone far more gentle that any Caro had used. Caro nodded.
The older man rapped out a command. The younger one
rose and limped toward the woods. The older man followed
for two steps, then turned to bark the same command at
Tag. With a flick of his hand, he indicated that Tag should
accompany them.

"What?" Tag looked to Caro for an explanation.

"They are going hunting," she said in a toneless voice.
"You are to go with them."

"Hunting! Dammit, this boy is dying. They are the walking wounded and you want us to go hunting." She had to
be insane. "We can miss one meal."

"Just go with them, Elmgrove." She sounded too tired
to fight with him.

"Let them go by themselves. Someone needs to stay
with the boy, and you don't seem to give a damn."

The older man rumbled a question at Caro. She answered. He glared at Tag. His hand moved toward the knife
at his belt. He spoke again, or maybe just growled. The
younger man narrowed his eyes and raised the bow he had
picked up when he stood. They definitely wanted Tag to
go hunting with them.

Still Tag hesitated. "I'll go, if you promise to . . ." The hell with it, Tag decided. In an hour what she did or didn't do wouldn't make any difference to the boy. He crossed the clearing and followed the two Indians onto a path that wound along by the river.

Caro hadn't bothered to introduce his companions. Tag decided they looked like the ragged remains of the French army, so he christened them Napoleon and Bonaparte.

Bonaparte, the younger man, quickly found a stout branch to use as a cane, but he didn't need it long. They went only two hundred yards when Napoleon stopped by a fallen tree. The two Indians exchanged a few quiet words. Bonaparte sat. Napoleon led Tag another hundred yards; then he too found a comfortable spot and positioned himself with an arrow notched into his bow. Tag sat and drew his pistol. Obviously, they were to wait for the game to come to them.

Ten minutes later, Tag had seen only a few flashes of movement, but his guide had bagged two rabbits. He motioned Tag to follow him back to where they had left their companion. Instead of continuing on to camp, Napoleon gestured for Tag to sit, then found a flat rock where he gutted and cleaned the rabbits. Like Bonaparte, when he finished, he settled back and sat staring into space. Maybe they believed Caro would regard them more favorably if she thought they had hunted for hours.

Just after sunset, a trill birdcall rent the air. Without a word, Napoleon stood and led them back to camp. Caro had built a fire, and was kneeling beside it scrubbing at the front of her dress with a wet rag. Behind her was the covered body of the dead boy.

She stood up, accepted the dressed rabbits, and skewered them on a stick she had prepared. She moved about making other preparations for dinner. The two Indians regarded her uneasily as if they would like to help, but were afraid they might break something if they did.

Tag tended to his three horses, then returned to the fire where she had again settled to scrub at her dress. The rasping sound irritated his already frayed nerves. Couldn't she even spend a few minutes to mourn a boy who'd died before he had begun to live?

"The boy died," he said.

"Yes."

"Any respectable Englishwoman would have had hysterics two hours ago. Do you want to talk about it?"

"No."

"Do you want to tell me what happened to them?" He pointed to the wounded warriors on the far side of the fire.

"They were returning to the village with the furs they had been trapping all winter. The Iroquois we saw attacked them. That's all there is to tell." She turned the meat, and the juice sizzled into the fire.

"Don't you care about anything?"

"Don't talk about what you don't understand."

"I understand that you watched a boy die with the same emotion as you're cooking dinner."

She looked at him for an instant, every muscle as taut as the string of a bow. The older brave jumped to his feet. She turned her head and spoke sharply in Shawnee. Looking back at Tag, she said, "I told him to kill you if you speak to me again."

Tag studied the brave's coiled posture and decided she had told him exactly that. She certainly didn't like criticism. He shrugged. It didn't matter. In the morning she would leave with them, and he would go back to the world he understood. A world where women had the vapors at the sight of a cut finger and sobbed for days over the death of a puppy foolish enough to pester a horse.

Caro took the cooked meat from the fire, divided it into portions, and distributed the bowls. The two Indians began eating immediately. Tag held his serving at arm's length, waiting for her to join them. She said something to the older brave in Shawnee and walked off toward the river.

The hell with you. Tag thought, and began to eat. His refusal to wait while she completed her ablutions gave him a small sense of satisfaction. She deserved a cold dinner. He didn't.

At least he would fall asleep tonight without torturous thoughts of her softness. A man needed more than physical curves. He had to believe a woman felt something.

Tag finished his dinner in silence and put the bowl aside. He noticed the rag Caro had discarded, and picked it up to clean his greasy fingers. "Uck." Watery blood dripped from his fingers.

He frowned. Her dress hadn't been mottled with blood when they left. Perhaps she had ministered to the boy while they were gone. He looked toward the spot where she had disappeared. She should be back soon. Even a lingering bath shouldn't take this long at this time of year.

He waited. "Caro's been gone a long time," he said aloud. Both looked at him blankly. He tried to distract himself with thoughts of Englishwomen in long gowns, whose eyes would fill with tears when he told them about the dying boy.

His uneasiness grew. He stood and circled the campsite. The sky had turned from rose to crimson to indigo, and would soon be black. She had been gone too long. He looked again toward the river.

The older Indian had risen and stood in exactly the spot Tag had last seen Caro. His hostile posture suggested he planned to be difficult.

Not this time, Napoleon. Tag walked toward him. As he expected, the warrior stepped into his path.

"Caro," Tag said, and pointed.

The older Indian shook his head and pointed to the fire. Equally determined, Tag tightened his jaw and pointed in the opposite direction. ''Caro may be in trouble. I'm going that way.''

Something in Tag's stance must have convinced the brave they were not just rattling sabers. If the man wanted to stop Tag, he would have to kill him. The man's eyes flitted sideways as if searching for a superior officer, and Tag knew he had won.

A second later the brave stepped aside, spitting a stream of angry Shawnee syllables.

Tag moved past, not even certain what drove him. He had been ready to fight to the death for his right to search for Caro, and she was undoubtedly just sitting someplace making a list of the people she was going to kill. The hollow reassurance did nothing to quell his uneasy certainty that she needed him.

When he reached the river, he turned upstream. It just seemed the right thing to do. In the near-darkness he couldn't see more than ten feet, but he searched the shadows. Her sun-bleached dress would stand out.

''Go away, Elmgrove.'' Her voice came from the darkness directly in front of him. She was alive and well enough to tell him to go away.

Tag didn't even consider it. Some raw need in her tone countermanded the order. Several more paces and he could see her outline where she knelt on a sandy half-moon of land by the river. He walked steadily forward.

''Go away. I need to b-be . . .'' She could barely force the trembling words out. The day's last light reflected off the yellow sand. Her lightning-quick glance at him revealed the silent tears streaming down her face.

''It's all right,'' he said, some part of him not surprised how wrong his every thought had been. ''You shouldn't be alone.''

''I am alone.'' She doubled over as if convulsed by a physical pain, her agony all the more devastating because it was inaudible.

Tag bent, gripped her shoulders, and drew her tightly into his arms. For a moment she resisted his embrace, then something shattered like the fragile shell of a egg. She burrowed against his chest, shaking and sobbing.

"Shhhh. It's all right." Tag stroked her head and back, whispering meaningless words of comfort. "It's all right." He held her and tried to stop her convulsive shaking with his strength. Eventually her sobs slowed to shuddering gasps. "Was it the boy?" he asked. "Did you know him?"

"He was mine."

Tag wondered, but he had to wait for her shuddering to ease again before he could ask. "Yours?"

She raised her head, and the wetness from her tears chilled his chest. "My brother. My son. Just mine. White Fish gave him to me." She stepped back, but her shaky leg refused to support her, and she had to clutch at Tag's shirt for support.

Without thinking, Tag scooped her up into his arms. Instinctively he knew she wouldn't want to return to camp. He turned completely around and found a natural bench where the bank dropped sharply to the sandy beach. He set her down there, oddly reluctant to let her go. Settling beside her, he took her in both of his arms. "Tell me about him."

"His mother died when he was five. I told White Fish I wanted to know how she did it—how she died. At the time I wanted to die too."

"You were only a child yourself."

"Loneliness seems worse than death to a child. My father had brought me to the village a few months before. I thought we would finally be a family, but he left only two days after we got there."

"The bastard. How old were you?"

"Ten. White Fish understood I had to have something to love, so he gave me Billy Boy."

"That was his name? Billy Boy?"

A ghost of a smile appeared on her face. "He was mine.

102

I named him after a doll I had. Nobody even remembers his real name anymore.'' She sat looking at the river for a long time, until Tag wondered if she had forgotten him. Then she spoke softly. ''I wasn't good for him. At first everybody smiled at the way I used to carry him around and beg for clothes to dress him in. Then they saw him becoming too much like me. Too soft.''

Her hand clenched in his. ''I tried to stop loving him. I really did. He . . .'' Her chin began to tremble again. ''He wasn't a very good warrior. He hated the ugliness and the killing. I thought after I went away he would be stronger, but now . . .''

Tag tightened his grip until the spasm of pain passed and her hand relaxed. Any words he could think of were too meaningless to voice. He slid his arm around her shoulders, but when she stiffened, he just held her hand and awkwardly stroked her forearm. ''You should not have sent us away.''

''Even the warriors understood I couldn't do him any more harm if I held him while he died. They understood I needed that time.''

''God, Caro, why didn't you tell me when we came back?''

For the first time she tore her gaze from the river and faced him directly. Her eyes held pain too ragged to mend. ''Some things have no words, Elmgrove.''

''Tag,'' he said softly.

''What?''

''Elmgrove is the name of my title. My friends call me Tag.''

''Are we friends?''

''I understand you better now.'' He understood her too well to deceive her. ''We are friends for tonight. Tomorrow I want you to return to your village with these people.''

''No.'' She snatched her hand away from his.

He couldn't believe she still had the strength to fight him

103

after the brutal day she'd had. "Nothing has changed. If you kill your cousin Edwin, you will be caught and hanged. If you don't, he may kill you. Either way, it is too dangerous."

"I am not afraid."

Tag smiled. "I didn't think you were. But I am." He covered her mouth with his hand to block her protest. "So afraid that I must insist you do as I say. Seven Feathers gave me the authority to order those warriors to escort you back to the village."

"They are my friends. They will not—"

"They will recognize Seven Feathers's token." He patted her shoulder. "It will not be forever. Somehow, when I get back, I will find a way to deal with your cousin. When it is safe, I will send for you."

She stood and turned to face him, her arms folded across her chest. "You won't send for me because I will either be with you or there before you. You cannot make me go back."

"I can and will." He drew the silver arm bracelet out of his pocket. "Those men may be your friends, but they will recognize his authority." He softened his tone. It would save arguing in the morning. "A few months won't make any difference."

"My grandfather may die."

"And he may not. Either way he wouldn't want you in danger." He stood. "Come. It has been a long day." He held out his hand.

To his surprise, she took it and let him lead her back along the river. Only when he turned right toward the glowing beacon of the campfire did she twist her hand from his. "You go. I still must wash."

He hesitated, considered the short distance, and nodded. He headed for the fire, surprised at the small wrenching inside him at letting her out of his sight. Tomorrow would be even more difficult.

The two Indians stiffened at his approach and questioned him with their eyes. "She is all right," he said. They probably didn't understand his words, but relaxed at his tone. They continued to watch the opening in the brush from which she would appear.

While he waited, Tag unrolled the buffalo robes they would use for sleeping. Remembering her anguish, he set his out next to hers. If she woke in the night, he would be there to comfort her. After checking the horses, he joined the others to wait for her return.

She stepped into the firelight, and Tag's chest tightened. She had scrubbed her face and loosened her hair so it cascaded in flaxen waves about her shoulders. Worse, she had removed the breeches she wore for riding and her legs were bare from the knees down. She looked as she had on their wedding night. Exactly.

He tried to force his mind to remember her innocent vulnerability as she told him of her love for the dead boy. But his traitorous body remembered only her softness when she trembled against him. His gaze flitted to the sleeping robes he had set out together.

His mind pictured her turning to him for comfort. He would take her in his arms and hold her as he had at the river. But if she stirred against him? If she tilted her head up to hear his words? If his hand remembered how easily he could raise that short dress? Comfort wouldn't be what he offered her.

He didn't dare sleep that close to her tonight. He had only to control the attraction for this one more night. Then she would return to her village with the others and be nothing but a very pleasant—and arousing—memory.

As she moved about quietly seeing to the needs of the others, Tag casually retrieved his sleeping robe and carried it to the far side of the campsite. He fell asleep congratulating himself on the wisdom of sleeping as far from her as he could.

He regretted that decision as soon as he opened his eyes the next morning. Caro gave him a wickedly innocent smile from the far side of the clearing.

Without looking, he knew she had outwitted him.

Chapter Six

"Good morning, Tag." Caro barely had time to say the words before she saw understanding dawn in his eyes. She lowered her gaze so as not to taunt him with her triumph.

"Where are the others?" He flung aside his blanket and jumped to his feet.

"Gone."

His head snapped from side to side as he searched the campsite. "Without you?"

"Did you honestly believe I would go with them meekly just because you showed me a little kindness last night?"

"Not because I was kind to you, but because it is the only thing to do. We can catch them." He hopped about on one foot while struggling to draw his boot into the other. "We have the horses. We can catch them." He stomped the booted foot on the ground, his eyes wide with a new suspicion. "The horses!" Without waiting for her response, he dashed toward where he had hobbled the horses, his right boot dangling from his hand.

Caro smiled. He would rant and lecture. She would have to listen to how his model Englishwoman would never have given away the horses, but in the end they would go on. She turned her attention to the moccasin in her hand. She would have time to finish it before he would be ready to continue.

"Dammit, where are the horses?" He ruined his attempt

to stamp angrily into the clearing by hopping to avoid bruising his bare foot.

"Those men were wounded. They need the horses more than we do."

"You gave away the horses?" He slammed his loose boot to the ground and muttered a series of phrases Caro knew weren't meant for her ears.

"Except for the packhorse," she reminded him calmly.

"Useless creature. We could never catch—yes, we can." He glanced toward where Billy Boy's body had lain. "They will have to travel slowly. Get ready. We can catch them."

Caro ignored the stab of pain at the thought of the lifeless body of the boy she loved. She would look forward, not back. "Not if they don't want to be caught. And believe me, they don't want to be caught."

"I am sure you saw to that." He exhaled with a shuddering windy sound. "Tell me, what are we supposed to do now?"

She carefully kept the triumph out of her voice. "Go to England."

He huffed another explosive breath. "I should have known you would say that. How do you propose we get there?"

"We walk."

"Walk to England. Of course. I shouldn't doubt you could do exactly that if you set your mind to it."

"Detroit is only a hundred miles."

He stalked across the clearing, and again ruined the effect by cursing when a sharp stone dug into his foot. He whirled to face her. "Which would give you what? Five more nights to seduce me into being your husband?"

Caro stifled a laugh. She had not considered that particular benefit. "An interesting suggestion. Though not at the moment if you don't stop glaring at me."

"Well, it's not going to happen." He sat, drew on his boot, and rose to stare down at her. "And I have no intention of walking all the way to Detroit. We still have the packhorse, and it will give me great pleasure to ride while you walk.''

''Unfortunately, the poor animal can't carry all this and you too.'' She swept her hand to indicate the goods strewn around the camp.

''I am aware of that. I am going to wash.'' He brushed the loose dirt and twigs from his breeches. ''You have half an hour to select what you can carry.'' He walked to the edge of the clearing and paused, his eyes narrow. ''I mean it, Caro. I am not the one who gave away the horses.''

Caro stared after him, then slowly collected everything into a large pile in the center of the campsite. Half an hour later she had moved everything several times, but discarded nothing.

Tag returned, leading the packhorse. ''I assume you are ready. Show me what you mean to take.''

''I have tried. Truly I have.''

''But?'' He stalked over to look down at the pile.

''I need it all.''

''Things can be replaced.''

Caro bit her lower lip. ''Not if they are all you have.''

He bent and hoisted the largest sack. ''This must weigh fifty pounds. What the hell is in here?''

''Books.'' Caro grabbed for the sack, but he held it just out of reach. ''My father brought me a book every time he returned to the village.''

''They stay here.'' He threw the sack so it landed with a resounding thud six feet away. ''I will send you all the books you want from New York.'' He bent to an open bundle and drew out a faded calico dress. ''And this? What is this?''

''My dress.''

He gave it a disbelieving shake. ''Your dress! Only if you plan to be ten years old again. Get rid of it.''

Caro closed her eyes against the memory. "It is the last dress my mother made for me. I need it."

His eyes softened, but the flinty look returned almost immediately. "Stop playing on my sympathy." He thrust the dress into her hands. "Sort out the things we need for the journey. Blankets, food, whatever. I will take that." He marched over and plunked himself down on the log bench. "Anything you are not ready to carry in ten minutes stays here."

Damn him. Half an hour later, Caro tucked in the last corner of a heavy awkward pack. Tag regarded her coldly from the back of the horse while she worked her arms into the straps and heaved herself to her feet. She couldn't smile, but at least she didn't groan with the first step.

She led the way. The first mile passed easily enough. The day grew warmer. Sweat drenched her armpits and trickled down her back. The straps gnawed into her shoulders, and she had to consciously force herself to draw long slow breaths. She decided she could probably walk until noon before she fell on her face and died.

She walked for less than an hour before Tag rode up beside her. "Do you always win?"

Too tired to reply, she ignored the question.

He dismounted and walked beside her for a few steps. "I know you will regard this as a sign of weakness." He stopped her with a hand on her arm. "It is not. I merely calculated how long it will take us to reach Detroit at this pace." He eased the pack from her shoulders, and she sat drawing long breaths while he distributed the weight on the packhorse.

Relieved of her burden, Caro could have walked until midnight. But late afternoon she noticed the slight limp Tag had developed getting increasingly worse. Lines of pain splintered out from the corners of his eyes. His boots had to be chafing abominably.

They came to a wide stream. Instead of crossing the

rocks that formed a natural bridge, she followed the bank until they came to a welcoming expanse of grass. "We should camp here for the night."

Relief flickered in Tag's eyes, but he made a weak protest. "We have a few more hours of daylight."

"But we have water here."

He nodded. After tending the horse, he dropped onto an uneven patch of grass with the rolled buffalo robe pillowing his head. Within minutes he was asleep.

Caro bathed, changed out of her travel clothes, and set a stew to boiling. Sitting cross-legged, she completed her preparations to return his kindness of the previous night. She had never just sat and watched a man sleep before. His quiet vulnerability startled her with unexpected waves of tenderness. She imagined pillowing his head on her knees while she soothed the worry lines from his forehead.

He opened his eyes and met her gaze. For a long minute they just looked at each other as if his thoughts could talk to hers in words far gentler than either of them had ever spoken. He flicked a glance at the fire. "I'm sorry. I should have helped."

"You were tired." She shook off her wistful mood. "More than tired. Remove your boots."

Just the word made him wince. "I'm not sure I can. My feet feel bigger than wine barrels." He sat up and tugged at his left boot.

Caro gathered up the things she had set out and went over to kneel at his feet. Patches of blood dotted his white stockings at the heels and across the toes. "I thought so," she said. "Here, let me." She reached out and drew off his stockings, gently peeling the material away from the raw patches.

She bathed the blisters with warm water and rubbed on a soothing balm. "They will be better in the morning. Now if you will relax, I will work out some of the knots." She began to knead his feet where she could without causing pain.

With a contented sigh, he lay back. "Mmmm." He closed his eyes and surrendered to her touch. He moaned in contentment whenever she found a vulnerable spot.

Finally she stood and walked to where his hand lay on the ground to present her final offering. "Wear these tomorrow." She held out the moccasins she had just completed. "Walking will be much easier."

His eyes widened with pleasure. He accepted the gift and looked back at her with an expression of almost wonder. "You are a saint." His gaze slid down her body, and his free hand reached out to grip her ankle. "And you have the most beautiful pair of ankles I've ever seen."

Her whole leg tensed under his touch. She held her breath.

"Beautiful." He stroked the front of her ankle with his thumb, sending shivers of sensation up her leg. "You like to be touched, don't you?" He caressed the back of her calf. "Don't you?"

"Yes." Her voice was a dry whisper. Her heart pounded against her chest. She didn't dare move for fear he'd stop.

"As long as I don't sit up we're probably safe enough. I can't reach any higher than this." His fingers played along the back of her knee. The shiver reached her shoulders this time. "When a woman shivers like that, it's an invitation to a man. Did you know that?" His grip tightened on her calf. "Even if you knew what I was thinking, you wouldn't stop me, would you?"

"No." If this was all she would ever get from her husband, she wanted it to continue forever.

"Because you like it or because you want me as a husband?"

"Both." She wanted to call back the admission, certain he would snatch his hand away.

But he continued to stroke her lower leg. He had to be

feeling the goose flesh his hand raised. "I am sorry to disappoint you, but perhaps I have more control than either of us thought," he said. "I find this reasonably sweet torture, but harmless enough." He looked at her with a tight-lipped smile. "However, pleasant as it is, I thought we agreed you would wear both the dress and breeches until we reached Detroit."

"Only for traveling." She had to consciously draw enough breath to talk. But if he thought his touch didn't affect her, he would allow her a few more delicious moments. "I can't wear them at night. They are too confining. My legs can't breathe."

He laughed. "I am having a little trouble with that myself." He gave the back of her leg a light slap. "Suppose you go sit over there so I can sit up."

Caro needed time to quiet her rapidly beating heart. She crossed to the fire and spent a long time scooping the stew into bowls. One leg felt so much colder than the other. She looked up to find him smiling at her.

"Thank you for the moccasins." He allowed his gaze to drift slowly down her body. "And for a treasure trove of pleasant fantasies."

She still couldn't think of anything to say, but her face heated with the warmth of his smile. A little nervous that he might touch her again, more concerned that he might not, she carried him his dinner.

His fingers brushed hers as he accepted it. "It seems I must say thank you again." He laughed. "Though I doubt if I will be able to eat until you settle out of arm's reach."

Caro returned to the fire and took up her own bowl. She ate in silence, wishing she could decide where to look. When she looked away, she imagined his smug satisfaction that she could not look at him and eat. But when she met his still-warm gaze, the food knotted in a tight lump in her throat. He looked as if he were eating each mouthful with her. Finally, she gave up and set her bowl aside.

He did the same.

"I wish you would stop looking at me like that," she said.

"Like what, Miss Fenton?"

Miss Fenton, she noticed, not Caro. His gaze continued to make her face feel like fire. "You only call me Miss Fenton when . . ."

"An excellent observation," he said dryly. "Your formal name when I am thinking the most informal thoughts. You will make some man a splendid wife someday."

Finally she felt the sting of his rejection. "Some man, but not you."

"Unfortunately, no."

"Will all Englishmen find me as abhorrent as you?"

He gave a mirthless laugh. "I thought we had just established that I do not find you abhorrent at all."

Caro hated herself for asking, but she had to know. "Then why . . . ?"

His voice took on a sudden chill. "Why do I resist your charms? I have already chosen the woman I will marry."

"You never mentioned that."

"There is nothing official. I have not offered for her yet, but I plan to as soon as I return to England."

Caro bit down on her lower lip. It had nothing to do with her. It shouldn't hurt, but she felt as if someone had just stolen something from her. "What is her name?" She was proud of the steady tone in her voice.

"Isobel the Icicle."

"Theicicle," Caro echoed, testing the distasteful sound.

"Isobel the Icicle." He said the words slowly, separating the name into three distinct words. "It is a private joke. I christened her that for reasons you can probably guess."

"Why would you marry somebody you refer to as an icicle?" Caro frowned, suddenly angry at the only reason she could imagine. "You love her very much, and she is cold to you."

"I don't love her at all."

"Oh." Caro liked that much better. But still it made no sense. "How will an icicle love you enough for both of you?"

He smiled. "How young you are. She will love my fortune and my title. That will be enough."

She studied him carefully to see if he was teasing her. He met her look steadily with a slight tilt to his head as if defying her to argue with some logic she could not understand. But his rejection of their wedding night still rankled too much to let the matter drop. "You said you could choose your wife. Why would you want someone who will care only for such empty things?"

"She will consider it a good bargain. She will give me the heir I need. Then she will be content to stay in London and spend my money while I go off to wherever I go off to next."

Caro looked into the fire for a long time, trying to feel how that could make sense. She could not even feel any compassion for the woman who would make such a sad choice. Eventually she gave up trying. "I would not like that."

"I was sure you wouldn't." He laughed and stood up. "So you see, I do not abhor you. I am merely looking out for your happiness."

"As I will look out for yours."

He gave an exaggerated shudder. "That statement, Miss Fenton, scares the stuffing out of me. Now I believe it is time we go to sleep—separately, of course."

Caro savored the last seconds of his good humor. "That may be a problem."

He glanced up from where he was rummaging through the baggage. "How so."

"We have only one blanket."

He stood for a minute as if stunned, then threw his hands in the air. "Of course. I should have anticipated that. You

115

gave away the horses. You refuse to wear more than the absolute minimum of clothing. Why should I hope you would consider two blankets a necessity?''

''It is a large blanket. We can share.''

''Not on your life.''

''You will be cold.''

Rummaging through the baggage, he found a thin cured hide Caro planned to make into a dress. He wrapped it around his shoulders and sat by the fire. ''I may be cold, but you will keep your virtue and I will retain my untarnished reputation to present to Isobel.''

For a long time Caro lay awake that night, endlessly reliving the few precious moments before dinner. Tag had done more than caress her leg. With his hand and his voice he had reached out and stroked the loneliness inside her. The night didn't seem so empty because she could hear the sound of his breathing.

She thought of the cold Englishwoman who wanted his name and fortune. Poor woman. Caro wanted only one thing. She wanted him to be there when she woke in the morning.

The next three days passed uneventfully. Occasionally, Caro detected the sound of other travelers. She always invented an excuse to lead Tag off the trail and linger in the woods until the party passed. She learned to live with the terror they would meet someone who would recognize Seven Feathers's token and obey Tag's command to take her back to the village.

The warm golden moments they shared more than made up for the nagging fear. Tag had a deep voice and he sang tirelessly, insisting she learn the words and laughing when she couldn't learn the tune. After the first day he lost his awkwardness around her during the daylight hours, and reached out to help her as naturally as if they had been companions for years. He would take her hand to help her up a hill, then walk for a mile with her palm hidden in his.

The first time they came to a stream too wide to bridge with a fallen branch, he looked at it and laughed. "No point in both of us going about with soaking feet. And since my moccasins have yet to be christened—" He swept her up into his arms and splashed through the water, singing in her ear. She felt as safe and cherished as a small child. After that she had to resist the temptation to lead them on a tortuous route that would force them to cross every stream in the valley.

Only at night would his wariness return. Then he would find an excuse to move quickly out of the way if she came too close. He would call her "Miss Fenton," and insist she stay on her own side of the fire.

Late on the afternoon of the third day, the weather turned savage. Black clouds roiled across the sun, turning the world gray. The first rain fell in high slapping drops that quickly turned to a stinging mist of sleet.

"We've got to find shelter." Tag looked around anxiously.

The forest of tall saplings with infant leaves offered little comfort. "I think I remember a hill ahead," Caro said into the wind. "The overhanging rocks might offer some protection. We stayed there several years ago."

"How far ahead?"

Caro couldn't remember whether it would be an hour or a day. "Does it matter? We can't stay here."

Tag dragged the buffalo robe from the horse and handed it to Caro, then located the deer hide he had adopted as his own. They walked for an hour hunched into the wind, which whipped across their faces and tore at their wrappings. To Tag's credit, he never questioned her order to keep moving, though after the second hour he began to look longingly at some of the trees.

Caro spotted the jagged hill a little to the north of where

117

she'd expected it. "There." She pointed and quickened their pace.

Ten minutes later she led Tag under the overhang she remembered. The natural cleft sheltered them from the worst of the rain, but offered little protection against the chill wind.

"Wait." Tag pointed to a dark spot in the hill. "That may be a cave over there."

"I–I don't like caves." Caro retreated until the uneven wall of the hill pressed into her back.

"Not as much as I don't like winter nights in the rain without a blanket." Tag snatched her hand, leaving her little choice but to scurry with him.

The dark spot proved to be the narrow opening to a natural cave. Tag scooped up a large rock, threw it inside, and waited. The rock landed with an echoing series of thumps. He threw two more rocks. When nothing stirred and no further sound emerged, he looked at her in triumph. "We have a new home. I'll go first." He crawled inside. "Perfect." His cry emerged a moment before he did. "You go in. I'll unload our things and gather some wood."

"I'll gather the wood." Only good sense kept her from saying, *I'll unload the things, gather the wood, and spend the rest of the night out here.* In England she would spend the days in huge, stone houses. Caves. She would practice tonight.

Too soon, all the tasks had been done. Every muscle tense, Caro followed Tag into the cave. It was too small. The close walls made the air heavy. She had to breathe through her mouth in shallow gasps.

"Don't sit in the opening," Tag said. "You'll freeze in the wind."

The cool breeze was the only thing that made it possible to find a breath. Obediently she moved to the side. The move let in the last light of the fading day. She could do it, Caro decided. She could stay if she remembered to breathe deeply. In a few minutes it would be easier.

She sat so she could keep her hand in the passageway to the outside. The chill on her fingers reminded her the opening would be there if she needed it.

"Splendid shelter, this." Tag walked in a circle, hunched over, running his hand over the stone walls. "I stayed in a cave in Portugal once. Damp wretched place. The walls smelled like cat droppings." He sat and began to peel the bark off the wet sticks to get to the drier wood inside.

Caro tried to focus on his words as he talked of the cave in Portugal and the man who'd found it. She bit her lip to keep from urging him to hurry with the fire.

He struck a spark. It flickered and went out. He struck another. A small glow appeared. He nurtured it, crumbling small bits of wood onto the infant fire. Caro exhaled with relief and glanced toward the far wall. Her blood froze.

A pair of red eyes glowered at her from the corner.

Her mouth gaped open. She strangled out a weak sound, but couldn't form a word.

Tag looked at her. She pointed frantically. He looked and saw the eyes.

Without haste he picked up a smoldering stick and threw it. The eyes disappeared. Tiny feet scratched across the floor.

Warm fur brushed across Caro's ankles. "Aieeee." Her control snapped. Mindlessly she scampered through the opening on her hands and knees. As soon as she could, she staggered to her feet and ran blindly into the darkness.

She tripped, but the spongy earth cushioned her fall. She gasped in long heaving breaths.

"Caro. Caro." Tag's frantic call came from behind her.

"Here." The word had too much breath to carry more than a few feet, but he appeared at her side before she could do more than raise her head.

He gripped her shoulders and pulled her to her feet. "What the hell happened?" The darkness was so complete she couldn't see his face, but could feel his breath on her face.

She tried to smile. "I don't like caves."

"You mentioned that. I guess I didn't understand that you *really* don't like caves." He ran his hands down her arms to her wrists. "Are you all right?"

"I am afraid of rats."

"They won't hurt you." He ran his hands up to her shoulders. "You're still trembling." He drew her against him.

"I'm sorry. I thought I could stay in there." Her pounding heart slowed to a milder thumping.

He took a step and turned her back toward the cave, keeping a protective arm on her shoulder. "You have to come back. You'll freeze out here in the rain."

"It's not raining."

With his thumb he scraped the moisture from her cheek. "That's not sunshine."

"It's only a light mist. I can't go back."

His tone hardened. "You can if I carry you. I can't leave you here."

"No." She set her weight solidly on her heels. Her mind reeled with pictures of him dragging her back to the cave and tying her there in darkness. The trembling began again. "I'll go back to the spot I found before."

"Be reasonable. I can't even see you in this darkness. How are you going to find a place a hundred yards away? I won't let anything hurt you. I—"

"No."

"Please—oh, the hell with it. Stay here then." He stalked off.

Caro sank to her knees. She would either freeze or she wouldn't. She wrapped her arms around her shoulders, but the chill seemed to come from inside her. Minutes passed.

"Here, put this on."

The warmth of the buffalo robe enveloped her. Its

safe familiar scent filled her nostrils. "Thank you. I thought—"

"Please, if you thought I would leave you out here, don't tell me. I pride myself on my image as a perfect gentleman."

"I promise never to think ill of you again." She reached out and found his hand exactly where she thought it would be. "Go back now before you freeze."

"I considered that. Unfortunately my upbringing as a gentleman precludes that as well. I can't leave you out here alone."

"But you have only—"

"Just for tonight I have decided to relax my prohibition against sharing a blanket." She heard the faint smile in his voice. "I believe I can control myself if you will promise to do the same."

The buffalo robe was large enough to spread on the wet ground and still have ample material to draw over them. In a moment they both settled under its warmth. The rain had softened to little more than a light mist. True to her promise, Caro huddled as far away from Tag as she could. Though thoroughly chilled, she assumed controlling herself prohibited burrowing against him to share the heat he radiated. She clenched her teeth together to suppress all but an inescapable chatter.

"Dammit, Caro, you are more than a man can stand." He reached out and drew her into his arms. "I can't sleep until you stop shaking."

"I'm sorry." She wasn't. Not if it brought her the heated comfort of his arms and the pad of his shoulder muscle to pillow her head.

"Don't tell me you're sorry." He brushed a tangle of hair from her forehead and rested his chin against it. "Tell me why you're afraid of rats. I would have bet my inheritance I would never see you afraid of anything." His voice had a sleepy rumble in the night air.

121

"I don't really remember. I think it has to do with my last week with my mother."

His shoulder heaved with an almost inaudible laugh. "Your mother was a rat?"

The night had made the memory too vivid for Caro to appreciate his small attempt at a joke. "She was a wonderful person. I lived with her and my two sisters in a small settlement about thirty miles from Detroit. I don't remember much about those years. I just remember being happy."

"Until?"

"A neighbor came in one day. My mother had a fever and a sore on her face. The woman ran screaming from the house. My mother cried. I knew something was terribly wrong."

"Smallpox," Tag guessed.

"Nobody would come near us. Not even after my sisters got sick as well. They brought food, but would leave it in the yard. Nobody would come in the house."

"Who took care of—" She felt his gasp and his arms tightened around her. "Oh, Lord, Caro, how old were you?"

"Eight. I never cried after the first day. I just kept thinking how angry my father would be if I let them die." Her hand clutched at his damp shirt. He began to stroke her hair.

"How long?"

"I don't remember if it was days or weeks. I just remember being so tired I wished I could be the one lying there."

"They died?"

"First my sister, then my mother, then my baby sister. She was only three." Caro drew a long shuddering breath. The darkness and his comfort somehow made the memory more vivid. "Even after they died, the neighbors wouldn't let me come out of the house. I think something must have happened with rats the last night. I had only one candle. I just remember the darkness and huge moving shadows on the wall. The neighbors found me huddled outside the next morning. I wouldn't talk to anyone for weeks.''

"Didn't anyone go inside to find out what happened?''

"They burned the house and everything in it. I had nothing left but the dress I had on. For years I thought they did it to punish me for letting my family die.''

He tilted her chin up so she could see his face in the faint light of the cloud covered moon. "You didn't let them die.''

"I've learned enough about healing to know that now.''

"You didn't sound like you believe it.''

"I do.'' Honesty forced her to add, "Most of the time.''

"I wish . . .''

Caro waited through several seconds of silence. "What do you wish?''

"It's foolish.'' He released a long sigh. "No, it's not foolish. I wish I could go back and make it different for you.''

"I wish I hadn't saddened you with all of that. I'm sorry.''

"Don't be.'' Again he smoothed the hair from her forehead and placed a whisper-soft kiss there. "I've never felt so close to a woman in my life.'' He chuckled softly. "Of course, that could be because you are practically lying on top of me.''

Caro pushed against his chest to retreat. He tightened his arm around her shoulder. "Don't go. I'm rather enjoying it. And for some baffling reason, I'm not half-mad with lust.''

She hesitated. She had promised. "If you're sure . . .''

"Go to sleep, Caro.''

Caro drifted up from sleep the next morning dreamily aware of Tag's nearness. Her eyes fluttered open to find him on his side staring down at her, his eyes as gray and

123

dark as a rain cloud. His arm pillowed her head. His other arm stretched across her body and rested in the small of her back.

"Shhh, it's all right," he whispered so softly she had to almost read the word from his lips. "Right now, I want to hold you more than I ever wanted anything in my life." His liquid eyes held a tenderness Caro ached to experience. With a gentle pressure of his hand on her back, he rolled her onto her side.

His lips brushed her forehead and her chin came to rest against his shoulder. She inhaled, and a musky scent, his male scent, replaced the delicate aroma of dawn. The dull throb of his heart became indistinguishable from hers, and she could feel the shudder of the breath he released along the whole length of her body.

She banished everything but the awareness of him. Not just his hard body touching her everywhere, but a rush of tenderness that seemed to come from both of them.

Time passed in slow shallow breaths and honeyed sensation. After moments that passed too quickly, he relaxed his grip and eased her from him. He sat up, shivered, and rose. Several long strides carried him to a thigh-high boulder where he slumped forward to rest his weight on his arms and looked off into the distance.

Caro remained as he had left her. Thought returned fragment by fragment. She'd been too disoriented from sleep to recognize the opportunity she'd been waiting for. He'd been lying next to her like a husband. If only she'd turned her chin up, he might have kissed her. He might have claimed her for his wife. She might have savored her revenge.

"Tag." She whispered his name so softly he didn't hear it. *Tag*. Her mind repeated the name, and her heart grew heavy with a new understanding. She wished he had kissed her. She wished he had put his hands on her as he had on their wedding night. But not because she wanted revenge.

She wanted him to want her. She wanted to truly be his wife.

He turned to her, a bemused expression on his face, the yellow sunlight gleaming off his sunshine hair. "What the hell was that?" he asked.

She wrapped her arms around her knees. For her it had been her a hunger reaching out to him. But for him . . . ? "I thought you would tell me."

"I don't know." He shook his head. "I don't know. I never . . . I just woke up and felt I would die if I didn't hold you."

Suddenly Caro didn't want him to spoil the moment by believing she had been scheming. "It wasn't . . ."

He gave a confused laugh. "I know what it wasn't. I just don't know what the hell it was." He took a few steps toward her and shook his head again. "I'm not a religious man, but if I were, that's what I'd want religion to be like."

Chapter Seven

Caro disappeared to take care of her morning needs. The tingling awareness remained with Tag. He moved about instinctively, gathering their things and loading them onto the packhorse. But he paused constantly to shake his head and ask the same question. "What the devil was that?"

He had awakened hard and ready for a woman—a not unusual state for him. He'd woken with a woman next him. Also not unusual. But there the similarity to anything he'd ever experienced ended.

Instead of turning to do anything about either, he'd felt a wave of emotion that slowed every movement. He'd wanted—he couldn't even put into words what he'd wanted. Though his mind was still fogged with sleep and tumbling with images of half-remembered dreams, his body had been alive to every sensation. With some non-thinking part of his body, he knew two things. He had to hold Caro; and he would do no more than hold her.

And he had held her for some unmeasured time when everything outside the circle of his arms ceased to exist. He'd inhaled the forest-green smell of hair, tasted the dew on her forehead. His throat had grown warm with the moist softness of her exhaled breath, a breath that reinforced his need to put his arms around her and protect her from anyone or anything that would ever hurt her again.

Tag's stomach wrenched into a tight, hard knot. Give him good honest lust any day, not . . .

For the first time he thought not of his reaction, but of hers, of the look he'd seen in her eyes when he'd turned to face her. *Damn her*, he muttered, then cursed himself for blaming her. It had been his fault. With a single unguarded moment of tenderness he had conjured up the one thing that could terrify him more than the devil himself—a woman who could love him.

It had been there in her eyes, a glowing warmth that saw, not his clothes, not his fortune, not his title, but just the man. Tag gave an aggravated jerk on the thong he was tightening under the girth of the packhorse. The animal snorted and stamped impatiently. "That's right," Tag said, giving the animal a fraternal pat. "We both ought to throw off everything and ride out of here as if the hounds of Hell were after us."

He finished the knot and stood to stroke the animal's neck. "But you're a horse, and I'm a gentleman. We're both trapped—at least until Detroit, where I will find someone to escort her back to her village."

Whatever Caro's thoughts, she didn't try to alter Tag's mood that day. She matched his grim pace, and made only two attempts to intrude on his withdrawn silence. He insisted they push on until almost full darkness, when they both dropped, too exhausted to do more than build a small fire and chew on dried meat for dinner. Caro crawled beneath the lone buffalo robe without even her usual offer to share.

The next morning brought a miracle. An hour from camp they came on a small community of five cabins. One of the settlers had two horses standing in a rough-hewn corral. On receiving Tag's promise to leave them at the inn in Detroit, he agreed to "sell" them for only three times the price Tag would have paid for prime animals at Tattersall's. Given that that meant they would reach the fort that afternoon rather than spending another night, possibly two, on the trail, Tag thought the bargain a fine one.

Caro's anxiety increased with each brisk mile. She needed more time so Tag could forget the morning that had driven him from her. She had spent hours searching for a way to apologize, for anything she could say to bring back his easy smile. But no matter how long she thought, she could not think of anything she had done wrong.

She hadn't tried to inveigle him into performing the act that would make him her husband. She hadn't chastised him for holding her so close when he did not plan to claim her. She had done nothing but enjoy the wondrous moments, and if that was an un-English crime, she could not bring herself to say she was sorry. So she had endured his silences and accusing looks.

His withdrawal and the certainty he planned to abandon her as soon as they were inside the fortification made the approaching town even more terrifying. She had been there many times, but always with her father, whose buoyant personality made them welcome everywhere. Alone she would be a strangely dressed outcast, or worse, an enemy.

The residents hadn't forgotten the recent cruel wars. Breath of a Panther had talked for days of the hostile stares he'd received the last time he came to trade. And he had stayed only for a few hours, refusing to spend the night.

Coward, Caro chided herself. What did it matter if Tag stayed with her? She needed only to stay in the wretched town long enough to obtain the proper clothes and discover the fastest way to England. For those few days she could appear to fit in or she could endure the scornful looks.

As they neared the town, traffic in the opposite direction increased. People passed on foot, on horseback, and in heavily loaded wagons. Most offered a pleasant greeting, though Caro noted the smiles of the women seemed a little more forced than those of the men. A few of the women simply stared through her as if she didn't exist. When that happened Tag's smile became tighter.

They entered the town in the late afternoon. It was a dirty, noisy place, ruthlessly stripped of any trees that might have decorated it. Caro resisted the temptation to shrink into herself, and looked straight ahead as she prepared for Tag's pronouncement of where he would abandon her.

She forced herself to study the women who crowded the streets. To reach England, she would have to become one of them. A long gown, tight shoes that clattered against the wooden walkways, and a bonnet that would keep the breeze from her face and hair. She wanted to turn back. No grandfather was worth never feeling the sun on her face.

Tag continued to ride at the same crisp pace, turning without hesitation from one street to another. After several minutes he reined to a halt in front of a three-tiered building. "We will stay here tonight. Tomorrow I will find someone to escort you back to your village."

Caro barely concealed her sigh of relief. Whatever the reason for his resentment of her, he did not plan to simply send her on her way. She would at least have tonight to accustom herself to the confusion of the town before continuing on her own.

He dismounted and gave a whistle, which brought a young boy running. "Take the horses to the stable." He flipped a coin to the youngster and headed for the doorway of the building without looking back.

The command snapped Caro out of her frozen state. She had to dismount or be led off to the stables. She slipped to the ground and followed Tag inside to a large common room with a scattering of people, mostly rough-hewn men, at rough-hewn tables. After several steps into the room, she stopped to accustom her eyes to the dim light.

Tag approached a bony woman who stood indifferently wiping the same spot on a long bar. "Good afternoon, Alice. I trust you followed my instructions regarding my room.''

The woman gave a smile that revealed a missing front tooth. ''You're back, Elmgrove. Lucky for you orderin' me to hold your room for you. Now that spring travel's opened up, you won't find another room in this town tonight. People trompin' through here in droves lookin' to settle the new territory.'' Her gaze had already flicked past Tag and come to rest on Caro.

''I trust you can come up with another room somehow, Alice. I will need two, for tonight at least. Possibly longer.''

''Two?'' Her eyes narrowed to black beads. She nodded at Caro. ''If that's your companion, somebody shoulda warned you I don't let none of that kind in here.''

Tag didn't bother to look back. ''That kind?'' His voice had the chill of a November frost.

''Indians.'' She raked Caro again with her glare. ''Or like enough to.''

''Not that it is any concern of yours—'' Tag's November frost cooled to midwinter ice—''but Miss Fenton is as English as I am.''

Alice stepped out from behind the bar and circled Caro. ''If you say so.'' She tightened her thin lips. ''I guess she can stay. Though you'll have to give up on that notion of keepin' up appearances and share your room with your . . . lady friend.'' She'd paused just long enough before the words to let Caro know she'd been insulted again.

Even in the dim light Caro could see the crimson that colored Tag's ears. ''I'm sure you can arrange something,'' he said.

Alice gave a dry laugh. ''I told you I coulda let your room three times a day while you were gone. There's nothing—''

''Hey, Alice!'' The voice from the other side of the room came from a man whose dark beard and gnarled hair made him look like a black bear dressed in buckskin. ''If he is tired of her, you can put her in my room! Without them clothes—''

Tag had clenched his right hand around the man's throat and dragged him to his feet even before the chairs he had knocked over crossing the room stopped clattering against the floor. "If you finish that sentence, you will never finish another."

The bearlike man's strangled attempts at words filled the silent room.

"Tag," Caro said sharply to call his attention to the man's purpling face. "He's choking."

Tag slowly relaxed his grip. Only when his hand dropped to his side did Caro notice that the stranger was a good six inches taller. Obviously the man did not consider his size a significant advantage. He dissolved back into his chair. "Sorry," he said.

With a vein throbbing in his temple, Tag watched him for a full five seconds, then walked to Caro and turned her with his hand in the small of her back. "We are going to my room now," he said without looking back. "Please send word when you have made the additional arrangements."

Upstairs, Tag guided Caro to a door, which he opened with a key. She moved into a square room and crossed directly to a lace-curtained window overlooking the street. Not certain how much of his anger remained, she thought it wise to be as far away as possible.

He stepped in, closed the door, and rocked back against it. His head bumped the wood panel with a soft thunk. "I'm sorry. That was ugly."

"You might have been killed."

He gave a tired smile. "I find I am not usually killed when I get that angry. I'm not sure why."

Caro suspected it was because he produced the strength of a demon and a look in his eye that promised he could double that strength. She remembered how Gray Wolf had backed away from him. A small mirror hung over a shaving stand set against the side wall. She couldn't resist the impulse to go over and peer into it to see how she had appeared to the people below. Dressed as Tag had ordered, with her doeskin dress over her father's shirt and breeches, she could see nothing to provoke the stranger's assumption she would be willing to go to his bed. When she turned, she found Tag watching her with a look as critical as her own. "They thought I was your . . . ?"

"Say it." His eyes narrowed. "My whore."

She had heard the traders who came to the village talk of whores with painted faces and provocative manners. "Why would they think that?"

"Believe me, Miss Fenton, I've thought about that. Your attraction, I mean. It's more than just those breeches." He angled his head to study her thoughtfully. "It's an awareness you have of your body. Something in the way you stand or move that makes a man sense you would be like liquid fire in bed." He tossed his hands in the air, palms up. "No man could explain it. But trust me, any man alive enough to still be breathing can recognize it."

Caro looked into the mirror long enough to consider how she could move without being aware she was doing so.

"Dammit." His palms slapped against the door as he pushed himself away and took three stomping steps across the room and whirled to face her. "You've done it to me again. I have never talked about such things with a woman. With you I never know what I will say next."

"Well, I am sure it doesn't matter because what you say makes no sense."

"I suppose not. If you understood, you wouldn't be nearly so dangerous." He gave his shoulders an abrupt shake. "At least you see why you need a more appropriate dress. Respectable women don't dress in breeches."

"If that mean-spirited woman below is your idea of respectable, I will keep my breeches." Her vow to conform hadn't even survived her first encounter. She tried again. "You are right, of course." She crossed to the window and looked out at the busy street below. "I will go out now and find something." The only dresses she'd ever owned her father had brought back from his trips. She had no idea if she could even locate the shop where one purchased such things.

"I will go," he said. "You would probably start a town-wide riot, and I can't threaten to kill every man who finds you as irresistible as I do."

Words of gratitude sprang to Caro's lips, though whether for his offer to venture into the town or his confession that he found her irresistible, she didn't know.

Before she could speak, he crossed the room, opened the door, and turned back for a final word. "I will order water sent up for a bath. Please don't leave the room." He stepped out, closing the door behind him.

Caro dragged a straight wooden chair to the window so she could sit and watch the bustle below. Her father had laughed at her nervousness in the town and told her that England had bigger towns, cities that stretched as far as the eye could see. Surely her soul would die in such a place.

"Bah!" Her soul wouldn't die, and neither would she.

But it would be so much easier if she could change Tag's mind about taking her with him.

Why had she ever told him she planned to kill her cousin? Even if she lied and told him she had changed her mind, he would never believe her now. Noise from the street assaulted her ears. Even protected by the distance and the glass pane of the window, she felt small and vulnerable. Alone. Suddenly a tiny spark of hope flared.

Irresistible. He had said the word.

Irresistible meant he would want her with him even if he didn't approve of what she planned to do. He was her husband and she had neglected her plan to make him want her as a woman. She would never have a better chance.

Tonight he would see her dressed in English clothes. She studied the women below, pictured herself walking with their mincing steps. He would see that she could be like them. He would want to take her with him.

A knock sounded at the door. A grizzled man entered carrying a washtub partially filled with water, which he dropped to the floor with a solid thud. A sandy haired boy came in behind him, sloshing water from two buckets on the floor. He dumped what remained into the tub. Both turned and left without a word.

Caro hurried to the tub and put her hand into the rising cloud of warm mist and then into the water itself. Not the icy water of spring rivers, but warm water and a bar of pine-scented soap. She could learn to be English.

Two hours later Tag returned, a colorful assortment of gowns dangling from his arm and a parcel wrapped in brown paper teetering on top. He crossed to the bed, where he dropped everything with a dramatic groan. "I couldn't find any new gowns already made up. One of these will have to do."

Caro gazed at the pile in astonishment. "Where . . . where did you get all of that?"

"There is a woman in town who buys things people realize they won't need in the wilderness and then sells them. I had no idea what would fit, so I bought everything that looked like it might."

"I don't know what to say."

"Don't say anything. Just find something respectable so you can join me for dinner. What you don't want, leave here."

Caro glanced anxiously at the window and cursed the darkness. She should have paid more attention to what the women outside were wearing. "I wish you had brought only one." She picked up the large wrapped parcel.

His face colored with the merest hint of a flush. "Don't

open that until I leave." He turned quickly to the door. "I will send a woman up to help you dress. When you are ready you will meet me downstairs."

How naturally he assumed everyone would obey his orders.

He paused with his hand on the doorknob. "Oh. And please unbraid your hair so you look a little less . . ."

Annoyance replaced her nervousness. "Less Indian?" She tilted her chin, defying him to disparage the people who had raised her.

"A little more English, perhaps." He left before Caro could voice the angry retort that sprang to her lips.

As soon as the door closed behind him, Caro tore open the parcel that had made him uncomfortable. She smiled at the picture of him scurrying from the largest collection of undergarments she had ever seen in her life. Reluctantly, she turned her attention to the startling assortment of dresses on the bed. He might at least have stayed to select the one he liked.

With brisk movements she discarded three dresses, a black, a gray, and something that looked as if it had been made of sludge from a river bottom. No one could be irresistible in such colors.

The previous owners of the remaining two dresses must have decided to keep their practical clothing and leave the frivolous behind. Both gowns were lovely. She let her hand hover over a shimmering red dress trimmed with black lace. Before she could touch it, a timid knock sounded at the door.

"May I come in, miss?"

Caro hurried over to admit a black-haired girl, who looked about fourteen and would have been attractive if not for the spots on her face.

"I'm Becky. My ma works in the kitchen. Alice says it's too busy now for her to come and help you, so they sent me.'' She glanced beyond Caro to the gowns on the bed. ''Oh, my, ain't they pretty?''

Caro returned to the bed, where she let her hand hover again over the red one, which drew her like a moth to the light. ''I thought perhaps this one. Unless you think it's too . . .''

''It's beautiful.'' Becky cautiously reached out and caressed the material as if she expected it to bite her. ''But I don't think my ma would ever speak to a woman wearing a dress like this.'' She snatched her hand away. ''She'd say it's wicked.'' Her face brightened. ''But perhaps not for you. Alice says you lived with the Indians. Did they do wicked things to you?''

Caro winced with the unexpected pang of loneliness. She thought of the ''wicked'' things her adopted people had done. They had sensed her loneliness and given her one of their own to love. They'd shared their meager scraps of food with her in the hungry months. They'd carried her wounded father a hundred miles, and then grieved with her when she could not save him. ''No. They didn't do wicked things to me.''

She tossed the red dress into the rejected pile on the floor. ''It will have to be this one.'' Caro picked up a wine-colored silk dress.

''That's better,'' Becky agreed. ''Ma said I'm to brush your hair.''

Caro obediently sat and let Becky brush out her hair. When the girl finally put down the brush, the tight blond waves left by Caro's customary braid cascaded over her shoulder like sunlight on rippling water.

Becky bit her lip. ''I don't know.'' She studied Caro's reflection in the glass. It looks a little . . . wild.''

Caro remembered Tag's eyes feasting on her hair during their wedding dance, and decided a little wild might be just what she needed. ''Leave it.'' She pointed to a stack of white clothes she had set aside on a chair. ''You will have to help me with those. I'm not sure which of them I am supposed to wear.''

Obediently Becky walked over to the pile and began sorting. She laughed several times as she banished something to a growing pile on the floor. Caro took a small satisfaction in knowing Tag hadn't been an unqualified expert in selecting women's undergarments.

''Those will do for tonight,'' Becky said, pointing to slightly smaller pile she had set aside on the bed.

Caro gasped. ''So many?''

Becky flushed and looked quickly at Caro's bare legs. ''It's not really a lot,'' she said anxiously. ''A chemise.'' She moved one article a few inches. ''Drawers, of course.''

''I remember them,'' Caro said.

Becky's flush deepened, and she set the drawers aside. ''A corset. My ma says I don't have to wear one yet, but all the fine ladies do. And two petticoats.'' She must have seen the protest Caro bit back because she added hastily, ''You may not need two.''

Determined to do things correctly, Caro let Becky help her into the garments. She even smiled, knowing the poor child would turn scarlet again if she confessed she felt almost fully dressed the moment she put on the heavy cotton chemise. The drawers came to just below her knee, where they fastened with buttons. But everywhere else they were loose and flapped about the way her breeches never had.

The corset was the worst, heavy material that scratched the underside of her breasts and dug into her hips. Becky stood behind her and tugged on the laces, ignoring Caro's complaint that she couldn't breathe. The petticoats would surely trip her before the night ended. However, she endured everything, and Becky finally slipped the shimmering gown over her head. She had been looking forward to the sensuous caress of the water soft silk, but the gown touched her skin only in tiny patches.

Caro practiced mincing across the room. She moved like

a wounded animal, struggling for breath. "The corset is impossible, Becky. I can't breathe."

"Nobody can, but ladies have to wear them."

"If your mother says you don't have to wear one, I can do without it."

Becky looked uncertain, but she followed directions and helped Caro out of the hateful corset. Caro inhaled three life-giving breaths, and realized she could do without the drawers as well. Nobody would know, and they did make such an awful flapping sound. She bent and removed them, ignoring Becky's wide-eyed astonishment.

On her next trip across the room she realized she was kicking the petticoats out of the way with every step. That would never do. Tag had said he liked the way she moved. She could never be irresistible lumbering like a bear. She removed both petticoats and stood there only in the comfortable chemise. "This will be fine, Becky," she said, ignoring the fact the girl had both hands covering her mouth. "Nobody needs so many clothes for one night."

"I don't think—"

"Help me with the gown."

Becky helped, but she moved slowly and continued to look as if she might back away and protest.

"There," Caro said as she felt Becky secure the final button. "So much better." She walked across the room, feeling almost normal again.

"I'm not sure." Becky's eyes brightened. "Maybe just one petticoat." If Becky had her way, they would probably begin the whole process all over again.

"Thank you. You have been a wonderful help." Caro's gaze fell on the pile of discarded clothes. The ideal distraction. "I am sure one of those gowns would be perfect for you."

"Oh, miss, I couldn't." Her eyes pleaded that she could. Two minutes later the girl left clutching the first large gown Caro had discarded.

Caro crossed again to the mirror for a final check. The neckline of the gown no longer looked so attractive. Patches of lace from the trim on the chemise poked out, spoiling the smooth line. "Dammit," Caro cursed as she had heard Tag do. With her thumb she tucked the lace into the gown, and studied the mirror again. She looked like she had developed a row of skin boils across her chest. "Dammit."

By untying the ribbon that pulled the gown tight under her breasts, she found she could wiggle out of it without unfastening it at the back. She removed the offending chemise and squirmed back into the gown. The neckline fell perfectly, covering her breasts completely but curving to a vee between them.

Caro tested her walk with one more turn about the room. The long gown still contorted about her legs, but the liquid fabric drifted aside without any effort on her part.

She felt wonderful and irresistible. And English.

Chapter Eight

In the tiny maid's room he had intimidated Alice into allotting him, Tag shaved himself. He might not have a valet, but he had warm water. Civilization would return in small measures as he progressed east. For now, a hot bath seemed the ultimate in luxury. He would have ample time to enjoy it, as it would probably take Caro hours to sort through the gowns he had purchased so hastily.

After a long soak he began to dress in the clean, crisp clothes he had left behind. With a start, he realized he was whistling, looking forward to one last quiet evening with Caro. Visions of her as she would appear filled his head. How often had he pictured her dressed in proper clothes with her nose tilted in the air like a duchess? He smiled. He would have to do something to provoke that pose tonight.

The inn had no private parlors, and the stairs descended directly into the public room. Tag stood at the foot of the steps and scanned the room on the remote possibility Caro might have come down before him. Like the city now claimed by the Americans, the large dining room had attracted a wild assortment of people. British officers in full-dress uniform dined with their wives within arm's reach of French and American trappers, who looked as if they'd had their last bath in the Biblical flood. His Indian princess was not among them.

He identified his objective and strode across the room to

a small table, which offered an excellent view of the stairs. After signaling for a tumbler of wine, he settled back in the chair with his legs stretched out in front of him and his ankles crossed. His casual pose belied his growing eagerness for his first view of Caro.

He waited. He finished his wine and ordered more. The din in the room increased. No woman could take all this time merely changing into a gown. The noise level began to grate on his nerves. Not generalized noise, he realized, but increasingly raucous comments from a table of rough-looking men to his left against the far wall, all vying with each other to impress a blond trollop who sat with her back to him.

He ordered more wine to distract himself from the intrusive discord. If he had even a single companion to cover his back, he would do the room a favor and suggest the men take their business elsewhere. The woman too.

"Enough." The loud male bellow came from the renegade table. A balding man jumped to his feet, knocking over his chair as he dragged the woman next to him up with him. "I saw her first. She's coming with me. Let's go, lady."

The noise startled Tag upright and silenced the whole room.

"Go with him, lady," a voice shouted from Tag's right, "and let us have some peace." Mentally Tag echoed the suggestion. What followed happened almost too quickly for the eye to track. The woman twisted, jumped back, and kicked. The balding man doubled over with another bellow of rage.

"God Almighty!" Tag leapt to his feet, knocking over his own chair. The woman was Caro and she crouched, facing the table of men with a knife in her hand.

"No reason to get excited, honey," a black-haired man said, half-rising from his chair with a placating gesture. "You just had to tell him you'd rather go with me."

141

Tag resisted the impulse to tear across the room. He moved slowly, calculating the odds. Five men, six if he counted the one gagging and holding his groin. For the moment Caro's feral posture had them frozen in place.

With icy calm he moved in to stand beside her. "Sorry, gentlemen, I am afraid there has been some mistake. The lady is waiting for me." He shifted his eyes just enough to give Caro an incontestable order. "Tell them you are waiting for me."

"Tag." She straightened, her face brightening. "Of course I'm waiting for you." She gave her head an impatient shake, which undoubtedly distressed every red-blooded man in the room as much as it did him. "It took you long enough to get here." Her clinging dress left nothing to the imagination.

Tag knew he had no hope of convincing the table of aroused men she was anything but what she appeared. "Now tell them that you plan to spend the rest of the night with me." He visualized murder, and looked slowly at each man. "All night," he added, hoping his voice was heavy enough to carry his message.

"They will think—"

"Tell them."

"I will be with him." She sounded obedient, if slightly bewildered.

Tag waited a moment, and watched the tension drain out of the watching men. He secured Caro's hand on his arm, turned his back, and headed towards the stairs, his ears alert for any sound. His boots thunked on the wooden steps. Caro started to speak. "Later," he said sharply, every instinct focused on the tingling hairs in the back of his neck.

They reached the door to his room unchallenged. He unlocked it and stepped in. He gave her just enough time to slip in after him before slamming the door and locking it securely. Only then did he release a long, shuddering breath and turn his attention to her. "Now do you want to tell me what the hell you were doing?"

She took a step back. The wall prevented any further retreat. "You're angry."

"Angry? Angry because I took time for a bath and found you offering your services to half-a-dozen men?"

"I wasn't offering my services. I was only—"

"That's what it looked like to me and to everyone else in the room." The blood throbbing neck and temples made his neck cloth uncomfortably tight. He stepped back and tore off both his coat and the offending neck cloth. He said a small, not particularly soothing, circle in the room. "What did you think you were doing?"

"You weren't there when I arrived. You're going to leave me tomorrow. I thought one of those men might know someone who would escort me from here on."

"Escort you where?" Tag couldn't blame any man who volunteered to escort her. He couldn't wrench his own gaze away from the inviting line where the burgundy dress met the soft white skin above her breasts. "In that dress there's only one place a man would escort you."

"You bought the dress."

"I bought a lot of other things too. Where are they?"

She tilted her chin defiantly. "I didn't like them. They were uncomfortable. Nobody could tell I didn't—"

The pulse in Tag's temple began to throb again, and it wasn't anger this time. "Every man in that room knew"— he could not resist reaching out and running his hand down her side to her hip—"you had nothing on under that dress."

"With all those things, I couldn't move the way you like." She bit her lip. Her deep blue eyes widened with honesty. "I only wanted you to like me."

Such innocence couldn't exist, Tag thought. She had no idea how much danger she'd been in downstairs, and she would be in the same danger the next time he turned his back for five minutes.

He stepped closer. "Oh, I like you all right. The way every man in that room liked you." He put his hands on the wall on either side of her, his body hovering a few inches from hers. He let his breath quicken with thoughts of crushing himself against her. The inferno inside him had to be blazing in his eyes. A normal woman would scream or faint. "Does this frighten you? Do you know what I'm thinking right now?"

"I can defend myself."

Fool. Tag didn't know whether the thought was for her or for himself. He just knew she was going to learn something tonight and he was going to feel her against him one last time. "Then do it." Without warning he rocked his hips forward, pinning her to the wall. "This is how your bald friend would have done it. Up against a wall, or anyplace he could get you to spread your legs."

He thrust his knee between hers, to force them apart. He ran his hand up her neck and grabbed a large enough handful of hair to tilt her head up for his kiss. Not a first tender kiss, but a vicious, crushing kiss in which he immediately forced her lips apart and began to ravish her with his tongue.

She struggled against him, but that only made the surging contact between their lower bodies more intense. She tore her lips from his. "You're hurting me."

"Not any more than any man would if you flaunted yourself in front of him in that dress." He lifted her from the floor to take the leverage away from her struggles, with the added boon that he could settle her exactly where he wanted. He spread her legs and pressed in closer. "Feel that," he said, grinding so she had no doubt what he wanted her to feel. "That's what a man wants to drive into you, and he doesn't care how roughly he does it or how much it hurts you."

She opened her mouth to say something, but he wanted her kiss, not her words. Holding her against him with both hands, he plundered her mouth again, releasing her only when he wanted more. "But a kiss is never enough for a man," he said: "This is what he really wants." At least it was what Tag really wanted. He dipped his whole hand into the low neckline of her gown, cupping the breast he'd known he was going to touch from the instant he'd seen her crouched there with the cobweb-thin gown defining every curve.

In a sickening moment of self-disgust, Tag recognized the whole scene for what it was. His unbridled lust, cloaked in some improbably noble purpose.

With a groan he thrust her from him and stamped across the room to pound his fist against the wall. Of course, he'd done it this way. It was the only way he could ever touch her again without giving her some false idea about their relationship. Without giving her some false hope he would ever let her love him.

Later, he thought. Later he could castigate himself for his self-deception. For now he could only hope his specious ruse might have some basis in reality, that it might actually serve to keep her from some wildly dangerous predicament after he left her. He turned to her and let his disgust at himself color his words. "I hope you enjoyed that lesson in what men want from a woman."

She tugged her impossible gown up to conceal charms that couldn't be concealed. "Is it what you want from a woman, Tag?"

"It is what I would want from any whore." Even in his current mood Tag couldn't stand the appalled expression on her face. "Which is what you will appear to be if you insist on continuing this journey alone," he added.

She recovered and stood in the straight, proud pose he would always think of as exclusively hers. "And you will not let me accompany you to England?"

"Tomorrow I will go to the fort and hire the most honorable troop of soldiers I can find to accompany you back to your village. I will send for you when I have made arrangements in England."

"Very well." With her spine straight and the gown shimmering about her legs, she walked over and opened the door. "Then we have nothing more to say to each other."

Late the following morning Tag returned from the fort. It had cost him two months' pay for each of five soldiers, but he had arranged for Caro's escort. The commander had vouched for their integrity. At the inn, Tag knocked three times on the door to her room, and then opened it with his key.

The room looked very much as he had last seen it, the gowns he had bought strewn everywhere. Caro, of course, was missing. Again he'd been a fool to hope she might behave in any rational way. He cursed, but resignedly. She couldn't get into too much trouble in broad daylight arranging for an impossible journey.

He clomped down the stairs and found Alice as usual behind the bar. "Where is Miss Fenton?"

"Gone."

"That much is obvious, but gone where?"

"Back to the Indians. And good riddance, I say."

Tag cursed. "You let her leave alone! Are you sure she didn't just go out for a walk?"

She gave an impatient shrug. "Sure as a body can be. She took the two horses you rode in on. Said she'd return them. Also took the packhorse." She preceded her next announcement with a gloating smile. "Said you would pay the reckoning."

The gloating smile turned to a leer. "Don't reckon she'll be alone too long. Daniel Wheeler—you remember him, the man with the bushy beard you tried to strangle yesterday morning—he was here when she was leaving. He lit outta here about ten minutes after she did. Wouldn't take a lot of schoolin' to guess where he was going.''

Tag clenched his hands into fists, remembering a man about three times Caro's size. ''How long ago?''

''Two hours, maybe more.''

He couldn't waste time on fantasies of what he'd like to do to the smug woman. He had to get to the stables before they unsaddled the horse he had rented.

Minutes later Tag was tearing out of town. He tried to recall anything he had noticed about Daniel Wheeler. Nothing except his size and his unfortunate decision to make a crude remark at the wrong time. With luck, Wheeler would wait until they were far away from town before forcing himself on Caro. If not . . . Tag could finish the thought only with wave after wave of pure rage.

In the intervals when the rage subsided, he prayed. Not to some unseen, half-forgotten god, but to Caro. Aloud and silently, he repeated jagged phrases. ''Hold on. Just hold on. You said you could do it. Protect yourself. Just this once, and I promise I'll surround you with a whole regiment of the most stalwart men you've ever seen.''

A little more than an hour after Tag left Detroit, a slight figure stepped from the woods onto the trail so abruptly that he went thundering past.

Caro!

He whirled his horse, went pounding back, and jumped from the still-moving animal to land unsteadily on his feet at her side. ''Caro. Are you all right?''

''Good morning, Tag.''

Good morning, Tag. He'd been picturing her bruised and violated and she'd said good morning. She didn't even seem surprised to see him. ''You couldn't have seen me clearly before you stepped onto the trail. How did you know it was me? It could have been anyone.''

*   *   *

147

Another wave of weariness gripped Caro. She didn't want to answer him. She just wanted to go home. She wanted to sit in the familiar forest and gather her strength. With an effort she tossed her head and met his gaze defiantly. "Only a wild Englishman would scare the birds out of the trees for miles behind him. I could hear you coming for the last mile. Now please leave me." She began walking west, leading the train of horses out of the underbrush.

"Where's Wheeler? He followed you."

"Was that his name?" Even the memory of her brief encounter with the bearded man failed to stir her from her lethargy.

Tag took several awkward steps to match his pace to hers, then looked back with a start as Wheeler's horse joined the parade behind them. "Is that his horse? What did you do with him?" His head jerked as he searched the surrounding area. "Did you kill him?"

Of course he would think that. He always thought the worst of her. "I should have. He's a vulgar man and a fool."

Again he looked around, as if he expected Wheeler to step from behind a bush, but when he spoke, his voice had a hint of amusement. "What did you do with him?"

"I tied him to a tree about two miles back." How easy he made it to want his approval, but she would not fall into that trap again. She let the indifference she felt suffuse her voice. "I assume he will eventually free himself, so I had to take his horse. I would not want to have to bother with him again."

"Of course not. It would probably spoil your whole day. Why did you run away?"

She vaulted onto the back of her horse. "Go away, Tag." She spurred her horse into a brisk jog. She had lain awake all night, smarting from his words and the ugly way he had touched her. From dawn on she'd kept a vigil at the window, waiting for him to leave the inn so she could make

148

her own departure without ever seeing him again. She should have known he would insist on putting everything into words and more words.

As she expected, he mounted and rode up beside her. "You haven't answered me. Why did you run away?"

"For days you have been talking about my returning to the village. I thought you would be pleased."

"I never suggested you return alone."

"No. You called me some ugly names and couldn't wait to be rid of me." She had tried so hard, said good-bye to everyone she loved, endured Billy Boy's death, and steeled herself for the fact that wherever they went she would be regarded as an outsider. But his final rejection had seemed too much to bear alone. "Now you have your wish. Go back the way you came and leave me be."

"Dammit, Caro. There were six ugly men last night. Any or all of them might decide to follow you."

He didn't even understand that those men could never hurt her as he had. "None of them succeeded in being quite as ugly as you. You found a very effective way to convey your message."

He gave a barely audible groan. "I'm sorry about last night. I . . . I was angry. The wine . . ." He stiffened his shoulders and looked into her eyes with an honesty that made her breath catch. "There is no excuse. I behaved badly, and I'm sorry."

She forced herself to regard him coldly. "Badly, but effectively. You convinced me I cannot travel to England alone."

He grabbed her bridle. "You cannot even travel back to your village alone." As always, he would order and expect her to obey.

She snatched the reins back and took a moment to soothe the bewildered horse. "I was doing that quite nicely until you arrived, and will continue as soon as you leave."

"You will come back to Detroit with me."

Somehow arguing with him brought back the strength she thought she might never feel again. She laughed. "You insist on ordering the world to suit yourself. The next time I see you, it will be in England."

"You still intend to go to England?"

"Of course. My father is dead, but he still has many friends. With Seven Feathers's help I will contact them and make arrangements for the journey."

Tag considered her words for several long seconds. Then, to her amazement, he threw back his head and laughed. "Thank you very much."

She had no idea how to respond. She had expected anything but genuine amusement. "What is that supposed to mean? Why did you laugh?"

He pinched the bridge of his nose and shook his head. "Just that this situation is so impossible I had to do something to be sure I am truly awake. You won't return to Detroit, and now I can't decide whether to worry that you will be murdered on the way to your village, or hanged for murder when you reach England."

In spite of herself Caro responded to his good humor. This was the Tag she wanted to remember, the Tag of the golden days they had spent together before the morning he had withdrawn into silence. She smiled. "None of my father's books prepared me for quite how mad you English are. You laugh when you should curse, and . . ." She stopped herself before she could add, ". . . curse when you should make love."

Tag watched the smile reach her eyes, then flicker out. It shouldn't matter that the day had brightened for a heartbeat, then dimmed again. It shouldn't matter, but it did. Half-formed schemes tumbled through his mind, none the act of a rational man. But he could not spend the rest of his life traveling between Detroit and some remote Indian village. "You leave me no alternative."

"Oh?"

He gave as much of a formal bow as a demented man could from the saddle of a horse. "Miss Fenton, I would be honored if you would accompany me to England."

She stopped her horse and stared at him in astonishment. "You just asked me to go to England with you."

"I am aware of that. I don't know yet how we will manage it. We can obtain a chaperone in Detroit. We needn't be together all the time. And you will have to make an effort to stay out of trouble."

"I need more time. I am not ready."

"I doubt either of us are ready. But you are determined to go there, and I doubt I would ever sleep again without knowing you arrived safely."

She looked both east and west. Tag could see the emotions almost physically warring on her face. A hungry yearning when she looked west, a grim determination when she looked east. "You will accompany me to England," she said slowly, as if wanting to be absolutely clear, "but you will not be my husband?"

Tag smiled. "Not unless I am a great deal weaker than I believe."

"And when we reach England?"

He laughed. "Caro, I am concerned with getting us out of Detroit unscathed. We will cope with England when we arrive."

Still the doubt lingered in her eyes. "You will take me to England, no matter what happens?"

Tag winced, recalling how many times she had been abandoned, and aware how much his ugliness of the previous night must have wounded her.

"All the way to England?" she asked.

Relief surged through Tag. It shouldn't be so important, but it was. "All the way to England," he promised. He thought of the giant of a man still tied to a tree two miles behind them, and the balding man at the inn probably still bemoaning serious damage to his manhood. "All the way to England," he repeated, then smiled. "And God save England."

Chapter Nine

The packet boat thumped against the dock with a jolt that would have been painful if it weren't so welcome. Tag had made the journey from Calais to Dover dozens of times, but never had he arrived unchaperoned with any female, never mind a lady for whom he had to find a husband.

He searched the crowd on the dock for anyone who might recognize him, and glanced uneasily toward the passageway from which Caro would appear. Logically, he should not meet anyone who would insist on an introduction, nor should Caro disregard his orders and appear in her doeskin dress. But all his mental reassurance couldn't move these final hours quickly enough.

The gangplank hit the dock, sending another series of tremors through the boat. The man he had sent to find a coach scurried ashore before the plank had even stopped shuddering.

Ten minutes more and Tag could relax for the first time in four months.

He gave up his study of the small crowd waiting below and devoted his full attention to the passageway leading to the cabins. As if only waiting for the proper moment for her entrance, Caro appeared. She met his look with a bright smile.

Damn.

She'd done it to him again. Just when he had worked himself into a proper state of nerves over what she would do next, she'd appeared looking as demure and pliable as a miss two sunny days out of the schoolroom. She glided across the deck with the grace that endlessly astonished him, as if her feet never needed to touch something solid to propel her. Her eyes danced and sparkled with anticipation, seeming to scarcely see him as she studied the chaos below. "Oh. There is a lot of . . . of everything."

Tag couldn't tell from her tone whether *everything* was good or bad. He found himself hoping England pleased her. "Please don't judge by . . ." He gave up. What did it matter if her first impression of England was of a dirty port city? In a short time she would be someone else's problem. He would have kept his promise and could get on with his life without always waiting for the next crisis.

"Lord Elmgrove!"

Damn his luck. The next crisis had just called him by name. From the pier below, the formidable Mrs. Blanchard, surrounded by a mountain of luggage, frantically waved a white handkerchief to attract his attention. A dragonette whose welcome in society depended largely on her ability to collect and dispense gossip, she would be set up for months when she discovered him traveling alone with Caro. Once she finished spreading that tale, even the most degenerate wastrels would be insulted if he suggested they consider Caro as a bride.

Tag could only hope she was embarking on a trip around the world. He nodded an adequate enough acknowledgment to quiet the bellowing and scanned the immediate area for a bolt-hole.

He sighed. Though Caro could swim better than most seamen, she would probably object if he threw her over the side. Hell, disguised as an English miss, she looked so vulnerable he didn't even have the heart to order her to walk off the boat as if she didn't know him.

Mentally he practiced explanations: *I provided chaperones all the way from Detroit to Paris. Mrs. Collins took sick. . . . This was such a short trip that I thought . . . I was in a hurry. . . .*

Earls don't babble, he reminded himself. They don't explain.

He drew himself up to his full height and put his hand on the small of Caro's back. "We don't have time to discuss this. When we meet that woman, just nod and smile. And for God's sake, agree with everything I say."

She looked at him suspiciously. "What will you say?"

"Damned if I know. But your reputation depends on my thinking of something."

Tag and Caro joined the throng starting down the gangplank. He threw a last desperate glance over his shoulder and spotted an elderly Italian woman he had nodded to the previous night. He could. . . . It might work. . . . Even if the woman didn't want to cooperate, she spoke no English. Unceremoniously stopping Caro's progress by grabbing a handful of her dress from behind, he waited until the plump woman came abreast of them, clutching a black dimity bag decorated with brilliant sunflowers.

"Permit me." He smiled down at her, and without waiting for a reply, reached out and relieved her of her bag.

She gave him a startled look and released a mouthful of Italian, which was probably either "Thank you," or "Give me back my bag, you scoundrel."

Tag didn't care which. Either would keep her at his side.

Mrs. Blanchard bore down on them with the unerring instinct of a falcon.

"Mrs. Blanchard, what a pleasant surprise."

"Lord Elmgrove, you have been gone for an age, you naughty boy. Poor Isobel is just—"

"A pleasure to be home," Tag said, interrupting with his most practiced smile. He didn't have time to hear any lies about how poor Isobel was pining away. "Absolutely splendid to see you again." If the tabby was suspicious of anything, it would be his excessive affability.

"Allow me to present Miss Fenton. I am escorting her to her grandfather, Reginald Fenton."

Mrs. Blanchard gave an imperious nod. "A lovely dress, my dear." With her wrinkled nose, long slow look, and the slight flutter of her hands, she managed to convey Tag's own private opinion of the sadly out-of-date creation.

A spark of anger flared in Caro's eyes, and Tag returned to worrying about the present situation. She had astutely interpreted the censure. Not a knife-drawing offense, he prayed, but he held his breath. Caro muttered a short phrase in Shawnee, which he assumed meant something like, "May a bear chew your ankles."

"What was that, my dear?" Mrs. Blanchard leaned forward, but at the same time managed to convey a concern about coming too close.

Tag quickly angled his body to include the bewildered Italian woman in the group. "And this is her companion, Mrs. . . . ." He scrambled for a likely name. "Mrs. Botticelli."

The introduction drew an indifferent nod from Mrs. Blanchard and a torrent of Italian from the newly christened Mrs. Botticelli. The latter tugged at the bag, which Tag clutched securely in his left arm.

"No trouble at all," he assured the sputtering Italian woman. With what dignity he could muster, he bowed to Mrs. Blanchard. "I certainly hope we will have a chance to chat in London. You must be most put out with me for delaying you."

"Not at all. Perhaps I won't even go to Paris. I am sure Isobel will want to hear all the details of your trip." She turned her honeyed smile on Caro. "Isobel and Lord Elmgrove are—"

"Quite the best of *friends*," Tag finished.

More Italian and more tugging from Mrs. Botticelli. Tag gave her a reassuring smile. "All Gaul is divided into three parts," he said in Latin, praying it was still close enough to Italian to bewilder a non-critical audience.

Mrs. Blanchard ignored the exchange and continued with her coy comments about Isobel. "Of course. We mustn't be premature." Her knowing look was as premature as an announcement in *The Morning Post*. "Friends they are. Friends for ever so long. And we all know what will happen some day soon." Her smile became progressively more patronizing.

Caro produced her own version of a faux smile. "I am pleased to know Lord Elmgrove has any friends."

If Mrs. Blanchard heard the frigid sarcasm, she ignored it in favor of exploring the relationship. "How very curious. Has he not introduced you to any of his friends during your travels?" Her self-satisfied smirk conveyed her opinion of why that hadn't happened.

Mrs. Botticelli had seemingly resigned herself to her fate, content to look from face to face, as long as she could keep one set of fingers clutched around the cloth bag. From the corner of his eye, Tag spotted a coach fighting its way through the maze of vehicles and pedestrians. He pointed. "I believe that is our coach." He put his hand on the small of Caro's back again to ease her past Mrs. Blanchard's bulk, confident Mrs. Botticelli would follow as long as he didn't release her bag. "Splendid to see you again. I will certainly call as soon as I learn you have returned to town."

For a moment he feared Mrs. Blanchard might not step aside to let them pass, but outnumbered three to one, she gradually yielded. The motion activated Mrs. Botticelli's tongue, and he nodded and smiled at her as the way opened up before them.

They reached the coach. Now, he had only to convince their reluctant chaperone to enjoy their company for a few moments longer and he could congratulate himself on an exceptionally fine show. He helped Caro inside. Mrs. Botticelli had voluntarily relinquished her grip on the garish bag. Her darting eyes testified to a fierce internal debate.

He could not risk waiting to see if ownership would triumph over safety. He whipped the bag inside after Caro, gripped the woman about the waist, and carried her with him through the opening.

Mrs. Botticelli's long-delayed fear finally surfaced and she opened her mouth to scream. As gently as possible Tag clamped his hand over her mouth. He had heard of such things being done, but no one had warned him it might cost an unspecified number of fingers. "Ouch. Dammit," he muttered, but softly because he was so clearly the cause of his own misery.

"Tag," Caro said sharply. Even after weeks of training she only called him Lord Elmgrove when he insisted. When she was angry, he was always Tag in that particular tone, and she was now clearly as angry as the chewing Italian.

"Lord Elmgrove please, Caro, we are in England." With his free hand Tag pounded on the door. "Away," he shouted. The vehicle began to move.

"Why have you taken this woman prisoner? The other is the one who needs your hand over her mouth."

"Be still." Tag could only estimate how far they'd moved through the crowded street, but he released his grip on Mrs. Botticelli's mouth in the interest of saving what remained of his fingers. Even if Mrs. Blanchard heard the screams, she would put it down to the inherent insanity of a foreigner. "My apologies, Mrs. Botticelli," he said, knowing he could never explain in words.

The captive let out a few token screams, clutched her bag to her chest, and began pleading with Caro in Italian.

Tag fumbled in his pocket and found several guineas, which he held out to the frightened woman. *"Gratias,"* he said, hoping the ancient Latin came close enough to the modern equivalent.

The woman accepted the coins but continued to speak, her gaze darting rapidly from Caro to the door.

Tag felt the coach list as it rounded a curve, and relaxed

against the seat back long enough to exhale. With another shout he ordered the moving coach to halt. He paused only long enough to check his stinging hand for blood, then stepped out. Before he could turn back to offer assistance, Mrs. Botticelli—whose true name he would never know—scrambled to the street. She backed away from the coach, three incredibly long steps for a woman her age, then smiled for the first time since he had grabbed her bag. With a possessive fist she held up the coins he had handed her. *"Gratias,"* she said, and turned to hustle away.

Tag climbed back into the coach clutching his injured hand. Caro turned her head aside and folded her arms across her chest to show her displeasure.

"You can at least look at this," he said, holding out his hand.

She looked at the red and white indentations left by the woman's teeth. Ungently, she turned the hand over. "A Shawnee woman would have drawn blood."

"An English woman would say, 'Thank you, Lord Elmgrove, you saved my reputation.' She might even swoon."

"You lied to that repulsive woman."

"Very well done, I thought." He chuckled. "Your reputation is saved, Miss Fenton." *Good-bye, Mrs. Blanchard.* Tag settled back, only to find the memory of the intrusive woman would not be dismissed so easily. Something niggled at his mind. Something he should remember. He frowned. The elusive thought slithered away.

Caro leaned forward. "What's wrong? You seemed to be enjoying yourself, but now when nothing is happening, you look upset."

"It's nothing." And perhaps it was nothing more that the appalling recollection he had promised to call on one of the most plaguesome women in London. "It's nothing," he repeated with slightly more assurance.

"Well, then, stop frowning over nothing and tell me where we're going."

With a final effort, Tag put their long journey behind them. "I am going to take you to your grandfather, of course. We may even arrive there early enough for me to leave for London tonight. It may take some time to find you a husband."

Tag's brusque words hit Caro like a slap. She felt like a sack of grain to be delivered and forgotten. Immediately, she looked out the window so Tag would not see the hurt in her eyes. She had always known this moment would come, but not on such a pretty day. Not before she had time to enjoy the sunshine and the shadows on the green hedges, which separated the golden autumn fields. She watched the passing countryside until she knew she could face him without a flicker of emotion on her face. "You have kept your promise, Tag. Thank you."

"My promise?" He too had been watching the country-side roll past. He seemed genuinely surprised by her words.

"You promised to deliver me safely to England. You have done that." If they had to part, she would handle it as coldly as he. "Perhaps it would save you some time if you stop the coach and set me down here."

"Soon." The word had a distracted sound, as if he had already gone away from her in his mind. He looked at her vaguely as if he had not heard her words. "Naturally I will see you safely settled."

Suddenly Caro wanted no part of his officious ideas on how she might be safely settled. "I have decided not to stay."

She finally managed to capture his attention. "Mrs. Blanchard is not England," he said firmly.

It wasn't only Mrs. Blanchard, but all the people on the journey who had made her feel like an outsider. Most of all it was Tag himself when he talked of simply depositing her somewhere. "I would hate your English clothes, and your English rules and your tight stone houses. I will meet my grandfather.'' Her grandfather who didn't even know she existed and probably wouldn't care. ''Then I will do what I came to do and go home.''

''And what do you think you came to do?''

Caro remained silent. He didn't need her to put her mission into words, and anything she would say would bring about another of his tirades about English law and English courts.

He had not forgotten. ''If you think I am going to escort you to your cousin's house so you can kill him, you are very wrong indeed.''

''You don't need to escort me anyplace. Just tell me where I can locate him.'' But even before he spoke, Caro recognized the stubborn look that usually preceded an implacable no.

''I don't believe that would be a good idea,'' he said.

England had looked very small on the ship's map. Even without his help, she should be able to find the man herself—except for one piece of critical information she had never thought to ask for. She watched the countryside roll past, let some time elapse, then commented casually, ''All this time, I don't believe you have ever mentioned my cousin's full name.''

He smiled. ''No, I haven't.''

''Is it the same as mine?''

''No.''

''How curious.'' She let the silence linger while she tried to think of a subtle way to phrase the question. Nothing clever presented itself. She surrendered. ''What is his name?''

He laughed, reached over, and brushed back a strand of hair that had escaped from under the foolish bonnet that bound her ears to her head. ''I will give you Edwin's name on the same day I give you a husband strong enough to keep you from killing your cousin or him from killing you. Though I still hope you will voluntarily decide against either, once you have had time to become more accustomed to our English ways.''

''Damn you.''

''Accustomed to our English ways means you don't say, 'Damn you,' or any of the other things we've discussed. Now perhaps we can have a more pleasant discussion on what you require in a husband. Would you prefer dark hair or light?''

''I am sure you have already weighed the advantages of each. Now, if you don't mind, I would like to enjoy the ride without a quarrel.'' He could produce all the husbands he wanted, but she would be gone before he ever returned from London to marry her to somebody else. She chose not to spoil these final moments with bitter words, and then settled back to enjoy the peaceful world that would be hers for such a short time.

Late that afternoon, Tag stood in the Fenton drawing room, thinking there should at least be a clock to tick away the final moments. The journey had once seemed interminably long, time measured in months, then weeks, then days. Now, he could probably count the remaining seconds and still not distract himself from the vivid memories of Caro that danced in his mind. Memories of a journey he would never forget.

He looked across the room to where she sat, her hands demurely folded in her lap. She looked positively frumpy in the travel dress he had purchased ready-made from a store in New York. The layers of heavy material at the neck and shoulders made her seem top-heavy. He was glad he hadn't been in the room when she first saw the dress. At the very least, she would have told him to wear it himself if he thought it so grand.

He suppressed a sigh. Only a man who had been without a woman far too long would find anything to admire in the way the nubby material draped her figure. Perhaps he wouldn't go as far as London tonight. Perhaps he would stop at every inn along the way until he found a barmaid with blond hair and eyes as blue as—

"Is it rude for my grandfather to keep us waiting so long?" Caro asked the question without rancor, in the same tone she always used when questioning him about English manners.

"He is old. And sick."

"He will not be any less old or less sick because we wait." She wrinkled her nose. "This house smells of age." The house smelled not of age, but of neglect. The most recent attempt at cleaning had merely made swirls in the existing layers of dust.

Tag tensed. His evening in the arms of a willing barmaid depended on Caro liking the house, or at least being willing to stay here. "Of course it does. It is over three hundred years—"

"Not that kind of age. It does not appear to be crumbling, but it smells like invading death."

"Your grandfather has been ill a long time. The servants have grown careless." Tag lifted his hand from where it had come to rest on an occasional table, shuddered, and brushed at the underside of his sleeve, which had produced a dust-free island on the table. "Perhaps when you live here, you can—"

"Mr. Fenton will see you now." The lethargic manservant, who had appeared without a sound, regarded them with disinterest. Either he had not heard the criticism or considered it irrelevant.

Tag took a half-step toward Caro, prepared to offer physical support if she seemed nervous.

She slipped past him, her face as impassive as that of the indifferent servant. In spite of the bulky dress she glided after the man with her usual grace, and followed him up the stairs to where he paused outside a heavy oak door.

The man opened the door and stepped aside. Caro

slipped into the room, leaving Tag no choice but to follow.

Reginald Fenton lay propped against a mound of pillows, in the center of an enormous bed that dominated the opposite side of the room. In spite of the unnecessary fire in the fireplace, he had a heavy crimson coverlet drawn to his chest, concealing everything but the top of his white nightshirt. Whoever had kept them waiting while they readied him had certainly not spent the time combing his thinning hair, which poked like arrows from his head.

His hungry gaze skimmed over Caro, rested briefly on Tag, then shifted to the empty doorway. The very room seemed to hold its breath as he watched and waited. After several long seconds he broke the heavy silence with two desolate words, "My son?"

Tag couldn't find the brutality to answer the question. He let the empty doorway speak for itself. After several long seconds, the skin on the old man's face sagged, and his eyes lost their focus. The long whoosh of his exhaled air filled the room.

Tag listened to the silence, willing the man on the bed to remember to inhale. Only when he heard the ragged sound of indrawn air did he draw breath himself. He did so loudly, as if he could keep the man alive by example.

Caro walked to the bed without hesitation and looked down with the dispassionate expression Tag had seen only once before—when the boy she loved was dying. Tag joined her there, putting a supporting hand against the small of her back. He wanted to say something encouraging, but could think only of words she would know were lies. She had found her grandfather, but she would be losing him soon.

Fenton turned his head slowly so he could see both of them, but his eyes focused only on Tag. "My son?" he asked again. The whispered words were not even as loud as his last breath.

Tag hesitated. Would it maker if he lied? He glanced at

164

Caro. It would make the old man's last moments more peaceful, but Caro would insist on the truth. The old man would probably pass away unnoticed while they argued. "I'm sorry, sir."

If possible, the ancient face became even more desolate. Fenton turned his head and looked at the ceiling, dismissing not only Tag and Caro but the entire world. For several long seconds his fingers plucked at imaginary wisps on the crimson coverlet. "Nothing left . . . nothing . . ."

"Not quite, sir." Tag forced a false brightness into his tone. "Perhaps you haven't noticed. I brought a visitor."

Fenton turned his head again and appeared to see Caro for the first time. She continued to look down at him, her face impassive. Even Tag, after all these months, couldn't guess her thoughts.

"Your granddaughter, sir."

"I have no . . ." A spark of life brightened Fenton's faded blue eyes. "Wendell's daughter?" For the first time his words were more than soundless air. "My son had a . . . ?"

"You don't look like my father." Caro spoke in the same tone she used to offer her opinion of boiled cabbage. Perhaps she hadn't noticed the old man was dying.

From somewhere the old man found the strength to speak again. Not loud or steady, but at least audible. "No. But you look like my son. He had my wife's eyes. Emma's eyes." He stopped to concentrate on breathing. "Tell me about my son."

Caro's shoulders straightened as always when someone mentioned her father. "He was a warrior you could have been proud of."

"He died . . . ?"

"In a battle to save a small Shawnee village."

"A waste—"

Caro's eyes flashed. "You do not know the man your

165

son became. They will talk of your son's bravery long after you and I are gone."

"Tell me about him."

"Later." With no explanation, Caro threw back the coverlet he clutched in claw-like fingers. She bent and pressed her hands, palms down, across his chest.

Fenton twisted in protest. "What are you—" His eyes widened in fear.

"Stay still." Ignoring his struggles, Caro continued to probe with her fingers on his bony chest.

"Lord Elmgrove . . ." The effort to free himself of her touch exhausted the old man, and he looked to Tag for deliverance.

Tag shrugged. She couldn't do any harm. "Caro has had training as a healer. I think she only wants to help."

"But—"

"Save your strength, sir. When Caro decides to examine someone, she'll do it in the middle of St. James Square if she takes the notion."

Fenton melted back into his pillows, his eyes wide watching her face.

"That's better." Caro closed her eyes and moved her hands about his upper body, frowning or nodding in satisfaction. She ended by raising one spindly arm that Tag would never have dared to touch lest it break like a dry twig under his fingers. Without warning, she released her grip. The limp arm dropped to the coverlet.

Caro straightened and tossed her head contemptuously. "I have seen sicker men walk for a hundred miles carrying a child." Tag knew from her pose she had intended to speak scornfully, but her eyes glistened with life and something else—unadulterated relief.

Fenton twisted away from her. "Come to watch me die, have you?" But his attempt at withdrawal lasted only a moment. He turned back to regard her curiously. "Tell me about yourself. Where did you come from?"

166

"I think I should . . ." Caro looked about the room, her fingers twitching, but she did nothing more than dart to the window and throw open the drapes. Turning back to the bed she said, "Perhaps you're right. You must have many questions. I will answer them, but not while you're lying like a limp fish. Sit up straight." For someone who had never even seen a schoolmistress, she sounded as if she had been serving as one for ten years.

Fenton didn't even think about disobeying. He struggled to sit up. Tag moved quickly to help, and earned a disapproving scowl from Caro.

Once Fenton settled, Caro talked. She told enthralling stories of the man who had been her father, moving about the room to imitate his voice and his posture.

"I remember that look," Fenton said once. Later he interrupted to ask, "Did he ever say, 'God's breeches'? He used to say that all the time." Caro nodded, and they both laughed. But mostly Fenton just rested against the back of the bed and watched Caro, his mouth open and his eyes drinking her in. Finally his eyelids began to droop.

Tag spoke quietly to Caro. "Perhaps your grandfather should rest."

"No!" Fenton's eyes flew open with a hint of panic, immediately replaced by resignation.

Caro approached the bed. "There will be many other times."

"May I . . ." If it were possible for a man to blush without changing color, Fenton did just that, looking as uncomfortable as an adolescent asking for his first kiss. He held out a shaky hand. "May I just touch you once before you go?"

Silently, Tag slipped out into the hall. A moment later Caro stormed from the room with a look that made Tag wish he had relieved her of her dangerous knife. "Where is that wretched person who is supposed to be taking care of my grandfather?"

Tag decided he could not contain her anger in the small hallway. Putting his hand under her elbow, he guided her back to the sitting room they had just left, as if she needed consolation, not something to slice into small bits. "It is not his fault your grandfather is dying."

Caro pulled away from his patronizing touch. "My grandfather has done all the dying he is going to do."

Tag's throat tightened with the knowledge of how much this meant to her. He couldn't let her hope against reason. "He is an old man, Caro. Old men die. They—"

"You English haven't got the sense to tell death of a man's spirit from dying."

"I saw him. He couldn't raise his head. His arm—"

"If I tied you to a cloud of feathers for months, I could make you as weak as a newborn." Caro looked around the room. "That servant? How do you make that man appear?"

Tag smiled for the first time since entering the room. "I think that had better wait until you have calmed down a bit."

Tag watched Caro pace off her anger, and wondered how long it would take him to save the life of the worthless servant and be on his way. If Caro were right about Fenton, if he had simply given up on everything after the death of his son and grandson, perhaps he would be well enough to take control in a few days. Until then she would need . . .

He looked helplessly around the shabby room. She would need a housekeeper, a bevy of maids, a cook—the old man probably hadn't eaten since Tag left England—a trustworthy manservant to look after her grandfather. The list grew. A companion, a personal maid, a . . .

But first Caro would need to stop looking as if she wanted to chew the furniture into splinters. "It's been a long trip. I know how you feel about being closed up, so first I recommend"—he laughed—"I recommend you go for a walk and claw the bark off some trees. By the time you come back I should have some suggestions for you."

She hesitated, but glanced again toward the window, and he knew he had read her correctly.

"Go. There is nothing you can do while your grandfather sleeps." He opened the French door, and the temptation proved too much for her.

Tag watched her leave, already debating what needed to be done to make the house habitable. He looked about for the best way of summoning a servant. Failing to find either a bell or a pull rope, he decided on the always effective go-to-the-door-and-bellow. With the decision came the realization he would not be leaving for London tonight.

Several hours after Caro's first meeting with her grandfather, Mrs. Blanchard arrived in London. She directed her hired coach to an almost fashionable address and disembarked. "Wait for me," she ordered the driver. "This will not take long."

Moments later an astonished manservant showed her into a small sitting room. She wasted no time on preliminaries. "Don't look so astounded, you scoundrel. Did you think you could pass yourself off forever as Fenton's heir?"

Edwin Boyle hastily put aside his book and crossed the room to halt his future mother-in-law's menacing advance. "Phoebe! What are you doing here at this time of night?"

"Come to put an end to your lie about being Fenton's heir."

"Better than anyone, you know that is precisely what I am. You wouldn't rest until I was the old man's heir."

"Not unless you are a blond twit from God-knows-where—his granddaughter."

With a few strangled exclamations, Boyle prompted Phoebe Blanchard to spew forth all the details of her meeting with Lord Elmgrove and Fenton's granddaughter. She ended with: "And if you think I am going to let a scapegrace like you marry my daughter, you can think again."

"Your stepdaughter."

"My last chance for an entry into the world you claimed you would live in. Lord Franklin would have married her in a minute. He still inquires for her every time we meet."

"Don't talk like that, Phoebe. Lord Franklin is a beast. He has already killed one wife with his vicious ways." Boyle kicked over a chair and circled the room looking not unlike a beast himself.

"That is the only reason I even considered your suit in the first place. That and Rosalie's whining that she loves you."

Boyle slowly brought himself under control. "She is fragile. Even the thought of this will terrify her. Say nothing of this to her. I'm sure I can . . ." He clenched his fists at his side. "I will go down there tomorrow."

Chapter Ten

Hours later in the stuffy room the barely responsive maid had prepared, Caro lay with her eyes open and wondered how much time had passed. She felt as alone as she had the morning she had decided to return to her village. But that experience had strengthened her with the knowledge that someday Tag would leave her.

Excitement and the ship's motion had kept her awake the previous night, but this was worse. She would never understand why the English built big, beautiful houses, then made them into smothering caves. She endured the closeness until she could stand it no longer; then decided she could wait one more day before struggling to accustom herself to English ways. For now she needed to sleep outside against the breathing earth.

More alive than she'd felt in days, she hurried to her trunk and found her familiar doeskin dress. She drank in the faint smell of life that still clung to it. Hastily she slipped into it, and paused to run her hand over the familiar softness where it caressed her thigh.

As a precaution, she grabbed the long English cloak from the closet. She could use it as a blanket and wrap it around her when she returned. If any of the servants bothered to notice her when she reentered the house, they wouldn't gossip about her strange dress. Of course, she would have to hope they didn't notice her bare feet.

Moments later she was outside drinking in the familiar

171

pre-dawn smells. Fresh green smelled the same all over the world. A life-giving smell and taste that chased the spider-webs from her soul.

Soundlessly she crossed the carpet of grass, imagining the crystal color of the tiny droplets of dew she could feel but not see. Any tree would do. She studied the shadowy forms and selected one whose branches drooped to the ground like embracing arms.

Under an overhanging branch, she dropped to the ground just as the first streak of scarlet pierced the gray sky. With a sigh she molded her body to the earth. This is how an infant must feel nestled against his mother. Even the day ahead did not seem so formidable.

She would say good-bye to Tag, but she would have her grandfather and she would discuss with him how to protect them both. No matter how English he was, he would want her to deal with the man who had killed his sons.

She released herself to the welcome blankness of sleep.

Caro's eyes flew open. Every muscle tensed.

Danger.

She sat and listened again for the sound that had wakened her. Nothing. An Englishwoman would think she had imagined it. Caro knew better. But she hadn't been able to identify the direction of the danger. If she fled she might run right into it.

"Relax." She recognized the familiar laugh. "I thought I might find you here." Tag moved the low-hanging branch aside and stood there smiling. The early morning sun caused his hair to gleam like gold, and he wore a white shirt open at the neck. Comfortable clothes like those he had worn just before they left America.

Caro released her grip on the knife she had automatically drawn. She returned his smile. "At least you have learned to move more quietly than when I first met you."

172

"You taught me well. Which is more than I have done for you. Have you been here all night?"

"How did you find me?"

"I knew you would be up with the sun. When you didn't answer my knock, I just looked for the kind of tree you would like."

"Why aren't you frowning and telling me proper young ladies sleep in beds that curl their backs into knots?"

"Have I been so impossible?" He stepped around the branch and came to sit beside her, not cross-legged, but with his knees drawn up under his chin. "After today your grandfather will have to worry about such things." His eyes softened as he studied her face. Perhaps she had not imagined the note of sadness in his voice. "Will you hate England so much?"

Caro looked around and inhaled. Through the leaves she could see the grass sloping down to a rippled pond with flecks of golden sun dancing on the surface. "I don't hate it here."

"Unfortunately, your grandfather would object if you decided to live under his tree. Very difficult to assemble the proper number of young men for you to choose from."

"Will I ever see you again?" The likely answer seemed so impossible that Caro shut her eyes against it. She no longer believed in the fantasy she had built of finding a warm home in England. She would do what she must to save her grandfather, then either escape to America or kill herself before the soldiers could lock her in one of their prisons.

"Of course you will see me again."

She opened her eyes to study his face and admit to herself what she would mind most about leaving England. She would miss him in this mood when his eyes warmed and he sat so close she could remember his touch.

"You will come to London in the spring," he said. "We

will meet at balls and parties.'' His words became softer, slower.

Something in the way he looked at her made Caro's body come alive at the memory of his touch. She no longer believed he did not want her as a man wants a woman. Too many times he had weakened and let his hands caress her, but his determination they would part like this had always stopped him.

He turned his eyes away for a second, and when he met her gaze again, his tone had a false brightness. ''Perhaps you will even dance with me—''

Caro moistened her lower lip with her tongue. ''But it will not be the same.''

He leaned forward and brushed her cheek with his knuckles. ''No, it will not be the same.

''I thought I wanted to say good-bye out here.'' His fingers lingered on her ear, then slipped under her hair to cup the back of her neck. ''But I think we had better return inside now.'' Still he did not move. His eyes had a liquid softness that denied his words.

''I wish just once we could have—''

''No.'' He dropped his hand from her neck and stood abruptly.

For a moment she feared he might walk away, but he bent and offered a hand to help her to her feet. He stiffened when the gesture brought her to face him, so close his breath wafted over her face in warm, ragged waves. She did not give him time to withdraw, but drew her fingers softly along the side of his neck. ''Tag, I want you to hold me one last time.''

''God, Caro.'' He shuddered and reached up to grab her hand. Instead of pulling it away, he held it against his neck. The tiny hairs there tickled, and she played with their softness. Her fingertips touched only the velvety down, not the skin. His voice dropped to a whisper. ''Not here in your grandfather's house. Not just after I swore to myself—''

174

''My grandfather's tree,'' she reminded him. ''He will not mind.'' She said the words into his lips. The terrible tension in her relaxed as she felt him surrender. His arms slipped around her waist.

His lips against hers felt as soft as the down on his neck. The arms he held her with had no more weight than an eagle's feather. His clean male scent mingled with the green of the trees and the loamy smell of rich earth. For a long moment they stood like that, not moving, just savoring the final closeness.

''Caro, I—''

His words didn't matter, just the movement of his lips against hers. The tickle of his warm breath against the corner of her mouth. She touched his lower lip with her tongue to silence the words.

He groaned. His arms tightened around her, and he angled his head for a proper kiss. He parted her lips with his. His tongue darted into her mouth filling her with the remembered sensations, then retreated just as quickly.

She moaned in protest. Her hand crept into his hair until she could feel the silk against the webs of her fingers. ''Please,'' she whispered.

Whatever resistance he felt disappeared. He probed with his tongue, long satisfying thrusts that sent sensation everywhere. With one hand he stroked from her waist to her neck and back again. Once, then again, this time stopping his hand to tilt her head so he could pull her closer. Her breasts pressed against his chest through the thin material of his shirt. Her hips and thighs met his, close but not close enough.

Again his hand stroked her back, then dropped to join the other hand, cupping her buttocks. With both hands he drew her to him, understanding the need he had created, the need to search for him. She stood on tiptoe and felt him press against her exactly where she wanted. *Oh, yes.*

With the next thrust of his tongue he drew her to him

again, this time searching for her with his hips as she searched for him. She moaned and heard the same sound from him.

Nothing mattered but the wave after wave of sensation that roiled within her.

He broke the kiss, ignored her whimpered protest, and trailed kisses down her neck. His tongue played at the base of her neck, wetting it, driving her wild with need. He lifted her off the ground, his hands on her thighs now. He groaned. "Caro." He moaned her name against her neck. "Caro."

With both arms she clung to him. She squirmed, felt the raised dress pull free. His hand cupped her bare thigh.

"Oh, God, Caro, no." He shook his head against her neck, the scratch of his stubble sending its fire to the throbbing place between her legs.

Instead of releasing her, he allowed her to raise herself so she could embrace his thighs with hers. His hands on her bare legs supported her there while her body instinctively positioned itself against his hardness. His hand moved down so she could feel its heat against her flesh.

"Yes," he breathed, "just for a minute." His arms tightened around her as he held her against him. "Hold still, little one. I need to feel you there. Just for a minute." A shudder wracked his whole body. "Oh, God."

Caro rested against him, her eyes wide, not sure what to do next.

He raised his head so he could look at her face, and drew a series of deep breaths. "We must not do this." He inhaled again and held the air for a long time before he spoke. "I'm going to put you down now. When I do, I want you to step back and not touch me at all. I am not made of stone."

Caro resisted looking down. Between her legs he felt like stone. She waited, and he slowly lowered her to the ground, pushing her away from him at the same time. When she stood in front of him, he exhaled and shuddered again.

She felt his retreat in the coldness in her body and her soul. What did pride matter? She rested her hand on his shoulder. "Please, Tag, don't stop now. We have so little time."

He reached up and drew her hand from his shoulder, but didn't release it. "I think that's why I permitted myself to start. We have no time. We are in England now, and you must give up this ridiculous notion that I will be your husband simply because it is convenient."

The coldness in his tone chilled her. "Do you think that is why I want you?"

"Isn't it?"

Caro inhaled. If he did not understand, she couldn't explain. Later she would feel the pain. For now, she wanted to sting him back. "Perhaps."

"Forget it." He dropped her hand then. "And since we are talking about being in England, please remember that here you need to wear undergarments." His face flushed, his muscles tensed, and his voice came from deep in his throat. "Do you have any idea what that does to a man?"

Again the need to taunt him rose like water in a newly dug hole. "You did not like it?"

"Of course I liked it. Any man would. Most men would have thrown you to the ground and—hell, I cannot believe we are talking about this again."

"But you didn't throw me to the ground because you still believe I will take a stranger for my husband. A stranger I don't want." This time she didn't feel angry, only terribly sad.

"I would be the worst possible husband for you." He tried to stamp away from the words, but the low branches stopped him after three steps. He turned to face her. "Now come. No, stay. I am going back to the house alone. You put that cloak on and come back when you are ready to be less provocative."

His eyes had the fiercely determined look she had seen

177

before when he retreated behind the fort he'd built to keep her away. "This afternoon you will be your grandfather's problem." He started away, but paused and turned just before he passed under the final concealing branch. "Good-bye, Caro." With a nod, he stormed toward the house like a wind-driven thundercloud.

Caro planted her feet firmly on the ground to control the desire to run after him. Damn England. Damn their rules. Damn the country where a man couldn't want a woman who had to kill someone.

People had passed out of her life before, and she had survived. She would survive this time. Later, when time dimmed the memory, she would recall the good things they'd shared. She would smile at the echo of his laugh. His last soft words, *Good-bye, Caro,* would not cause her breath to catch in her throat.

"Bah!" She straightened her shoulders. She would not accomplish her mission mooning like a seven-year-old.

For the remainder of that morning, Tag endlessly circled the small bedchamber assigned to him. The cramped space confined him like a prison, but he didn't dare wait anyplace else for his final interview with Fenton. He could face Napoleon's army without a qualm, but he didn't have the courage to risk meeting Caro.

The bewildered hurt in her honest blue eyes would make him feel like the pond scum he was. Not because he had kissed her. Hell, he'd even sought her out knowing he would probably claim a final kiss, a reward for the honorable restraint he'd practiced for so long.

Honorable coward, he chided himself. He'd kissed her, then flayed her with vile accusations she didn't deserve.

The warm invitation he'd seen in her eyes had nothing to do with a manipulative desire to trap him into being her husband forever. She'd offered him nothing but an embracing love. A love he almost didn't have the strength to reject.

Her last memory of him would be of the ugly rejection. Of the way he'd stung the coldness back into her voice and given himself a chance to regroup. He couldn't even ask her forgiveness. He would see to her safety; he would watch her from afar, but he would never let her get that close to him again.

Tag read, he wrote in his journal, and he paced the room in the same endless circles. Finally, well after noon, a knock sounded at the door. "Mr. Fenton wants to see you immediately."

Immediately. Of course, immediately. Wait five hours, then come immediately. Tag obeyed the imperious command because he couldn't leave without seeing Fenton, and he wanted to leave.

He entered the bedchamber without knocking, thinking to save Fenton the exertion of responding. To Tag's surprise, Fenton appeared considerably better. Though he still sat engulfed in pillows, his eyes had a new resolution and his head seemed to sit straighter on his shoulders.

"You are alone, Lord Elmgrove?" The strength in Fenton's words matched the resolution in his eyes. Though he could never command troops with that voice, at least he projected the sound across the room.

"Miss Fenton will be here shortly." Tag crossed the room and sat. If Fenton wanted to take command, it would be easier if they were on eye level.

"I suppose you expect me to thank you for bringing my granddaughter."

"Yes." Since he had traveled several thousand miles, gotten married, and had faced down every man who decided he had as much right to Caro as Tag did, he felt entitled to that simple answer.

"Well I think you should be executed as a fool. You can just get her right out of here."

"Pardon me?"

"Have you given any thought to what I'm supposed to do with her?"

Since Tag had thought of little else for the past three months, he found that another easy question, and he made no effort to control his impatience. "Take her to London, find her a husband, and leave her your fortune. The same as every other grandfather in England."

Fenton scowled. "Unfortunately, we don't have time for that. The season won't properly begin for another five months."

Tag hoped he would have dealt with the situation long before the start of the season, but he liked the idea of Fenton accepting the responsibility. "If you will forgive me for saying so, you will need every minute of that and more just to accustom her to the idea."

"Bit like her father, is she?" The old man's face softened into a reminiscent smile. "She seems to like you well enough. As a matter of fact, that might be just the ticket. You're not married, are you?"

Tag almost tipped over his chair in his attempt to back away. Alarm warred with civility and led to a distinct speech impediment. "I . . . I . . ." He got up and took a turn around the room. He had faced equally direct offers, just none where he worried some demon inside him might leap out and say yes if he didn't clamp his hands over his mouth.

A deep breath and he regained control. "I am naturally sensible of the honor you do me, but . . ." Any polite lie would do. "I promised my grandmother I would not marry until I was"—he started to say forty, then decided not to take any chances—"fifty." Fenton would recognize the nonsense for what it was, but at least he had communicated his position clearly.

"I see." Fenton slumped back into his pillows, and the dying man Tag had met that morning reappeared. His hand fluttered helplessly. "Then you will have to take her away. Tonight."

"I am sure you will become accustomed to her in time. She is really a very . . ." Since he had no idea what quality Fenton valued most, he let the sentence trail off, hoping the old man would fill in his own fantasy.

Fenton looked down at the imagined creatures he plucked from the coverlet. "If you have your way, she won't live long enough for me to become accustomed to anything."

"I assume you plan to explain that."

"You understand well enough." Fenton raised his head and his pale eyes narrowed in impatience. "Less than a year ago you came to me with a tale of the murder of my son and grandson. Today you bring that little slip of a thing in here and propose to leave her to that monster."

"Boyle doesn't even know she is in England. Before he does, I assume a man of your position can make arrangements for her protection."

"A man in my position! In case you haven't noticed, I am rather occupied with this business of dying."

Despite the seriousness of the subject, Tag laughed. The man had no comprehension of the fate in store for him. People didn't die without Caro's permission. "I suspect you will have to rethink that once Miss Fenton takes charge," he warned.

"She won't have time to take charge of anything, because she is leaving with you today."

In spite of Caro's assurance that the old man was stronger than he appeared, Tag decided against an outright refusal, which might lead to a strength-sapping confrontation. "No need to worry about any of that immediately. No one knows you even have a granddaughter. Much less that she's in England." He rested back against a bureau, trying to convey by his posture his lack of concern for the situation.

Fenton huffed impatiently. "That will change the minute anyone lays eyes on her. She is the image of my son, who was the image of his mother."

The discussion had gone in circles long enough. Fenton might not consider Tag's wishes a serious enough impediment to his schemes, so he decided to call up the heavy artillery. "Even if I were inclined to fall in with your scheme, I doubt Miss Fenton would leave."

"She's a woman. She'll go where she's told."

Since Tag's primary goal was to rid himself of Caro, he decided against telling Fenton what happened to the black-bearded man who thought to take Caro where she didn't want to go. "Your granddaughter may be a trifle unique in that regard. I suggest you take a few days to let you get to know each other and then examine your options."

"Blast it, man. We don't have a few days. We don't even have a few hours." Tag sincerely hoped Fenton's current illness hadn't resulted from an attack of apoplexy, because if so, he seemed on the verge of another one.

"What's that supposed to mean?"

"My cousin Edwin's servant just arrived. Edwin is due here at any moment." Fenton shook his head and retreated into his dying posture. "Come to count the silverware, I presume. Make certain I don't take any of it with me. The minute he sees Miss Fenton . . ."

Tag cursed. "Today?" He knew he'd heard correctly. The question was just a last desperate grab at freedom.

"Can't understand why he isn't here yet. The whoreson always walks in here like he already owns everything he touches. Makes me feel ashamed I'm not already dead."

"And you can't—"

"Can't do anything. I suspect he's already started paying Albert's wages because that lobcock took the gun I always kept there." He pointed to a drawer in the bedside table. "Otherwise I would have—"

Tag didn't hear the rest. He had to get through the required number of oaths before he could begin to deal with the situation. He stomped to the window muttering creatively, one fist pounding the other palm. "We'll just have to—" Even if he could think of a reasonable excuse for intercepting the villain, he had no idea from which direction he'd come. Not that he had any worry about Caro. He was more concerned about her killing Boyle before he even realized who she was.

From what he knew of Boyle, the bastard would walk in barking orders like the master of the house. The minute Caro saw him . . . He cocked an ear toward the door. The scene might already be taking place. Caro wouldn't make much noise about it. Tag's shoulders slumped. He couldn't see himself calmly playing cards at White's the day they hanged her for murder.

He turned back to the crafty-eyed man on the bed and saw him nod in satisfaction. "I don't suppose you have any suggestion where I should take her? She needs—"

"Don't talk to me about what a girl that age needs. Anyone I knew who could deal with such things has been dead for twenty years. You brought her here. You can . . . I still think you should marry her. That would—"

"We have a more immediate problem than finding somebody to marry her. If you can think of a way to convince her to leave, you are a better man than I. She's probably even now gathering herbs to make you some foul-tasting tea."

Fenton smiled. "The last I heard you were some kind of hero. Chased the French from Waterloo all by yourself. Surely you can deal with one little girl, even if you have to pick her up and carry her out."

"You'd think so," Tag muttered dryly.

"Don't look so distressed, I am sure if you simply warn her of the danger . . ."

"If you warn her of the danger, Wellington himself wouldn't be able to get her out of here." Tag exhaled a long breath. "I will manage somehow, though you may have to help."

"Help how? I can't even get out of bed. My legs get all—"

"Just agree with whatever I've told her. And for pity's sake, don't even hint there may be any danger here unless you want her standing guard by your bed with a gun and a knife in her hand." Tag glanced again toward the door and scowled. "Right now I have to go and keep your bloody cousin alive."

He marched toward the door, but turned back as another thought ruined his exit. "And may I wish you a speedy recovery, sir, because like it or not, Miss Fenton belongs to you."

Primed for a confrontation, Tag couldn't decide whether to be annoyed or relieved to find the sitting room empty when he arrived. He paced the room, planning his strategy for convincing Caro to leave.

Strategy! He gave a dry laugh. He had no more strategy than a fool planning to take on the French army with three men and a goat.

He had spent so many weeks telling her that leaving her with her grandfather was the only possible plan, he couldn't turn-about now without some explanation. He shrugged. Like Wellington, he'd simply have to act as if whatever approach he came up with was precisely what he'd intended all along.

He glanced about for a clock, walked to the door, and bellowed for the traitorous Albert and ordered his coach readied.

Tag went back to contemplating explanations for a rather precipitous departure.

Of course he could declare an insatiable passion for Caro and insist he couldn't bear to leave without her. But that posed more danger than a daring daylight rescue from the hangman.

As if in response to the thought, Caro appeared at the door from the terrace. The skirts of her heavy dress trailed behind her. The bonnet she'd worn hung from her wrist, green leaves overflowing in all directions. If he succeeded in getting her out of here, Fenton would owe him another debt. The old man at least wouldn't have to drink the lip-puckering, nostril-stinging tea that would be made from those leaves.

Tag feigned annoyance. "I thought you would never return. I have decided against leaving you here." This first sally had a slim chance of succeeding—if she would just once behave like a normal woman and say *yes, Lord Elmgrove.* "It is long past time we were on our way."

"And I have decided we have nothing more to say to each other."

"We can talk about that. Fenton's an old man. Even now we have overstayed our welcome. What have you done with your cloak?" He bustled about the room, as if the sight of such last-minute activity might prompt her into motion. "Ah, here it is." He tossed the cloak over his right arm and held the other out to her. "Now, shall we?"

She took a half step backwards. "We shall do nothing but stand right here until you tell me what you are about."

"I can imagine nothing more obvious. I am leaving."

"And I am staying. If this is your idea of leave-taking—"

Tag's laugh sounded false even to his own ears. "I admit I had considered having you stay here. But this is a dreadful place. Look about you." He produced a dramatic shudder that would have had any Englishwoman agreeing and scurrying for the door. "Surely you can't imagine I would leave you here?"

Caro drew herself up with the thoroughly English dignity that Tag had been trying for months to teach her. "You forget yourself. This is my grandfather's house." Head high, she marched across the room and turned on him. "Where are your manners?"

In less dire circumstances Tag would have applauded her performance as worthy of a duchess. Perhaps all of his efforts hadn't been wasted. With reluctance he discarded his first plan and slipped into a more placating mode. "I meant no offense. And certainly we will deal with the situation here. But not today. The daylight is already beginning to fade."

He forced himself to slow his movements so she wouldn't feel pressured, but he crossed the room and put a guiding hand on the small of her back. "We can discuss several ideas I have in the coach." By the time the coach got under way he would have several ideas.

She stepped away from his hand and demonstrated her own ideas by seating herself firmly in an uncomfortable straight-backed chair. "Do you forget? We have already said good-bye. I left behind everything I loved to come here. And now you are suggesting I leave because this place offends your . . . your eyes? Your nose? What is it?"

"Both."

"Your English houses offend my eyes and nose, but I—"

"I know. You sleep under trees. That is all very well and good while I am here to protect you. But no one here . . ." He stopped short, knowing it would do little good to paint pictures of imaginary terrors. And the real threat would delight her beyond words.

Time for a slight switch in tactics. Even in the wilderness there must be some concept of imposing an unwelcome presence. "Actually, I have spoken to your grandfather. He feels we have come at a most inconvenient time. He is not up to receiving visitors."

Caro studied him as if by looking hard enough she could discern the thoughts behind his eyes. "A short while ago you were quite satisfied to have me stay. And then you thought he was dying. I cannot imagine a time less convenient than that.''

"That is because you were not raised English. Pride, you know. Even the oldest of us do not like others to see us in a weakened condition.''

"And my people have pride in taking care of their own. Now, if you would be on your way, I must find the kitchen and prepare what I need.'' She rose and again, her English blood obvious in her disdainful look.

Tag's desperation increased. If he picked her up and carried her out, he would have to marry her. Even the most slothful servants would have that all over the village by nightfall. If he didn't . . .

He became aware as they talked that he had been straining to listen for the sound of a coach that even now might be pulling to a halt in front of the house. If he didn't get her out of here, Boyle would walk through that door issuing orders. It would take Caro two heartbeats to figure out who he was. Tag quickly appraised the room to decide which shabby ornament she would use to kill Boyle.

Scattered images of the coming scene flashed through his mind. He could probably deflect her first attack. Boyle would understand who she was and launch his own attack, knowing he could claim to be defending himself. Tag would dash from one to the other of them saving lives until they all dropped from exhaustion. All because he couldn't think of a reason for her to leave now.

He needed something so outlandish, so foreign to her experience that she would have no choice but to let him cope with it. "It is not his health that makes it inconvenient. It is . . . It is the work that needs to be done here.''

She looked around as he had done earlier assessing the dismal state of the room. "We have stayed in far worse places. I am sure with a little effort . . .''

Tag huffed in frustration. He could almost see her rolling

187

up her sleeves to begin the unfamiliar household tasks herself.

"Perhaps we could even get someone to help," she continued. "Serving girls, like at the inns. You have said my grandfather is quite wealthy."

With her penchant for action, he had no doubt she would have the entire village in to clean within twenty-four hours. He pictured her happily spooning medicine into her shriveled grandfather while merry workers turned the house inside out. A little dust wouldn't bother someone with the lamentable habit of sleeping on the ground.

With a silent apology, he honed in on her only weakness, closed spaces and small creatures. All her pride hadn't kept her in the cave the night a rat had run across her foot. "It is not just dismal here. It's the rats."

"Rats! In this closed room?" Her hand leapt to cover her mouth.

"These old houses, you know. As it gets cold the rats come inside to live. They make the most frightful racket running about inside the walls. Of course they wander about at night."

"Oh."

"They get tangled in people's hair. Create the most dreadful messes." Someday I'll make this up to you, he vowed silently. Someday she'd be alive for him to make it up to her.

Her hand fluttered to her hair. "What can be done?"

He suddenly realized he had chased himself into a corner. He might get her away from here, but he would never get her to stay in another house. "Quite simple really. Just a matter of employing a troop of rat chasers. They come in with their instruments. Nothing more than big iron pots really. They make the most frightful din for a few days, but after that, no one ever has a problem until the next year. It's frightfully annoying while it's going on. The rats go insane and run all over the walls and floors."

* * *

Caro quickly scanned each corner and crevass in the room. Her stomach tightened. The walls of the room came closer. Her hands clutched the folds of her dress, but she resisted the impulse to lift the skirts and be certain the vile creatures weren't already tangled in the unfamiliar layers. "And this is going to happen here?"

"Tonight. That is why . . ."

She glanced toward the door. The impulse to dash outside became so powerful she could think of little else. But something in his voice stopped her. Would even the English be mad enough to remain indoors while . . . ? She shuddered at the unthinkable. "Will others remain here?"

"Oh, yes. It's not really so bad once one gets used to it."

"My grandfather . . . ?" Perhaps if she braided her hair and put on a tight bonnet . . . Her long skirts might protect her legs, but she would never know when a tiny furry creature might slip under them and scamper up her leg. If she wore her short doeskin, at least she could see. She could protect herself. She could . . .

"My grandfather . . ." she said again, unwilling to say the words that would commit her to staying in a dim, closed room trying to keep the rats away from both of them.

"Your grandfather will be fine. Probably even enjoy the excitement. But he specifically asked me to take you away. No proper English lady would remain."

And no proper warrior would run away from the horror, even if it was what he feared the most. She could do anything a pallid Englishman could. She drew a deep breath and tilted her chin as any warrior would when he had made his decision. "He needs me. I will stay with him."

"Dammit, Caro, he wants you to leave." He walked to the window, looked out, and threw up his hands in frustration. "We must go. Now."

189

"The only place I will go is to my grandfather. We must prepare for the horror."

Tag looked appalled as he always did when she flouted convention. He stepped quickly between her and the door. "Uh . . . Uh . . ." His mouth moved twice more but produced no recognizable sound.

"Please move. I must prepare—"

"Your hair is untidy," he snapped. "Go and fix yourself and I will prepare your grandfather." He gave a laugh, and a spark of his customary humor appeared in his eyes. "I will prepare him for your preparing him."

Caro needed courage, not humor. She stepped around him without bothering to respond and hurried out the door to the passageway.

Tag followed.

Entering her grandfather's bedchamber without knocking, she found him sleeping peacefully. Perhaps he had found his own way of escaping. Perhaps she could help most by brewing him a potion that would allow him to sleep through the nightmare.

She approached the bed and whispered softly so as not to startle him. "Grandfather. Grandfather."

He opened his eyes. "Emma," he whispered. Slowly his eyes focused on her face.

"No. I am Caro. Your granddaughter. Emma's granddaughter."

"I thought you had left." He struggled to raise himself on the pillow. "You must leave."

"There, you see," Tag said from behind her. "You must—"

Caro ignored him. "Ta—Lord Elmgrove told me what is to happen. I will stay will stay with you and protect you from the rats."

"Only one rat." His face tightened at the thought.

Tag had been wrong. Her grandfather did fear the coming night. "Perhaps none, if I can have one of the instruments for frightening them away."

"My gun—" He shook himself abruptly. "No, you must not use my gun. You must be gone before he comes. Leave quickly."

She stepped forward quickly and put her hand on his shoulder. His illness might be only of the mind, but he should not excite himself so. "Don't worry, I will protect you from the hordes."

"Hordes! What . . . ? Wh . . . ?" He looked frantically left and right. Only when his gaze found Tag did he find his voice. "Hordes. Lord Elmgrove do you know more of this than I do?"

"Considerably, sir," Tag said firmly. "But I suggest you follow your first instinct. Insist your granddaughter leave. Immediately. And put your best authority into it."

Caro whirled on him. "Oh, do be still. You only make a bad situation worse." She drew herself up to her full height. "I will not leave my grandfather."

Impatience tightened Tag's jaw. "You are a woman. You will—"

Her eyes flashed. "I will defend my grandfather. I will not leave him."

Tag folded his arms across his chest. He had seen that defiant look on Caro's face before, once when they crouched in the bushes and she prepared to defend them against the band of Iroquois. "No. I was a fool to suppose you would."

"No one needs to defend me." Fenton had managed to sit up and square his bony shoulders. "This is entirely expected. After all, he is only one ma—"

Tag took a thumping step forward, the movement giving force to his interruption. "There is no arguing with Caro in this mood. We must . . ." Even now they were running out of time. "We must . . . do what we must."

"Thank you for finally realizing that." Caro clutched at

her knife, which had suddenly appeared in her hand. She turned it over several times, then raised it helplessly as if she would toss it aside. "Now, if you will find the rat-chasers and tell them I am ready to begin."

"Rat-chasers? Who—"

"Say no more, sir." Tag looked around and assessed what needed to be done and the time it would take to do it. Impossible. Nothing mattered but leaving, and Caro would not leave without the old man. So be it.

He stalked to the bed, his step so determined that Caro had no choice but to move quickly out of his way. No words would stem the storm of protest she seemed preparing to unleash, so he pressed his lips together as he bent, put one arm under Fenton's neck, the other under his knees, and lifted. The burgundy coverlet, which Fenton clutched in his hand, came along and weighed more than he did.

"Put me down. Do you hear? Put me . . ."

"Sacre bleu . . ."

Tag prayed Fenton's flailing protests kept him from recognizing the colorful epithets Caro had learned from the French trappers, mixed with Shawnee curses.

Without looking back, Tag strode from the bedchamber, carrying his light but noisy burden. Caro kept up her multilingual protest, but followed. He hesitated only once, at the head of the stairs to catch up the coverlet that threatened to trip him.

Albert, for once available, met the procession at the foot of the stairs. "What are you—where are—pardon me, your lordship, but—" At least his awe and bewilderment had produced a proper title.

"Mr. Fenton has decided to take a short trip." Tag spoke unhurriedly as if Fenton frequently decided to journey about in his nightshirt.

"I have not—"

"Tag, put him—"

"He will need some things. Assemble them."

"Yes, my lord."

"Assemble them and send them to . . . send them to . . . Oh, bother, we will send for them." Tag started to brush past the man, but Albert sidestepped with the quickest movement he had exhibited to date. For a moment Tag feared he might block their exit with his body, but he merely opened the door with a flourish and bowed as politely as a butler bidding a formal party good evening.

Tag permitted himself his first smile, mildly curious as to where he would instruct the driver to take this bizarre crew.

Chapter Eleven

Caro followed Tag toward the door held by the servant with the accusing eyes. Her cheeks burned with shame. She should have the courage to defend her grandfather in his own home, but mental pictures of the closed room and furry creatures scurrying from behind every wall quickened her step.

A word from her might stop this insane dash from the house, but she could think only one word. *Hurry.*

She would not speak that word.

A small sigh of relief escaped her as she stepped though the door into the late afternoon sun.

Outside was better. Small creatures behaved predictably outside. Caro stopped at the top of the steps, expecting Tag to turn toward her and tell her where he planned to make their stand. Instead, he continued with unbroken stride toward the waiting coach. "Tag, wait."

He slowed for a single breath at the door the coach driver held open. Without looking back at her, he took a giant step and disappeared inside, still carrying her grandfather like the corpse of an honored brave.

By the time she settled in the seat opposite the two men, her terror of the rats had subsided enough for her to consider what she should have done. The others would have stayed in the house. Her grandfather would have stayed if she and Tag hadn't come. She could have stopped Tag when he lifted her grandfather. She could have insisted they stay. She should have. . . . She could have. . . .

"Just drive, Joseph," Tag called out the door. "I'll tell you where when we get to the main road."

She was still a coward because she refused to look up and see the scorn in her grandfather's eyes. The coach began to move. She could not ride forever looking at her hideous shoes. Slowly she lifted her gaze to see her grandfather settling himself into the cushions in the corner. An amused smile created deep crevices in his face and caused his pale blue eyes to sparkle with renewed life. He was looking not at her but at Tag. "I assume you are aware I am dressed only in my nightshirt."

Tag flashed an answering grin. "I noticed."

"And you don't consider your action a bit precipitous?"

"Naturally not. Though I would prefer to discuss it later." Both men chuckled, confirming Caro's suspicion that all Englishmen were mad.

She couldn't do anything about the madness, but she was certainly responsible for the wild dash from the house. Both men would have stayed if Tag hadn't known about her irrational fear. "Grandfather, I'm sorry. I . . . We can go back . . . we can—"

"Not at all, my dear. I'm sure I will quite enjoy this outing. So long as your friend has a plan." He looked again to Tag. "You do have a plan, don't you? You realize there are a limited number of places where I can call in my nightshirt."

"Of course I have a plan." Tag hesitated, then grinned. "It's just that at the moment I'm not quite sure what it is." He glanced out the window to watch a coach rumble by in the opposite direction. He didn't speak again until the noise died away. "I guess what we do now partly depends upon you, sir. Can you travel?"

Her grandfather raised his eyebrows and glanced about the obviously moving coach. "It appears so."

"I meant your medical condition. Do you need a doctor?"

Again grandfather's eyes sparkled. "Not as much as I need some clothes." His face sobered. "Forgive my levity. This small adventure is certainly an improvement upon waiting in a small room to die, which is what I have been doing for the past six months. To answer your question, I do have a doctor. He comes in once a week to see if I have cocked up my toes yet. So far he hasn't done any harm, but he hasn't done any good either, so I assume I can get along without him."

"Splendid. Then we will—" Tag put his head back against the seat and stared indifferently at the roof. "We will all look at the inside of the roof while I think about what we will do."

Like a mindless Englishwoman, Caro glanced at the roof, then shook herself at her foolishness.

Tag angled his head to study the older man. "I don't suppose you would consider an inn, sir?"

"I would prefer something a little less public."

The coach ground to a halt. "Which way, my lord?" The disembodied voice of the coachman came from outside. "We've reached the main road."

Tag turned to the open window. "Remind me, Joseph, precisely where are we?"

The coachman rattled off a series of unfamiliar place names and distances.

"Of course." Tag sat forward rubbing his hands together. His mischievous grin that indicated he was enjoying himself immensely. "I have a friend—"

Caro responded as she always did to his good humor. "Improbable, but occasionally true," she said to her grandfather.

Tag acknowledged the interruption with a nod that promised retribution and continued. "I have a friend who prides himself on being positively imperturbable. The look on his face when we arrive should more than make up for a few hours' ride.'' He nodded an enthusiastic agreement with himself and gave directions to the driver. With a self-satisfied expression, he settled back to contemplate delights only he could see.

Caro automatically watched the road, memorizing the route for a return journey. She wondered if Tag had felt as helpless when traveling in America as she did now.

They stopped once to change horses and send the driver in to purchase an inedible meal of greasy meat and dried bread. The journey took more than three hours. When the coach finally rocked to a bumpy stop, Tag reached over to gather up her grandfather and the coverlet.

''I can walk,'' the old man protested in a voice jagged with exhaustion.

''Nonsense.'' Tag leaned forward and prepared to step from the coach. ''You would ruin a perfectly splendid tableau. And in your present attire I doubt if walking would add much to your consequence.''

Caro followed Tag from the coach, stiff and sore from the jolting journey. In the darkness, the house appeared as a gray wall that stretched infinitely into the shadows. Before they reached the top of the stone steps, a door opened, bathing them all in soft yellow light. A stocky man in dark formal clothes guarded the entrance.

''Good heavens!'' He jumped aside quickly. ''An accident. Come in quickly. I'll get help.'' He looked frantically around the hall.

Tag stepped in calmly. ''No need to fuss, Mason. I merely—''

''Lord Elmgrove! Are you . . . is he . . . ?''

''Nothing of the sort.'' Tag rocked back on one foot and favored the man with a devilish grin. ''I merely thought it time I paid a call on Rexford. Is he about?''

''In the library. You . . . I'll . . .''

''Compose yourself, Mason. Just show us to him. I am

rather looking forward to seeing his expression when we make our entrance.''

''Sorry, my lord. It's just . . .'' With a visible effort the man managed to make his face a blank page. ''If you will follow me.''

In spite of her weariness, Caro hurried behind Tag, eager to see the reaction his entrance produced. Only Tag could make a sport out of a disgraceful flight from those hideous creatures. Though she didn't always understand his humor, she had laughed more in the past weeks than in all the years before she met him.

She trailed him into a room the size of a Shawnee longhouse. A tall, darkhaired man, sitting by the fire, rose to his feet.

''Egad! What—'' He took three steps forward, his face creased with concern. ''Tag—'' He skidded to a halt in the middle of his fourth step and angled his head to the side. His brows pulled together and his eyes narrowed. Suspicion yielded to a triumphant smile. ''Tag, you're pulling the wrong pig by the ear. That corpse you're holding just smiled at me.''

''Dammit, Marc, I bet myself a thousand pounds you'd at least—''

''At least send for tea for your friends? Certainly. Mason, if you would.'' He nodded his order at the servant, who stepped out the door, murmured a few words, and returned to watch with glowing eyes and an impassive face.

''And now, perhaps you will introduce me,'' the stranger said.

Tag, still holding her grandfather and the crimson coverlet, which now drooped to the floor, threw back his head and laughed. ''You really are provoking. You could at least humor me by doing a little fumbling.''

The smiling man ignored the comment, marched across the room, and drew himself up to an impressive height in front of Tag. He focused his attention entirely on Caro's grandfather, and gave a crisp bow from the waist. "I am Marcus Blackerby, Earl of Rexford. And if this young man has kidnapped you, I vow he will return you before morning."

Though his movements were sharply restricted, her grandfather gave an equally crisp nod to acknowledge the introduction. "Reginald Fenton. This young lady is my granddaughter. And I would be satisfied if you could just convince Lord Elmgrove to find a place to put me down."

Rexford gave a deeper bow to Caro, who was so astonished by the formality under the circumstances that she could not remember the proper way to greet an earl. She just smiled.

Rexford had already turned his attention back to Tag. "Tag, do you have other calls to pay this evening, or am I to assume you plan to spend the night?"

"Enough, Marc. Though Mr. Fenton is not particularly heavy, the sooner he is settled—"

"Of course." Rexford made a formal quarter-turn to face Caro. "Miss Fenton, I regret my wife has already retired and is not here to issue the invitation personally. But I assure you that she would be honored to have you stay with us." A wide smile softened his words. "She would even be willing to put up with this Bedlamite"—he angled his head toward Tag—"for one night."

Caro involuntarily smiled at the combination of formality and warmth. In spite of the strange circumstances, she felt comfortable in an English house for the first time. "Thank you."

"Mason, show these people to whichever rooms are made up." Rexford extended his arm toward the door. "And bring Lord Elmgrove back here—at gunpoint, if necessary."

A few minutes later, Tag returned to the library, grateful for the coincidence of geography that had brought him to his closest friend and the one person best suited to help untangle this snarl. Marc had already located a crystal decanter filled with amber liquid. Always sensitive to a man's most urgent needs, he poured a full glass and held it out as Tag entered the room. "I believe I forgot to say welcome back to England," Marc said.

"Understandable under the circumstances." Tag accepted the glass, downed its contents, and returned it.

Without a word, Marc filled the glass and watched while Tag took another large swallow before speaking again. "From the way you are guzzling my imported hell-broth, I assume you did not stage that entire diversion just to provoke me."

Still carrying the glass, Tag collapsed into a chair by the fire. "No. Under other circumstances I would have put that off for another day."

Marc settled himself more slowly into a matching chair. "From the fact you arrived with only one Mr. Fenton and a rather unexpected young lady, I gather Fenton's last son—"

"Died about a year ago. The girl is his only issue."

Marc muttered an inaudible oath and bared his teeth in a grimace of pain. "I don't believe it was a good idea for you to bring that pretty little thing back with you at this point."

"I'm not sure why you should say so, but I know it wasn't." Tag took a long drink. "But she wanted to come, and I had little choice. Will Boyle be a threat to her, do you think?"

"I am sure of it. I believe he has killed again since you left. Do you remember Mackenzie at Waterloo? A big Scotsman? Wounded at Quatre Bras?"

"Of course," Tag said. "I saw him in the hospital after the battle."

"Evidently Fenton told him the same story he told you. Mackenzie got well and came back here and confronted

200

Boyle. I don't know the details, but one of them challenged the other to a duel. That should have taken care of Boyle, but Mackenzie never made it to the hill. He was set upon by ruffians that night, found dead in the street the next morning. That's too much coincidence for me."

"Damn him!"

"Yes, damn him. But in the meantime, I wouldn't let that pretty little girl you brought with you stand between Boyle and something he wants." Marc's eyes brightened. He picked up his glass and raised it in a tribute to Tag. "I failed to commend you on a dramatic entrance. You might have had me flummoxed if I hadn't recognized Fenton. I deduced you chose a hasty retreat as the best way of protecting those two from Boyle."

"Not precisely."

"Oh?" Marc's eyebrows rose.

"The hasty retreat was also to protect Boyle from Miss Fenton."

"Miss Fenton?" Marc's wide eyes registered all the astonishment Tag had wished for earlier.

Tag laughed. "You don't make many mistakes, Marc, but I suspect you have the wrong impression of the delicate Miss Fenton. She is not your average English miss."

Marc's lips pursed. "She seems normal enough to me. Except for a rather unfortunate taste in dress."

Tag grinned, temporarily enjoying himself immensely. "It might help if I tell you her taste in clothes runs to short doeskin dresses and no undergarments."

"I'm just going to let you explain that rather than make a fool of myself by asking any more questions."

"Wendell Fenton wasn't much of a parent. Except for occasional appearance, he left the raising of his daughter to a tribe of Indians in the Ohio Valley."

"Savages," Marc said with a disapproving frown.

Tag tensed, then remembered that had been his own original expectation. "Not savages. Extraordinarily civilized actually.'' He smiled. "Except, as you say, for a rather unfortunate taste in attire.''

"They all go about in doeskin dresses?''

"Actually, the men wear a lot less. You could design a complete wardrobe for a man from your average handker-chief.''

Marc laughed. "But that still doesn't tell me what you were protecting Boyle from. You didn't expect him to cock up his toes at the sight of a strangely dressed female?''

"It's not just her clothes that are different. It's the think-ing, though I didn't completely understand that when I agreed to bring Caro back with me.''

Again Marc's eyebrows rose in a question. "Caro is it?''

"Hell, we've been traveling together for four months.''

Marc gave an amused nod. "Remind me to ask you about that later.''

"I won't.''

"Anyway, proceed with her different thinking.''

"The people who raised Caro have a rather Biblical con-cept of justice, which she seems to share. And they don't waste much time gathering proof. If someone injures a member of the tribe—and Caro is a member by adoption—the chief sends someone off to deal with the matter. Pref-erably by bringing back the scalp of the enemy.''

"So you are saying there is some sav—Indian out there now stalking Boyle?''

"Not precisely.''

"Stop playing games with me. Did the chief send some-one to kill Boyle?''

Tag shrugged. There really were no ideal words to ex-plain Caro. "The chief couldn't spare a warrior, so he sent Caro. Everybody agreed it was her right because it was her family.''

"Good heavens! You don't think she'd actually go through with it, do you?''

"I didn't at first. Now I'm convinced the only reason she

202

didn't leave me at Dover and go looking for Boyle is because I never told her his full name.''

"You have to talk her out of it."

Tag gave a disdainful laugh. "Tomorrow I will introduce you to Caro properly and let you try to talk her out of something she has taken a notion to."

Marc spoke twice, just syllables of disbelieving protest; then he sat back with a shrug. "Perhaps that's the solution then. Just point her in his direction and be prepared to help her get out of the country."

"Dammit, Marc, Caro's not a murderer!"

"I thought you just said she was."

"Well, she's not. She just thinks she is. She's a . . . she's . . ." Pictures without words tumbled through Tag's mind. Caro with her head thrown back laughing, Caro in the sun with the wind slapping her hair against her face, Caro lying next to him, curled into him for warmth. *She's mine.* "She's a lady," he finished lamely.

"I see." The drawn-out words and Marc's knowing expression suggested he hadn't missed the way Tag bit his lip to rid himself of the images. The clock ticked off several long seconds. "What do you plan to do about her then—when you run out of friends to wake up in the middle of the night, I mean."

"I was hoping you might help me with that."

Marc laughed. "And I was hoping I had already done my part."

Tag gave the comment the impatient look it deserved. "As I see it, she only needs a little more time to get used to our ways. Understand how we feel about killing people. And then we can—"

Marc held up his hand palm outward. "Stop right there. *We* drink brandy together. *We* play cards. *We* can even go fishing together if you want. But when it comes to dealing with young women who want to kill people—"

203

"She doesn't want to kill *people*. Just Boyle." Tag figured since he had arrived safely in England, he could discount the times Caro had threatened to kill *him*.

"Of course. Silly of me. I assume you will continue explaining my part in this whether I invite you to or not."

"A few weeks to get used to our ways, get some clothes and perhaps a little polish, and we can find her a husband. She is a considerable heiress, you know. It shouldn't be difficult. We—"

"Again stop! You are talking nonsense. It is not our place to find her a husband."

"Her grandfather hasn't been out of bed in six months. He insists there are no relatives, though I admit we did not have much time to discuss it. Besides, you and Amanda are perfect."

"No, Tag."

This ideal solution had presented itself with the decision to come here, and Tag did not intend to be turned aside by a simple no. "Amanda is so sensible. Caro will listen to her where she wouldn't to you or me." Tag rubbed his hands together and wished he could see an answering spark of enthusiasm from Marc. "It shouldn't take long. I thought perhaps Alan McSoley—"

"Alan McSoley announced his betrothal a month ago."

"Hopkins, perhaps. Though I think he's a bit pompous, don't you?"

"No."

"Well, I do. Caro would never put up with anybody who blathers 'dashed splendid idea' all the time."

"I meant, no, we can't help you out. No, we won't help. We can't."

"But . . ." Something vital and alive in Marc's expression stopped Tag's protest. "You needn't look so elated about it." He tried to frown, but Marc's grin made that difficult.

"Sorry, but I am elated. Amanda is . . . I . . . I'm going

to be a father, Tag.'' The imperturbable Earl of Rexford sat
grinning like a stupefied country lad.

"A father!" Tag leaped from his chair to pound Marc
on the back. "I never thought . . . but of course . . ." He
returned to his chair, his smile at least as broad as Marc's.
"I assume you are hoping for an heir."

"You would think so, wouldn't you. But"—he drew his
brows together in amused confusion—"every time I look
at Amanda, I picture a little girl tossing her head and looking back at me with those eyes. I sometimes think I want
that more than an heir." His face grew serious and he took
a long drink from the glass he had set aside. "To tell the
truth, the whole thing scares the hell out of me. I'm so
afraid something will go wrong." He stared at the carpet
for a moment and shook his head. "Nothing should be this
important."

Tag resisted the temptation to offer false reassurance on
something he knew nothing about. "When does this . . . this
thing happen?"

"Not soon enough for your purposes, I fear. We still
have several weeks left, though I plan to take Amanda to
London tomorrow. The only doctor within thirty miles of
here is always drunk as an emperor by midday. So it will
be months before Amanda could even consider getting in-
volved launching your protégée. Besides, I'm not certain I
see how a husband would cure Miss Fenton of her unfortunate desire to kill people."

"Not people, just Boyle. And I told you she will get
over that once she gets more accustomed to our ways. She
has lived outdoors most of her life. Hates being confined.
I thought a tour of Newgate might change her view of murder and its consequences in a hurry." Tag rubbed his hand
across his brow to banish the thought of Caro even knowing
such a hellhole existed. "She belongs in—it doesn't matter
where she belongs. I am more concerned with finding her
a husband who will keep her safe until we can do some-

thing about Boyle. You know, the kind of man we fought with at Waterloo. A Scotsman maybe. She would like Scotland. Those men are all little mad about protecting their women. One of them would . . ."

Marc had begun shaking his head, and he let Tag babble to a halt. "You are missing the most obvious solution," he said with a slow smile.

"What's that?"

"Marry her yourself."

The blow came out of nowhere. *"Et tu, Brute."* Tag stood up and stomped across the room, only to find himself confronted with a wall, which forced him to turn and face Marc. "Bloody hell, Marc, I expected better from you of all people. I expected—"

"Sit down and be reasonable," Marc said firmly. "You have been threatening to marry for years now. I only met the chit for a minute, but she can't be any worse than Isobel the Icicle or some of the other frozen fish you've taken up with. It is obvious you care for Caro—"

"I don't *care* for her. I'm responsible for her. There is a difference." Tag had no intention of sitting or even standing still. He paced to the corner of the room.

Marc waited with an amused slant to his eyebrows. "You forget, I can see your face when you mention her name. That's not just responsible. That's a woman you want to hold on to."

"Will it satisfy you if I confess to a mild physical attraction?" Like a moth held a mild interest in a lamp.

But hell, a man could control a little lust. As soon as he rid himself of Caro . . .

"Remember, you're talking to *me,* Tag. I've seen you two minutes before you disappeared with your latest Aphrodite, and it never put that possessive expression on your face. That girl you dragged in here is as different from your other women as diamonds from dust."

"She's . . ." *She's nothing special,* Tag tried to say, but the traitorous words wouldn't come. She was indescribably courageous, fiercely loyal, and when she wasn't threatening to attack anyone, had enough warmth and love to blanket the world.

Everything a man could want, and the embodiment of Tag's every nightmare.

Tag faced the wall again and closed his eyes to block out the memory of his father's voice. Not just the words, but every intonation exactly as he had heard it twenty-two years ago, through his anguish over his mother's death. *You must stop blaming yourself, Taggart. It is not your fault. She made the choice herself. She did it because she loved you.*

No amount of talk could change the fact his mother would be alive if she hadn't loved him. Give him a selfish woman every time. A selfish woman and a life without gut-wrenching guilt every time he saw his father looking at her portrait.

"Tag." Marc's too gentle voice came from behind him.

Tag turned, determined to answer Marc's question about Caro casually. "She's nothing special," he managed to grind out through clenched teeth, his hands still fisted with the memories.

"Tag, I know—"

"No. I know. I know exactly what you're going to say." *Unfortunate. A dreadful tragedy. A child's view of being responsible, but . . .* Marc had said it all before, and Tag had believed him because he'd wanted to. Believed him and let an adorable, courageous French woman love him He had proposed to her, promised her an idyllic future, and buried her.

He couldn't change the past, but he could make damn certain it never happened again. "Never again," he said aloud in a tone final enough to end the discussion with anyone but Marc.

Marc's lips narrowed. He glanced at the ceiling and exhaled a long breath. "Tag, I respect your judgment. I admire just about everything about you. But you are letting two unfortunate occurrences ruin your whole life."

"I won't discuss it, Marc. Not even with you." Tag set his feet more firmly on the floor, prepared to stalk out of the room if his friend said even one more word on the topic. "Tomorrow I'll figure out a way to be rid of her."

For a moment Marc looked as if he might ignore the warning. Then he grimaced. "I guess it's every man's right to mix his own poison." He stood. "I suspect we are not going to solve anything tonight. So if you will excuse me, I have a wife waiting for me."

Tag glanced down at the rug so Marc wouldn't see the flash of envy in his eyes or guess how his stomach lurched at the thought that Caro could be waiting for him. He managed a civil "Good night."

He waited until Marc left, then did what any right-thinking man would do. He cursed, looked around the four walls, and cursed again. Marc's abrupt departure had left the room so full of memories of Caro. "Dammit, Caro, get out of my head." He should be thinking of how to get rid of her.

Instead, he wanted to call Marc back and talk about her. His mind kept flashing pictures. His tongue kept forming sentences, all of which began with, "You should have seen her when . . ." A few more muttered curses and Tag surrendered. He could control his actions, but not his thoughts.

He pictured her in the bedchamber where he had left her an hour ago, perched on the edge of the large bed in the room next to her grandfather, her eyes pleading with him not to leave her. Every muscle tensed with the compulsion to go to her, not to make love to her, just to lie beside her as he had so many nights on the journey. To take her in his arms and assure her that he would protect her from the strangeness that was England.

Not to make love to her.

Thrill to the most sensual, adventure-filled Historical Romances on the market today...

FROM 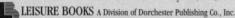 LEISURE BOOKS

As a home subscriber to the Leisure Historical Romance Book Club, you'll enjoy the best in today's BRAND-NEW Historical Romance fiction. For over twenty-five years, Leisure Books has brought you the award-winning, high-quality authors you know and love to read. Each Leisure Historical Romance will sweep you away to a world of high adventure...and intimate romance. Discover for yourself all the passion and excitement millions of readers thrill to each and every month.

SAVE AT LEAST $5.00 EACH TIME YOU BUY!

Each month, the Leisure Historical Romance Book Club brings you four brand-new titles from Leisure Books, America's foremost publisher of Historical Romances. EACH PACKAGE WILL SAVE YOU AT LEAST $5.00 FROM THE BOOKSTORE PRICE! And you'll never miss a new title with our convenient home delivery service.

Here's how we do it. Each package will carry a 10-DAY EXAMINATION privilege. At the end of that time, if you decide to keep your books, simply pay the low invoice price of $16.96 ($19.98 CANADA), no shipping or handling charges added.* HOME DELIVERY IS ALWAYS FREE.* With today's top Historical Romance novels selling for $5.99 and higher, our price SAVES YOU AT LEAST $5.00 with each shipment.

AND YOUR FIRST FOUR-BOOK SHIPMENT IS TOTALLY FREE!*

IT'S A BARGAIN YOU CAN'T BEAT! A Super $21.96 Value!

LEISURE BOOKS A Division of Dorchester Publishing Co., Inc.

GET YOUR 4 FREE* BOOKS NOW—
A $21.96 VALUE!

Mail the Free* Books
Certificate
Today!

4 FREE* BOOKS 🌹 A $21.96 VALUE

Free Books Certificate*

YES! I want to subscribe to the Leisure Historical Romance Book Club. Please send me my 4 FREE* BOOKS. Then, each month I'll receive the four newest Leisure Historical Romance selections to preview for 10 days. If I decide to keep them, I will pay the Special Member's Only discounted price of just $4.24 each, a total of $16.96 ($19.98 in Canada). This is a SAVINGS OF AT LEAST $5.00 off the bookstore price. There are no shipping, handling, or other charges.* There is no minimum number of books I must buy and I may cancel the program at any time. In any case, the 4 FREE* BOOKS are mine to keep—A BIG $21.96 Value!

*In Canada, add $7.95 US shipping and handling per order for first shipment. For all subsequent shipments to Canada the cost of membership in the Book Club is $19.98 US plus $7.95 US shipping and handling per order. All payments must be made in US dollars.

Name _____

Address _____

City _____

State _____ Zip _____

Telephone _____

Signature _____

If under 18, Parent or Guardian must sign. Terms, prices and conditions subject to change. Subscription subject to acceptance. Leisure Books reserves the right to reject any order or cancel any subscription.

(Tear Here and Mail Your FREE Book Card Today!)*

Get Four Books Totally
F R E E* —
A $21.96 Value!

(Tear Here and Mail Your FREE* Book Card Today!)

PLEASE RUSH
MY FOUR FREE*
BOOKS TO ME
RIGHT AWAY!

Leisure Historical Romance Book Club
P.O. Box 6613
Edison, NJ 08818-6613

The tightening in his groin identified that as his biggest lie of the day. If he ever permitted himself to lie next to her again, there wouldn't be enough honor in all of England to prevent him from finishing what they had begun at dawn.

With an audible groan he surrendered to the memory of her open thighs wrapped around him, her eyes liquid with trust and desire. If he hadn't had to thrust her from him to release his own clothing . . . If he went to her now, she would welcome him, open herself to him in exactly the same way. He would . . .

Tag clenched his fist, bit his lip, and shuddered. Caro would sleep alone tonight, the innocent sleep she deserved. And for him the nightmares he had held at bay for years would return.

Chapter Twelve

Upstairs, Caro lay awake in the darkened room. She had been so exhausted while settling her grandfather, she'd thought she would fall asleep as soon as someone showed her a place to lie down. But the minute Tag and the servant had left the room, every sense had come alert with the pounding of her heart. This was far worse than the night in Tag's father's house because then she hadn't known about the rats.

Caro lay awake and waited.

She waited until the candle burned out, then waited in the darkness, listening to every sound. She waited, dreading not just the night, but the dawn. In the morning she would have to face the earl's wife with too little sleep and too much hunger for the warm friendship of the women she had left behind. Alone in the dark she surrendered to her longing for the easy companionship of another female.

She listened with the door slightly ajar to the sound of masculine voices and then to the muted padding of footsteps on the carpeted stairs. Not Tag's footsteps. She sensed that, knew she would recognize his sound and respond, the way she responded to his scent behind her even in a crowded room.

After a long time she heard his unmistakable step, different because the house echoed noises differently, but definitely his. He walked slowly, without his usual bounce.

Perhaps he too resented the walls that imprisoned them and made the air heavy and stale.

The door to a room near hers scraped open, then closed with a gentle bump. She waited only long enough to be sure Tag would not reappear, then slipped into the passageway, taking several long seconds to shut her door silently. Even to her sensitive ears, her bare feet made no sound on the steps, and the lock on the front door cooperated by opening with only two metallic clicks.

The night air embraced her. Her first breath infused her with strength. She followed the moonlit path, searching for a site far from the house where no one would find her. Without warning, the path opened on a wide clearing with a stone outbuilding in the center. She could lie in the shadow of the building and still draw comfort from the familiar stars.

She slept.

Much later, a three-noted whistle that didn't belong in the forest snatched Caro from a dreamless sleep. The unfamiliar sound transported her back to a world where an unrecognized birdcall could be the first and only warning of a hostile attack. Without a single betraying movement, every muscle leaped to attention. She listened and heard only natural morning sounds, but the hairs on the back of her neck warned her of another presence.

Slowly she opened her eyes to narrow slits. Ten feet from where she lay, a woman stood in a loose flowing gown, her rippling hair the color of a newly opened chestnut. A flock of birds, thirty or more, circled overhead.

The woman whistled again, the same three notes that had wakened Caro. The birds circled again, then dove directly toward the woman. One even landed on her outstretched hand.

"Oh." Caro could not suppress her gasp of delight.

The woman turned with a smile as rosy warm as the

211

newly risen sun behind her. "I was afraid that might wake you, but I could not let them fly all day."

Caro rose slowly so as not to startle the birds. No, she thought, she rose slowly because she did not want to startle the woman. A gamekeeper or serving girl perhaps, but one who could assuage her loneliness if only for a few minutes. "The birds, they come to you?" Caro flushed slightly at such an obvious comment.

The woman hesitated long enough to smile at a white bird on her shoulder. "They are homing pigeons. But come and meet them. They grow very impatient if I ignore them too long." She shooed the flock through a window into the stone building. "This is a pigeon cote," she explained. "For as long as they live, these birds will return here. Even from hundreds of miles away."

Though aware that keeping company with the servants was as unacceptable as sleeping on the ground, Caro followed the woman through a wooden door to a fenced enclosure. The birds came waddling from the stone building into the courtyard to mill about their feet, pecking impatiently at their feet. Perhaps the woman felt the same kinship Caro did, because she asked no questions about Caro's unexpected presence. She merely scooped out a handful of grain from a burlap bag and demonstrated how to hand-feed the birds. For the next hour the woman moved about, laughing at the antics of the birds and chatting with Caro as comfortably as an old friend.

Finally the stranger stood and brushed the flecks of grain from her hands. "Come, we have pandered to these insatiable creatures long enough. And I must sit down. I am . . ." She blushed and finished the statement with a self-conscious glance at her obviously bulging waistline.

"I noticed." Caro laughed, secretly pleased she had guessed the reticent English would discuss something as natural as childbirth only in the most roundabout terms.

The woman led Caro from the enclosure to a bench in

the shade of a fragrant bush. She sat with only a hint of awkwardness and offered Caro an inviting smile. "Sit with me for a moment."

Caro resisted the pull of the tempting invitation. "I must get back to the house."

"So soon? It is still very early."

Caro glanced at the sun, which had just begun to turn a soft yellow. "If I don't go now, someone may catch me slipping back into the house."

"And that would be so terrible?"

"Oh, yes. If Lady Rexford discovers I sleep outside"— Caro glanced at her dirt-smudged feet—"and wear no shoes, I will be socially ruined. The English are terribly fussy about things like that." Belatedly, Caro remembered her new friend was also English, though not stiff and patronizing like the women on the ship. "Not the ordinary people. The ones Tag refers to as the *ton*."

The woman's eyes danced with amusement and her voice burbled with laughter. "And Tag told you Lady Rexford would personally see to your social ruination? I must have a talk with him."

"Not her personally. But English women are—" In mid-sentence the reason for the woman's laughter dawned. Flight was impossible and the ground refused to open and swallow Caro. She had no choice but to wait and pray she hadn't made another wretched blunder. "Please tell me you are not—"

"Lady Rexford. I am afraid that I am. But if it is any consolation, I shall be too busy in the next few weeks to see to anyone's ostracism."

"But . . . but you are a countess." Caro's heart plummeted with the knowledge she had just met her hostess, the woman who should expect her to behave so correctly. She wrapped her arms about her to keep out the sudden chill of the morning air.

"And as you pointed out, quite ordinary." Lady Rexford

patted the bench beside her. "Now come and sit. Let us enjoy the time we have before the others wake."

"Lady Rexford," Caro murmured, still not able to believe that the welcoming smile wouldn't change to a haughty sniff of disapproval. "You are a countess, and you found me sleeping on the ground. You didn't even ask my name."

Lady Rexford's warm laugh filled the morning and softened the ice that had begun to form around Caro's heart. "You are Caro, of course. And you must call me Amanda, not Lady Rexford. I admit to being startled at first on finding you here, but I expected we would meet sooner or later. My husband told me about you last night. Now sit and tell me about your home."

Within a few minutes Caro realized her new friend was no more intimidating than any expectant mother. Amanda kept her hands protectively across her stomach even when making polite inquiries about Caro's homeland. Her eyes widened with interest when Caro mentioned she was a healer among her own people, and the conversation kept returning to the expected child.

"You have no idea how glad I am that you are here. I am so terribly nervous about this." Amanda's interlocked fingers tightened across her stomach. "And there is no one I can talk to."

"Your husband? Surely he would—"

"Oh, dear, no. He is the worst. Earls are used to being in charge, and he can't take charge of this. He gets very blustery at even a hint that something might go wrong and changes the subject as quickly as he can. I think underneath all his words he is as worried as I am."

"You have had visions? Dreams of your own death?" Caro's heartbeat quickened with the chill memory of all the people she had known who had predicted their own deaths. Women did die in childbirth. But it would not help Amanda to pretend her fears didn't exist.

"Oh, no, nothing like that. I've never even thought to worry about myself. It's the baby." Amanda's eyes glistened with unshed tears. "I never expected to have a child. I don't think I could bear it if something happened to him." Her hands fluttered nervously. "To her."

"Perhaps I can reassure you," Caro said. Her hands had reached out automatically to examine the baby's position, but she flushed and drew them back. Here, where every town had a doctor, there was no need for her kind of healing. "I am sorry. I didn't mean to be so forward."

"Please, don't draw away. If you know of such things, if you could just tell me I am being silly, I would be so grateful."

Despite the plea, Caro hesitated. Tag would surely frown at her putting her hands on the belly of a countess. The English had such strange notions about touching. "I would need to feel the child."

"Of course." Amanda rose quickly and turned to face Caro with her arms invitingly open at her sides. The hope and trust in her eyes banished the last of Caro's doubts.

She closed her eyes and mentally recited the ancient prayer of her people for the unborn spirit. With the prayer, Caro's attention turned to the unborn baby rather than the woman carrying it. "How soon?" she asked too brusquely, then softened the question with a smile.

"Not for a few weeks. Maybe more." Amanda flushed. "I don't really know. I wasn't thinking of such things at the time."

Caro nodded. She reached out and put her palms along the outside of Amanda's swollen belly. With the first touch she felt a darkness that almost made her turn to see if a cloud had stolen the light from the sun. A heartbeat later she recognized the darkness as one of feeling, not sight.

She closed her eyes to shut out everything but the living world under her fingers. Slowly the dark feeling evolved into wordless pictures. Little Squirrel, whose lifeless daughter had been born at dawn; Singing Water, whose silent infant had taken only a single breath and passed on. Caro had known with them, as she knew with Amanda, that the inevitable process of birth had already begun. Too soon.

She kept her eyes closed and pretended to continue the examination. Not to be certain, but because she needed more time to decide what to say to Amanda. With one of her own people she would simply look up and speak the truth. The woman would patiently wait for the spirits to decide whether to let the child live. Her body would work in harmony with nature to give her child every chance.

But could an Englishwoman understand this? The English who fought with nature, chopping down trees and changing the course of rivers? Would her fear make her body a rigid boulder that the hapless infant would have to batter his way through before he would have even a hope of life?

Caro didn't know the answer, but if there was a senseless way to bring a child into the world, the English would find it. Her fingers tensed with her decision. She had promised reassurance, and she would give a lie.

But the lie would give the child precious hours to begin his journey. Amanda would relax and let her body work in the way of nature until the time came when she had to help. And then?

Caro stared at the ground, picturing sunshine and fields of wildflowers until she could look up without even a hint of apprehension in her eyes. She smiled. "It will be a very special baby." She whispered a silent prayer that she had spoken the truth.

Tag sat with Marc in the blue breakfast room. Both of them had chosen chairs that enabled them to look across the south lawn to the path leading into the woods. A fortunate choice since it eliminated the necessity of standing up and walking to the window every two minutes.

"Amanda is late this morning." Marc, once renowned for his engaging conversation, had already said the same thing three times. Repetition had not made it any more fascinating.

"She has probably met Caro." Not probably, definitely. Tag had gone out soon after sunrise to assure himself that Caro had slept safely under whatever bush she had chosen. He had seen the two women happily draped in birds.

Before he could share this information, the same two appeared on the far side of the lawn, chatting amiably. The knowledge that Caro had found a friend at last warmed him.

Marc rose, opened the door, and stood tapping one booted toe, his arms crossed on his chest. "You're late," he growled as the two women stepped into the room.

Amanda tamed her husband with a look as soft as a kiss, and hurried to greet Tag. "It is marvelous to see you returned safe and well. And thank you for bringing Caro to me. I was not aware how much I missed the company of another woman. And she is charming. I am sure we will be wonderful friends."

Caro looked anything but charming in a crumpled gown twenty years too old for her, her bare toes peeking out from beneath its drab folds. Her once-neat braid had abandoned any look of control. Her golden hair escaped and danced in all directions with the breeze, which came through the open door. "Yes, she is charming." Tag agreed, uncomfortably aware he thought her much more than simply charming.

The women delayed breakfast a second time by asking for "just a minute to freshen up."

In a surprisingly short time they returned. Caro looked demure and innocent in a lemon muslin gown borrowed from Amanda. Her hair, brushed until it gleamed, tumbled over her shoulders in ripples of matching sunlight. Even Marc's eyes widened with approval.

Skillful hosts, Marc and Amanda plied Caro with questions about her home, and in a short time she was making the people who raised her come alive in the cheerful room. Tag contributed little, content to watch Caro enjoying herself.

Too soon, Marc reluctantly pushed his chair back from the table. "Distressing as it is, I am afraid I must end this discussion. All this delay has put us behind times." He ignored his wife's disappointed frown and turned to Tag. "As I explained last night, we must be off to London today. You two, however, are welcome to stay as long as you like."

Caro gasped. "London? How far is London, Tag? I thought you said it was a long way."

Rexford stood. "About seven hours, my dear. That is why we must start almost immediate—"

"Don't go." Caro's crisp words sounded more like a command than a plea.

Rexford shook his head. "From the expression on my wife's face, I suspect she shares your sentiments. But on this issue, I am afraid I shall have to overrule you both."

"But—" Caro threw a nervous glance at Amanda and lost her imperative air. "But Amanda and I have had such a short time together. Please wait a few days."

Rexford smiled. "I assure you, there will be many days. You must visit us in London as soon as we are settled. But for today we must be on our way."

"But you must not go." She sent an even more desperate look at Amanda.

"Amanda, please tell him you want—"

"No protests, please." A sharp slice of Marc's right hand underlined his determination to cut off any argument. "I am sure you have noticed my wife's condition. There is not a competent doctor within fifty miles of here, and I will not get a comfortable night's sleep until I can summon at least a dozen at a moment's notice."

Still the explanation didn't satisfy Caro. She stood, her

hand clutching the edge of the table so hard her fingertips whitened. ''But the journey. In a bumpy coach. Surely she would be better off here.''

Marc's jaw tightened so his words came with exaggerated distinctness. ''Miss Fenton, on every issue not involving my wife's safety, I am prepared to indulge you. On this, however, I am inflexible. Amanda . . .'' He said his wife's name as a command and nodded toward the door.

''Amanda, don't go.''

Tag cringed at the desperate note in Caro's voice. She never begged. She never even asked for help. He tried to soften the tension with a laugh that sounded false even to his own ear. ''Caro, these people will think you are bored with my company.''

Despite the fierce expression on Marc's face, Amanda crossed the room and put her hand on his arm. ''Caro and I have had such a short time together. Perhaps one more day—''

''Not one more hour. Now go and do whatever you must to leave immediately.'' Rexford stood impassively until he saw Amanda's slight nod of submission. Then he looked over her shoulder at Caro. ''Miss Fenton, I must confess I am disappointed at your insistence. At a time like this, your concern should be for my wife, not for your own desires.''

Tag's stomach tightened with the rebuke. A violent protest rose to his lips, but he too was taken aback by Caro's behavior. At the same time, he longed to comfort her with his arms and assure her that he would supply whole rooms full of friends.

He said nothing.

Caro's cheeks reddened, but she bit lip and drew a deep breath.

Amanda walked to her with a too bright smile. ''We can talk while I make my final preparations. And you can join us in London at the end of the week. Come.''

219

Caro forced a too tight smile. "You go. I will join you in a moment."

Amanda hesitated, nodded, and left the room without looking back. Marc crossed the room and pretended to be fascinated with the view from the window. Caro continued to stare at the door for several seconds after Amanda left. When she finally turned to face Marc, she appeared to have grown several inches.

No longer desolate, she said his name firmly. "Lord Rexford." She waited until he turned around and gave her his full attention before speaking again. "You must not take your wife to London today."

"We have already established that I plan to do precisely that. And all of your trifling desires—"

"This has nothing to do with my desires. I permitted you to think that because the real reason would only make your wife more anxious."

"The real reason." Rexford formed the words of ice. "I am sure you plan to explain."

Caro's chin rose. "I am a medicine woman to my people." She said the words in the same tone Napoleon would have said, *I am the emperor of France.* "A journey today would be dangerous for Amanda."

Marc's eyes narrowed. "You have examined my wife? She has symptoms?" His exclamation of disgust sounded like a dry cough. "Tell me about these symptoms."

"I have examined her. Yes."

"And?"

Caro stood at rigid attention, unaffected by Marc's burning stare. "I know what I know."

"Examined her how? Found what? Come, Miss Fenton, don't toy with me."

"I put my hand on the place where she is carrying your baby, and I suspect your child will arrive early. Possibly even today."

"All the more reason to get her to London immediately.

You are not claiming the process has begun, are you? Surely, she would have told me.''

Caro closed her eyes and shook her head. ''It is impossible to explain to one not raised in our ways.''

''Try.''

Finally, Tag could no longer stand to watch the blazing confrontation. ''Marc, please. Caro is only trying to—''

Marc responded to Tag with a scathing look. ''Trying to convince me of something she wants by claiming some kind of mystical knowledge.'' His attention flashed back to Caro. ''Tell me what you found when you put your hands on my wife's stomach. Tell me so I can verify it. Surely, if you felt something I will feel it too.''

''You are not trained. You cannot know . . . it is a dark feeling, a knowing.''

''And because of this dark feeling, I am to keep my wife here. Exactly as you want. And if we stay here and if nothing happens, you will just throw up your hands and say, 'Oh dear, I must have been mistaken.' ''

Tag had never seen Rexford so angry. Caro merely stood there and met his gaze impassively. ''And if nothing happens *because* you stay here, your child may live.'' Caro's voice softened. ''Lord Rexford, it doesn't matter what you think of me. What matters is your child's life. I only hope you will stay here. Despise me to your heart's content if you wish, but stay here.''

Marc turned to the window with an oath. He stood staring out for a long time, only his shoulders moving with each long breath. Finally he turned to pin Tag with his questioning stare. ''I trust you, Tag. What do you think of all this? Do you believe in dark feelings?''

Ten years of friendship and respect rose with the answer. Twenty years of solid English thinking. Of course he didn't believe in mystical feelings. ''I . . .''

The answer Marc demanded wouldn't come. Tag believed in Caro. Her goodness, her unselfishness, her solid faith in herself. "Irrational as it is, Marc, I trust Caro. I think you should listen to her." Not irrational, he remembered. "A man fell from the rigging on our ship to England. A bad fall and he broke his arm, but he got up and walked around. Convinced everybody he was all right. Caro examined him and quietly told me he'd be dead before dawn. He was."

"That was different. He probably damaged something inside. I could have—" Marc broke off to stare openmouthed at the door to the hall.

Tag whirled. Amanda stood there, her face alabaster white. Her lips quivered with the faintest smile when she looked at Caro. "You didn't think I would leave you at his mercy, did you?" Amanda said.

Marc recovered first. He hurried to his wife and took her hand. "Amanda, this isn't for you. You should not—"

Amanda ignored him and looked at Caro over his shoulder. "I have only one question." She spoke so softly Tag had to strain to hear. "How often are your feelings wrong?"

Caro stood without answering. Everyone in the room looked at her. The silence of the unanswered question trembled in the room.

"How often?" Amanda asked again.

"Never." Caro whispered the word on a long soft exhale.

Marc murmured inaudibly to his wife. She permitted him to take her arm and lead her to a chair. Then he straightened to face Caro again. "It appears my wife has chosen to take your alarms seriously. I have no choice but to accede to her plea to remain here."

Again Caro met his gaze without flinching. "I am aware I do not know much about your country, but it appears you are unnecessarily insistent on this journey to London. You are going only to be close to your chosen doctors?"

"Correct. And—"

Caro's upraised arm indicated the luxurious room with a

222

sweeping gesture. "And with all of this you cannot simply bring the doctors here?"

"Our doctors are busy men. They are unlikely to undertake a journey from London on the whim of a visitor from a strange land."

Caro exploded an impolite syllable from her native tongue. "They will come for you. You will kidnap them if you have to. I will do it if you are afraid."

"That will not be necessary." For the first time Marc gave a faint smile. "As you say, they will come, and I suppose the idea is a good one." He looked down at his wife. "I think this is all a cartful of nonsense, but I assume you will be more comfortable if I sent for a doctor."

"Please."

"Then it is done. Now, Miss Fenton—"

"Caro." Amanda broke in, frowning at her husband. "You sound much less threatening when you address her as Caro."

"Caro, then. Since we have temporarily decided to accept your *feeling*—" Marc managed the word with only a hint of his earlier contempt—"you will tell us what you would do about this situation if you were with your people."

"I will mix a potion that occasionally quiets a baby intent on arriving too early." Caro looked at Amanda, knowing the herb would likely do little more than make Amanda's fear more tolerable. "And you must stay as quiet as possible."

Amanda's head bowed in agreement. Then she looked up and glared at her husband. "And we will not be gloomy."

Marc's face softened with his smile. "I have been well and truly routed. We will not be gloomy."

"And you will send for the modiste from the village," Amanda added. "It will give us all something else to think about."

"I will not . . ." Rexford broke off at Amanda's look, which promised rebellion. He laughed. "I will not be gloomy and I will send for the modiste from the village. Do

223

you have any more orders, or may I content myself with those two?''

"You may kiss me once before Caro and I retire to prepare a vision of loveliness to grace your dinner table."

By late afternoon Amanda had drunk the bitter tea Caro provided, and Caro had discovered just how irksome preparing a vision of loveliness could be. Either Rexford or Tag had decided that, since the ladies could not go shopping, every single article of feminine apparel in the village should come to them. The modiste arrived with two assistants and an overburdened servant to carry in bolt after bolt of material.

For the first time, Caro did not merely have to decide between two or three ready-made dresses that almost fit, but had to consider a whole host of things. In reality she did little more than stand and consider while the modiste and her assistants pushed and prodded and held up an endless succession of materials. Amanda sat comfortably against the bolster and pillows of her bed. The choice of materials seemed simple compared to the endless variety of ways they could be sewed together.

Too frumpy. Too flouncy. Too plain. Too flamboyant. Too . . . Too . . . Caro had never imagined there could be so many toos for something as simple as a dress. But eventually the fluttery dressmaker and her assistants departed for a distant room with a bundle of soft blue silk, which they promised would be a dress by evening, and orders for a dozen more.

After that, Amanda amused herself for another hour selecting gloves, shawls, bonnets, ribbons, and dozens of other items that Caro couldn't even name, much less imagine wearing. Eventually Amanda pronounced herself satisfied, "for today." She packed everyone off and summoned a maid to deliver the towering array of things they left behind to Caro's room. With a yawn, Amanda confessed she could sleep. Only in that last moment before Caro left did

Amanda's eyes betray the fear that must have haunted her all day. "You won't let Marc chase you away if I let you out of my sight, will you? Promise you'll stay, at least until we know . . ." she said, taking Caro's hand.

"Of course," Caro promised lightly.

Caro slipped quietly from the room, grateful the enormous fuss had finally ended. She would never stay in England long enough to wear all that Amanda had insisted on ordering, but had endured the fuss because it distracted the expectant mother.

Though the prospect of resting tempted her, Caro decided to visit her grandfather. Despite his protests, the journey had exhausted him, and he had been sleeping both times when she had visited him earlier. The sound of Rexford's raised voice stopped her before she reached her grandfather's door. She had no desire for another confrontation with the earl.

She listened.

"Dammit, Fenton." Tag's voice now. "I don't care how safe you've been until now. Caro changes everything. If you die before she is married, Edwin Boyle will be her guardian. And nothing Marc or I can do will keep her safe. You can't go back there now."

Edwin Boyle. Caro froze, not even daring to breathe. They were discussing the man she had come to kill. They would stop if they knew she could hear. Furtively she looked up and down the hall, ashamed to be caught listening, but prepared to silence anyone who gave her position away. The spirits were kind because the hall remained deserted.

"I don't see why you're so determined to go back there. At least not today." Rexford was with Tag. Both of them were arguing with her grandfather They didn't want her grandfather to go back to some place. His home?

"We don't even know he is there," her grandfather said. Caro stifled the impulse to ask where.

"But you think he is," Tag said. "You think he would stay even if you are not there?"

225

"He comes to see if I have made any progress towards dying. He stays to drink my brandy and dump his seed into my housemaids. I doubt if he will leave before tomorrow."

Caro's knees weakened in relief. She had all she needed to know. Her evil cousin was at her grandfather's house and would be there until tomorrow. Quietly she opened the door to her own room. She had to make her plans.

Inside, she fell to her knees, resting her head and shoulders on the bed, taking comfort for the first time in something soft and English. Until this moment she hadn't realized how much she'd feared she would fail, feared she would be unable to find the evil man and feared Tag would persuade her to abandon her mission. Most of all she'd feared she herself would change, become too soft, too English.

Now, a short ride and she could confront the evil one in the only place in England she could reach on her own. She stood and walked to the window. Rexford would not mind if she borrowed a horse. Even if he did, she would be guilty of a worse crime before he discovered it.

Amanda. The sudden thought of her new friend brought a rush of guilt.

Caro brushed the intrusive thought aside and searched the room until she found her shabby bundle, which the scrupulous maids had tucked out of sight. With eager fingers she pulled out the well-worn leggings and tunic. English women didn't ride astride, but dressed in her travel clothes, she would look like a country lad.

A country lad on a splendid horse? No matter. She could not plan for everything. If a crisis developed she would solve it then. For now she could only do what she must.

Amanda. With the persistent thought the dark feeling of the morning returned. How much time did she have before Amanda would need her?

"No," she whispered, but she heard again Amanda's words. *You will stay with me, won't you?*

226

Chapter Thirteen

Two hours later Caro woke to a soft tap on the door. She had made the only decision she could, refusing to listen to the niggling whispers of temptation that insisted she could be to her grandfather's house and back before Amanda needed her. Clutching her doeskin dress for the comfort of its familiar scent, she had slept soundly in an English bed for the first time.

Tap, tap. The sound came again, more insistent this time. Caro sat up and hastily tucked the worn garment under a pillow. "Come in."

The door opened and an apple-cheeked maid entered. She held one hand high above her head so the rustling gown she carried would not trail on the floor. "I am Sally. Lady Rexford sent me to help you dress." She swooped the dress onto the bed and began opening drawers and pulling out garments with the cheerful air of a person who enjoys her work and does it well. Within minutes Caro had stepped, backed, or wiggled into more clothing than she usually wore in a week, and still Sally hadn't even looked at the gown on the bed. "Now sit," she instructed.

Caro obediently sat on the bench in front a dressing table with a large mirror and a startling array of jars and bottles, which had mysteriously appeared since morning. Sally took Caro's hand as comfortably as if it were her own and began massaging it with a cream so cool and soothing Caro closed her eyes and surrendered to the sensations.

With an equal ease of manner she brushed Caro's hair until it crackled and small wisps rose to meet the brush. "It's so lovely, miss," she said, smiling with pleasure. "I can do anything I want with it." She wanted to pile it on top of Caro's head in a style as intricate as a woven basket. Caro shifted her head awkwardly with the unaccustomed weight.

"Now stop that," Sally scolded, "You'll get used to it. I am afraid we can't do anything about the color you've let the sun turn your face. But if you won't tell anybody I said so, I think it suits you. Makes your eyes as blue as a milkmaid's bonnet, it does."

With a last pat to the elaborate hairstyle, she directed Caro to stand. Seconds later Caro turned about in the shimmering blue gown, which felt as light and smooth as the lotion Sally had used on her hands.

Caro glanced down in alarm. Light and smooth because it didn't even exist over most of her chest. She gripped the fabric with both hands and tugged. "Sally, should it be this low?"

"Of course it should, miss. Men like to see a lot of bosom. No one knows why, it's part of what makes them men." Sally smoothed a final wrinkle that couldn't possibly exist in the liquid fabric. "Now look." She turned Caro to face the mirror and beamed with pleasure at Caro's gasp. "As grand as a queen, and that's a fact."

Caro didn't dare move. Though ashamed of her vanity, she knew she would be disappointed if the exquisite creature in the glass didn't mimic her movements. "Thank you, Sally," she whispered. The mirrored lips moved, giving Caro courage to breathe and turn her head. Just for tonight she could be the lady in the mirror.

"It was simple when I had something good to start with." She turned Caro around for a final inspection. "Lady Rexford said I was to bring you to her. I think she knew you would look like this and wanted to be there to see the gentlemen's eyes fall out of their heads.''

Caro followed Sally to Lady Rexford's room, but hesitated at the door. Thoughts of the alluring woman in the mirror disappeared, and Caro became once again the Shawnee medicine woman about to enter the *wegiwa* of a sufferer. She would not alarm her friend by showing even a hint of concern on her face.

"Don't stand there, Caro. Come in and let me see you." Amanda jumped up from the bench in front of her own dressing table without a hint of discomfort. "Oh, you are even lovelier that I expected! How I envy you, so delicate and feminine.''

Caro exhaled with relief. Certainly Amanda looked as if she had nothing more on her mind than elegant gowns and intricate hairstyles. Perhaps just this once Caro would be wrong. Perhaps tonight Amanda would be nothing more than the gay English hostesss and Caro could be an elegant English lady. The kind of lady Tag would want for a wife, if only for a short time.

Amanda hurried to Caro's side. With a hand on Caro's shoulder she turned her around and smoothed an imagined wrinkle as Sally had done, as if that were part of some mysterious rite. "Perfect," she said, "but let us go now and give the gentlemen something to think about besides their tedious politics.'' She glanced at the porcelain clock. "We must hurry. Marcus will be growling.''

If Rexford had been growling, their appearance startled him so that Caro could only hear the soft whoosh of air as he exhaled. "Upon my honor, you have been busy." He hurried to his wife's side. "My dear, you look lovely. And Miss Fenton''—he executed a formal bow—"you are absolutely . . . you are . . .''

Caro lost whatever he might have said, interested only in Tag's reaction. He had yet to move except for a silent movement of his lips.

"Caro . . .'' He said her name as if he had to force the

word around an apple core stuck in his throat. His lips moved twice more and he managed to say her name again, this time in a strained whisper. "Caro. Your gown—you are—"

Rexford laughed, looking over his shoulder at Tag and back at Amanda and Caro. "I always said the man should be an orator." He half-turned and gestured at Tag to join them. "Come along, man. I have confirmed that this is the same young lady who left us earlier. And I am sure she is hungry."

Tag took the five long strides necessary to cross the room, and bowed as elegantly as Rexford had. "Good evening, Lady Rexford, Miss Fenton." His voice had regained its usual warmth. "You both look absolutely splendid."

"I believe we have already established that. Now if you don't mind . . ." Rexford cocked his elbow and Amanda put her hand lightly on his arm.

Tag imitated the gesture, and after a moment's uncertainty, Caro claimed his arm with the same possessiveness with which Amanda had taken her husband's. Tag hesitated a moment before following the others. Perhaps seeing her dressed as a lady truly would let him accept her as his wife. The thought set her heart to pounding and colored her face with a warm flush.

Rexford led them to a room only slightly larger than the one where they had breakfasted earlier. Caro remembered to smile at the footman who held her chair. She didn't just look different. For the first time she felt as if she could be the proper Englishwoman Tag talked about so incessantly. Felt as if she wanted to be that.

Her changed appearance had an added benefit. The others no longer treated her like some visitor from a distant tribe who had to be the center of every conversation. The other three talked about their country, their parliament, and the returning soldiers who for some reason had to starve when they couldn't fight. Caro let the words drift around her and simply enjoyed the way Tag kept watching her.

Eventually Rexford noticed the same thing. "Dammit, Tag, will you look at me occasionally when I talk to you? Caro won't be able to eat a bite if you keep looking at her like you want to—"

"Marcus!" Amanda said sharply.

Caro, already flushed, felt even the tips of her ears burn. She had been only too conscious of Tag's looks, which made her stomach tighten with the memory of his touch on her thigh. If the others could simply disappear, she would feel him easing her legs apart again. And this time, his molten looks said he would not stop.

"Sorry, my dear, but you have to admit it's a little disconcerting to be talking to somebody whose mind is—"

"Marcus, if you say another word, I vow you will be eating dinner in the stables."

Tag frowned. "Enough, Marc. I admit I was thinking about Caro. But I was thinking about a husband for her. Perhaps Manfried. I know he's a duke and all. But if he could see her tonight—"

Rexford interrupted. "He'd look at her exactly the way you are. And you'd probably be obliged to call him out."

Caro's fingers tightened around her butter knife. There was only one way to contend with Tag's stubborn insistence on his own plans. "I don't need a husband. I have a husband."

Rexford's eyebrows almost disappeared into his hairline. "Does Tag know this?"

"Caro!" Tag's knuckles whitened against the table. His eyes glared a fierce warning.

"Tag knows. Tag is my husband."

Rexford gulped down the wine he had just sipped. "Tag? Did you forget to tell me about this?"

"We are not married. I am not her husband," Tag said through clenched teeth. "I am not your husband," he repeated to Caro. "You have to forget about that."

Rexford gave a short laugh. "A little hard to forget about something like that. Also a little hard to mistake a wedding for anything else. So either you are married or you're not. Which is it?"

"We are."

"We are not."

"Try to remember, both of you. Did you go through a ceremony?"

"Yes." Caro looked only at Tag, though Rexford had asked the question.

He returned her glare with equal intensity. "Damn Indian ceremony. Not even a wedding, it was a dance."

"You seemed to enjoy it enough at the time," Caro said.

From the corner of her eye, Caro caught Rexford's wink at his wife. "Strange. Tag never did care much for dancing," he said.

Caro's comment had silenced Tag. His eyes turned liquid again and his fingers stroked his wineglass.

Despite her anger, Caro's flesh tingled with the memory of how those fingers had moved over her body during the dance. Her fingers caressed the table, as smooth and firm as his chest in the firelight. Her tongue darted out to moisten her suddenly dry lips.

Tag exhaled a long shuddering breath and tore his gaze away from Caro to look at Rexford. "Even if somebody did want to consider that a wedding ceremony, we never consummated the thing." He looked back at Caro. "And we're not going to."

"Enough." Rexford raised both hands, palms outward. "I believe Amanda and I are beginning to understand. This is definitely something you two have to settle for yourselves." He laughed and spoke directly to his wife. "Though I must confess this is one of the reasons I regret living so far from London. There is no one to accept a wager on this consummation business." He captured Tag's attention with a tale of a sizable wager he had won.

232

Suddenly, Amanda gasped, attracting Caro's full attention. If Caro hadn't been so intensely aware of her friend's condition, she might have mistaken the sound for a delayed expression of shock at the turn in the conversation. But the lightning flash of pain and terror in Amanda's eyes caused Caro's dinner to settle in her stomach with a thud. The men, obviously unaware, continued to argue about horse racing.

"No." Amanda's sharp word and her warning glance at Rexford stayed Caro's instinctive impulse to rush to reassure her.

Rexford chose to accept the word as a rebuke. "Correct as usual, dear. This is definitely not a topic to interest you ladies. I apologize."

The men turned the conversation to horses they owned or used to own. Caro listened and waited for a cue from Amanda. Time dragged. Amanda smiled and managed to respond with a word or two to questions from her husband, but finally her fingers again tightened on the table.

Caro waited until the grip softened and then stood. Amanda would never relax sitting at the table. "I have a bit of a headache," she lied. "I believe I will go to my room."

Tag jumped to his feet. "Caro, you never have headaches."

"I do now. And I am going to my room. Amanda, would you come with me, please?"

"Of course. If you gentlemen would excuse us. . . ." Amanda rose so slowly Caro was certain Rexford would notice, but he merely rose and nodded

Once standing, however, Amanda sailed across the room as proudly as a queen. Not until they were safely out of sight of the doorway did she stop and clutch Caro's arm, all her horror clearly written on her face. "Caro, it's— please, Marcus mustn't know. He will be upset."

"Tag will keep him occupied," Caro assured her, keeping her voice steady and unemotional. "Let us get you upstairs."

A waiting footman hurried over. "Are you all right, my lady? Can I help?"

Amanda straightened and forced a smile. "I would be grateful for an extra arm up the stairs, Walter." She put her hand in crook of his elbow, but did not release her grip on Caro. Fortunately, the stairs were wide enough to accommodate the three of them. Amanda paused at the top of the stairs, and her fingers dug into the flesh of Caro's forearm.

The footman must have felt the same pressure because his face paled. "What? What should I do?"

"Just wait," Caro said. "She is fine."

Almost with her words, Amanda let out a long breath and nodded. Walking almost normally, she led the way to her room. "Thank you, Walter."

"Are you sure you will be all right, my lady? Shall I fetch Lord Rexford?"

"Of course not. I'm just a little tired." Amanda waited until Walter had closed the door firmly behind him, then began to tremble so violently she had to hold on to Caro for support. "Oh, Caro, it's happening now, isn't it? It's too soon." Her eyes filled with tears, which would destroy her last remnant of control.

Caro closed her eyes, fighting the temptation to put her arms around this woman who wanted her baby so desperately and weep with her. She forced a stoic coldness into her voice. "You will stop that right now. Your baby is about to be born. And if he is to live, he will need all your strength."

As she expected, her words had the effect of a slap. Amanda bit her lip and controlled the trembling. "Marcus must not know. He will be terrified and will throw the whole house into a commotion, bellowing orders everywhere because he doesn't know what else to do."

"That's better," Caro said, referring to the fact that Amanda's color had begun to return. "But we must tell him so he can send for the doctor." The morning performance had convinced her Rexford would be beyond furious if even the local doctor did not arrive in time.

"No." Amanda's grip tightened again. "That doctor is not only a fool, but a butcher. I won't have him near me."

"Then is there someone else?"

"A local midwife, but . . ." Amanda bit her lip, silent until the tightness of pain began to recede from her eyes. "From this morning I thought that you could . . ." Her mouth opened, and Caro sensed the return of the earlier panic. "You can deliver this baby, can't you? You have delivered babies, haven't you?"

"Frequently. But you are English and I thought you would want—"

"I want you." Amanda's grip relaxed. She exhaled and looked around the bedchamber as if she had never seen it before. "Now tell me what we must do."

Caro helped her out of her elegant clothes, but insisted she don a light dress. "We have several hours at least, and you must walk about as much as possible."

"But I can't. I—"

Caro refused to let her face show the slightest compassion. "You are strong. You will do what is best for the baby."

Grimly Amanda nodded, and with the next contraction circled the room with her hand resting only lightly on Caro's arm. "That was better," she confessed as the pain eased.

Caro glanced at her own gown. She couldn't do anything with all these cumbersome clothes. "I must go and change. I will not be gone longer than five minutes. Just sit and think of the loveliest place you ever visited."

"Hurry."

In her room Caro found Sally dozing. The maid jumped

up when Caro entered and glanced at the clock in alarm. "You're early, miss. Is something wrong? Did the gentlemen not like—"

"Help me," Caro ordered, turning so Sally could unfasten the line of tiny buttons at the back of the gown. She could not keep the event secret from everyone in the house, and Sally appeared as sensible as anyone she had met. "I believe Lady Rexford is going to have her baby."

"Oh, the poor thing." Sally stopped unbuttoning and wrung her hands together. "What's to be done? Who is going to . . ."

"I am. Now, help me out of these clothes." She located a packet of herbs. "Please make a strong tea with these, and then we can only wait."

As soon as she had shed the confining garments, she reached under the coverlet on her bed and located her familiar dress. Ignoring Sally's startled gasp, she slipped it over her head, drawing strength from its comfortably familiar touch.

"Oh, miss." Sally's hand covered her mouth and she shook her head. "You can't wear that to a birthing."

In spite of her tension, Caro smiled. "It has been to many birthings. Leave me now, Sally. I need to be alone." She looked up to find Sally watching her uncertainly. "And don't tell Lord Rexford. Now, go."

"I will. I mean, I won't. I mean, I will leave and I won't tell Lord Rexford."

Caro waited until the maid left, and then extinguished the lamp and walked over to open the window. She had no time to go outside, but she stood in the darkness drawing strength from the moon and the night air. Joining with the night spirits in the ancient prayer of her people.

When Caro returned to Amanda's room, the expectant mother had her eyes closed, a single large tear running down her cheek. She sensed Caro's presence, and wiped the tear away with the back of her hand. "I will be all right, I just . . ." She glanced at the door through which Caro had just entered. "Could you lock that door, please? So Marcus doesn't come wandering in accidentally." She shook her head sadly. "It will be the first time I have locked him out."

"Sometimes a woman's man can help. When he cares for her as much as Rexford cares for you."

Amanda smiled. "He cares for me, but Marcus gets dreadfully angry at things he cannot control. I am not sure I would have the strength to worry about him right now." She waited until Caro had locked the door and returned to the chair beside the bed. "What will happen now?"

"Now we will wait. The pains will gradually get worse, but they are easier if you move about and think of something else. I do not think it will be too long."

"What should I think of?"

Caro had no idea what Englishwomen thought about when they needed strength. "I can tell you of my people." For the next two hours Caro recited stories she had heard as a child, carefully selecting those about women whose courage and determination had saved their families or even the entire tribe.

Though Amanda smiled at the obvious attempt to give her strength, her eyes grew clear and the muscles of her face tightened with resolution.

"NO-O-O-!" The shouted word reverberated through the house, not muffled even slightly by the solid door. Heavy footsteps pounded on the stairs like rapid musket shots.

Amanda looked at Caro and gave a resigned smile. "I believe Lord Rexford is about to join us."

A moment later the handle on the door turned and a heavy body thudded against the locked door. "What's going on in there? Open this door!"

"Not now, Marcus," Amanda called, her voice more commanding than it had been in two hours, "we're busy."

"Open this door before I break it down." Fists pounded on the door to illustrate the threat.

The smile reached Amanda's eyes. "I don't believe we have a choice, and we may as well spare the door." She nodded to indicate Caro should respond to the shouted command, then grimaced and breathed her way through another pain.

Caro unlocked the door and stepped back quickly. Rexford practically fell into the room. "What's going on in here? Walter said . . ." His gaze flew to where Amanda stood supporting herself against the wall. "Walter said you were ill. Are you . . . ?" This time he did not miss the grimace that tightened her facial muscles. He just stood with his hands on his hips, looking at his wife as if furious with her for defying him.

"Calm yourself, Marcus. I do not have time for your marching around giving orders. Please leave."

Rexford whirled on Caro. "She is having the baby, isn't she? This is all your fault." His face had turned a deep crimson and veins throbbed at both temples. "Why isn't she in bed? Get her into bed."

Caro reminded herself that, in his own way, he was as frightened as Amanda. "She will be all right," she assured him firmly, wishing she could say as much for the baby. Certainly the commotion wouldn't strengthen his desire to open his eyes in such a world.

"Well, I won't hear of it. Get your things, Amanda. You are not having the baby here. Not without . . . not with . . . say something, Amanda."

"Please go, Marcus." Amanda gasped out the words. Her expression went rigid with another contraction, and she lost the calm determination that had carried her through the earlier ones.

"No!" Rexford's face contorted with a pain that mimicked his wife's. "Do something," he roared at Caro.

Caro did the only thing she could. She took the knife

238

from the sheath at her thigh and pressed the point of it directly into Rexford's chest. "She asked you to leave. You are upsetting everyone with all this furor. Now go."

Twice her size, Rexford could easily have disarmed her at such close quarters. Instead he stared at her with jaw-dropped astonishment, and backed up a step when she increased the pressure.

"Go." Caro took a step forward, again increasing the pressure. They moved like that toward the door, one step at a time, until Rexford had backed into the hall. Over Rexford's shoulder Caro located Tag leaning back against the far wall. "Please close the door, Tag," she said calmly.

Tag obeyed with a resigned shake of his head. "Caro, you have to stop taking out that knife every time somebody annoys you." He reached out and gently drew it from her hand.

Caro didn't even look at him. She allowed her body one furious shudder, then put her index finger on Rexford's chest in place of the knife. "Rexford, your wife is going to have that baby whether you give her permission or not." Her hand trembled as her body had a heartbeat ago. "She is terrified and needs your help now more than she has ever needed it before."

"You admit she is having the baby. Why is she not in bed? Why is she standing against the wall?"

Caro drew herself up to her full height. "Your doctor is not here. Unless you can bring this child into the world yourself, we will have to do it in the only way I know." Her voice softened. "Believe me, it is a better way. I have given her an herb tea to ease the pain. She is doing very well."

Before Rexford could speak, Tag put his hand on his friend's shoulder. "The Shawnee medical practices are regarded very highly in America. Even white men have been known to seek them out."

Rexford's face crumpled. His eyes reflected his naked

emotion. "I love her more than my life." In a voice that cracked with the tortured words, he asked, "She's not going to die, is she?"

"I am sure she isn't." Caro bit her lip. For all his emotion, Rexford was a strong man and deserved to know the truth. "I am afraid I cannot be as certain about the baby. It is coming too soon."

Rexford winced and buried his face in his hands. Tag tightened his grip on Rexford's shoulder, but eased it when Caro frowned at him. Rexford would find his own strength and share it with his wife.

Finally Rexford looked up, his words no more than a whispered plea. "How can I help? She won't even let me in the room."

Caro put her hand on his arm. "She won't let you in the room because she knew you would behave exactly as you did, and she doesn't have the strength to deal with your outburst."

"What can I do?"

Caro relaxed. "You can go in there and tell her she is important to you. Tell her you will keep her and care for her no matter what happens."

"You will let me go in now?"

"I want you to."

His face clouded with doubt. "But I thought men weren't supposed to . . . I don't know if I can."

"I will tell you when it is time to leave. Until then, the little one may sense the strength of the spirits in the room. His life may depend on how hard he is willing to fight for it. My people believe we can share our strength even with the unborn."

Rexford's jaw tightened. He squared his shoulders, took a step, and put his hand on the knob of the closed door. Before opening it, he turned and looked at Tag. "Stay here, will you, Tag? I may need your strength." He shook his head. "God damn it, I would never have bedded her if I knew how terrified I would be at this moment.''

Without waiting for Tag's promise to stay, he opened the door and marched into the room.

Tag watched him go, then looked questioningly at Caro. ''Shouldn't you go in there?''

Caro glanced into the room and saw Rexford put his arm around his wife and begin to speak with his face close to hers. ''No. He can help her now far more than I.''

Tag stepped closer. ''Thank you, Caro. Thank you for helping my friends.''

''They are good people.''

''You are good.'' Tag took her hand and looked into her eyes. ''Did you mean it? Will she be all right?''

Caro pulled back from his touch. ''Do you think I would lie to him about a thing like that?''

Tag refused to release her hand. ''No.'' A faint grin replaced his intense expression. ''Cut him a bit with a knife perhaps, but not lie to him.'' He brushed back an unruly tendril of hair that had tumbled across Caro's cheek.

She felt again the weight of the unaccustomed hairstyle. No wonder her head felt heavy and off center. Reclaiming her hands, she reached up and began to draw out the hairpins.

Tag clasped her wrists and lowered her hands to her sides. ''Here, allow me. I may not be able to help in there, but at least I know how to take down a woman's hair.'' He proceeded to take out the pins one by one and drop them into Caro's waiting hand. As he released each section, he let it flow through his fingers all the way to end, drawing the tension from Caro's head and neck.

She lifted her chin and tilted her head back to savor the flow of sensation. He stared down into her eyes, his warm breath caressing her cheek. She couldn't stifle a soft moan of pleasure.

Even after he had released the last pin, he continued to run his hand up the back of her neck, massaging her scalp and letting his hand drift through her hair. The tip of his tongue appeared between his lips. His eyes softened. "I should not be thinking what I am at such a time."

"Life is very precious at such moments." Too precious even to breathe, Caro thought.

Tag seemed to echo the sentiment, standing motionless looking into her eyes, the pads of his fingertips just a whispered caress on her scalp.

"Excuse me, miss." The twang of Sally's familiar voice shattered the moment. "We were talking in the kitchen and they all agreed I should be the one to help. I been with my mother five times already and not too long until number six. I've brung the water and some nice fresh linens."

Caro turned and smiled at the maid, who stood patiently holding a basin of water, a stack of snow-white linens draped over one arm. "Thank you, though we won't need hot water for a while yet."

"This is cool, miss, because birthin's hard work."

Though reluctant to disturb the couple inside the bedroom, Caro knew the young maid was right. A cool cloth would feel soothing to Amanda and give Rexford something to do.

Reluctantly, she followed the maid into the room. Rexford sat in a chair next to Amanda, clutching his wife's hand and whispering soft words. He turned to look as Caro and the maid entered. His eyes had a desperate, help-me expression when he looked up at her, but he had sense enough to show only gentle concern when he turned back to his wife.

He took the basin of water from the maid and carefully squeezed out the cloth before handing it to his wife. Fine beads of perspiration had begun to form on her forehead, and she accepted the soothing material gratefully.

After checking and finding Amanda's progress satisfactory, Caro told the maid she would send for her when the time came, and returned to the corridor to wait with Tag,

but he had never learned the art of patience. At unpredict-
able intervals, he would turn from her to pace the length
of the hall and stomp his way back to ask again, "Do you
think it will be much longer?"

His abrupt movements destroyed her serenity. Eventually, she left him to do his pacing alone, and went to sit
cross-legged in a corner of the bedroom. Time passed.
Amanda's pain became unremitting and she was unable to
smother the tortured moans. Rexford's face turned the color
of cold ashes, and Caro finally yielded to his plea that he
be allowed to help Amanda to the bed.

"Go," Caro said to him, "and send for Sally. It won't
be long now."

He hesitated as if he might debate this with her. Caro
ignored the hesitation and walked to the window to give
him a last few private moments with his wife.

Caro turned back in time to see him fling open a connecting door to the next room and storm through it. "Tag,"
he shouted, "Tag, get in here."

After that things progressed rapidly. Amanda strained
and screamed. She followed the scream with a jagged plea.
"No, not me. The baby. Take care of the . . . ahhhhhh . . .
the baby."

The baby's head appeared. Caro moved quickly to twist
the shoulders into position. The tiny form shot into her
waiting hands. Fearing the worst, Caro turned so her body
would conceal the child's condition.

Amanda had fought valiantly for her baby's life and she
refused to be denied. "My baby." She fought to sit up. "Is
he . . . is she . . .."

"It is a little boy," Caro said. *A very still little boy.*
Behind her she heard Rexford burst into the room. "Tend
to your wife," she said sharply. "Don't let her sit up."
Quickly she cleared the mucus from the infant's nose and
mouth. *Breathe*, she commanded silently. *Breathe.*

Beside her she heard Sally gasp. "He's not—"

243

"Quiet," Caro commanded the girl. "Breathe." She spoke aloud this time with the power of every tense muscle behind the whispered word. The infant shuddered in her hands.

"Marcus." Amanda called her husband's name in a voice that held all the anguish of every woman who had ever lost a child. "Do something. Do something for the baby."

Marcus came and stood by Caro's shoulder. "Breathe, dammit, breathe."

The room echoed the indrawn breaths of the watchers and nothing, nothing at all from the too-still infant.

Caro looked up at Marcus, knowing he would see the torment and despair in her eyes.

"No!" Rexford's rage reverberated through the room.

Chapter Fourteen

Caro heard Rexford's cry. Heard not the pain, but the rage. The fury transported her back to the campfires of home to the story she had heard so often about the man the chief had chosen to be her husband. About the rage that gave him life.

With an effort she blocked out the sight of Rexford towering over her, his hands clenched as if he would bring the roof down upon them. She retreated into herself and allowed her own anger to consume her. Through a fiery haze she looked at the almost weightless form in her hands and cursed in the language of her people. "Breathe, you worthless, lazy, miserable creature. Breathe."

"Breathe." With trembling hands she raised the baby to her mouth and forced her own breath into his body. "Breathe." The babe ignored her shouted command. Again she breathed her fury into his lifeless form. Again. And again.

He trembled with her anger. She raised her head to curse again and felt it, a shudder from his tiny body. He drew his own first ragged breath.

Awestruck, she held him in unsteady hands and waited for a few seconds of eternity. The child drew another breath without the stuttered hesitation. His body warmed in her hands. This time his naked chest rose visibly.

Time ceased to exist. There was only the whispered sound of indrawn breaths. From beside her Caro could hear

Amanda and Rexford, like her, drawing each breath with the new life.

"Aaa." The sound came so faintly it might have been the scrape of fabric, except that no one had moved in the still room. It came again on the next exhalation, unmistakably the first hint of an infant's cry.

"Aaa-laa." It came again. The most beautiful sound Caro had ever heard, the angry cry of an infant. This time the baby thrashed with twig-like arms and legs. Caro looked up.

Rexford stood motionless, staring at her as if he had seen the face of God. "He's alive."

"He's alive," Amanda echoed in the same awestruck voice. She smiled. "And very angry."

Rexford held out his hands as if he would take the baby, then drew them back quickly. "What . . . what now?"

Except for breathing, the still-wet infant had little to attract even the most devoted father. Long and thin as a birch branch with a bulbous head, he continued to wail. "Take him, Sally," Caro said to the young maid, who had not moved since Rexford entered the room.

Sally accepted him into a spotless white cloth, and carried the baby across the room to the table.

Rexford looked momentarily bereft.

"Go with her," Caro said with a smile, "while I tend to your wife. I promise Sally will make him quite presentable."

Rexford hesitated, then hurried after Sally like an eager puppy.

Caro turned her attention to Amanda. One of Amanda's hands still covered her mouth, but she had relaxed back against the pillows. Her face had regained a faint hint of color. "My baby. He is . . . will he be all right?"

"I am not—" Caro knew she shouldn't raise false hopes, but she felt a certainty as absolute as the morning's foreboding had been. "I am sure he will."

Amanda scarcely noticed Caro's ministrations. Though Sally and Rexford blocked her view of the child, Amanda watched every move they made and smiled at the chance comments drifting across the room. Finally, Caro bundled away the soiled linens and covered Amanda with a light sheet. "Lord Rexford," she called, "I believe your wife would like to meet her son."

Rexford introduced his son to his wife, and seconds later remembered the friend who had waited with him through the torturous hours. "Elmgrove," he shouted, startling both Amanda and the baby. "Elmgrove," he repeated, this time shouting in a whisper, "get in here and meet my son."

As if only waiting for the invitation, Tag, carrying a bottle of amber liquid and two glasses in one hand, strolled through the connecting door with a bounce to his stride.

Rexford met him halfway across the room. "I have a son, Tag."

Tag used his free hand to clap Rexford on the back. "So I heard." Despite Rexford's attempts to guide him toward Amanda and the child, Tag remained rooted in place, looking at Caro. "What happened? What did you do?"

Rexford released his grip on Tag's arm. "Yes. What did you do?"

Caro flushed, remembering her shocking anger, and wondered if she could explain. "I thought of the man I was to have married. He never should have lived."

Tag's brow furrowed, but he gave a soft laugh. "Precisely my opinion. Big ugly brute, I thought he was."

Caro ignored the light comment. "My people often tell the story of his birth. His mother, Calling Dove, was making a journey with Tecumseh when the infant chose to arrive. Tecumseh was a great chief, but not a patient man. He grew angry at having the journey interrupted and kept storming into the hut to tell Calling Dove to hurry."

"Fortunately we are more patient than Tecumseh," Tag said to Marc. "She will eventually tell us what happened

247

here. She just sometimes has to go back several generations to make her point.''

Caro ignored the interruption. "Tecumseh waited for many hours, and on one of his visits to the hut, the babe arrived. Like your son, the babe refused to breathe. Already angry at the delay, Tecumseh erupted into a rage at having wasted so much time on a child who refused to breathe. He seized the baby and reviled it as I did, blowing his own air into the child's mouth. The child returned.''

"Like my son," Rexford said reverently.

"Yes. I thought . . .'' Caro hesitated, knowing she hadn't really thought, and trying now to add reason to her actions. "I knew there was nothing more I could do. I thought if I got angry enough, the spirits might return him.''

"Like Panther Breath," Tag said.

"Breath of a Panther," Caro corrected. "He is called that because he lives with Tecumseh's breath—Tecumseh's name means Panther in the Sky.''

Tag laughed. "Without even knowing the story, I thought his name remarkably apt.''

Rexford didn't even smile. "I am not sure I understand, Miss Fe—Caro, but you gave me my son. I will be forever in your debt.''

"That is not necessary. I only did—''

"Enough," Tag declared. "This is far too serious a discussion for such an occasion. We haven't even toasted your heir.'' With a small amount of juggling, he succeeded in pouring two glasses of brandy from the bottle in his hand. He handed the bottle to Caro, then passed a glass to Rexford, and the two men moved to the bedside.

There they toasted the child, the mother, and the child again. Finally, Amanda looked up with a weary smile. "You gentlemen may want to drink all night, but I believe I will sleep.''

Rexford looked around slightly startled. "Here?''

"Of course.''

"But . . . but where will I sleep?"

Amanda gave a small chuckle and closed her eyes. "Just for tonight, Marcus, I am not going to worry about that."

"Naturally not. I will handle everything." Donning his customary air of command, Rexford began issuing orders for a cot and whatever else he needed for his comfort.

Caro smiled. Clearly she would not have to worry about Amanda or the baby tonight. Quietly she slipped from the room.

Caro's departure left Tag awkward and oddly bereft. He said a polite good night to Rexford and Amanda and hastened after her. "Caro, wait." He heard the front door close, and realized he had waited too long.

Surely she didn't expect him just to walk to his room and sleep? He had scarcely seen her all day. They had to talk about . . . for the life of him he couldn't remember what they had to discuss.

Ignoring the uncomfortable, nagging incompleteness, he turned toward his room. He actually got as far as sitting on the bed and removing one boot before he acknowledged he had lost whatever battle he was fighting. He wanted to go after her. Pacing the room and pretending he didn't made no sense.

A blanket. If she planned to spend the night outside again, he could at least bring her a blanket.

Outside, Tag's restlessness disappeared. The silver moonlight made the sky twilight-bright, and the cool dark smells soothed his ragged nerves. No wonder Caro sought solace in the night.

Without haste he followed the path she had taken last night. He would find her. He smiled. Or more likely, she would appear from behind a tree demanding to know why he was clomping through the woods like a white man.

After a comfortable stroll, he reached the dovecote. Drenched in moonlight, in the exact center of the clearing, Caro sat with her legs crossed and her head thrown back.

Tag knew better than to intrude. He had seen her seek this private time often enough to know that she would ignore him until she had renewed herself. He spread the blanket on the ground, content just to be near her.

He sat for an hour or more and watched. Occasionally she would raise her arms and chant softly in the language of her people. More often, she simply sat motionless, part of the night. Tag had no words for his thoughts, just a sense of peace and fullness. Finally, she stood with the ease of a drifting cloud.

She showed no surprise at seeing him, just walked toward him and didn't stop until he stood and wrapped his arms around her and she rested her head on his chest.

Tag could have held her that way until dawn.

She raised her head. "I can't come back to the house with you tonight. I need . . ." She waved her hand at the night around them.

"I know. I brought you a blanket. Sit with me for a few minutes." He took her hand and led her to the coverlet he had taken from his bed. She sat and he dropped down beside her.

For a long time they sat in silence. She looked like she had never known a moment's discontent. "Are you angry with me?" he said at last.

Even in the dim light he could see her slight frown. "Angry? Why would I be?"

He silently cursed himself for spoiling the moment. "Because of dinner, when I refused to be your husband."

"Ah," she said, and nodded with the memory. "It seems such a long time ago. I was angry, but I am not now. I assume you have your reasons."

"Thank you. Truthfully, they don't seem so real right now."

"You are here. So I know it is not because you dislike me. Can you tell me what I have done?"

"Not what you've done. What you are."

Caro's jaw tightened. "Because I am so different. Because—"

"No. Never say that." Tag shook his head violently. "Because you are a woman who could love a man completely. The way Amanda loves Marc."

"And that is bad?"

Tag felt his own jaw tighten and the muscles in his face harden. "For me it is a burden I will never accept again. Never."

"Tell me why."

The night had drained the horror from the memories. Tag could picture the incidents but couldn't feel them tearing at his gut. Words would bring it all back. "Another time, perhaps. I have felt too much today. Right now, I would just like to . . ."

She looked at him, her face utterly serene. "What would you like to do?"

"I would like to hold you until you fall asleep."

"I would like that too." Soundlessly she relaxed into his arms.

Tag lay back, drawing her with him. She stirred several times before settling comfortably with her head on his shoulder. He wrapped his other arm around her and watched a wispy cloud drift across the moon. He held her without passion, content to bury his chin in her hair and drink in her clean lavender scent. Gradually, her breathing grew more regular.

Tag's last conscious thought before sleeping was that he would return to the house as soon as he could think of a way of moving without waking her.

"Mmmm." Tag moaned and the sound woke him; the sound and the knowledge that something was terribly wrong. Without conscious thought, his body shifted and he understood. Still drugged with sleep, he understood, but could not keep himself from straining with his hips toward the softness. "Mmmm."

251

Exhaustion, the brandy, the lunacy of moonlight had convinced him he could lie with Caro without passion. While he slept, without the conscious control of his mind, his body had taken full advantage of the situation.

He had turned on his side and insinuated one leg between hers. The movement had pushed her short dress to the tops of her thighs, silver white in the waning light of the moon. His hand cupped her breast and he had wakened at the moment any normal man would have spread those thighs and moved between them.

And he was all too normal.

He had only to roll over and claim her for his wife to wake up like this every morning. His hand, which he had drawn back in horror when he first woke, hovered inches above the delicious temptation, the dark line where her short dress met her thigh. His groin tightened with the thought of following that line to the juncture between her legs.

He would stroke her there until she began to stir and arch toward him, searching for more with languorous sleepy movements. Slowly, ready to reclaim it instantly if she woke, he lowered his hand to her exposed thigh. It was incredibly soft and smooth. He held his breath and savored the way the flesh warmed under his palm. He could not imagine wanting to lie with any other woman. Could not imagine wanting any other woman for his wife.

His wife. The possibility chilled him.

Caro. Not some cold woman who would produce an heir, dispose of his excess income, and spend as much time away from him as possible, but the woman he wanted to wake with a whisper-soft touch every morning. His wife. The thought thrilled and terrified him.

Rexford said he was insane to believe he could never dare to let a woman love him. Unlucky and a little demented on the topic of women and love. Unlucky, but not some kind of Jonah bringing destruction.

If he could believe that . . .

Caro. Caro, whose love could give breath to a stillborn child. Caro, with enough love to fill the emptiness that had consumed him the day his mother died and had never quite left him.

If he could believe Marc's assurances, he could reach out and claim all this as his own. He slipped his thumb under the hem of Caro's dress to the crease between her leg and body. If he followed that line to the nest of curls his thumb sought, he would have no choice but to make her his wife. He would wake up like this every morning. She belonged to him.

He let his hand stroke more firmly, less concerned now that he might wake her.

"Ohhhh." At first Tag thought the sound came from him, but he looked up and found Caro watching him, her eyes wide. "Don't stop."

Don't stop. He hadn't even started except in his mind. But he abandoned any attempt at restraint, letting his hand glide freely over her abdomen, just brushing the top of the fringe of curls. *Damn, no man could ever anticipate the smoothness of a woman's body.* His woman's body to touch like this every morning. "Caro," he whispered.

"Have you finally come to me as a husband?"

Yes, he had come to her as a husband. He answered with his touch. A lover's touch. Letting his hand glide over her breasts, to the valley between them, and then down lightly over the curls to rest motionless between her thighs. A husband's touch.

His wife.

His wife, and he was claiming her for the first time in an open meadow, like a farm boy with some disreputable slut. She deserved better. If it killed him, she deserved better. "Not yet, my love, but soon."

"Oh." Her voice held all the disappointment he felt.

"Soon," he promised, "but now . . ." He couldn't leave

her yet. "But for now, just open your legs and let me lie between them for a moment. I promise I won't ..." He knew his promise had no meaning for her. She had no reservations. She would welcome him into her body with the same warm openness she welcomed his touch. But he would not take her for the first time like an animal in the field.

With his knee he jostled her legs apart. Shifting his weight to that knee, he moved between her legs and lowered his weight. She gave a small gasp of surprise, and her thighs tightened just for a moment as if she would shut him out. "It's all right," he assured her, and the rejection turned into an embrace. She accepted him into the cradle of her body.

Safe with the material of his breeches between them, he let his hardness search for the entrance he needed, pressing himself into her with ever-increasing intensity.

For a moment she lay there too startled to move. Then her face brightened. "Like the kiss," she whispered in a breathless voice.

"Yes, like the kiss." This time when he drew back to rock toward her again, she rose to meet him. Again he drew back and again she met him in the rhythm of his deepest kiss. "Yes," he whispered. "Oh, yes."

"Ohhhh." She began to moan, her breath coming against his cheek in soft pants. "Ohhh." The cradle of her thighs widened, seeking more.

He slipped his hand between them to the welcoming moistness, reveling in the way her body sought his touch. "Yes," he whispered. "Come to me." Her eyes widened and she convulsed around his hand. "Yes," he whispered, kissing her lightly on each fluttering eyelid.

Gradually, her body quieted and relaxed under him. Slowly, he raised his head to find her smiling at him.

"Was that ... ?"

He laughed. "No, my love, that was not all there is. But

it is all we will do for now.'' With a final brush of his fingers, Tag disentangled himself from Caro and dropped into a sitting position beside her, his knees drawn up almost to his chin. He carefully averted his gaze while she rearranged her short dress. The rising sun had tinted the puffy clouds a soft pink, and the entire world had taken on a rosy glow.

A tuneful whistling interrupted Tag's reverie. Across the clearing a stocky young man appeared, shambling toward the dovecote. His appearance produced a rush of blood that caused even Tag's fingertips to tingle. If Tag had followed his insane inclination a few moments ago, the lad would have discovered them on the ground rutting like mindless dogs. Never again, he vowed.

After today there would be no need. The shame disappeared in the delicious contemplation that sometime today—perhaps not until tonight—he would claim her for his wife in deed as he had in his heart an hour ago. ''As of now, my love, you must be a proper English lady, so I suggest you make yourself presentable.'' He nodded in the direction of the approaching lad.

Caro had already risen to her knees. ''I saw him.'' She brushed at the skirt of her dress. ''Amanda must have sent for him to tend to the birds.'' She glided to her feet. ''I must go and help. I am sure she would want me to.''

Tag gave a soft smile. Only Caro would come this close to being caught making love in an open field and then worry about who was going to feed a flock of birds. ''Of course. I will wait for you here, if you don't mind. I like my birds either on a dinner plate or two hundred yards away.''

She did not even turn to favor that comment with the smile it deserved. Tag rested back on his arms and surrendered to the pleasure of just watching her move. She flowed across the clearing with the easy grace of one born to move with the breeze.

His wife, and for the rest of his life he would bask in her warmth. He would wait as he waited now for the first glimpse of her smile. He shuddered at the thought of the terrible mistake he had almost made.

Within a few days, he might have gone to London, determined not to look back. He might have married before the year was done. Some cold beauty like Isobel the Icicle. Beautiful, dark-haired Isobel, attractive only because she would bear his heir and never love him. Hell, she wouldn't even grieve overmuch at his death so long as he left his fortune behind.

Caro wouldn't care a fig for his title. It would probably take him months even to coax her into letting people address her as Lady Caro. He smiled and watched the flock of birds circling in the morning light above her head while she chatted amiably with the lad who had come to tend them. She wouldn't care about his title, but she would love him.

He clenched his fist at the realization of how much that mattered. Until a few hours ago, he had never given a thought to the emptiness he had held at bay for years. Then, with a decision as simple as resting his hand on her thigh and turning toward her warmth, he had filled that emptiness with the certainty she would love him.

As he loved her.

What a beautiful, surprising morning. His heart soared with the rise of a bird toward the red-streaked rising sun. He loved her. Perhaps he had since their wedding night. Since the moment she had looked at him with her wide, innocent eyes and threatened to leave the *wegiwa* and find somebody to teach her how to love him as he needed to be loved.

His muscles tensed with the need to spring to his feet, run to her, and share this astonishing insight. He checked the move. He would run to her, probably take her in his arms, and then . . . Of course, first he would have to knock the country lad unconscious before he let his hands slide down and raise the hem of her dress. Before he eased her to the ground and . . .

He laughed. Definitely not proper thoughts about a lady who would one day be a countess. With a mock frown, he forced himself to make a few slight changes to the fantasy.

With all his English dignity, he would ask her to join him in the sitting room after breakfast—properly dressed, if you don't mind. With maybe a few extra corsets in case his unruly hands had fantasies of their own. There he would propose to her in a fashion worthy of her station. He would use the same speech he had planned for some cold future wife, only in this case, they would not be merely formal phrases. He would proclaim his love with his heart full of memories of the hundred times he might have said he loved her—if only he had realized it then.

The country boy trilled out a musical whistle, and the flying birds circled toward the cote. Caro watched, her head thrown back, her loose hair gilded by the sunlight. So beautiful. So full of love for even those worthless creatures.

Perhaps, Tag thought, by the time he met her in the sitting room, he would even have regained enough control to promise to wait for a proper ceremony before possessing her. Of course, that thought would go up in flames if she so much as put her ungloved hand on his arm. No need to wait for a proper ceremony. She had married him months ago in her Indian ceremony and never wavered in her willingness to let him possess her. Anytime, anyplace.

He smiled at her willingness to open herself to him at his slightest touch. No need to wait. He had married her in his heart an hour ago, and he would bury himself in her before the next sunrise.

A cloud passed over the sun, bringing with it a sudden chill. Doubt assailed Tag. Had he believed Marc's assurances too easily? Believed them selfishly because he wanted to so badly?

"No." Tag whispered the word aloud, but the tiny hairs on his neck that had risen with the thought refused to lie down. An hour ago he had responded without thought. Responded not to Marc's assurances, but to his own pounding need to drive himself into Caro's waiting body. Responded to his own lust.

Suppose he was right and Marc was wrong.

"No," he said again, and stood to wait for Caro. He would not surrender to the fear. He would not let a childhood fear rob him of this one last chance at happiness. "Dammit, Caro, hurry." She would banish all his doubts.

Tag glanced at the sky, expecting to see a mountain of clouds swirling in to consume the sun. But the lone cloud had passed, a solitary threat, quickly dispatched by the sun.

"Good-bye, Jeb," Caro called. "I will be here tomorrow."

The country boy, who had already started back the way he had come, turned and acknowledged her words with a slight wave and a nod in Tag's direction.

The sight of the lad's departing back freed Tag to seek Caro in the grain shed to which she had turned for some housekeeping task. With each step he practiced the formal words he would use. *Miss Fenton, perhaps you would oblige me by joining me in the green sitting room after breakfast.* He smiled in anticipation of her blushing confusion as she tried to interpret his message.

She turned and smiled as he entered. "I am sorry we have been so long." She hurried across the small room and stopped so close in front of him that her warm breath caressed his chin. She rested one hand on his shoulder. "I . . . I thought this morning you would make me your wife."

Tag caressed her cheek, "Don't worry, little one, you will not have to wait long, but we will do it in the proper English fashion, beginning with the proper words." He straightened to a formality he couldn't feel but knew such an important occasion merited. "Miss Fenton, perhaps you would oblige me by joining me in the green sitting room after breakfast. I will have something important to ask you."

"And then . . . ?" Caro looked up at him, her eyes shining with hope.

"Just wait."

She nodded. Then her eyes danced with mischief and she imitated his formal manner. "Then perhaps you would oblige me with a small favor now."

Though his body had already hardened at her touch, Tag maintained his starched manner and officious tone. "Naturally your slightest wish is my command. What can I do for you?"

"Kiss me."

"Pardon me?" Tag tried to look properly affronted, though his hand moved automatically to her waist and his breath caught in his throat.

"I have been thinking all this time. Though I liked everything you did to me"—her face turned the softest shade of scarlet—"you barely kissed me."

Tag's other hand trembled as it found the familiar curve of her hip. Too well he remembered what he had done to her only a short time ago. He abandoned all pretense at coolness and could not control the raspy sound of his voice. "If I had kissed you as I wanted to, nothing could have stopped me—"

"But I thought . . ." She spoke so close he could almost feel the movement of her lips on his chin. "I thought you wanted me."

"I want you." His voice ached with his hunger. Over her shoulder he could see the stacked sacks of grain that made too inviting a mattress. "But not here. Not like—"

Her tongue darted out and moistened her lips. "You have kissed me before. It tasted like—"

Tag drew her to him so he could look past her, feeling

just the soft tickle of her hair on his cheek. Perhaps she would have the control to keep him from taking her right here with the soft coo of the birds in the background and the heavy scent of grain in the air. He had never known her to break a promise. "I will kiss you, if . . ." Her body molded to his and he knew he would kiss her no matter what she answered. "If you swear no matter what happens, no matter what you feel, you will not let me raise your dress." He made his own private vow she would never again wear that dress outside their bedroom.

"That would be so bad?" She turned her face so he could feel her lips against his cheek.

"Swear." He eased his head back so he could meet those lips.

"I swear." Her lips met his, warm and welcoming.

Slowly, he reminded himself, just enough to awaken a hunger she would carry all day. Just enough so . . . Just enough so the world exploded in sensation. Her lips parted immediately, welcoming his searching tongue. Dimly he realized he had walked her backward two steps so the sacks of grain braced her thighs, pressing her body against him as if they had been molded together from the same mound of clay.

He ran his hand up her back to grip her head and angle it slightly. She began to make a soft purring noise in her throat and moaned softly. Her lips moved against his, inviting him, drawing him in. Fiercely he stroked her back, then dropped his hands to her buttocks to lift her higher against him.

"No." The muffled sound against his lips sounded like no. He ignored it. She twisted her face away from him. "No." She said the word emphatically and distinctly this time.

"No, what?"

"My dress. You're raising my dress. My promise . . ."

Tag glanced over her shoulder at his hands clutching her

buttocks. They were indeed raising her dress. "Forget your
promise. Take the goddamn dress off. If we don't finish
this thing right now, we will both go mad." Tag relaxed
his hold to help her rid herself of the cumbersome thing.

Instead of cooperating, she began to struggle against him.
"No, I don't think—"

"Dammit, Caro."

As he turned his head to curse, she took advantage of
the opportunity to twist away from him and take several
quick steps across the room. She stood there, her arms
crossed on her chest, breathing in rapid pants. "I'm not
sure I understand why, but you said . . . you said the
dress . . ."

"I know what I said." He turned and dropped down to
sit on the burlap bags of grain. "You don't have to explain.
Just wait for me outside. I'll survive." *And in a few days,
I may even be able to breathe again.* Caro obediently
turned and left. Tag took a series of deep breaths. In a few
minutes he found he could stand without clenching his
teeth.

No wonder she had made him abandon his vow never to
let another woman love him. She could make him abandon
his left leg just by moistening her lower lip.

He took a final deep breath and stepped outside to find
her standing comfortably with her weight on one foot,
watching something in the sky. She fell into step beside
him. Did she even remember that he had invited her to
receive his proposal immediately after breakfast?

No harm in being certain. He certainly didn't want to
wind up proposing to a parlor maid come to dust the occasional tables. Halfway across the clearing he stopped her
with just the lightest touch of his fingers on her arm. She
turned toward him so both of them stood sideways to the
woods leading to the house. "Caro, I do hope you remember—"

From the corner of his eye, Tag caught the blur of motion. A dark shadow bounding across the clearing toward them.

"No!" Caro screamed the word, and used a thrust of her hand against his shoulder to give impetus to her leap toward the moving shape.

Tag's world came to a frozen halt. No time. No sound. Just the paralyzing reenactment of the most terrible day of his life.

Eight years old. Standing with his mother on the lawn. The monstrous shape. The ferocious noise. Her hands thrusting him behind her. "Run, Tag, run." He hadn't run, just stood there screaming while the snarling beast launched itself at his mother. Her screams mingled with his. The sound of snapping bones, tearing flesh. The rusty smell of blood. Screaming. Screaming. Screaming.

"Noooo." The sound of Tag's own scream tore through his paralysis. Caro was already on the ground, her arms around the huge beast's neck. Twenty years of rage and frustration gave Tag the strength of a colossus. With a shriek of primitive fury, he reached down, tore her from the beast, and literally threw her behind him.

Teeth clenched, he launched himself at the beast, clasping it around the neck and wrestling it to the ground. The animal struggled and emitted soft growls, not nearly as loud as the ravaging sounds etched on Tag's soul.

The animal wiggled free and retreated with a series of yelps. Tag attacked again, determined to tear it apart with his bare hands. Again he fell to the ground in a flurry of sound and fur.

"Tag! Tag!" Dimly Tag became aware of something pounding him about the head and shoulders. Someone calling his name. "Tag, stop. You'll hurt him." The red haze engulfing him lessened. The dog growled, but softly. Tag's death-grip slackened.

The animal pulled free and bounded away to drop to the ground a few feet away with a bewildered whine. Caro circled Tag and sank down next to the dog, running her caressing hands over him, and speaking softly in her own language. Finally she looked up at Tag, as confused as the bewildered animal. "You tried to hurt him. Why did you try to hurt him?"

Tag shook his head to clear the fog. "He was attacking. He was . . . You shouted."

"He's Rexford's new dog. He likes the birds." Caro's face assumed a pleading expression. "He doesn't hurt them. He just bounds around and drives them into a frenzy. Amanda said . . ."

Tag backed away. He didn't need any more explanations. He'd been a fool. Rexford's dog, a playful, gentle creature had—Tag turned and stalked away. The creature had come just in time to show him what a fool he'd almost been.

For a few brief hours he'd believed he could let a woman love him. There had been no danger this time, but the incident had shown him what he'd known in his heart all the time. The adventurous spirit that had led him to America, to Waterloo, and to a dozen other places was as much a part of him as his blond hair. He would be the worst kind of villain to let Caro love him.

With her quick reactions and instinctive courage, she would always step between him and any danger. And someday she would pay for that love and courage with her life. She would die, bravely like his mother, or needlessly like his fiancée.

Tag reached the edge of the woods and looked up with a start. *Fool,* he berated himself. He had reached the edge of the woods—the wrong edge.

He would have to turn and walk back across the clearing to reach the house. Back past the spot where Caro still huddled on the ground, stroking the dog. He would have to stop and say, "Excuse me, Miss Fenton, I do believe this morning has been a terrible mistake. If we could just . . ."

Surely he deserved the time to splash some cold water on his face and maybe have a glass of stiff brandy before facing that scene.

With all the dignity of a king, he began the trek across the clearing. He passed within a few feet of her, but merely nodded. Let her make of it what she would. He needed some time.

Mentally he practiced the words he would say. "Caro, this morning was a dreadful mistake."

Chapter Fifteen

Caro clutched the dog and watched Tag's retreating form. Explanations too rapid for words galloped through her mind.

He was afraid of dogs. But he had attacked the dog.

He hated dogs. But she had seen him scarcely notice when the dog brushed his leg in the library.

He'd thought the dog was going to . . . She couldn't finish that sentence. The frenetic animal would have done nothing more than lick them both to death.

Reluctantly, she gave up. Whatever happened was simply something too English for her to understand.

But she had understood Tag's touch on her body under the tree.

He wanted her. He had covered her with his body and slid his fingers into her until her womb cried out with a hunger for his seed. The memory began an aching pulse between her legs. His body had throbbed with a need as deep as her own, but he had shuddered and eased himself away from her. Perhaps Englishmen had to prove their manhood by controlling even such natural things as this. Only his promise that she would not have to wait long kept her from running after him.

To live in his world, she would have to understand his customs.

She rocked back on her heels and looked at the expanse of green around her. Tag's world. It would soon be hers.

For the first time, it did not seem new and strange. The open spaces, and well-tended fields had a formal beauty of their own. She could learn to love it as she had loved her own land.

She would have to accustom herself to many things. Forests that extended for only a few miles rather than forever. Roads that gashed the landscape. Walls and hedges that penned the fields. But . . .

But even the small stone houses had a feeling of permanence she had longed for. Tag told her some people had never been more than a few miles from the house where they were born. She would grow old with the same trees that greeted her as a new bride. Her children would welcome their children on the same paths she had walked when only dreaming of children.

Yes. She could live in this strange land because Tag would be at her side, and his voice glowed with warmth when he talked of his home. Their children would love his home as he did. They would grow up in the same house as Tag's father and grandfather and great-grandfather. She would find more friends like Amanda and Marcus. She would . . .

The dog woofed impatiently, reminding Caro that Tag would not wait forever while she dreamed of being his wife. "Come on, Caesar," she said, keeping a tight grip on his ruff as she stood. "You have to go back to the house, and I have to go and become a proper Englishwoman."

She slipped into the house through a back door, shooing the dog before her. Nails clicking on the stone floor, he hurried off to where he usually spent the day. With furtive glances, she moved as silently on her bare feet as she would through the forest. If she planned to be a grand English lady, it wouldn't do to meet even a servant dressed as she was. She paused and brushed her tangled hair back from her face, and smiled at the futility of the gesture. Only Tag could want such a ragged creature.

266

Twice she pressed her back against the hard wall to avoid being seen by a scurrying maid, but she finally reached the hall leading to the bedchambers. From behind Amanda's closed door, she heard voices. Rexford's was firm and commanding, Amanda's softer but strong, and finally there was Tag's. He must be telling them of his plans.

Delighted at the prospect of seeing Tag again so soon, she raised her hand to knock, then hesitated. If he had come directly from the meadow, his clothes would be peppered with the same small flecks of grass she had tried to brush from her own. One glance and Rexford and Amanda would guess exactly how they had spent the night.

Caro imagined that knowing look, and knew she would flush with the warm memory of Tag's hands on her body. He would fumble for an explanation, though the truth would be as obvious as the rising sun. And perhaps Rexford, for all his talk of consummation, would be as shocked by her behavior as Tag had predicted.

She smiled and lowered her hand. She wanted this morning to be perfect. Just this once she would trust Tag and try to be the kind of woman he wanted for a wife. Cool and dignified.

She hurried to her room, changed into the nightgown the maid had left on the bed, rolled her own dress, and tucked it into her bundle. She could deal with it later. Momentarily satisfied, she glanced around, then laughed at her reflection in the pier glass.

Now she looked like a hoyden who had spent the night on the ground and hastily changed into a gown to fool the maid. And if she didn't banish that satisfied smile from her face, she would not fool even the most unimaginative servant.

A few minutes later, satisfied she had eliminated all traces of the most glorious morning of her life, she pulled the rope to summon the maid. Almost before Caro could settle into the bed she had hastily disarranged, Sally appeared, carrying a cup of hot chocolate and another new dress.

"Sally, could you help me dress, please? I must look absolutely perfect this morning."

"Of course, miss."

Absolutely perfect took about four times as long as Caro wanted to permit. She repeatedly quelled her impatience and allowed the chattering girl to fuss. Finally Caro sat before the dressing table in a blue wool dress, softer than anything she had ever seen in America. Would Tag even recognize the stranger who stared back at her from the glass with her hair piled on top of her head? She brushed her fingertips across her forehead as Tag had done when he swept her hair from her face.

With an apologetic smile at Sally, Caro loosened the edge of one curl so the loose wisp would invite his touch.

"Oh, no, miss."

"It's all right, Sally. I must hurry now." Caro glanced at the clock. It had been more than an hour. Surely Tag would be waiting impatiently. Men did not have to fuss with such an impossible number of buttons.

At the head of the stairs, Caro found a footman in crisp livery. A refined lady would not slink around by herself to find the correct room. "Can you show me to the green sitting room?"

"Of course, miss." His measured pace slowed her winged steps. She gave an inaudible sigh. She would learn decorum, even if she had to learn it from the servants.

"Right in there, miss." The young man pointed to an open door.

"Thank you." Caro paused and tilted her nose up as she had seen the English ladies on the ship do. A smile danced at the corners of her mouth. She might enter graciously, but in a moment she'd be in his arms.

Tag stood on the opposite side of the room. His rigid bearing and the tight set to his jaw stopped her before she'd taken her second step into the room. Her foot hovered in the air a fraction of a second too long. "Tag?"

"Come in."

Caro finished her step and closed the door behind her, knowing instinctively she didn't want to share this moment with anyone else. Her hand lingered on the doorknob and she had to open her mouth to breathe. The whoosh of air left her mouth stiff and dry. She couldn't have spoken even if her mind could have formed words.

For a long moment she stared at him across the empty silence. It was Tag, but not Tag. The man who had caressed her with his hands and his words had gone, leaving behind only an empty image of himself. Caro's heart pounded against the wall of her chest.

"Miss Fenton—Caro." His gaze darted away and his fists clenched as if it required a physical effort to force his eyes to look at her. "This morning was a mistake." The words had a wooden sound, as if they came from someplace outside him. "I can't be . . ." He drew a long shuddering breath, and impossibly, his bearing became even straighter. "I only waited long enough to tell you. I will be leaving for London immediately."

His words came from a long way off. The rest of the room disappeared until Caro could see only Tag's face. His moving lips. He continued to talk. She caught jagged phrases. ". . . should never have happened . . . know what you thought . . . so wrong . . . leaving . . . leaving . . . leaving."

Gradually Caro's senses cleared. The walls and furniture shifted back into view. The doorknob had turned wet and slippery under her clutching palm. "Why?" Her lips formed the word, but no sound came out.

"I have spoken with Marc and Amanda. They are terribly grateful to you for giving them their son. They have offered you a home here as long as you care to stay."

He paused. The clock ticked off seconds without mean-

269

ing. "I suggest you remain here until your grandfather is well enough to plan your entrance into society. Amanda will help." Again he paused, his gaze searching her face for a response. "Dammit, Caro, say something. Don't just stand there like you're carved from wood."

Not wood. Stone. Brittle stone that would crumble if she tried to move or speak. The only word she could think of screamed through her mind. *Why?* Calling on years of training in simply enduring, she fought to suppress the question that trembled on her lips.

He didn't want her. Why didn't matter. "Why?" she whispered, then louder because she had to know. "Why?"

"Please don't ask. You would not understand."

"I would try." She waited. The silence made the air so heavy her chest ached with the effort to breath.

Several times Tag looked as if he might speak. His facial muscles twitched as he formed and rejected words. Finally he turned his palms up in a small gesture. "Very well. I will tell you. You will not understand, and I will not discuss it." He walked to the window and turned to face her. "I am leaving because you love me."

"But . . ." But he had accepted her love and reveled in it.

"Years ago I vowed never to let another woman love me."

"But you have said you must have an heir. You must marry."

"I will marry, but I will choose a woman who will love my title and my fortune. A woman who will not care if I live or die."

"That makes no sense." She clamped her lips shut. She didn't understand because he didn't want her to. Something in her insisted she fight him, if only with ragged words. "Why? You were happy this morning. I could not be wrong about that."

"I was happy as a boy with a mother who loved me and

died because she did. Just as you would have died if a different dog had burst from those bushes.''

He sounded as if he believed what he said, but the morning had been only sunshine and life to Caro. ''There was no danger.''

''Not this time. But someday . . .'' His facial muscles tightened and his eyes looked behind her at some specter she could not see.

Caro held her breath and waited for him to explain what had changed him from the laughing man she knew to a stranger who spoke in wooden phrases.

''Very well,'' he said, as if she had prompted him. He continued to look at the wall behind her head. ''When I was eight, my mother and I went to the river. I dallied on the return. A dog burst from the bushes, exactly as Marc's dog did this morning, only this dog was rabid. My mother screamed for me to run, then threw herself between the dog and me. The beast tore her to pieces.''

His gaze found her again. ''I will never forget standing at her grave, knowing it should have been me they were lowering into the ground.''

''How awful.'' Caro longed to comfort him with her touch, but his rigid posture warned he would reject any advance. ''It was a horrible sight for a young boy, but I don't understand—''

''She died because she loved me.''

''But that was long ago. You were not responsible.''

He turned to the window and drew several long breaths before facing her again. ''I finally did believe that. At twenty I went to France. I thought it would be a lark to carry messages for the British. I thought I would live forever.''

This time Caro had to turn away from the naked pain in his eyes.

His voice came from behind her. ''There was a Frenchwoman. We planned to marry, but I was away the morning the French dragoons came for me. I was only half a mile away, but she refused to tell them where I had gone. I learned later that they'd beaten her to death trying to learn my whereabouts. She'd died needlessly. Even had they captured me, my friends would have gotten me away.''

"I'm sorry." The ritual words for grief seemed as inadequate as always.

"So am I. I vowed on her grave no woman would ever again die because she loved me."

Caro realized he thought he had explained why she would face the rest of her life without him. "What you have told me has nothing to do with now."

He looked at her with the eyes of a stranger. "I did not expect you to understand. Can you deny that you would try to protect me if I were in danger?"

"I deny that you would be responsible for what happened to me."

"But I would. Even if I retired to the country and lived without excitement, something would happen. You would do something very brave and very foolish as you did this morning when you stepped between me and that dog. I will not go through that again. Not even for you."

"I am not like the helpless women you have known."

He waved his hand in an abrupt gesture of dismissal. "Enough. We could put a thousand words to it, but it would change nothing." He glanced at the door and tugged at his gloves as if he would brush past her.

Where was her pride? She, who had been raised to face any torture with stoic indifference, was standing here longing to throw herself at his feet and beg him to stay with her. She needed anger, not whining. "Of course not. Because you want to leave. You lying English can always twist the past to suit your whims."

He stiffened as if she had struck him. The corners of his mouth whitened. "Believe as you will, Caro. I explained only because you insisted. Once you have adjusted to England you will find a man who—"

"Elmgrove, you are babbling." Caro pictured words chipped from a frozen lake. "You said you were going. Please go."

He drew out a leather purse. "Your grandfather left home with no purse. You may need this for . . . for whatever women need." He held the purse out to her. When she remained immobile, he set it on a side table with a melodic clinking.

Caro didn't think of coins, but of soft metal that could be pounded into arrowheads to pierce his cold heart. "You owe me nothing."

"I owe you . . . I just want . . ."

"You promised to bring me to England. You have done that. Now go."

His lips moved as if more words would change anything, but in the end, he did not speak. He just nodded and walked toward her. His steps had a funereal cadence.

Caro knew she had to move or block his passage. Her feet seemed rooted in the wooden floor. She gouged her fingernails into her palm, forcing herself to take the two shuffling steps that would move her from his path. *Go, go, go,* her mind shrieked, even as her fingers ached with the need to reach out and clutch at him.

Rigid as a lance, she stood while he moved past her, not even reacting to the caress of the air his passing produced. She stood listening to the sounds from the hall. The clatter of his boot heels upon the marble floor. The sharp bite of his words to the waiting servant. And finally, the solid thunk of the door closing on his back.

Alone. Alone to dissolve into a boneless bundle on the floor and sob every drop of moisture from her body.

With a vicious kick she banished the image of herself huddled on the floor. "Damn him." Damn him for turning her into a whimpering white woman.

Judy Veisel

She stamped across the room, snatching a porcelain shepherdess from a table as she passed. A string of French curses fueled her building rage. Whirling, she hurled the fragile figurine at the black slate fireplace. She didn't need him. She had never needed him.

She would do what she had come for and go back where she belonged. Back to a land where people did not say one thing with their bodies and another with their words.

Almost before the thought was born, Caro began to make her plans.

Rage would defeat her. She needed calm. Closing her eyes, she pictured herself as a warrior preparing for a great coup. She spread her arms and prayed for the guidance of the spirits.

Only when her breathing slowed and she felt a deep inner peace did she rise, knowing precisely what she would do. She would borrow a horse from Rexford, ride to her grandfather's house, and dispose of her murderous cousin. Only then could she put this unwelcoming country behind her.

The same young footman as before led her to Rexford's study. She entered and he rose from a sturdy leather chair. "Caro. Come in. You have spoken to Tag?"

"Yes. He left a short time ago. I will miss him. He was kind to me."

"I assure you that Amanda and I will do whatever we can to make your stay a pleasant one."

"That is good of you."

"If there is anything . . ." His anxious expression made her request almost too easy.

"I had hoped"—Caro struggled for just the right amount of wistfulness—"I might ride sometime today."

"Of course. Unfortunately, I will be occupied most of the day, but I will send a message to my groom. He will be happy to ride with you."

"That won't be necessary. In fact"—she permitted a small catch in her voice—"I prefer to ride alone."

274

"Tag would have my head if I allowed you to ride alone. But my groom is most unobtrusive. I doubt you will even notice he is there."

"But . . . Very well." She gave her agreement reluctantly. Later in the day, when a horse turned up missing, Rexford would remember and assume she had simply disregarded his orders and slipped away to ride off her disappointment at Tag's departure.

A few minutes later, dressed in the leggings and shirt she had worn in America, she mounted one of Rexford's horses without inconveniencing a groom by suggesting he accompany her.

The long ride through the pleasant countryside soothed her spirit as nothing else could. Everywhere she saw the English passion for order and permanence. Sunny, comfortable homes with smiling women and well-fed children. No sign of famine or watchers lurking in the trees, alert for a hostile attack. Peace. Mile after mile of peaceful countryside. If only . . .

Every time her mind drifted to "if only," she ruthlessly slashed the thought away. She could never be English. She could never belong. Even Tag, who understood her better than anyone, found her wanting.

She clenched her teeth and refused to admire the country. She would make her murderous cousin pay for his crimes, and return to the land where . . . where she didn't belong either.

Damn, damn, damn.

She banished the thoughts and rode on doggedly to her grandfather's house, where she tethered her horse in the woods on the edge of the estate.

The most difficult part of the journey proved to be struggling back into the crumpled gown she had stuffed into her pack. She didn't need a looking glass to suggest she shouldn't present herself at the front door. Whoever answered her knock would certainly alert the household to her strange and memorable appearance. That would spoil her plan for a hasty dash to the coast, where she could find a ship to take her to America.

On feet trained to stealth from childhood, she made her way to the house, unseen even in the midday sun. Circling the building, she found several unlatched windows, but had to guess at the room least likely to be occupied. Choosing the one with the heaviest drapes, she slipped in and listened for any sound.

Though used to stalking only in the forest, she applied the same rules. Move silently, never leave one place of concealment without having the next one in sight, and always listen. It was absurdly easy.

Within an hour she had searched the house from top to bottom. She had watched a maid painting her face in an upstairs bedroom, listened to two women gossiping in the kitchen, and found her grandfather's valued manservant dozing in the study. The cloying odor of a recently smoked cigar hung in the air.

Cursing silently, she considered her options. Her cousin certainly wasn't in the house at the moment, but he might return later. On the other hand, she couldn't afford to spend days waiting. She had to know for certain whether he would return.

So far she had broken no laws, unless one counted the theft of Rexford's horse, and he couldn't even count it as a theft unless she didn't return it. The only consequence of making her presence known would be that the servants could identify her. That would matter only if she succeeded in cutting her cousin's heart out—which she couldn't do if she couldn't find him.

Obviously, locating her cousin took precedence over secrecy.

Caro shuddered at the thought of the English prisons Tag had described. Dark holes where the captives never saw the light of day. Rat-infested . . .

No matter. She would do what she had to.

With a determined stride, she headed to the front door, which she threw open and closed with a resounding slam. "Good morning," she shouted. "Is anybody here? Good morning!"

The disreputable servant scampered from the study, closing the door behind him. With one hand he straightened his twisted waistcoat; with the other he brushed specks of ashes from his thighs. "What ... who ... where did you come from?"

Caro tilted her nose slightly toward the ceiling in a conscious imitation of a countess Tag had pointed out in France. "Albert Manning, isn't it? I knocked, but no one answered. You really should be more efficient."

"Who the devil are ... Oh, Miss Fenton. Where ... ?" He looked over her shoulder at the closed door.

"My grandfather is not with me." Caro realized she had neither a pelisse nor gloves to hand him to remind him he was a servant. To cover the oversight, she added more drawl to her words. "I heard a rumor my cousin, Edwin Boyle, was staying here. I am most anxious to meet him."

"You missed him by a fair amount. He left this morning."

"Oh, dear." *Oh, dear indeed.* He needn't look so pleased about it. "Perhaps you could tell me where he went."

"Perhaps I could. If I knew. But a lofty gentleman like that doesn't tell the likes of me where he's off to."

"Oh, dear." Such a feeble British expression that was, but it didn't soften the smirk that had begun to form around the man's down-turned mouth. He had obviously had time to appreciate her appearance.

No help for it but to continue with the role she'd chosen to play and hope someone had the good sense to lift his scalp someday. "My only relative. I did so look forward to seeing him."

A greedy light came into the man's eyes. "Now that you

speak of it, he was a bit surprised to learn of you too. Most anxious to learn where you and your grandfather lit off to in such a hurry. He said if I was to hear from you"—the fingers of his right hand rubbed against his palm—"I should let him know at once."

Caro's shoulders stiffened. "And where would you let him know?"

"I'd have to send a message to several places. But word would catch up with him eventually. If you will just tell me where you are staying, I'm sure he will call on you." His words came a little too quickly, and Caro wondered if her cousin had promised to pay him for any information he sent on.

She resented the idea of any alliance with this man, but she could scarcely ride all over England looking for Boyle. Like Tecumseh setting a trap for the long knives, she would have to let her cousin find her. But before she spent days waiting, she had to test the man's eagerness to deliver her message. "I think not. I will call again another day, and perhaps be fortunate enough to find him here."

The panic she anticipated flitted through the man's eyes. "Oh, no, miss. Mr. Boyle was most explicit. If I learned of where you went, I was to let him know directly."

Caro's tension eased. Boyle would receive any information she left. He would find her. Now she had only to be certain he did not wait an eternity to do so. For this she had to be a simpering English miss.

She did it, though it galled her to appear to care as much as a feather what this dolt thought. "You must think us absolutely dreadful for flying off like that. But everybody says I can be terribly silly sometimes, and my grandfather insisted on having me under Lord Rexford's protection until he can get me safely married." She offered a confidential smile. "And that will be soon enough, I assure you. Why, already—but how silly of me. You don't care about that."

"Staying with Lord Rexford, you say?"

"Yes. I will be there until I am married. Now, I really must be off."

Manning's brow furrowed. "Your carriage is waiting? I didn't hear . . . ?"

Caro tossed her head and barely remembered in time to keep her arm tucked in to her side. "Oh, no. I told you, I do have a mind of my own. I walked from the village."

"But that's—"

"A long walk, but extremely pleasant." She had not passed a village and prayed that it was not seven or eight miles. She turned and let herself out the door before the gaping man could question her further.

Despite the failure of her mission, Caro felt a curious lightness on her return trip. It took her several miles to recognize the source. She hadn't killed Boyle and she didn't have to leave England today.

England and Tag.

Tag, who wanted her body, but had ridiculous reasons for not wanting her as his wife. Her whole being rebelled at the idea of leaving before he realized what he had lost.

Now, perhaps she wouldn't have to. English ladies were nothing more than women in fancy gowns. She could learn to wear gowns and speak with fancy airs. Tag would return eventually, if only to present whatever insufferable man he had chosen as her husband. However wretched a candidate he presented, Caro vowed to herself she would force Tag to watch her flirt with him. He would watch her offer herself to another until he was sick with knowing what he had lost.

Tag could no more hide from her than Boyle could.

Chapter Sixteen

On Monday, Tag made an abortive visit to a woman whose charms had always set his blood to boiling. The experience left him standing at the window, cold and indifferent. On Tuesday, he started drinking in the early afternoon and continued through most of the night. Wisely he chose to do his drinking alone so he did not bore anyone with his drunken ramblings about a blond Indian girl with a touch like the wing of a bird.

Tuesday's effort left him with a throbbing headache on Wednesday morning, but by afternoon he felt well enough to win a fortune at faro, and lost it again that night. Neither experience seemed worth more than a passing thought. Thursday he combined drinking and gambling, earning the grandfather of all headaches, which made him forget whether he had won or lost at the tables.

By Friday, he acknowledged that the world had yet to devise a pursuit that could make him stop thinking about Caro, and he contented himself with walking the streets of the city. He saw her everywhere, in a young girl carrying a basket of flowers and a ragged urchin dressed in breeches whom he followed for half a block before the boy's hat fell off and revealed his black hair.

After that, he refused to allow himself to act on the quickening of his pulse that insisted the woman ahead or in the shop window must be Caro. The meaningless days tumbled into weeks, each longer than the one before. A different woman, a different bottle, a different gaming hell, but always the same memories. He might have starved to death if he hadn't had servants to remind him to eat, and he began spending more and more time in his study thinking of his ridiculous promise to find her a husband. He could find her a husband, all right, but then he'd probably kill the man before he let him touch her.

He had known the morning he left that he would miss her, but not like this. He had never encountered a woman he couldn't ride away from with only a fleeting regret. How was he to know he would wake every morning searching for a missing part of himself?

"Dammit all," Tag said to no one for the eleventh time one gloomy Wednesday morning. He restrained himself from throwing his empty glass against the wall of the study. Unless he exercised some control he would reduce the entire household to drinking from horse troughs.

The study door opened and Tag's butler poked his head in. "Excuse me, my lord, there is a young man here—"

"I am not at home."

"But sir—"

Tag scowled. "I am not at home. Are those words so difficult to understand?"

"This lad is from Lord Rexford. I thought perhaps—"

"Blast it, man." This time Tag did throw the offending glass. "Why didn't you say so?"

Baxter limited his response to a pitying glance and dodged out the door.

Seconds later, a dripping boy Tag recognized as one of Marc's stablehands appeared. "A letter, my lord. Lord Rexford ordered me to deliver it myself. He didn't want to wait for the mails."

Tag snatched the sealed parchment and tore it open. He read the missive and exploded into a flurry of oaths. "The fool. What does she think she's doing?" What did Marc

281

mean by letting her? He read again, more slowly, certain he must be mistaken.

"Baxter," he bellowed, "order my horse."

Baxter appeared instantly from the hall. "If you are thinking of going to Lord Rexford's, my lord, may I remind you, it is raining."

"I didn't ask for the weather. I asked for my horse." He probably wouldn't even notice the rain. Caro needed him again, and he felt alive for the first time in weeks.

Several hours later, Tag pounded into Marc's study. "Marc, what the devil is going on?"

Marc looked up from the papers he was studying. "Tag! I didn't expect you for hours yet." He raised his eyebrows. "Nor did I expect you to stand there dripping on my carpet. Can't you—"

"No, I can't." Tag belied his words by handing his greatcoat and hat to the butler, who had followed him into the room. "What is this about Boyle? Why did you wait a week to tell me?"

"Because I didn't know until this morning." Marc turned to a cabinet behind him and drew out a decanter and two glasses. "And all your thunder isn't going to change anything, so you may as well relax while we decide what's to be done."

"Where's Caro?"

"Quite safe. I presume she is upstairs doing something terribly feminine."

Tag had never seen Caro do anything "terribly feminine," but his curled fist unclenched. Marc wouldn't give the assurance if he wasn't certain. "Tell me about Boyle. Your note said—" He lowered himself into a chair and accepted the offered glass.

"Apparently he appeared in the neighborhood about two weeks ago. Caro has met him several times."

"Surely Amanda would have told you something like that."

"Amanda is not able to go about yet. But our neighbors, Mrs. Bradshaw and her daughter, have taken quite a fancy to Caro. I thought you would be pleased that Caro appears to be making quite an impression, at least in our small circle."

"Needless to say, I was not aware that your small circle included Edwin Boyle."

"He came down as part of a house party at the Grangers'. I heard a group had arrived, but never thought to inquire about the makeup of it."

"Caro has not seen fit to mention it?"

"Not until this morning. And only then because the man had the audacity to call. I encountered him in my own hall this morning asking for Caro."

"I assume you sent him packing."

"I was about to, but she came down the stairs before I could get the cobwebs out of my mouth." He gave a disbelieving shake to his head. "I must say, Tag, she is not at all what you led me to expect."

"I never tried to predict anything about her."

"From your description I would have expected her to leap down the stairs shrieking a war cry and brandishing a knife."

"A little overdramatized, but not entirely improbable."

"Then we are certainly not talking about the same young woman. She greeted him as elegantly as she would in a receiving line at Carlton House. Then she introduced him to me as blandly as you please. 'This is my cousin, Edwin Boyle.' As if I should thank her for inviting that blackguard into my house."

Marc ignored Tag's disbelieving look and continued. "He came before the rain in a fancy carriage to make arrangements to drive her to the Bradshaws' this afternoon."

Tag leapt from his chair and crossed the room. He

whirled and faced his friend again. "You forbade it, I assume."

Marc gave a self-deprecating shrug. "I should have, but she agreed and had him out the door before I could do more than mumble a few syllables."

"But after he left?"

"After he left, I sent for you." Marc accompanied the words with an apologetic shrug. "It is not really my place to forbid the young lady anything."

Tag's face suffused with heat. "Dammit, Marc! You would have let her endanger herself like that?"

Marc rose and made a soothing gesture with his hand. "Steady, Tag. I would not have let her go, but frankly, I'm glad you're here. I don't know quite what to make of the situation."

"Well, I do. This is precisely what I feared would happen. She thinks she is invincible. We've got to . . . I've got to . . ."

Marc again put out a restraining hand. "From what I have learned since this morning, it may not be the kind of danger you fear."

Tag's voice chilled. "By all means, tell me what you've learned."

"Mrs. Webster called on Amanda and mentioned Caro has been paying Boyle some very flattering attention."

"What is that supposed to mean?"

"Mrs. Webster hinted very strongly at a match."

"Dammit, that's insane. You said they have only known each other for two weeks."

Marc shrugged. "Marriage is so much more socially acceptable than murder," he said dryly.

"Caro would never—" Tag left the words hanging in the air. He had no idea what Caro would do. The room seemed too small to contain his swelling emotions, but he moved back and forth in the limited space, muttering to himself. Most of the phrases began or ended with "dammit.'' Finally, he looked to where Marc stood with a questioning expression on his face. "We have to do something.''

"My sentiments exactly.'' Marc smiled. "Though I thought I did my share when I sent for you.''

Tag exhaled a long breath. "Remind me to mention this next time somebody is touting your fortitude. Will you send for her? Please.''

"I will if you stop pacing like a bear on a chain.'' Marc took the few steps necessary to step into the hall and speak to a waiting servant.

As ordered, Tag resumed his seat. Again the chair seemed too confining. In spite of the frustrating situation, his pulse quickened at the prospect of seeing Caro again. It might take her a while to get over being angry at his abrupt departure. And then . . . Perhaps he should just take her away for her own good. With the continent safe again for travel, they could go about for years with no danger of encountering Boyle. Years of waking up next to her every morning. Years of being whole again.

"I thought we established I like you better when you are not pacing.'' Marc's voice startled Tag back to the confining study.

A little surprised, Tag realized he was circling the room again, his stomach tight. "Sorry.''

"I am a trifle vague on how you left things with the young lady. Do you want me to stay, or would you prefer to meet her alone?''

"I . . . I don't know.''

"Good. Because I have a decided preference. I will be with Amanda if you need me.'' Marc disappeared, leaving Tag free to sit or pace as he chose.

Tag did both, scarcely aware of his movements, trying to imagine how Caro would react to him. Probably with a string of curses and threats to cut his heart out. Odd how he liked her in that mood as much as any. All life and fire. How he loved the honesty of her emotions.

"Good morning, miss." From the hall came the voice of a servant. Tag sidestepped quickly behind Marc's desk, both to provide a barrier should Caro suddenly decide to throw a knife and to keep himself from immediately sweeping her into his arms.

His lungs ached. *Breathe, you clodpole.* He'd never known another man who simply forgot to breathe. Where was she?

As if swept in by the thought, she stepped into the room and hesitated, framed in the doorway. Her blond hair had been trimmed and framed her face in soft curls. She wore a green gown with a gathering of lace at the throat. Time had softened the effects of wind and sun on her face. Vanilla cream, Tag thought, and ran his fingers across the desk top as if he could almost feel the velvet texture.

For a fleeting second she posed there, her eyes flashing with the fire he remembered. The fire turned to the ice blue of a Scottish lake in winter. "Lord Elmgrove, how delightful to see you." She floated across the room with her hand extended.

Without thinking, Tag stepped from behind the desk and took her hand, "Caro."

She withdrew her hand before he had quite finished breathing her name. "Oh, my, sir." Her voice had the artificial quality of a ballroom where strangers pretended to be friends. "I suppose I must let you presume on an old acquaintance and use my first name, but it certainly won't do in public."

Light dawned. She was demonstrating how much she had learned in the weeks they had been apart. "Caro, you do look splendid. A perfect English lady."

"I am pleased you think so."

"But we must talk."

"Of course. But"—she gave an exaggerated, feminine

shudder—"you look a bit damp. Perhaps after you have changed . . ."

"Now." He barked the command more sharply than he intended, but the false note in her voice irked him beyond reason, as did her portrait smile.

"As you will, my lord."

"As you will, my lord," he mimicked. "What happened 'What do you want to talk about, Tag?"

"Oh, please, don't remind me how ingenuous I was when we first met." She brushed the happiest months of his life aside with an unnatural wave. "Perhaps we should sit." She took two small steps to a chair and sat without looking behind her.

"Blast it, Caro, stop the playacting. We need to be honest."

"That should be novel." She leaned forward and the frost in her voice melted slightly. "Very well, Tag. What do you wish to talk about?"

"Edwin Boyle."

"I thought we would come to that."

Tag slammed himself into the chair opposite her so abruptly she started. "You thought it would come to that, but I can't imagine why it has. I can't imagine why you are even seeing him."

"He's my cousin."

"He is a murderer."

"I find him charming."

"Dammit, then he's a charming murderer."

"I have only your word on that."

This time, Tag started as if *he'd* been struck. "I told you—"

"I know what you *told* me." The unnecessary emphasis confirmed the insult.

Tag sprang from his chair to keep from striking anything fragile with his clenched fist. "Bloody hell. Are you doubting my word?'' Her cool gaze answered the question. "If you were a man, I'd call you out for that."

"How fortunate that I am a woman. We both know your word is whatever pleases you."

Tag reeled under the near truth of the accusation. "I never lied. Even that last morning. I admit—"

"You never lied?" The ice in her voice made all of her earlier affectations as warm as a caress. "I suppose introducing that little foreign woman on the boat as my companion was your idea of the truth. Or all the times you introduced me as your younger sister. Also the truth?"

The knot in Tag's stomach uncoiled. At least she had focused on something any reasonable person could understand. "Excuse me. Those were emergencies. To save your reputation, I might add."

His movement about the room forced her to turn in her chair to watch him. God help him, even as he defended himself, he could think of little but the white curve of her neck and how easily his lips would fit into that hollow.

"... the rats in my grandfather's house."

"Pardon me?"

"I said, I suppose the rats in my grandfather's house the day we left were also an emergency."

"Oh, blast." He had forgotten that one. "How did you find out about that?"

"Amanda found me sleeping next to the baby one morning. I told her I was protecting him from the rats. You made me look like a fool. But, of course, that doesn't matter because it was one of your little emergencies."

"It seemed like a good idea at the time. Edwin Boyle was due to arrive that afternoon and I didn't know what either of you might do to the other." Tag crossed the room and sat down, prepared to plead with her to understand. He had only been concerned about her safety. He leaned forward.

She turned her body, increasing the distance between

288

them. Her slowly exhaled breath chilled the air. "Which brings us full circle. Mr. Boyle is here now and you still have no idea what either of us might do."

"Yes, I do, because you're not going to see him."

She gave a dry laugh. "I'm sure you feel you have some right to say that and I am simply too slow-witted to see it."

"I have every right. I—"

"You gave up any right you might have had a month ago."

"Three weeks ago," Tag whispered, then glanced at the clock. "Three weeks, two days, and three hours." Adding more volume and firmness to his voice, he said, "If you won't listen to me, then Rexford will forbid it."

Caro nodded. "A better possibility. He can refuse Mr. Boyle entrance to the house, though that would be unforgivably rude. But his authority over me stops at his front door. It may interest you to know I have not been idle since you left. There are any number of places where we can meet. Now, if you will excuse me, I have an engagement in less than an hour." She rose, and Tag stood automatically.

Only a few inches separated them. He could either strangle her or kiss the smug expression off her lips. She took the decision from him and eased past him so closely that the skirt of her gown brushed his calves. *Don't go,* he wanted to shout, but before they could talk about the anger between them, the more pressing problem of her appointment had to be resolved.

"Your grandfather," he said to her retreating back. "Your grandfather will—"

She turned, again framed by the doorway. "My grandfather wants only to see me married. He will scarcely consent to having me locked in my room either here or at his estate." She produced another cold, infuriating smile. "Accept it, Tag, you are only a spectator." She nodded and

289

glanced down at his hands. "And you should have that hand tended to."

Tag looked at his clenched fists. At some point he had picked up a letter opener from the desk. A small trickle of blood from the bent instrument dripped to the carpet.

He stared at the empty doorway, clutching the twisted metal, until he could control the impulse to go after Caro and shake her until her teeth rattled. But a word with her grandfather might save him the trouble of killing Boyle today.

He found the old man propped up in bed. His blue eyes, a faded version of Caro's, gleamed when Tag stepped purposefully through the door. "About time you returned, young man. You have made a perfect botch of things."

Tag had no time to waste on formalities. "I am relieved you are well enough to recognize something must be done."

"I am not well at all."

"Well enough to speak. You are aware Caro has been meeting with Boyle and that she plans to drive out with him this afternoon."

"I am aware she has been meeting him. When Rexford mentioned it to me this morning, I suggested he send for you."

"You let it go on." Tag threw his hands in the air. "You are the only one who has the authority to protect her."

"What would you have me do?" Fenton's sweeping gesture indicated the tousled bedcovers and the table littered with vials of potions and pills.

"You can begin by forbidding her to go anywhere with him this afternoon."

"And tomorrow?"

"And every day for as long it takes for her to come to her senses."

The old man shook his head. "I may not have that much time. Which brings us to the discussion we began the day we met. Only a strong husband can protect her.''

Tag froze in the center of the room. ''Am I to understand you permitted this to continue merely to prompt me into offering for her? She could be killed.''

Fenton returned Tag's fierce gaze without flinching. ''I doubt you will let it come to that. You obviously care for her or you would not have come winging down here.''

''The man is a murderer. You are a madman.''

''No.'' Fenton let the long pause linger and shook his head sadly. ''No, I am a desperate man. And you are the best choice available.''

Cursing himself for having wasted precious minutes, Tag stormed from the room and ordered his horse brought around. From Rexford's study, he borrowed one of a pair of dueling pistols. Boyle would have to pass through him to call for Caro.

The rain had stopped and the sun gleamed off the emerald trees. Moisture dripped from the overhanging branches, and the newly washed air had a crisp tang. How could anything evil could be abroad on such a day?

The crunch of wheels alerted Tag to how wrong he might be. Within seconds a curricle turned into the drive. The driver, a lanky man in a fashionably fitted coat, held the reins carelessly in thin hands.

Tag urged his horse onto the drive. ''Mr. Boyle?''

Boyle muttered a sharp oath at the abrupt movement, but collected himself quickly. ''I am afraid you have the advantage of me, sir. I don't recognize you.''

''I am Elmgrove. Miss Fenton asked me to deliver a message. She will be unable to accompany you this afternoon.''

Boyle's eyes narrowed. ''She appeared willing enough this morning.''

''And unwilling this afternoon.''

''You will forgive me if I prefer to hear that from the young lady herself.''

Tag remained firmly positioned in front of the horses. "You heard it from me."

Boyle raised the reins in preparation for urging the horses forward. "We are not acquainted, so if you don't mind—"

Tag returned his icy look. "We have not been formally introduced, but I know you rather well. I was with Oliver Fenton at Waterloo just before he died."

Boyle stiffened. His mouth tightened into a thin line. "A regrettable tragedy."

"There are those who say you did not find it entirely regrettable. At least not until Miss Fenton appeared as her grandfather's heir."

If Boyle's look had been a sword, it would have sliced Tag in two. "I believe we begin to understand each other, Lord Elmgrove. You would not be the unidentified officer responsible for some very ugly rumors about me last summer, would you?"

"If I admit it, would you challenge me to a duel?" A duel would be the ideal solution.

"Unfortunately, no." Boyle gave a disapproving frown, keeping his tone very casual. "Dueling is illegal and I can scarcely afford to tarnish my reputation further." The creases in his forehead became dark valleys and his tone hardened. "But if I hear a hint of such rumors in this neighborhood, I shall certainly insist you substantiate them."

Tag's teeth clenched. "You have taken great care to make that impossible."

"Precisely why nobody with any sense gave them a moment's credence. Now, if you will excuse me, I do have an appointment to keep." He flicked the reins of the curricle, causing the bewildered horses to edge forward, physically jostling Tag's mount.

Tag's stallion danced three steps, then quieted. "I have said the lady does not wish to see you." Tag snapped out each word.

His tone failed to produce any change in Boyle's determined expression. "And I believe she does. In spite of whatever lies you have poured into her head." Disdainfully, he glanced around. "Since she is not with you, I can only suspect you are jealous because she prefers my company to yours."

"At the moment, my concern is for her safety. Mr. Fenton's heirs have a regrettable tendency to die when they turn their backs on you."

Boyles eyes flashed fire. "Bastard."

Tag waited.

Boyle relaxed and laughed. "Even if your accusation were true, you forget she is merely a female. When her grandfather dies, I will be her guardian. I will inherit not merely his fortune, but the charming Miss Fenton as well."

"Not if she marries first."

"A possibility, I admit, which is why I am waiting so patiently for you to move aside so I may press my own suit. I must confess, the prospect of bedding her is not entirely unattractive."

Tag's hand jerked. His well-trained mount reared and probably saved Boyle's life. A man on an uncontrolled stallion could not draw a gun and fire, no matter what his flaming temper demanded. By the time he had the horse once more under control, the red haze had disappeared. "You will not go to that house today, Boyle."

"You have no authority," Boyle said through whitened lips.

"Lord Rexford also asked me to deliver a message."

"You are full of messages, aren't you?"

"This one is most important. Look around at the trees, Boyle. You are on Rexford's property, and he doesn't like you any better than I do. He has ordered his servants to shoot you on sight—as a poacher."

"A poacher! That's absurd."

"Perhaps. But I doubt you will want to test it. Unfortunate errors do occur."

Boyle glanced to the left and right.

No rational man would believe the empty threat. But a coward who had shot innocent men in the back might have some imagination. "Feel it, Boyle. Don't the hairs on the back of your neck warn you of danger? You don't think Rexford would have let me come out alone to meet you?"

Boyle looked around again, less covertly this time. His hand made a faint, involuntary move toward his neck. "You are certainly demented enough to do something so foolish. As I never provoke madmen, I will allow you to give my regrets to Miss Fenton." He gathered the reins and began to turn the curricle. "I will, of course, apologize personally tonight."

Tag waited until the crunch of the curricle wheels faded into the distance, then turned his horse toward the house. Before he had gone two steps, Marc stepped from behind a towering oak, clutching the mate to the pistol Tag had borrowed.

"Really, Tag! A poacher? I doubt we have had one in these parts in the last hundred years."

Tag grinned and dismounted. "It seemed better than claiming you would shoot him for the cut of his coat. You might at least have let me know you were there."

Rexford laughed. "As you said, you didn't really think I would let you come out here alone, did you?" He began walking, and Tag fell into step beside him.

"And if I had shot him?"

Rexford grinned. "Then I guess we would have had to try your poacher story, weak though it is."

"What did he mean about personally giving Caro his apology tonight?"

"Caro has any number of engagements planned. Tonight, I believe it is a ball at the Bradshaws'." Rexford gave an amused shrug. "I suspect you will have a busy week if you plan to keep Boyle and Caro apart at gunpoint."

Chapter Seventeen

Completely dressed for the Bradshaws' ball, Caro dismissed her maid. She needed to be alone.

Tag had returned, so tonight it could all end. Boyle would die in the Bradshaws' Grecian temple where she had agreed to meet him at midnight. Why could she feel no satisfaction? The firelit nights of her childhood seemed too far away. She had spent her life as a healer; now she would kill. Only the fact that Boyle would die peacefully and painlessly made her believe she could do what she had to.

Because Boyle had chosen to present himself as her suitor, she would have her revenge on Tag as well. Before the evening ended, Tag would suffer the anguish of believing she had given her body to his enemy.

For him that would be worse than the easy passing into an endless sleep that she planned for Boyle. Tag might not want her for a wife, but she knew that the thought that another man might possess her would enrage him. For all his English civility, the man could barely unclench his jaw when she spoke Boyle's name.

Thanks to Clarissa Bradshaw, Caro had learned the art of flirting well. She would see Tag had ample reason to clench his jaw tonight.

Sally hurried into the room without knocking. "The gentleman is waiting, miss."

Caro inhaled and prepared to join Tag, who had insisted on escorting her to the ball. Automatically her hands leapt to the scooped neckline of her dress. Her breasts pushed at the tight material as if they might escape, and Tag with his sharp eye would quickly guess she wore nothing under the soft material. He would have good reason to remember the last morning they had spent together, when his hands had set them both to trembling.

She caught her lip between her teeth and bit down hard. If she thought of those moments with him, she would never get through tonight. During the long hours since Tag's arrival, when he alternately pleaded with her, then ranted at her, she had found a way to control her thoughts. She thought of ice. Ice and cold and the long hungry winters with her adopted people, when they walked through snow.

Tonight, she would think of ice, and he would think of fire.

"Your reticule, miss," Sally said.

"Thank you." Caro snatched the purse before Sally's sensitive fingers could detect the rough packet of herbs beneath the thin material. "Don't wait up for me. Lady Rexford will help me with my dress."

Sally's face clouded with disapproval. What did it matter what she thought about who might help Caro undress? At least she would not rouse the household when Caro didn't return.

With all the dignity it had taken her weeks to learn, Caro descended the stairs to where Tag waited.

Half an hour later, she moved through the receiving line with Tag so close behind her she could feel his breath on her bare shoulders.

"Oh, Caro, you've come at last," Clarissa said. "Isn't it exciting? Who will you dance with first?"

Caro produced her first natural smile of the day.

Clarissa needed no reply. "Just look. So many gentlemen. Life has been so exciting since you came to stay. I hope you dance with Mr. Edwards first. He is so handsome tonight, and even Mama admits he is quite taken with you. Wait until he sees you dance. You scarcely even needed those lessons. Mama says you are so graceful because some people are born graceful.''

A slight pressure from Tag's hand in the small of her back moved Caro on.

Tag followed her into the crowded room. The strains of the orchestra sounded in the background. ''Did I overhear Miss Bradshaw say you planned to dance?'' he asked.

His surprise made it easy to answer coolly. ''I would scarcely come to a ball otherwise.''

''Then perhaps you will allow me.'' He held out his arm as Clarissa's dancing instructor had done, but hesitated when he saw the lines forming. ''Unless you would prefer to wait for something less complex.''

She laid her hand on his arm with a condescending look. ''It is hardly that difficult.'' They joined the others and began to move through the intricate but repetitive steps of the dance. He moved flawlessly and Caro longed to break through his cool detachment.

With a wicked smile, she realized precisely how she could do it. They separated. When they came together again she let the hunger she had once felt for him burn in her eyes and said something very suggestive in Shawnee.

His eyes widened. ''What did you say?''

''I was remembering our first dance.'' She moistened her lip and lowered her gaze slowly to his thighs. ''I said—''

''Dammit, Caro.'' His ears flushed red. ''Don't look at me like that.'' He stumbled a few steps, leaving his next partner standing with her hand extended.

Each time they met, Caro murmured in Shawnee and produced the heated look of the marriage dance. By the time the music stopped, his face had taken on an unhealthy crimson hue, and a purple vein throbbed in each temple.

She had lost count of how many times he'd muttered, "Dammit, Caro."

His icy control returned as he led her from the dance floor. "I hope you enjoyed that disgraceful exhibition."

She gave one last glance at the obvious bulge in his breeches. "You appeared to, though not as much as you enjoyed our first dance."

"You will save both waltzes for me."

She laughed. "I am sure you are aware, my lord, it would be most improper to dance with you three times."

"Then you will sit one out."

"You will eat bad fish and die." Caro offered her favorite curse in Shawnee, hating the fact she felt alive for the first time in a month. Mr. Edwards joined them to claim his dance.

For the next hour Caro moved through the formal English ritual, dancing with whoever asked and watching Tag watch her. She danced with Boyle only once. During their dance, she whispered a confirmation of her promise to meet him at the appointed hour. Tag glared at her through the entire set, looking hot enough to sizzle a buffalo haunch.

The strains of the first waltz began. Tag appeared at her side "My dance, I believe." He swept her into his arms before she could refuse.

In spite of herself, Caro's blood warmed at his familiar touch. She looked up and met his heated gaze. Was he remembering the way his hand had stroked her? Knowing her response would drive him wild, she let his touch enflame her. "Mmmm." She surrendered to the soft sounds of the music, the heady scent of flowers, and the liquid hunger in his eyes. "If nothing else, you taught me to appreciate a man's touch."

His grip tightened on her hand and her waist. "God, Caro, you must stop looking like that. You will turn every man in the room into a rutting stallion."

"Not every man. They don't know me as well as you do—yet."

His gaze shifted from her face to the décolletage of her dress. "They know that dress is shockingly revealing."

Caro forced herself to savor the revenge she had planned. "But not what I wear under the dress."

He produced the now-familiar shade of vermilion. "If you are implying that I even know what you have on under your dress, you are mistaken."

"You ought to. You chided me about it often enough."

"I chided you about wearing noth—" He snatched his hand back as if her dress had burst into flames. "Good heavens! Are you saying you have absolutely noth—dammit, even you wouldn't dare."

"People are staring, my lord."

He looked around and realized he had stopped in the center of the dance floor. They stood with couples swirling around them, just the tips of their gloved fingers touching.

"We must dance, my lord."

"Surely, you don't expect me to put my hand on you in front of all these people. You are mad." He twisted his right hand awkwardly as if searching for someplace impersonal where he could put it.

Caro laughed at his confusion, and if the laugh had a bitter sound, she ignored it. "Courage, Lord Taggart. Surely you won't touch anything you haven't felt before."

With a determined grimace he pulled her to him. For an instant his hand hovered in the air behind her. Then, with a groan, he surrendered, spreading his palm over her back, verifying with his fingers that she spoke the literal truth. "You are doing this deliberately. To torment me."

"Yes."

His eyes softened into molten pools. "Then let us both enjoy it." His fingertips pressed into her back, and Caro danced in a swirl of sensation, her hand clasped tightly in his, his breath warm on her face. Caro concentrated on snow, on frozen lakes and bitter north winds, and refused to admit she would trade the rest of her life to lie in his arms one more time.

The dance ended and he led her from the floor, her hand trapped firmly between his arm and his body. "We have to get out of here."

Snow and ice, she thought. Snow and ice. "Hardly. I am enjoying myself."

Mrs. Bradshaw forestalled any answer he might have made. "Lord Taggart, Clarissa is just devastated you haven't danced with her yet. She has heard so much about you from our dear Miss Fenton. Come along now."

"Miss Fenton and I were just going to get a breath of air."

Drawing her hand from his arm, Caro smiled sweetly. "Yes, do dance with Clarissa, Lord Taggart. I feel a bit of a headache coming on. Perhaps, I will just . . ."

Just go out and kill Mr. Boyle, she finished mentally.

Desire warred with British civility on Tag's face. Civility triumphed. "I will return directly."

Caro let him take two steps before calling him back for a final jibe. "Lord Taggart." She lowered her voice and waited until he moved closer. "Don't worry too much about our little secret. Before the evening ends, I vow you will not be the only man with that knowledge."

"No." Air whooshed out with his fierce reply. For a moment she feared he might strike her. But he just stood there, his fists clenched so tight his arms trembled.

Mrs. Bradshaw tugged on his arm. After a searing look that promised further discussion, he turned and followed Mrs. Bradshaw.

Caro glanced at the clock. Boyle had left the room five minutes ago. Gracefully refusing several requests for the next dance, she made her way to the far side of the ballroom. Lifting two glasses of champagne from the table by the door, she slipped out onto the terrace.

Several couples stood chatting in the flickering light of a dozen lanterns. She firmly ignored them and descended the steps to the freshly cropped lawn. The more soothing light of the half-moon illuminated the crushed-stone path. Though her mind urged her to hurry, she had to move slowly or there would not be enough liquid left in the crystal glasses to dissolve the powder she intended for Boyle.

She felt no fear of meeting with her wicked cousin. As long as he thought her as compliant and witless as Clarissa, he would wait for a more opportune time before harming her.

The white columns of the folly came into view. Edwin Boyle stepped from the shadows. "At last. I feared you might not escape your watchdog."

Without permitting her step to falter, Caro hurried to him. "How could I not when I knew you were waiting?"

He clasped her shoulders and bent to brush her lips with a kiss, drawing back at the sight of the two glasses in her hands. "What is this, my dear?"

"I thought perhaps we could celebrate my first ball." Caro remembered to drop her gaze shyly from his face.

He took the glasses from her hands and placed them on the waist-high wall behind him. "A splendid idea. But I will show you a better way to celebrate." Again he clasped her shoulders. This time his lips found hers. They were too thick, too moist. Repulsive.

Caro resisted the impulse to grab her knife and slash at him. "Oh, my." She took refuge in apparent innocence. "Is that proper? This is all so new."

"Not quite proper. But I find it impossible to resist. I want so much more for us."

"I feel the same. But what can we do?" Caro had little patience for the conversation, but she could not simply walk up to him and say, "Drink this and die."

"We can marry, of course. You must know how I feel about you. I have loved you from the first moment I saw

302

you. I live for the sound of your voice, the sight of your smile.'' He said the words as if he were reading from a familiar book.

Caro felt no anger at the lies, only a tremendous sadness. How often she had pictured Tag saying exactly those words. How different his voice would have sounded.

She pushed the thought away. Tag could not be permitted to intrude here. She had to answer so they could drink and she could begin the long journey back to the land she thought she had left forever. ''I have admired you.'' She choked on even that mild lie. She had to do better. Forcing a brittle brightness into her voice, she tried again ''Marry. How wonderful. Let us drink—'' She tried to twist her shoulders from his grasp.

He laughed. ''Not so fast. I knew you would be eager, but there is a slight problem.''

Whatever his problem, his cigar-laden breath produced a more severe one for Caro. She wanted to be ill. Her shoulders wanted to crawl from beneath his clutching fingers. ''Oh, dear. A problem?''

''Your grandfather refuses to receive me.'' His mouth tightened into a thin line. ''I fear your loathsome protector has been filling his head with lies. Your grandfather may not give his consent.''

Caro resisted the impulse to drag him to the drink like a reluctant horse. ''I shall talk to my grandfather.''

''You mustn't. If he even suspects what we are planning, he might set that seething firebrand on me. Did you know Lord Taggart tried to provoke me into a duel this afternoon?''

''How wretched of him.'' How wretched of Tag to care enough to risk his life and his reputation for her. In a moment she would commit a deed so abhorrent to his English morals that he would despise her forever. She shuddered at the thought of the contempt her act would bring to his eyes.

''Do not be alarmed, my dear. There is another way.''

"Tell me quickly." *Tell me quickly, so we can get on with this.*

"You must come away with me. If we spend the night together, everyone will insist we marry." He brushed his hand along the neckline of her gown, letting his fingers linger at the cleft between her breasts. "And I promise you will enjoy it."

Hideous man. He planned to enjoy her body while deciding whether to kill her or make her his wife. She forced herself not to cringe at his touch. How different from Tag, whose fierce sense of honor had kept him wrestling for weeks with the temptation of making tender love to her.

"Do not look so frightened, my dear. Truly, this is the best way." Boyle's hand slid to the back of her neck. "Say you will come away with me."

Caro repressed another shudder. He would be suspicious if she agreed too quickly. "But is that quite proper?"

"How little you know of our customs. It is always done when people want to avoid a lot of fuss and bother."

"Then we shall do it. But now we must celebrate."

"This is the celebration you came for." His hand tangled in her hair, turning her head toward his open lips.

Caro struggled harder, pushing and turning her face away so she could speak. "Oh, no, sir. The English always celebrate with champagne. That much I have learned." His grip relaxed slightly. "And if I am to be your wife, I must learn to wait on you. Please, sit over there in the moonlight." She pointed to a bench on the far side of the folly.

"Silly woman." His laugh had little humor, but he crossed the marble floor and lowered himself to the bench. "You will meet me here at noon tomorrow and we will make our escape. To your grandfather's, I believe. What a delicious irony that will be."

The moment had come. But with her back to the murderer, she saw only Tag's face. If she killed Boyle here, Tag might do something incredibly foolish. He might feel

304

his honor demanded he endanger himself to help her escape. Boyle had offered her another choice. She could kill Boyle tomorrow, far away from here. Far away from any chance Tag would ever suffer for what she had to do.

The powder tingled in the palm of her hand. She turned and looked at Boyle. Tomorrow would be soon enough. She would meet him here as they had done before, but he would not touch her again. For now she needed only to get away from him without arousing his suspicion and without enduring any more of his clammy touches.

She poured a small portion of the powder into his glass and carried it to him. He accepted the glass. Even his smile made the flesh on her shoulders feel as if tiny creatures were crawling over it. "To tomorrow," he said, and drained his glass.

"To tomorrow," she echoed.

"Be sure to tell no one of our plans," he said, the words already beginning to slur. He slid to the stone floor, saving Caro the trouble of answering.

Tag stood motionless on the stone terrace. Twice he had searched the ballroom for Caro before realizing Boyle was also missing. A hasty search of the grounds had produced neither of them. He would not find Caro until she was ready to be found.

For the first time in his life Tag understood the terror some soldiers experience on the battlefield. Every sinew in his body urged him to run, screaming like a madman. His mind whirled with pictures of murder or seduction, but he could do nothing but stand at rigid attention and wait.

A movement in the shadows caught his attention.

Caro. She was alive. For a moment he knew only surging relief. He took a step toward her. No. He would see her too soon as it was. If he went to her he would lose control.

He waited.

She mounted the steps to greet him with the cool false

Judy Veisel

smile he despised. "Good evening, Lord Taggart."

"Where have you been?" His jaw trembled so he could scarcely get the words out.

"Where I promised. With Mr. Boyle." She gave a provocative smile. "Does that annoy you?"

She was taunting him. He wanted to shake her until her bones rattled. "What have you been doing?" Strands of displaced hair fell about her shoulders.

Her laugh sliced him like a knife. "What have I been doing? Is that any question to ask a lady? You of all people should remember how easily I respond to moonlight and a comfortable bed of grass." Her tangled hair and skewed gown made the memory all too vivid.

"Dammit, Caro, I should kill you." He didn't even dare take the single step that separated them.

"But you won't. You are far too civilized."

"You didn't let that gutter vermin touch you?"

She tossed her head in a haughty gesture she had learned too well. "You will never know, will you?"

A swirl of white skirts on the hill from which Caro had come distracted Tag. A young woman appeared, hurried up the steps, and spoke in an animated whisper to a man similar enough to be her twin. He gave her a look that suggested he had a great deal more to say on the subject of where she had been, and sent her scurrying inside. As soon as she disappeared, he raised his voice to address the scattering of people on the terrace. "One of you gentlemen may have to come and help me with Mr. Boyle. Mr. Franklin has found him as drunk as an emperor in the folly. He can't rouse him and doesn't want to leave him there all night."

Exhilarating relief surged through Tag. That foxed Boyle couldn't have been responsible for Caro's bedraggled state. She greeted his questioning glance with stony indifference.

His heartbeat accelerated. Boyle couldn't be drunk. Tag had watched him all night. Boyle hadn't consumed enough

306

to make a three-year-old lightheaded. Blood rushed to Tag's head. Boyle couldn't be roused, the man had said. Had Caro killed him?

"Get out of here," he whispered, turning her by the shoulders. Whatever she had done, he would protect her. "Go to Marc's. I will join you there as soon as I can."

He watched her enter the house, took one step to follow the men who had set out after Boyle, then quelled the impulse. No point in linking himself and Caro with a dead man. He waited, and during the eternally long minutes mentally prepared himself to look as bewildered as everyone else.

Finally, two men appeared, supporting Boyle between them. Boyle's clothes, though disarranged by his awkward position, showed no trace of blood. *Is he dead?* Tag clenched his teeth. He would know soon enough.

The ribald comments of the men reached him first, their tone totally inappropriate if the men had been carrying a corpse. Tag's pulse gradually slowed.

Caro hadn't done her worst. He would have to commend her on her good sense—if he decided not to shake her for bringing him to the brink of heart failure.

He glanced at the animated crowd that had formed around Boyle. Boyle dozedly took a glass of water from someone. His eyes had the heavy look of someone dragged too abruptly from a deep sleep. "I . . . how did I get here? What happened?" He sounded as dull-witted as the average jug-bitten schoolboy.

Tag turned his thoughts to Caro. *Enough.*

Enough lies. Enough games. Tag stalked off to find her.

For once in their short acquaintance, Caro had followed orders. A driver waiting outside the house informed Tag she had sent for Marc's coach and ordered the driver to take her home. "Don't worry, my lord, I heard her tellin' him ta come back for you."

Just as well she left, Tag thought. The kind of confrontation he had in mind shouldn't occur in a public place. In fact, it shouldn't occur until he'd been locked in a closed room and allowed to bang his head against the wall for a few days.

But he had to decide what to do. And he had to do it tonight. He paced. He stomped along the line of coaches until he made the horses so restless most of them were also stamping and snorting. And they hadn't even met Caro.

Incredibly, Tag's mood began to lighten. She hadn't killed Boyle. And she hadn't let the man make love to her either, no matter what she wanted him to believe. Those two certainties made him feel like shouting with relief. At least for two and a half seconds until he recalled the rest of her behavior since he'd arrived.

She'd goaded him and tormented him and, for a final insult, might have gotten herself killed, because she had certainly met Boyle. Like a runaway horse with the bit between her teeth, she had no awareness of her danger.

He had left her a month ago in order to protect her from some possible future danger, but he had left her alone to fight this very real battle in a world she didn't understand.

Fool, he berated himself. *Fool*. What would his sacrifice matter if she didn't live out the week?

He thought of the morning he'd almost made her his wife. How noble he'd felt. *What a noble ass*.

Tag paced some more. The horses nickered, and the solution became disgustingly obvious. He silently blessed the dilatory coachman for giving him time to think.

Caro was in danger because he had so virtuously walked away from her, so nobly refused to endanger her by asking her to be his wife. How often today had she reminded him he had abdicated any right to control her behavior?

He had abdicated, and he could damn well unabdicate.

Such a simple act would have given him control. He stalwartly refused to let his hand stray toward his groin, and the mild ache that had been troubling him all night. By giving in to the desire to pound his body into hers, he could claim the right to control her behavior. He could become her husband.

As her husband, he could command her obedience.

He could be her husband simply by stripping that wretched gown from her body. His blood boiled and he shuddered at the thought she might resist. But she wouldn't. She couldn't.

In her own eyes she had married him months ago, and he had married her in a meadow on a mist-shrouded morning.

Tag strained for the first sight of the coach that would take him to her. Tonight he would brand her as his own, and in the process teach her how very vulnerable a woman alone could be.

Chapter Eighteen

Caro sat cross-legged on the floor of her bedchamber still wearing her green silk gown. Murmuring the familiar words of her childhood, she sought communion with the spirits who had always guided her. But the stone walls of the house imprisoned her and she couldn't feel the presence of her familiar spirits.

For the first time in her life, she felt truly alone.

She searched for the sense of righteousness she expected to feel. It had seemed so perfect this morning when she'd resolved to combine her vengeance against Tag with her mission to destroy Boyle. But the sense of victory she'd sought now crumbled like dry clay in her hands.

Tag's reaction when she lashed out at him had been everything she'd hoped for. His rage and frustration had blazed in his eyes. But she had to fight to recall that look. The moment she relaxed, the other look intruded. The only one that mattered.

Nothing about the night mattered. Nothing but the few brief minutes that stood out with the vividness of a red bird in the snow.

Then let us both enjoy it, he had said the moment before they both surrendered to the music of the waltz. Everything had disappeared but the feel of his hand on her back, the sight of his teeth biting circles of white into his lips, and the stormy passion in his eyes. Her knees had weakened with the certainty that, in his mind, he was touching her as intimately as on the last morning they had lain together.

Even her bare toes tensed with the memory.

She might have yielded then. Thrown her pride to the winds and begged him to take her outside, to hold her once more, if only for a minute.

But the music had stopped. The silence had brought reality. He wanted her body. Nothing more. Freedom from his touch had allowed her to recapture the anger she could only feel when her pulse wasn't pounding in the same rhythm as the vein at his temple.

Why couldn't she feel that anger now? Why did her body have such different memories from her mind?

Whoosh. The whisper of sound from the other side of the closed door came so softly that Caro wouldn't have heard it if she hadn't been subconsciously listening. She'd known he would come. He would not let the night pass without trying again to control her.

The door opened and Tag stepped in. She resisted the temptation to scramble to her feet. Muscles tense, she simply looked up at him.

He had removed his outer clothes and his shoes. The dead white of his shirt and the fair skin of his neck and face emphasized the difference between him and the men she had known in her world. So different, she told herself, so civilized.

But that was before his gaze locked with hers. The gray-steel hardness in his eyes warned that if she taunted this warrior, she had better be prepared to kill him. She rose with the infinite care of an unarmed brave confronting a wild bear in the woods. "What are you doing here?"

Moving only his right hand, he reached behind him and locked the door. A muted click in the silent room. "Where is your maid?"

Caro curled her toes into the carpet to keep from retreating. "She just left a moment ago. She will return immediately."

311

"Phumfph." The explosion of air might have been either a humph or a dry laugh. "Do you know your eyes shift when you lie? But if she does return, you will tell her to leave," he said through tight lips.

"I will tell *you* to leave." Caro's voice gathered strength, though she had to fight the dryness in her mouth. She couldn't be afraid of him. Not Tag.

But he didn't move, and his searing gaze made the dark green dress suddenly seem as transparent as air. Anything was better than the silence. "What are you doing here?" she repeated, the last word little more than a whisper.

"You invited me."

Caro's hands twitched with the impulse to shield her breasts from his burning gaze, but she clasped her fingers together at her waist. She would not let him intimidate her. "I most definitely did not."

"Oh, yes." He took a step toward her. "You invited every man in the ballroom every time you moved." Another step. "Now let's see if you meant it."

Cursing her cowardice, Caro matched each advancing step with a retreat until she felt the wall at her back. She pressed her palms against the smooth grain of the wood. "Tag." She used too much air just saying his name, and had to take in another quick gulp. "You should not be here. We will talk in the morning."

He brushed her cheek with his knuckles and leaned forward to rest his palm on the wall behind her. "That's not what your eyes said when we waltzed. Your eyes promised things most men only dream about."

Caro pressed her back against the wall and brought her hands in front of her chest to block him if he tried to crush himself against her. The tone of his words frightened her. His jaw trembled and he looked as if he would take her right here against the wall without warmth, without tenderness. "Stop, Tag. You're not like this. You are English. Always civil."

"That's always been your mistake, Caro." His free hand moved to rest lightly on her waist. "You underestimate the English. Mistake civility for weakness. Now, let's talk about tonight. Let's talk about how Englishmen treat women who behave as you chose to." His hand slipped intimately around to the small of her back where it had rested when they danced.

Caro gasped. Even in anger the heat of his hand could set her insides to quivering. Set her to thinking that they had only tonight. "You're bluffing. You wouldn't—" Not like this. Not with all her bitter thoughts between them.

"Wouldn't what? Be interested in what you have on under that gown? You forget. You've already told me. Even invited me to determine for myself." His fingers glided over the silk of her gown to caress her buttocks. "But in a ballroom I couldn't do this, could I?" He released his grip on the wall and ran that hand down her spine to join the one already stroking her.

In spite of herself Caro's buttocks tightened. "You don't want to do this."

He blew a heated stream of air through his pursed lips. The warmth brushed her cheek like the gentlest breeze. "Oh, I want to do it all right. But perhaps it isn't me you want. Perhaps it's Boyle." His fingers tightened. "Tell me about tonight. Did you kiss him?" His lips hovered enticingly close to hers.

His accusing tone helped her regain control. English ladies did not entertain gentlemen in their bedchambers. In her mind she could hear herself imitating Clarissa's teasing tone. "Oh, scandal, my lord, you certainly don't expect a lady to discuss something so private."

His hands cupped her buttocks and tensed as if he would pull her toward him. "I would expect a lady to wear more than I'm feeling here. Did you kiss him?" He watched her lips as if he could see evidence of Boyle's slobbering kiss.

Caro repressed the impulse to draw her hand across her

mouth. Tag's lips hovered so close to hers, a single touch from them would cleanse away the repulsive memory. But a confession might drive Tag to do something they would both regret. "No. I . . . No." Caro had to put her fingertips on his chest to keep from closing the distance between them. She had wanted him for so long. Her tongue darted out to moisten her lower lip.

"You forget your eyes give you away when you lie. He kissed you. Like this?" He brushed his hard mouth across hers in a touch so fleeting Caro had to grit her teeth to keep from begging for more. "Not like that, was it?" Tag said, his breath like baby kisses on her mouth and chin. "We both know Boyle. He takes what he wants. It was more like this, wasn't it?"

Tag bent his head for a long bruising kiss, his closed mouth working to open hers. "Open your mouth to me," he ordered, "the way you did to him." The words softened Caro's lips until his tongue could dart in to flick at her clenched teeth. "Open your mouth. It was like this, wasn't it?"

"Yes."

His tongue plunged fiercely. Caro felt his anger. She had neither words nor breath to explain she meant yes, she would open her mouth, not that Boyle's kiss had felt anything like his. In a minute she would explain. In a minute she would be able to control the arrows of sensation shooting through her. Her body arched toward him, but he held her firmly away with his hands at her hips.

He tore his mouth from hers and drew his head back to look at her, his eyes even more angry than when he'd come in.

"Tag, please, it wasn't like that."

"Oh, no? That's how I imagined it while I waited for you on the terrace."

"We have to talk. You—"

"We have to talk, but about you, not about me. Kissing

a man like that is dangerous. But maybe you don't understand that."

Caro pushed against his chest with both palms. "Enough. Get out of here now." It was like pushing on a thousand-year-old oak.

"We established you kissed Boyle. But I want to know more. Where were his hands?"

"They weren't—"

"Here?" His hands slid over her buttocks to grip her again, fiercely this time. "This is where any man worth his salt would want his hands. So he could do this." He pulled her to him, pinning her hips to his. "Now kiss me again." He bent to claim a fierce demanding kiss, pressing her back against the wall.

Even as her body responded, Caro struggled. She wanted him with every tingling nerve, but not like this. Not when he was merely taking revenge because she had let another man kiss her. "No." Her twisting movements merely ground her lower body into his, sending rivulets of sensation spiraling upward.

"Good, but not good enough," Tag said into her mouth. He used his tight grip to lift her off the floor, then pinioned her to the wall with his hips. His hardness throbbed against her. Her body softened in response.

"Yes," he said, "that's where a man wants a woman. Right there, so he can use his hands for more important things." He stroked the outside of her thighs. "A man wants his hands here so you will open your legs when he touches you."

"I don't—"

"Then he can find something better than silk under your gown. Like this." He began easing the gliding silk up, his lips heating her neck with butterfly kisses.

"No, Tag. Not like this." Caro's words were a whispered lie, for her body strained toward his touch. His hands found her naked thighs as he raised the gown to her waist.

"Now that's silk." He caressed her in long strokes. Her legs opened automatically, allowing him to insinuate himself more firmly between them. He clasped her to him and thrust upward. Her thighs tightened around him.

She moaned and let her aching body search for more. In a minute she'd have the strength to fight him, but just for now she had to feel him against her.

"Yes," he murmured. "This is where every man in that room wanted to stand." His lips trailed kisses toward her breasts. Then he stopped and raised his head. "But how could I forget the enticing neckline of that dress. A man would want your legs around him, but not yet." Tag brought his hand up and put just the tips of his fingers into the low neckline of her gown. "Do you want me to touch you here?"

"No." Her hands rested lightly on his shoulders. Her breath came in short gasps, her chest straining toward his hand.

"Do you want me to touch you? Remember, I'll know if you lie."

"Yes." Caro would have said anything to prompt him to move his fingers, which hovered so close to her aching nipple.

His fingers crept closer. "Do you want me to take you to bed?" His body throbbed against hers.

"Yes." Every straining muscle reached toward him, but she could not let him believe she would respond so to any man. "But not like this. Please. Not while you are so angry."

Tag froze. He eased his head back so she could see his face. The harsh angles melted into gentle curves. His eyes warmed. "I'm not angry." He bent forward to nuzzle her breast. He reached down with his palm to raise it towards his lips. "I'm not angry, Caro," he repeated. "How can I be angry holding you like this."

"When you came in . . ." She bit her lip to cling to the

316

thought with her body moving in a building rhythm against his. "Your eyes when you came in . . ."

"Even then I was only angry because of the dangerous game you were playing. You wouldn't listen to me and I had to make you understand."

"You thought if you came to me like this, I would listen?" Her words dissolved into a moan as his tongue circled her nipple.

"You are so fierce, Caro. So certain nothing can happen. I just had to teach you. This was the only way I could think of."

The words jolted Caro from her delicious languor. "You're not angry? You are . . . This is another of your tricks to make me do as you order?"

His tongue produced a coldness where there had been fire. "Never to hurt you. Only to show you how vulnerable a woman can be. Now let us get on with this."

Understanding completely, Caro let her anger build. "This is another of your English lies." He had deceived her again. He'd used the way her body responded to him to force his will up on her. Her fists pummeled his shoulders. "You bastard." With one leg she swung back, kicking against the wall to give her strength. Off balance, he staggered half a step and fell. Caro twisted from him, knocking over a small table in her effort to get away. She took three steps and whirled to face him again. "You bastard! You came here like this because your words did not succeed."

She would kill him.

She reached for the knife strapped to her leg, then remembered she had removed it with her stockings. Two more steps brought her to the dressing table where the knife lay on top of her discarded hose. She snatched it from its sheath.

Tag had already drawn himself to his feet. "Ah, the knife. I expected that would appear at some point."

Caro drew back her arm for the throw. "I will kill you."

He took a cautious step toward her. "I don't believe you will."

She shot the knife toward him. God help her, she didn't even dare throw it close enough to nick him for fear he might move into its path. The knife clattered against the wall.

He laughed. "I thought not." He advanced.

She grabbed a top-heavy vase of white roses and flung that after the knife. Her aim was more accurate this time. The silver urn struck his upraised arm, drenching him with petals and water before it clattered to the floor at his feet.

Footsteps pounded in the hall. "Caro, are you all right?" The knob of the locked door rattled. "Caro." It was Rexford's voice. Caro, are you all right?"

Tag froze at the sound.

"Caro, are you all right?" Amanda repeated her husband's question and the door shuddered again.

"Go away," Caro shouted. She wanted no interference. She would kill Tag herself with her bare hands.

Tag hesitated only a moment. "Go away," he said, echoing Caro's command.

"Ahhhh." Rexford's drawn-out syllable contained comprehension. He chuckled. "I believe they want us to go away, my dear."

"But—"

Rexford cleared his throat. "We thought we heard something, my dear, but we didn't. So back to bed with you." Seconds later Rexford and Amanda's retreating footsteps sounded in the hall.

"Now, where were we?" Tag asked with an infuriating grin.

Caro's interrupted rage returned. "I'll kill you. You . . ." A string of Shawnee curses gave her strength. She launched herself at him like a bobcat. Her weight carried them to the floor, forcing a surprised rush of air from his lungs.

She didn't give him time to recover, but straddled him and grabbed two handfuls of his hair. He gripped her wrists and tore them to the sides. Short wisps of hair remained in her clenched fists.

He laughed and rolled so that he mounted her. "You'll have to be a lot stronger than that if you intend to kill me." He released her hands, but threw his head back in time to dodge the sharp blow she aimed at his jaw. "You do what you want with your hands, and I'll do what I want with mine."

He plunged his hand into the neckline of her gown to squeeze her breast.

"Get off me." She writhed on the floor to free herself of his weight.

"Certainly"—he stretched across the length of her, wrapped his arms around her, and rolled again—"if you insist on being on top." He laughed again. "Did I ever tell you how much I enjoy rolling around the floor with you?"

She could have escaped then, but in her rage she could see only the temptation of pounding her fists into him. He blocked most of the blows with his forearms, gripped the neckline of her gown in both hands, and tore at it.

The harsh ripping sound mingled with his satisfied exhale. "There. I have wanted to do that all night." He gripped her wrists together in one hand while he stroked her exposed breasts with the other.

For the first time it occurred to her he might actually take her by force. "Damn you. This is rape."

"I doubt that. Rape is when a woman is fighting for her virtue."

"I am fighting for my—"

"You are fighting because you are angry at me." He shifted beneath her. "And frankly, I don't really care about that right now. I only care about where you're sitting."

With a gasp, Caro realized exactly how she was sitting. She had straddled him again, her skirt hiked up to her

Judy Veisel

thighs, his male hardness throbbing beneath her. She tugged against the hand holding her wrists.

"Don't even think about leaving. It's much too late for that." Perversely he released her hand.

She jumped to her feet. The bed blocked her path to the door. She scrambled across the white and pink coverlet. He dove after her and caught her ankle, pulling her back. A second later the slats creaked as he landed beside her.

"Just as I hoped. You wanted to be more comfortable. Now, we have wasted enough time." He imprisoned her between his thighs and sat up to hastily remove his tangled shirt. His breath, like her own, was coming in rapid pants, and his damp hair hung down over forehead.

In a moment she would find the strength to fight him, but now she could think only that he was the most beautiful male she had ever seen. Her eyes followed the direction of his heated gaze, and she realized he was staring down at her naked breasts.

"You're beautiful," he whispered, "and you want me inside you."

"No." *Maybe*.

"You will." He took the sides of her torn dress in his hands and ripped again, easing his weight from her enough to complete the job.

She took advantage of the momentary release to try to wriggle free, but he tightened his thighs around her. "Not yet, my sweet, first I need to look at you." He stroked her from her breasts to her hips. "So beautiful. I've imagined you like that on a thousand nights." He continued to stroke her with both hands, slowly draining her of any will to resist.

"That's better," he said, easing himself down to lie beside her, but keeping one leg firmly tangled with hers. "Now I'm going to kiss you. Slowly, the way you like it."

She could bite him, she thought, the instant before his lips found hers. But his chest met her breasts at the same

320

time. Her mouth rounded with the unexpected warmth. A hundred tiny hairs produced prickles of sensation. His hard muscles set her nipples tingling, and her body softened to receive him.

He had taught her to kiss too well. Her mouth waited for his tongue, welcomed it, and hungered for it when he quickly withdrew it. He didn't keep her waiting long. His tongue plunged and retreated with the rhythm he had taught her meant intense pleasure.

She heard a soft moan she recognized as her own. Her hand slipped around his neck.

"That's right," he said, "that's how to tell me you want me." He whispered the words into her neck, kissing her there in the hollow and sending gooseflesh down her back and arms.

"I don't . . ." Caro whispered the lie and knew it didn't matter why he had come, only that he stay.

"Yes, you do, because when I kiss you here"—he sucked on the curve of her neck—"I can feel this"—he cupped his hand under her breast and touched the aching tip—"straining toward me. Your body is telling me exactly what you want."

If she could hurt him only with words, she would use those as a weapon. "Not you. It is just what any woman wants from a man."

"It doesn't matter. Tonight I won't disappoint you."

He took her breast in his mouth and began to suckle. With his hand he made slow circles on her stomach and abdomen, each circle coming closer but never touching the warm place between her legs. She began to moan and arch toward him as if she could force him to fill the void his sucking created.

"The other thing," she whispered, "the thing you did that morning."

"Soon, my sweet, soon." He lowered his hand to caress the inside of her thighs. Again too far from her need. But each long stroke came closer. His fingers brushed her curls. Her thighs parted wider. She strained toward his hand.

After an eternity, his hand returned and lingered there, letting her move against him. She closed her eyes and let the sensations roil through her. Everything felt soft and warm and moist, except for the throbbing pulse that matched the rhythm of her heart.

Suddenly, Tag's hand disappeared, then his breath and even the warmth of his body. "No." Caro's involuntary protest escaped. She snapped her eyes open. He could not leave her now.

"Shhhh. Only a minute." He stood at the side of the bed, fumbling with the buttons of his breeches.

Caro sank back into the bed. Two more breaths and she would find the will to resist him. She would not simply lie here and do his bidding.

He dropped his discarded clothing to the floor and stood before her, totally, unselfconsciously male. "Sorry. I should have done that before, but the moment never seemed right." He bent, gripped her ankles, and spread her legs apart. For a moment he stared down at her, an awed expression on his face. Then he gave an appreciative shudder. "I have finally run out of things to say."

Slowly he lowered himself to lie between her legs.

Before Caro could clasp her legs to refuse him, that male part of him touched her where his hand had been. His breath warmed her breast and his tongue circled her nipple. Her arms slipped around his head to draw him closer.

Her body moved against him in the rhythm of his slowest kiss. Straining, knowing there was more and not quite sure how to reach for it.

His hand slipped between them, not stroking now, but searching. "That's it," he whispered, "tilt toward me." His finger slipped inside her, bathing her in remembered sensations. She rose to meet it.

"Slowly now, Caro. Wait for me."

322

But she couldn't wait. She opened her legs wider, searching for more. Suddenly his finger disappeared, leaving her rubbing against his hard maleness. With his fingertips he opened her even further. "That's it, Caro," he whispered. "This is what you want."

She felt it then, a fullness and a throbbing. She arched toward it.

His hands cupped her face in his hands. "Easy now," he whispered into her lips. "I'm having a hard enough time holding back. Hold on to me. This may hurt for a moment."

She felt a sudden thrust and a sharp, tearing pain. "Ow." She stifled the startled cry even before his hand covered her lips.

"I'm sorry. There was no easy way to do that."

"I know," she said, disappointed that what she'd waited for so long could be over so quickly.

"Lie still. It will pass in a minute." He supported himself on his elbows, holding his weight off her body.

She closed her eyes and obeyed, conscious of the fullness, the receding pain, and his warm breath on her neck. They could not stay like this all night.

She twisted her hips to dislodge him. A wave of sensation washed through her. She gave a soft exclamation of surprise. "Oh."

He responded with a soft laugh. "Yes, oh. Open your eyes. I need to see what you feel."

She opened her eyes to find him smiling down at her. "What was that?"

"I think you moved. Did it hurt?"

"I don't think so." She moved again. "Oh. It's rather . . . startling."

His smile widened. "I think you're ready to continue, but stop me if I hurt you." He moved slowly at first, watching her face, his teeth biting into his lower lip.

After a time, Caro lost all thought in the spiraling sen-

323

sation. Her body moved with its own rhythm until the throbbing fire took her to a pinnacle where thought and breath didn't exist and the world exploded in a throbbing drumbeat of pure feeling. A moment later, Tag collapsed against her and buried his head in her neck, his heavy breathing a windstorm in her ear.

Enough breath finally returned so Caro could speak. "That was good." Not adequate words, but words didn't exist to express the wonder. "I am glad you were the first."

Tag did raise himself then, a fierce scowl on his face. "I don't know what the hell that is supposed to mean, but we can discuss it in the morning. Right now I'm too tired."

Not tomorrow. For them there would be no tomorrow. Caro brushed her hand down his naked back so even her fingertips would remember this night as long as she lived. "Yes. You must go now."

A slow smile replaced the scowl. "Finally, you credit me with more strength than I have. I have no intention of going anyplace."

"You can't stay here."

For an answer, he untangled himself from her and rose, pulling her with him. He kissed her lightly on the forehead, bent, and snatched up the coverlet so suddenly that the rush of air chilled her naked body. "Get in."

"But—"

"Or you can stand here arguing for another hour and then get in."

Naked and too tired for words, Caro had no doubt that would be the outcome. Or perhaps she simply could not resist the prospect of spending the night in his arms. She obeyed.

He closed the lamps. The bed rocked under his weight, and a moment later his arms enfolded her. "Sleep now." He kissed the back of her head.

Impossibly, Caro slept. Sometime during the night she woke with her back nestled against Tag's hard body.

Dreamily she understood he had drawn her from sleep with feather-soft caresses. She stirred.

"Shhhh," he whispered into her neck. "Just let me touch you."

It seemed an hour before he allowed her to turn and open herself to him. Again she fell asleep in his arms.

The rasping of the curtain being drawn intruded on Caro's languorous dream. Warm light bathed her face. She opened her eyes to see Tag standing by the window, dressed in his breeches and the shirt he had discarded so hastily the night before.

"Good morning." He offered a smile as warm as the sunlight.

Yellow light. Too bright for early morning. "My maid!" Caro sat up with a start, searching the room for the familiar figure.

"I am sure Marc suggested she wait until you sent for her this morning." Tag laughed. "Not that anybody will have much doubt what went on here last night." His sweeping gesture indicated the stained coverlet, Caro's tattered gown, which lay in a heap on the floor, and the general chaos of the room.

"Oh, dear." Caro's face heated. He would mind the embarrassment so much more that she. "I'm sorry. Perhaps we could fix it."

"I'm not. Sorry, that is. You look thoroughly enchanting. If we did not need such an early start, I would join you in that bed." His gaze feasted on her breasts until he shook himself. "But come, we must be on our way."

Caro hastily drew the coverlet to her neck. "On our way?"

"To my father's house."

"Your father's house!"

He chuckled "Really, we must do something about your

conversation. You are beginning to sound like a mountain echo.''

Caro just stared.

''Of course, my father's house. He would never forgive me if I married without him in attendance.''

''Married?''

''You did it again.'' Tag threw back his head and laughed again. An exultant sound that infuriated her. ''But never mind, we must go.''

''Don't laugh at me. What are you saying?''

''Silly goose.'' He smiled and walked over to sit on the edge of the bed. ''We must leave this morning for my father's house, so we can be married tomorrow, or perhaps the next day.'' He cocked his head at her frown. ''Purely a formality, I admit. You became my wife last night, but society demands just a bit more ceremony.''

Three weeks of listening to the scandal bandied about in country drawing rooms had given Caro a very clear idea of what she had become. ''I did not become your wife. I became your light-skirt. One of dozens, I believe.'' A note of bitterness crept into her tone.

He startled back. ''What are you . . . ? Who told you about that?''

''Mrs. Bradshaw takes great pleasure in relating tales of your exploits. She will be the first to congratulate you on another conquest.''

''Dammit, last night wasn't a conquest.'' He sprang from the bed and took a turn about the room, looking as if he might devour Mrs. Bradshaw for breakfast if she happened to appear. Finally, he faced Caro from three feet away, his hands stiffly at his sides. ''My past has nothing to do with what happened here. In any case, we must marry.''

''Oh?''

''By nightfall, everyone in the neighborhood will know what went on here last night. Your reputation will be ruined unless we are married by this weekend. So put on your things and let us be on our way.''

Caro clutched the coverlet tighter against her chest to ward off the coldness that wrapped itself around her shoulders like a mantle. ''Would your eagerness to marry be related to what else happened last night? The fact that I refused to obey your command not to see Boyle again?''

''I admit that is part of it.''

''You came here intending to do exactly what you did, so that this morning you could strut around here giving me orders.''

''I did not. I—why I came here doesn't matter. What matters is that we get away from here and marry before your reputation is completely destroyed.'' His tone softened, and his eyes heated. ''Besides, I want to spend tonight in your arms, and I am not certain how tolerant Marc plans to be.''

A world of temptation opened up before Caro. She could ignore her appointment with Boyle and spend the day anticipating the feel of Tag's hands on her body. She looked at his long fingers and her body heated, remembering the sensations. Her rational mind rose to protest. She could spend tonight savoring his touch, but the rest of her life knowing she had abandoned her duty, the rest of her life obeying his imperious commands.

She clenched her hands and felt the muscles in her jaw tighten. She would meet Boyle at noon, do what had to be done, and escape to the coast. ''What matters more? That we save my reputation or that you take me away from Boyle?''

''Dammit, they both matter. Please don't be difficult. Even now the servants are probably gossiping.'' He raised his voice for the first time. ''Dammit, you have no choice.''

His tone decided her. Naked and in bed, she could scarcely pretend to be an elegant lady, but she did have a choice. "I have every choice, my lord. And I choose to stay right here."

"You chose last night. Society demands—"

"Your society demands."

"You will be an outcast." He flung the words at her.

She ignored the pain of the image. "I am already an outsider. Last night changed nothing."

"You are the one who insisted you are my wife."

"And you insisted I was not, until it suited your convenience. Please leave now. I am not going with you."

He slapped himself down into a fragile chair, which creaked in protest under his weight. "I am going nowhere without you." He crossed his arms over his chest.

Caro glanced at the clock. She had two hours before her appointment with Boyle. Tag could spend every minute of those two hours using his underhanded methods to secure her compliance. Rather than fighting him, she would be wiser to give him a bit of his own back. "I see you are determined. Perhaps in a few days." Let him not think her too eager. "It seems a bit abrupt to simply leave without warning."

His fierceness evaporated and he jumped to his feet. "Thank heavens you decided to be reasonable. I am sure Marc and Amanda will understand if we don't linger." His step had a jaunty bounce as he approached the bed. "Now hurry, let us be on our way."

Caro gave an exaggerated gasp. She needed only to occupy him for two hours until she could make her escape. "Surely you don't expect me to travel like this, my lord."

Tag looked down at her, his usual mischievous twinkle sparkling in his eyes. "Much as I would enjoy it, I admit the rest of the world would be more comfortable if you put on a few clothes." He sat again on the edge of the bed and eased the coverlet from her fingers to devour her breasts with his gaze. "It does seem a shame, though."

"I will need to send for my maid."

"I can help you dress."

Caro's anger flared at the thought of the number of women he had probably helped in precisely the same situation. She forced a smile. "I am sure you can, but I would like to look perfect for you this morning."

He twisted a lock of her loose hair in his fingers. "You look perfect. Flushed and inviting." He snatched his hand back. "But that is for later. I suppose you want me to leave."

"I believe that would be best," she said. *Don't go,* her mind screamed.

He half-rose, then relaxed his weight onto the bed again, and cupped her cheek in his palm. "An hour then. A long hour, and I will be waiting in the hall."

Again Caro produced her grand lady tone. "My lord, when have you ever known a lady to dress in an hour?"

He flicked his thumb across her lips. "I have known you to dress in three minutes."

"But that was before you invited me to be a countess. I shall need at least three hours."

"Three hours!"

"You want my hair arranged with some semblance of style."

His eyes melted into the liquid pools she had lost herself in only hours ago. "I want you on top of me with your hair tumbling over my chest." He bent toward her. Before Caro could draw her next breath he jerked himself back. "But that is for later. You have your three hours." His eyes became teasing again. "But trust me, if you do not appear in the hall at precisely one o'clock, I will come up here and carry you out over my shoulder. Stark naked if necessary."

Caro's resolution wavered. Laughing, his eyes dancing in anticipation, Tag looked like every good memory of their time together. She reached out and slipped her arms around his neck to draw him into one last fierce embrace. Irrepressible Tag. He had lied to her, abandoned her, and come last night to take her by force if that was the only way he could command her.

Damn him.

She loved him with every drop of blood in her body—and she could not even tell him good-bye.

Chapter Nineteen

Tag circled the spacious entrance hall and glanced at his watch again. Caro had exactly two minutes to descend those stairs before he kept his promise and carried her from the house over his shoulder.

A demanding knock at the front door warned him he might be delayed. A waiting servant leapt to admit the visitor.

Mrs. Bradshaw sailed in. "Lord Taggart. How delightful to see you again so soon."

Trapped, Tag bowed. "My pleasure, madam." Hoping for a prompt rescue, he turned to the waiting footman. "Please inform Lady Rexford she has a caller."

Mrs. Bradshaw raised her hand in a halting gesture. "No need to disturb Lady Rexford. I merely wanted to assure myself Miss Fenton had arrived home safely."

"Fetch your mistress." Tag commanded. He had no intention of being saddled with the neighborhood prattle-box, no matter what her mission. He turned to her with a patient smile. "I assure you that I personally escorted Miss Fenton home last night."

"Not last night. This morning, after her meeting with Mr. Boyle."

"I beg your pardon?"

"Oh, dear." Mrs. Bradshaw brushed her lips with her fingertips. "I do hope I am not talking out of turn, but the entire neighborhood knows those two have been meeting in my garden. It is such a short walk from the back of Lord Rexford's park.''

Tag's blood chilled. He raised his eyebrows, but maintained a stony silence.

Mrs. Bradshaw hurried on. ''I saw no harm in it. Miss Fenton is such an independent young lady. And young people must have some freedom. I thought—''

Tag had no intention of listening to her every thought. ''I am waiting most patiently to learn what alarmed you today.''

''Mr. Boyle came in a coach. He said he would be leaving the neighborhood this morning. Well, he spent only a few moments in the house, though he did tell me most graciously how much he enjoyed the ball. When he asked to walk in the garden, I thought he merely wanted to say a private goodbye to Miss Fenton. But then the coach went around back. Of course I couldn't see anything. But it was most curious. When the coach passed the house again, the curtains were drawn. I thought . . .''

Tag's heart and temples pounded with his own thoughts. Shouldn't he have guessed Caro would not give up her plan for revenge so easily? Had she met Boyle? Left the neighborhood with him? He refused to let the chattering woman voice her own suspicions. ''I am certain whatever you thought, you were wrong,'' he said.

He controlled the impulse to dash up the stairs and assure himself he hadn't been mistaken.

Mrs. Bradshaw refused to be denied. ''With any other young woman I might have thought . . . but Miss Fenton is so sensible. Mr. Boyle is such an acceptable young man. There would be no reason for them to slip off together. I just thought—''

Mercifully, Amanda appeared in the hall. She glanced immediately at Tag's face, and her step faltered. ''Tag, what is it?''

How could he have believed Caro would have taken

three hours to dress? She could have slipped from the house by any of a dozen doors. ''Nothing, Amanda: But perhaps you would take Mrs. Bradshaw into the sitting room and assure her Caro is safely upstairs.''

Amanda looked both frightened and bewildered. ''But what—''

''Into the sitting room now,'' he repeated. He regretted the sharpness of his tone, but he could apologize later. Mrs. Bradshaw was probably memorizing his every facial expression to share with the local tabbies.

Amanda produced a gracious smile. ''Come along, Mrs. Bradshaw. We will have a lovely chat. I must hear all about the ball.''

Tag waited until the drawing room door closed behind the two women, then bounded up the stairs.

Caro. He shouted her name in his mind, but his clenched jaws kept the sound from reverberating through the house. Without knocking, he flung back the door to her room. The pounding of the knob against the wall produced the only sound in the silent chamber.

''Caro. Dammit, Caro, where are you?'' He recognized the futility of the question even as he spoke it. She had gone with Boyle to do precisely what she had planned from the moment she had left her village.

He wrenched open her wardrobe searching for the shabby bundle of possessions he had toted halfway around the world for her. She would not have left without it.

By the time Tag completed his search, the room looked as if he had ridden his horse through it and he had confirmed his certainty. She did not plan to return.

He sat on the bed and buried his face in his hands. Last night had meant nothing to her. She'd never planned to marry him.

No. She'd never lied. She had never promised a marriage that would last forever. Only until her mission took her

Judy Veisel

from him. She had given him one night, knowing the time had come for her to leave.

For one despairing minute Tag thought he could let her go forever. But every piece of furniture in the room reminded him of how easily he had overcome her in their struggle last night.

She might not kill Boyle. She might be his victim.

An hour later, Tag discovered Caro's only mistake. She had been reluctant to carry her mangy bundle of possessions to her meeting with Boyle. Under Tag's questioning Marc's head groom reported that he had overheard Caro asking a local lad to deliver something to her grandfather's estate. She obviously believed her final confrontation with Boyle would take place at that isolated manor house.

Whether she liked it or not, Tag would be there.

Caro followed Edwin Boyle into her grandfather's great stone house. She inhaled, grateful she would not have to stay long. The hall had the same musty smell as on her first visit. The dingy windows let in little light, and the walls threatened to close in on her.

A shuffling sound announced the arrival of the manservant a moment before he appeared.

"Ah, Albert," Boyle said, "playing the master of the house again, were you?"

Albert tugged at his coat in a vain attempt to eliminate the wrinkles. "Sorry, Mr. Boyle. I didn't hear you knock."

"I didn't. Did you follow my orders?"

"Your messenger arrived this morning. I have sent the other servants into the village. They will not return until tonight."

Satisfaction flashed in Boyle's eyes, but he quickly concealed it with a cold smile. "Now, Albert, if you will bring us some tea, you may be on your way as well."

Caro barely concealed her disgust. How could he think her so witless? Even silly Clarissa would be uneasy with a

334

man who made such careful preparations to spend an afternoon where no one would hear her scream. Caro gave a mental shrug and assumed the vacant expression of a sated hedgehog. His preparations suited her quite nicely.

It seemed entirely fitting that she should kill him in the house he had murdered two people to inherit. She would be well away before anyone discovered her deed.

The coming days stretched as flat and empty as a winter landscape. She would return to her people, but even the prospect of relating her adventures in front of the late night fires held little appeal. She wanted . . . she wanted what she could not have.

For now, she must concentrate on the moment.

Boyle ushered her into the sitting room and made a solicitous attempt to brush the dust from her chair before she sat. Perhaps he intended the gesture to compensate for his plan to rape or murder her. He followed the direction of her gaze as she glanced about the room. "A rather hideous room, I agree. But we will discuss some changes once we are married." His voice always held the same bland note whether he was proclaiming undying love or discussing the condition of an indifferently kept room.

"That will be nice," Caro answered because she could think of nothing more insipid to say. He accepted the comment. She studied him, trying to find the evil she had anticipated. Instead she saw only the empty bark of a hollow tree, a man whose spirits had abandoned him.

Albert arrived, filling the silence with the clatter of the tea service. "If that is all, I will be on my way."

"Just go." Boyle dismissed him with an impatient gesture.

"Very good, sir." Albert disappeared and seconds later the muted thud of the front door closing echoed in the hall.

Boyle clattered his teacup to the table and rose. "Pleasant as it would be to sit drinking tea all afternoon, we must

get on with what we have come for.'' His tone gave no
hint of his intentions.

Caro drew herself to her feet. Her calf tingled under the
sheath of the knife she had strapped there. Time to walk
over and plunge that knife into her enemy's heart. Now
that the moment had come, her mind rejected the idea,
struggled to find reasons to delay what she must do. Perhaps Tag was right. Perhaps it would feel more right if she
waited until he attacked her.

She waited. The silence in the room grew heavy.

''It is not enough that we merely ride away together,''
he said. ''Your grandfather might still find a way to hush
up the episode. We must make certain he insist we marry.''
He studied her intently now across the low table between
them, his weight poised on the balls of his feet, anticipating
any movement.

She looked around the room, memorizing every feature.
When she returned to her village, she would have to describe every detail of this ending to her quest. ''And how
shall we do that?''

''Patience, my dear. What we shall do next must take
place upstairs.'' His eyes shifted warily, as if even now he
expected her to bolt from the room.

Caro had no intention of escaping. She suppressed a
smile and produced her own mental images of what would
take place upstairs. Anticipating pleasure, he would naively
remove his clothing. The warriors would laugh at her account of a captive who stripped off his own clothes. His
assumption that she would let him touch her finally made
her think she might take some pleasure in killing him.

Caro did smile. Perhaps she could persuade him to tie
himself to the bedpost as well. ''If you think we must,''
she said with feigned reluctance. She reached across the
table for the hand he held out for her.

His tight muscles relaxed under her touch, though she
had to draw her lips into a thin line to keep from recoiling

at the moistness of his ungloved palm. He led her from the room and to a large bedchamber upstairs. Though she knew now the house sheltered no rats, her skin crawled as if the vermin might come pouring from the walls at any moment.

Boyle released her hand to close the door behind them; then he turned back to her with a look that made her feel as if he had already torn off her gown. "This may be a bit difficult, my dear, so I suggest you just clench your teeth and follow my directions."

Caro had no idea what a timid English girl would do at this point, but she nodded silently and waited for him to continue.

"First, you must take off your clothes."

She produced a startled look. "All of them?"

"Of course. Unless you want me to do it for you." He took a half-step toward her.

She resisted the impulse to retreat. For the first time she recalled Tag's repeated warnings. Though not as large as Tag, Boyle would attack like a hungry wolf if he scented weakness or fear. "All of them?" she repeated. She tried to infuse her voice with just the right amount of nervous willingness.

"Right down to the last thread." His wiped his palms on his breeches in anticipation.

She let her hands flutter anxiously in front of the buttons at her throat. "Only me, or will you do the same?"

His smile set her teeth on edge. "Both of us. It is more pleasant for a man that way."

"Oh, dear." She twisted the top button of her gown with fingers she hoped appeared too clumsy for the task. "I . . . I am a bit nervous. Perhaps if you removed yours first I would not be as uncomfortable."

He took another step forward as if he would tear the gown from her body.

"Oh, dear." Caro sidestepped and worked even more

frantically at the tiny buttons. "I do so want to do this right."

Boyle stopped and turned his palms upwards. "Very well. Perhaps you will feel less uncomfortable if I remove my boots and shirt. There is really nothing to be alarmed about." He crossed the room to two armchairs separated by a rosewood table. With his back to her, he struggled out of his morning coat, revealing a pistol tucked into the small of his back. This he casually laid on the table.

Caro let the gesture pass without words, but made careful note of it to retell later how easily she had disarmed her captive.

He dropped into the right-hand chair and began to tug at his boots. "Bloody hell," he muttered, "I should have kept Albert long enough to help with this."

She held her breath and willed him to succeed. An Englishman was so much more helpless without his boots.

With a slurp of air his foot jerked free. He dropped the first boot to the wooden floor, adding a thunk and the slap of leather to his grunting noises.

Caro made no effort to conceal her smile. She took several steps so the high bed concealed the lower half of her body from him. Bending as if to remove her own shoes, she slipped the knife from its sheath to conceal the blade in her sleeve and the hilt in her palm. *Foolish man,* she thought, *my only danger is that I will find the sight of you too revolting.*

He stood and drew his open-necked shirt over his head. Though his chest and stomach could not be whiter than Tag's, they had the soft, flaccid look of the underbelly of a fish.

Boyle puffed up his chest and looked at her as if expecting some simpering comment.

"You have the breasts of a woman," she muttered in Shawnee.

"What's that?"

"Magnificent," she said more clearly. She would have to wait until he moved away from the gun before expressing her opinion more adequately.

"And the brains of a flea," she added in the language of her childhood. "Truly magnificent," she translated without being asked.

"Thank you," he said, strutting toward her in his breeches and stocking feet. "And now I believe we can make this more interesting. You have not accomplished much without me."

Caro readied the knife, planning precisely where she could slash without killing him immediately.

Thump. The loud noise came from the hall below, followed by pounding footsteps. "Caro!" Tag's voice bellowed out her name. "Caro!"

Damn him. Not now.

Boyle backed hastily to the table and snatched up the pistol. "It seems we are to have company. Call him in here."

"Tag, go away!" She glanced toward Boyle, who stood with the gun pointed squarely at the closed door. "Tag, go away!" she shouted more loudly.

Naturally, Tag did precisely what she should have predicted. He pounded up the stairs toward the sound of her voice.

She tried to slide the knife down into her palm. The tip caught on the lace at her cuff, robbing her of the precious second she needed to draw back and throw it.

Clutching the pistol, Boyle took three steps across the room and caught her around the neck with his free hand. He dragged her back from the door through which Tag would burst at any second.

"Tag, go!" Her strangled cry mingled with the crash of the door hitting the wall.

Tag burst through, his pistol aimed directly at her heart. He came to a skidding stop.

He and Boyle faced each other across the room, Boyle shielded by her body, Tag open and vulnerable.

Chapter Twenty

Tag froze. Even a careless breath might cause his finger to shudder on the sensitive trigger.

"Tag, please go away." Caro's cool command held not the slightest quaver of fear. "I do not want you here."

"The hell I will." Tag shifted his gun so that it pointed at Boyle's head, fully exposed by Caro's shorter stature.

Boyle's eyes followed the movement, and he turned his pistol so the steel tip pressed into Caro's temple. He smiled. "You can shoot me, Lord Elmgrove, but I will die pulling the trigger." He smiled.

Tag clenched his teeth. "But you will die."

"And I will not mind that she dies as well. But I believe you will. Now put down the gun."

"Dammit." Caro shouted. "Am I nothing in this?" She stamped her foot, but missed Boyle's unbooted toe. "Just turn and go, Tag. He will not spend his only bullet on you." She looked tiny and fragile, but furious rather than afraid.

Boyle tightened his grip on her neck. His lips tightened with the effort, showing clenched white teeth. "The gun. Now."

"Release her and I will put it down. You have my word on that." He had to give Boyle a reason for releasing her. "Everyone believes you abducted her," he lied. "If she is harmed, they will come for you."

"She came willingly enough. Now, I would rather have

your action than your word—before I count to three. One . . .''

Tag bent forward to obey.

"Not on the floor. Over here on the table." Boyle backed up four shuffling steps, dragging Caro with him. She would be just out of Tag's reach if he followed Boyle's direction. "Two . . ."

Tag had no choice but to do as Boyle ordered. He crossed the room slowly so as not to startle Boyle, laid the pistol on the table, and wondered if the solid sound of metal on wood would be the last he ever heard.

"Thank you. Over there now." Boyle relaxed and gestured, the gun carelessly aimed as if it no longer mattered whether it pointed at Tag or Caro.

It meant the world to Tag. Caro had unexpected strength. If he could force Boyle to use the bullet on him, perhaps she would have a chance to reach the gun he had surrendered. "You are a bastard, Boyle."

Boyle grinned. "But a relieved bastard now. There was always a chance you would realize surrendering the gun would accomplish nothing."

Tag returned to his place by the door so the gun would have to point solidly away from Caro. "You promised to let her go."

"I promised nothing. Your arrival merely helped me decide what to do. A neat scenario. Your love ran off with me. You came after her and killed her. Though overcome with grief, I managed to kill you. Very convenient."

"Damn you. No one will believe she preferred a slobbering toad like you over me."

Boyle laughed. The comment seemed to please rather than infuriate him. "But she did. She came here willingly. That's what truly galls you, isn't it? I regret I cannot permit myself the luxury of letting you watch me enjoy her before I kill her." He took deliberate aim at Tag's heart.

Tag mentally commanded Caro to seize the moment and

braced for the impact. Caro struck at Boyle's arm. The gun pointed momentarily at the floor but did not discharge. She twisted from his grasp and dashed across the room. There, she whirled to stand in front of Tag, a human shield with her arms straight out from her shoulders.

"Dammit, Caro." Tag grasped her waist and tried to thrust her behind him. But Caro could turn into a leaden weight when she chose, and he succeeded only in moving her to his side. Still, Boyle could shoot only one of them and he was the wiser choice. "Get out of here. Now."

Caro drew back the arm closest to Tag.

Boyle's gun shifted with Caro's movement. Tag stepped in front of her jostling her arm. The knife clattered to the floor behind her, though her arm completed the throwing motion. Boyle fired and dove forward to avoid the knife that had flashed in the sunlight.

Tag felt a stab of fire in his thigh. He took a second to assess the situation. His gun had skittered under the bed. He had no idea how long it would take Boyle, already on the floor, to untangle himself from the table and retrieve it.

Caro turned and scooped up the knife. Tag had no time to give commands she would disobey anyway. He grabbed her shoulder and pushed her in front of him through the open door. His body would shield hers if Boyle located the gun.

Caro dashed down the hall. He hurried painfully after her. The flight of stairs had never seemed so long. Her long skirts slowed her steps. Tag reached the bottom of the stairs just as Boyle's shadow appeared behind him.

Tag slipped on the marble floor of the hall and realized blood was streaming from his thigh. Caro noticed too, but she urged him on without sympathy. Together they pounded through the front door.

He had left Marc's stallion untethered on the drive in front of the house. "The horse," he said, and pointed.

Caro put out a hand to slow Tag's pounding pace. The

skittish beast raised his head and danced nervously. Caro made soothing sounds. Her deceptively long strides completed her approach before the horse could decide whether to stand or run.

"Hurry." Tag glanced over his shoulder. Boyle appeared in the doorway brandishing both guns.

Tag grasped Caro's waist and threw her onto the horse. "Go." He slapped the animal on the rump.

The stallion erupted into motion. Tag had no time for concern. Even off balance, tangled in her skirts, and clutching her bundle, Caro would control the animal.

Tag whirled to face Boyle.

Boyle aimed and fired.

Tag dove. The bullet sliced the air above him. Hooves clattered on the stone drive beside him.

Caro shouted down at him, "Dammit, Tag. Get up. I almost trampled you."

"I told you to go." Tag pushed himself to his feet, conscious of a weakness in his right leg.

"I will as soon as you get up behind me." Caro had hiked up her skirt so she could ride astride.

"Go now. Boyle—"

"We have time. He has gone to reload."

Though Tag had assumed as much, he threw a fast glance at the empty doorway. Clasping the hand she offered, Tag managed to vault onto the horse. "Go," he ordered.

She turned the horse off the stone drive and headed across the expanse of lawn towards a tangle of woods at the far side of the estate. They entered the cover and he ducked to avoid a branch that threatened to slap him in the face.

"Where are you go—" A jolt of pain from his thigh cut off his words.

Caro urged the horse less than a half of a mile into the clutching underbrush and halted beside a large rock in a tiny clearing. She swung her leg over the horse's head, and dismounted. "Get down."

"What are you doing?"

"It will do us no good to escape if you bleed to death. We have time. Boyle cannot follow without his boots and a horse."

Tag looked at his leg. While not a dangerous wound, it could become so if it continued to bleed. Even with the care he took to dismount, the leg almost refused to support his weight.

"Sit there." Caro pointed to the rock.

Tag limped the few necessary steps and sat down. He looked up in time to see Caro throw the reins over the horse's neck and give him a resounding slap. The animal shot off in the direction from which they had come.

Tag lurched forward with no hope of catching the fleeing animal. "Dammit, Caro! What are you doing?"

"Merely insuring you don't insist we run away." She frowned as if he, rather than she, had just committed an unforgivable act. "You shouldn't have come."

Only Caro could be annoyed at being rescued from a man about to ravish or murder her. "Of course not," he said. "You were coping admirably on your own."

"Actually, I was."

"In another minute, Boyle would have had your clothes off."

"No. I would have had his clothes off. It is a quite different thing." As casually as if she were alone in her bedchamber, Caro raised her skirt and removed her petticoat.

"What were you planning to do about him then? Hope he would die of embarrassment?" The unreality of the situation struck Tag, and he cursed. Caro, with her spectacular legs and unperturbed manner, had made him forget Boyle would come after them at any moment. "We haven't time

Judy Veisel

for that. We must get as far away as we can." He pointed. "Go that way."

She stood her ground. "Don't be absurd." Using her teeth, she tore the petticoat into strips. "We have ample time. He will take an eternity to put on his own boots. He has dismissed the servants, so he will have to ready his own horse."

She nodded at Tag's leg. "Even if we planned to run away, there would be little point in going much farther with you leaving a wide trail of blood." Though her words were harsh, her fingers moved gently as she bent to wrap the white strips around his thigh.

To distract himself Tag asked again, "What would you have done? With Boyle, I mean?"

"Truthfully?" She looked up and smiled.

"Yes."

"I had the knife in my hand when you arrived. I would have killed him."

Tag shuddered. Assuming they survived, she would never be a conventional wife. "He should have looked more grateful for my arrival," he said. The wound was beginning to throb, and he had to bite his lip to roll back a wave of weakness.

In the distance Tag heard the sound of their horse crashing through the neglected woods. "Perhaps you were right to release the horse. We can move more silently on foot."

He took a single step forward. Again his leg shuddered under his weight. Suppose his leg wouldn't hold him? Suppose he couldn't go on? "I have a plan," he said. His plan consisted of little more than standing and throwing rocks at a man who had just tried to kill him twice. But she didn't need to know that. "You go on. I will delay him here."

"Why would either of us go on?" She tossed her head impatiently. "Even your weak English law will permit you to kill a man who is trying to kill you."

Again she ignored the obvious. "The law is not the problem here. By now Boyle has two loaded guns and who

346

knows what other weapons he has managed to collect.''

"Weapons," she said with the word in the same scornful tone she used to refer to petticoats.

"Please, Caro, we will argue about weapons later. I insist you get away from here. Immediately."

"And I refuse."

He detected the distant sound of a snapping branch. The picture changed, filling his veins with frigid water and his mind with despair.

Suddenly he understood his growing terror. Nightmares were sent by demons to give men a foretaste of the agony to come.

Boyle would find them. Indomitable, courageous Caro would step between him and Boyle. Boyle would shoot and she would die.

Then the nightmare would truly begin.

Her death would be only the beginning of the horror, because he would survive. He didn't know how, but some cursed fate would let him live to watch them lower her into the ground, knowing she had died because she loved him.

He buried his face in his hands to black out the flood of images, past and future.

It would all happen exactly as he saw it—unless he could convince her that, for him, there were worse things than dying.

He raised his head and gripped her hands and drew her towards him, forcing her to look at him and see the truth in his eyes. "Caro, I can't let you do this."

"You can't stop me."

"Dammit, Caro, you of all people should understand. This is the only thing I have ever feared."

She frowned in disbelief. "You have faced guns before."

"Not guns. You."

"You are afraid of me?" She looked genuinely bewildered, and Tag wanted to shake her for not seeing the reality of his nightmare.

347

Judy Veisel

"You will stay here because of me. And you will die like the only two other women who ever mattered. You will die because you love me and will not leave."

"Ahhh." The scornful syllable expressed both comprehension and disdain. "Perhaps I should let you die because you are so foolish as to compare me to those helpless females."

"Please, don't make light of it. We don't have time. Even now I can hear Boyle over there." He pointed to the right where he had detected distant sounds.

Again she responded with a scornful syllable. "He will search like a white man. We will be ready long before he finds us."

"But he *will* find us." Tag closed his eyes against the picture of Boyle breaking from the cover of trees and pointing his gun at Caro's heart. "He will find us, and for the third time in my life the woman I love will die."

"You love me?" Caro's face radiated joy.

"Of course I do. Now—"

A stern frown replaced her beatific expression. "Then you will not compare me to those others. Your mother was helpless against that dog. I would not have been." She tilted her head at a defiant angle. "And you know that is true."

He barely remembered Boyle in time to suppress a chuckle. "Had it been you, we would probably have eaten the beast for dinner."

She nodded, then drew her brows together thoughtfully. "I cannot say about your young woman and the French soldiers, but certainly several of them would have died with me."

"Again a possibility," he admitted, "but what has that to do with now?"

"Boyle is no threat to me."

Traitorous hope stirred in Tag's breast. He killed it swiftly. "Boyle has a gun. Probably two."

348

"And he moves like a white man." The approaching snap of twigs and slap of branches confirmed her words.

"Surrender, Elmgrove. This is a small woods. I will find you eventually," Boyle called. Nearer than Tag hoped, but still distant.

"Go," Tag whispered, "he will kill us both."

Caro lowered her voice as well, though not enough for Tag's comfort. "In my village even the smallest girls were taught how to protect themselves against a white man with a gun."

"You have no weapon."

"*You* have no weapon. I have my knife. Now please be quiet so I can hear Boyle."

Tag's will to resist crumbled. "You are staying?"

She laughed. "Did you ever doubt it? I must go now and determine exactly where he will come from."

Tag made a tentative effort to rise, and recognized the futility of trying to accompany her. "Be careful."

"I will." She paused. "And thank you."

"For what?"

"For respecting me." She turned, took a step, and turned back to him with her enchanting smile. "Do you really love me?"

"More than my life."

"Good." She disappeared as silently as her smile.

Tag waited uneasily. Rationally he knew Caro could evade Boyle, but it still felt wrong not to be at her side to protect her.

Boyle continued to call for their surrender.

Caro materialized soundlessly at his side. In her long gown she might have been a perfect English lady except that she carried the wicked Indian knife in her right hand. Her face glowed and her eyes danced with excitement. "I have seen him." She pointed. "He will be here soon. You must move over there."

She helped him to the far side of the clearing. A fallen

log stretched out from behind a concealing bush. "Sit." She pointed back across the clearing. "Boyle will come from over there." Wrapping the remnants of her petticoat around the tip of a long branch, she handed it to him. "When you hear him, you will wave this. Just once, quickly. Being a witless Englishman, he will step from his cover and fire at the cloth. I will be over there." She pointed to a position five yards to his right.

"An excellent plan. But suppose Boyle comes from behind us?"

She laughed. "I have ensured that he won't."

"Naturally." Her confidence made it too easy to forget the reality of the danger. Tag sobered. "How did you accomplish that?"

Her eyes twinkled. "One of my many complaints about the English. They cannot find a person in the woods unless somebody builds them a road." She gave a careless toss to her head. "And since I did not plan to spend the next several hours waiting for him, I built him that road. I left him a trail even a white man can follow."

No niggling doubt would betray him into robbing her of her confidence. They would live or die, but they would do it with abandon. "I would have expected nothing less. If Wellington had you, he might have sent the rest of us home." He eased himself down onto the log she had indicated.

Her obvious excitement irked Tag. "You are quite enjoying this, aren't you?"

She glanced at his leg. The blood was beginning to seep through the bandage.

"I am sorry about your leg, but yes, I am enjoying this." She pointed. "He will step from cover over there and I will throw my knife."

"Perhaps I should throw the knife. You conceal yourself, and be prepared to get away if I miss."

Her disdainful look told him she shared his lack of confidence in that plan. "I have been throwing knives since I was twelve. And you?"

In spite of himself he smiled. "This would be the first time."

"You will have to trust me."

Tag studied her taut body and confident expression. He felt a curious lightening of his spirit. They would live or die by her hand.

He was not afraid to trust her.

Tag saw Boyle first in a shadow of dark movement exactly where Caro had predicted. The man had dismounted, obviously realizing that the low-hanging branches of the neglected woods made riding impractical.

Seconds passed and Tag caught more frequent glimpses of his enemy as he moved through the trees and undergrowth. Boyle carried a long branch and his frequent slashes set the bushes to trembling. He certainly didn't lack for confidence.

Tag appreciated the absurd fact that Boyle had taken time to don his morning coat. At least he had dressed properly to murder two people.

Tag looked to his right and saw Caro standing only partially concealed with the knife ready. Involuntarily his hand tightened on the branch that would attract Boyle's attention. Perhaps he could attract the bullets from both of Boyle's guns.

Caro saw the movement and shook her head.

Tag counted off the tense seconds as Boyle moved nearer. Finally, Boyle hesitated at the far side of the clearing.

Tag whipped the branch through the air. The white petticoat snapped above his head.

Boyle jumped into the clearing and fired. The sound echoed.

The bullet sliced through the branch Tag held only

351

inches from his hand. Caro should not have counted on Boyle being a wretched shot.

Her knife sang through the air.

Boyle screamed. The gun bounced to the ground. Boyle's head slammed back against the tree that had half-concealed him. Caro's knife had sliced through the fleshy part of Boyle's shoulder. He slid to a seated position at the base of the tree, clutching his shoulder.

Boyle continued to scream.

Caro darted out from her cover and snatched the second pistol from Boyle's waist. "Come out, Tag, and help me decide how long we should take to kill him."

"No, Caro." Tag struggled to his feet and used the log to support his first few steps until his leg agreed to cooperate. "No, Caro," he repeated before she could do any serious damage with the gun. "We are safe now. I can watch him while you go for the authorities." He dragged himself across the clearing and supported himself against a conveniently bent tree.

"Why go for the authorities?" Caro demanded.

Boyle stopped thrashing and sneered. "So they can hang you two for attacking me on my own property."

"My grandfather's property."

"It doesn't matter. It will be mine soon and you two have tried to kill me." He clutched the shaft of the knife and tried to pull it free. "Get this out of me and I will persuade them to merely transport you."

Caro ignored his struggles. "Will you be very angry if I kill him, Tag? It is what I have come for." She sounded utterly reasonable for a woman about to murder a helpless man.

He could possibly disarm her, but given the weakness in his muscles, only possibly. "We have a law."

"Of course we have a law," Boyle shouted, "and you two will hang if we don't reach an agreement."

"Shut up, Boyle." The fool didn't realize Tag was trying

to save his life. Caro glanced at Boyle and then back at Tag. "Is it true that they could punish us?"

Tag had no idea what the law would decide. "Of course not. We can convince people he kidnapped you. He did shoot me."

"So they will not hang us. But will they hang him?"

Tag wondered if he could get away with a lie, and decided probably not. "Hell, Caro, I don't know. But I am getting damn tired of standing here."

"Then we have to kill him."

"What is all this talk about killing?" Boyle whined. "I didn't do anything to you two." He looked at Caro. "You came with me willingly enough." He wisely neglected to mention he had planned to kill them both.

"You killed my uncle and my cousin." Caro discarded the gun and produced another smaller knife from somewhere in her clothing.

Boyle eyed the gleaming blade. "You can't prove that."

"That's what Tag says. That is why I have to kill you."

Boyle directed his panicky look at Tag. "She is insane." For the first time he seemed to comprehend his danger.

"Not insane, but different from anyone you have ever met—" Tag said. "You should have paid more attention to her background."

"What has her background to do with getting me out of here?"

"She was raised in America by Shawnee Indians. They have their own idea of justice. If you have a jot of sense, you will help me convince her you will die soon enough."

"You are mad."

Caro stepped toward him and sliced through the clothing on his upper body as neatly as she would make the first cut in skinning a rabbit. "Our captives sometimes take days to die. Tell me about my uncles. Something that will satisfy Tag's law." She let her knife hover just below his throat.

"You wouldn't dare," Boyle bellowed.

"Not wise, Boyle," Tag muttered. He should have warned Boyle about issuing a challenge to Caro, but perhaps her threat would work. She had sounded as if she would let Boyle live if he admitted his crime.

She etched a thread-thin line from Boyle's throat to his navel. He screamed as if she had sliced through his heart. Droplets of blood seeped out to define the cut.

"Tell us about my uncle," Caro demanded.

"Tell her, Boyle. Her people remove skin an inch at a time." Tag needed to end this. He had heard too many stories about Indians to doubt Caro meant precisely what she said. "Perhaps this could wait," he said quietly to Caro. "I believe my leg is beginning to bleed again."

Briefly distracted, Caro glanced at his leg, but obviously decided it could wait. "Not as much as this scoundrel will bleed." She made a minuscule cut in the white flesh of Boyle's breast. Of course. Tag grimaced. It wasn't her leg, and her people took pride in enduring pain. She made another small cut.

Boyle screamed again. "I killed them. Is that what you want to hear?" Caro looked at Tag. "Is that what your authorities need?" she asked as blandly as if inquiring what he would have for dinner.

"Yes." Clouds swirling in Tag's brain dimmed his wits and prompted him to add, "If they believe us."

"They might not believe us?" Caro didn't wait for Tag's reply, but turned back to Boyle with the hovering knife. "They might not believe us." She poked at his nipple with the tip of the knife.

"Dammit, Boyle," Tag said, "tell her something only you know so I don't have to stand here and listen to you scream."

"No." Boyle screamed again. "Yes. The oldest son I killed him as well. Nobody ever suspected. Rob Mac-Cracken helped me bury him in Scotland. He can tell you where."

Caro looked again at Tag. "They will believe that?"

"They will believe that." Tag nodded wearily and almost pitched forward. "Now perhaps you will come over here and keep me from falling on my face."

With a swish of the low-hanging branches, Marc stepped from the trees, followed by another man. "Tend to him, Caro. I will deal with this scoundrel." He crossed the clearing with a purposeful stride, and wrenched the knife from Boyle's shoulder. Boyle tumbled forward with a piercing shriek as his chest hit the ground.

Tag ignored the noise and steadied himself with a hand on Caro's shoulder. "Marc! How long have you been there?"

"Not long enough to see everything. We saw the horses and assumed you were in the woods, but we had to wait for the screams to lead us here."

The man with Marc crossed the clearing and positioned himself under Tag's other arm. Following Caro's unspoken direction, he helped Tag to the log he had used before.

"Why didn't you show yourself earlier?" Tag asked.

Marc handed the whimpering Boyle his neck cloth to use on the wound in his shoulder, but otherwise paid him scant attention. He pointed to the stranger standing beside Tag. "This gentleman here is a magistrate. I thought we might need a disinterested witness, so I took time to go by for him. When we got here we started hearing some very interesting things, so we waited."

"God, Marc! Suppose Caro had . . ." The horror of having his wife arrested by his best friend for murder overwhelmed Tag so he could not complete the sentence.

Marc laughed. "William here served with me on the Continent for several years. I have reason to know he can be very selective about what he hears and sees."

"But Marc . . ."

"I believe the rest of your questions can wait until we have cleaned up the mess you have created here." Marc eyed the bandage on Tag's leg. "You will live until we can get you back to the house, won't you?"

Tag reached out and drew Caro down beside him. He slipped his arm around her waist and, for the second time that day, surrendered control. Marc would organize everything. "Not Fenton's house, if you don't mind. My father's house." He smiled down at Caro. "We have a wedding to arrange."

Chapter Twenty-one

Two days later Tag limped into the sitting room of his father's house for his first private moments with Caro in what seemed like a lifetime. He reached behind him and turned the ornamental key in the lock.

Its satisfying snap caused her to look up with a start from the shirt she was mending for him. "You should not be out of bed, my lord."

"My lord! Since when have I been 'my lord,' and not 'dammit, Tag, why are you out of bed?' "

She smiled and relief coursed through him. She was here. She would stay and he would not be able to hold on to his anger very long. "Very well. Dammit, Tag, why are you out of bed?"

"Because it is the only way I can be sure you are not out slaughtering villains. Or worse—" he paused to recognize the sickness that gripped him as he voiced his true fear—"sailing to America without me."

"You know I would not leave without seeing you."

"Then, dammit, why haven't you been in to tend me?" In spite of his vow to remain sternly aloof, he crossed the room to stand before her.

She refused to take his outstretched hand, and glanced down at her sewing. Her cheeks colored with a hint of a blush. "Your father said it would not be proper."

Tag exploded with oaths in three languages. "That old rake. When did he become your chaperon?"

"When you told him you would marry me. He said the best way to ensure an eager bridegroom was to—"

"That old fox. I will show him eager." Tag bent, snatched the crumpled shirt from her lap, and threw it on the floor. Ignoring her attempt to evade him by arching back in her chair, he took her hands and drew her to her feet. Her nearness tempered his anger. "He thought I would not be eager enough, did he?" He released her hands so he could caress her hips as he had imagined twice an hour for the past two days.

"Oh, no, he said he could tell by your looks you were impatient enough, but—"

Tag managed merely to mutter his uncomplimentary opinion of his father. "But he thought if you didn't visit me in my bedchamber I would stay that way?" He let his hands glide over her gown. Too many petticoats. He cursed every word he had ever said about the virtue of undergarments.

"No. I told him you had promised to marry me only to keep me away from Mr. Boyle, but once you remembered Marc had taken Mr. Boyle away, there would be no need for you to actually do so."

"You didn't really believe that, did you?"

"He didn't. That's when he made me promise to stay away from you. He said if I did that, he would see to getting you to the church." She flushed and looked away from him. "I think he suspected about the night that you . . ." She shook her head. "It doesn't matter. I will not let him force you to marry me."

Tag couldn't decide whether to be amused or infuriated by his father's turn toward respectability. Caro's exhaled breath warmed his chin and his father suddenly seemed unimportant. "He won't have to force me to do anything." He drew her to him so he could feel her thighs against his.

She put her hands on his shoulders and looked unflinchingly into his eyes. "It is all right. I know that you love me, but can't marry me because of those other women. I understand you can't let yourself be near a woman who loves you." She pressed with her hands on his chest and pushed back as if she would leave him.

He tightened his grip on her hips, holding her to him. He had no intention of letting her go. Not for a long time. Her movement had forced her lower body even more firmly against him, and a surge of desire jumbled whatever he might have replied.

She ceased her struggles to free herself and looked at him with a flare of hostility, more familiar than her sweet compliance. "I mean, I don't understand. I think it is unbelievably beetle-headed, but I will accept it because you say it is so."

He kissed the tip of her nose. "Well, you don't have to accept it, because it's no longer true."

Her eyes flashed with delighted triumph. "You mean what I said about being different convinced you?"

"Not what you said." Tag struggled for words to express what he had come to understand in the past two days. "Not even what you did."

"What then?"

"It was something I felt. I can remember the exact moment. I looked at you and knew I trusted you. To take care of yourself. To take care of me. And someday to take care any children we have."

"I told you that—"

"Let me finish because it's important to me. I realized if anything bad ever happens to either of us, it won't be my fault. And it won't be your fault. It will be some ugly twist of fate, and I'm not going to let that spoil a single minute of what time we do have."

He kissed her then to show her exactly how he planned to spend that time. She responded with her usual fire, and he cursed the ocean of material between them. He broke the kiss and began a determined campaign to raise her skirt and whatever devil-designed garments she had on underneath.

She reached for his hands. "Tag, I'm not sure that's a good idea."

"I am." Long-suppressed desire made his voice as ragged as the petticoat she had bound his wound with. "I have thought of little else for two days." His hands reached the second layer of petticoats, and he wondered how far he dared take this delightful pursuit in the sitting room. "Neither of us is leaving this room until we have dealt with my father's misbegotten idea of making me more eager." He pulled her to him and shuddered with the satisfying touch of her center against his hardness.

"No." She turned her face away from his kiss. "I promised your father I would not let you do this until we were married."

"Well, unpromise him."

"No."

He sought again for her lips and caught only the tip of her ear. "We are married, remember. You told me we were often enough."

"And you told me often enough that would not satisfy your English notions."

"I was wrong." His hands tightened on her hips as he held her against him. "I held you exactly like this the night we married. And you had on a lot less then than you do now."

"Did it bother you?" Her resistance softened with the question.

"You mean did I want you the way I do now?" He spoke the hoarse words into her neck and felt the tremor that rippled through her.

"Yes."

"So much so that we are fortunate I did not tear down your village when I found out I couldn't have you."

"Well, now, you will just have to tear down your father's house, because I gave your father my word.''

"Well, you can just . . ." His protest died unspoken. She had given her word, and her courage had earned his respect. He could not tempt her to break her promise. "Dammit." He glanced down at their intimate position and loosened his grip so she was not so firmly melded against him. "At least tell me you didn't promise we wouldn't stand here talking like this.''

"No, but I am not sure I can think of much to say in this position.''

"You can answer one question for me." He pulled her firmly against him again, then released his grip with one hand and pressed against her chest so she arched back as she had during their Indian wedding dance. "What did you say the first time you felt me against you like this?''

"I don't remember.''

"That was when you abandoned English and began speaking in Shawnee. I have always wondered what you said.''

She flushed and he knew he was right. She had said something very unladylike.

"Tell me. I can see you remember.''

"I remember, but I believe your father would insist I wait until after the wedding to tell you." She twisted away from him, and her skirts swished about her legs. She brushed at the wrinkles.

"Damn my father. I would like to wring his neck.''

She laughed, walked to the door, and unlocked it. "But not until after the wedding, I presume.''

Three days later Tag dragged his officially sanctioned wife away from a tangle of wedding guests to a waiting coach. The following day they would begin a wedding journey that would take them through a series of cities on the Continent and, eventually, to America for a visit with her people. But he had his own plans for the balance of the balmy afternoon.

The coach ground to a halt two miles from his father's house. "Out," he commanded.

Caro looked for a moment as if she would protest, but she obviously decided that would not be a wise way to begin a marriage. Tag jumped to the ground in her wake, carrying a buffalo robe. He turned and called to the coachman, "Two hours, Channing, no more." The coach drove off and Tag pointed to a path.

"Tag, surely you don't expect to—"

"Silence, woman."

Caro interpreted his command literally, and followed the series of narrow paths in silence. Less than half a mile from the road they came upon the lake that formed the back boundary of his father's estate. He spread the buffalo robe on the soft ground.

Caro looked at him, alarm warring with delight. "Tag, surely you don't expect to—not here."

He grinned. "You are my wife now. Even my father would agree I may choose when and where to exercise my rights as your husband."

She looked unconvinced. "Someone might come."

"This is a secret place. I used to come here often as a child. No one will disturb us."

Her voice dropped to a whisper. "It's beautiful, but why here?"

He took her hand and drew her down with him to the warm robe. "I thought it fitting after all the days and nights I lay on the ground thinking I would go mad with wanting you."

She threw herself into his arms with an eagerness that tumbled them both backwards. "How perfect." She reached for the buttons of his shirt.

He gripped her hands. "Not so fast, vixen. You still haven't answered my question."

"What question?"

"The night of our wedding dance, what did you say when you first felt me against you?"

"I said many things."

He laughed. "I am sure you know the one I mean. It was clearly about my attributes. Did you say I was as big as a buffalo?" He grinned impudently.

"No." She shook her head. "I did not say that."

Tag shrugged away a mild disappointment. "What did you say?"

She let her gaze drift to the area in question. "I said a buffalo would look at you and die of shame."

MADELINE BAKER

Beneath A Midnight Moon

Winner Of The *Romantic Times* Reviewers Choice Award!

He comes to her in visions—the hard-muscled stranger who promises to save her from certain death. She never dares hope that her fantasy love will hold her in his arms until the virile and magnificent dream appears in the flesh.

A warrior valiant and true, he can overcome any obstacle, yet his yearning for the virginal beauty he's rescued overwhelms him. But no matter how his fevered body aches for her, he is betrothed to another.

Bound together by destiny, yet kept apart by circumstances, they brave untold perils and ruthless enemies—and find a passion that can never be rent asunder.

_3649-5 $4.99 US/$5.99 CAN

Dorchester Publishing Co., Inc.
P.O. Box 6640
Wayne, PA 19087-8640

LOVE FOREVERMORE

MADELINE BAKER

The West–it has been Loralee's dream for as long as she could remember, and Indians are the most fascinating part of the wildly beautiful frontier she imagines. But when Loralee arrives at Fort Apache as the new schoolmarm, she has some hard realities to learn...and a harsh taskmaster to teach her. Shad Zuniga is fiercely proud, aloof, a renegade Apache who wants no part of the white man's world, not even its women. Yet Loralee is driven to seek him out, compelled to join him in a forbidden union, forced to become an outcast for one slim chance at love forevermore.

___4267-3 $5.99 US/$6.99 CAN

**A WANTED MAN.
AN INNOCENT WOMAN.
A WANTON LOVE!**

Renegade Heart
Madeline Baker

When beautiful Rachel Halloran took Logan Tyree into her home, he was unconscious. A renegade Indian with a bullet wound in his side and a price on his head, he needed her help. But to Rachel he was nothing but trouble, a man whose dark sensuality made her long for forbidden pleasures; to her father he was the answer to a prayer, a gunslinger whose legendary skill could rid the ranch of a powerful enemy.

But Logan Tyree would answer to no man—and to no woman. If John Halloran wanted his services, he would have to pay dearly for them. And if Rachel wanted his loving, she would have to give up her innocence, her reputation, her very heart and soul.

_4085-9 $5.99 US/$6.99 CAN